He heard the whisper of a footstep just before the question came from behind him. "May I help you, sir?"

Slowly Alec turned, put on guard by her tone of voice. Frigid with scorn, it wasn't nearly as polite as the question. Sure enough, his eyes fell first on the pistol in her raised hand, pointed right at his chest. He had faced pistols before, though, and more than one of them had fired—not usually at such close quarters, but he had learned to ignore the urge to flinch and dive for cover. It was much more prudent to be ready to strike back, should the opportunity arise . . . as well it might, he realized, finally looking the woman in the face.

She was tall but slim, and not half as old as he had expected. Her heart-shaped face was framed by long tendrils of brown hair, pulled loose from the knot on top of her head. The heavy pistol trembled almost imperceptibly in her grip, but her eyes—luscious eyes the color of cinnamon and gold and amber—were utterly calm and level. Alec's interest rose a notch; he'd never been shot by a woman

Romances by **Caroline Linden**

A VIEW TO A KISS
FOR YOUR ARMS ONLY

CAROLINE LINDEN

For Your Arms Only

AVON

An Imprint of HarperCollinsPublishers

This is a work of fiction. Names, characters, places, and incidents are products of the author's imagination or are used fictitiously and are not to be construed as real. Any resemblance to actual events, locales, organizations, or persons, living or dead, is entirely coincidental.

AVON BOOKS
An Imprint of HarperCollins*Publishers*
195 Broadway
New York, NY 10007

Copyright © 2009 by P. F. Belsley
ISBN 978-0-06-170647-9
www.avonromance.com

First Avon Books paperback printing: December 2009

Avon Trademark Reg. U.S. Pat. Off. and in Other Countries, Marca Registrada, Hecho en U.S.A.
HarperCollins® is a registered trademark of HarperCollins Publishers.

Printed in the U.S.A.

10 9 8 7 6 5 4 3 2

To my dad, whose military history library would have come in handy during the writing of this book; and to my mom, who taught me to love the local public library (which DID come in handy during the writing of this, and every, book)

For Your Arms Only

Prologue

July 1820

It was said that every sort of vice could be found in London, if one knew where to look. In the filthy rookery of St. Giles, one didn't have to look very hard.

The fight had already started, a bare-knuckle match between two street fighters in a grimy pub cellar. The favorite, an Irishman native to St. Giles, was short and stocky and known for fighting dirty; in St. Giles, fighting dirty was applauded. The challenger was an African, dark and formidable, and jeered by the crowd. The cellar was packed with men who had paid their farthing at the door and were intent on recouping their money by placing bets with any and all takers. A musty odor of old smoke, spilled beer, and dried sweat clung to the walls; before the night was over, there would probably be a sharp scent of freshly spilled blood as well.

One spectator, pasty pale and a little too short to see over the rest of the crowd, wormed his way through the room. From time to time he bobbed on his toes for a glimpse of the fighters before resuming his search for a better vantage point. At last he seemed to find one that suited him, settling into a place against the wall opposite the stairs.

"Five quid on the Moor," he said to the man beside him, a tall fellow in the hard-worn clothes of a drayman.

The taller man removed the cigar from between his teeth and blew out a puff of smoke. "The Irishman's favored."

The newcomer, Mr. Phipps, scoffed. "Bloody idiots, the Irish. Look at the Moor—solid muscle, a long reach, and such ferocity! He could beat a dozen Irishmen." In timely demonstration, the African fighter struck, pounding several quick hits to his opponent's belly. The Irishman staggered and looked for a moment as if he would fall to his knees. Phipps raised a fist in triumph.

His companion shrugged. "Perhaps. But the crowd wants the Irishman to win, Mr. Phipps. If the African wins, the losses will be heavy."

"You've got no appreciation at all for the sport, have you, Brandon?" Mr. Phipps said crossly.

"No." In the ring, the Irishman landed a punishing blow to his opponent's chin, and the African fell back to his seconds, reeling in pain. The frenzied crowd roared, and even the colorless Phipps let out a shout. Brandon didn't move, his eyes still restlessly roaming over the spectators.

"You're the only man I know who wouldn't relish this assignment," Phipps told him in a low voice. "There's men out doing a lot worse than watching a good mill." Brandon just gave a quiet snort. Phipps shook his head and sighed, reluctantly turning from the fight. "Well, where is Pearce?"

"There." Brandon tilted his head, indicating a balding man in a green coat across the room. "He met them just a bit ago and took a packet from them. Paid in coin."

"And the Blackwoods?"

"By the ring, near the corner." Brandon dropped his cigar and ground it under his heel. "They bet very heavily on the Irishman."

Phipps nodded. "Good work." He pushed up the brim of his cap and wiped his forehead, and his other men, scattered around the room, took note. With practiced ease they maneuvered toward the three men just identified. The two Mr. Blackwoods and Mr. Pearce would spend the night in Newgate Prison, although none knew it yet. Like many others before them, the Blackwood brothers had been brought low by their gambling, but unlike more ordinary sinners, they had resorted to embezzling stocks from the bank where both worked as clerks. Simon Pearce, a partner in the bank, was likely the architect of the scheme. Sir Thomas Broughton, another partner, was anxious to have Pearce removed while avoiding any embarrassing publicity that might ruin his bank. For discretion he had turned to John Stafford, chief clerk of the Bow Street Magistrates Court and spymaster for the Home Office, and Stafford had set Brandon to discovering how the Blackwoods transferred the stolen stocks to Pearce.

Brandon eased away from the wall. His job was done now. "I'll leave you to it." Keeping his head down, he started to head for the door at the back of the crowded room.

"One moment." Phipps pressed a folded paper into his hand. "Condolences," he muttered.

Brandon automatically closed his fist around the paper and shoved it into his pocket. "Why?" He looked back at Phipps, but the shorter man had already disappeared into the crowd surging toward the ring. A scuffle on the far side had broken out and was growing larger as more men turned from the staged—and probably fixed—match between the African and the flagging Irishman, and enthusiastically joined in the fight going on among the spectators.

He had no interest in joining that fight; his responsibility had only been to keep an eye on the Blackwoods and Pearce until Phipps could arrive to arrest them. That was Brandon's specialty as a spy: watching. Now Phipps and his men would spirit the thieving clerks and banker away, to face who knew what, and no one in the disorderly crowd would notice or care.

Around him the roar grew louder, punctuated by cracks of a whip as the fight organizers tried to keep order. Brandon pushed through to the rickety stairs, taking them two at a time. When he came out into the back of the dingy pot-house, the owner gave him a sharp glance. The bare-knuckle fight going on in his cellar was hardly secret, but it was illegal all the same. Brandon's lip curled at what the man would think if he knew several fellows from Bow Street were down there right now. Instead of leaving and fixing suspicion on himself, he leaned against the counter and motioned the publican over.

"When does the African fight again? He's lost me some blunt tonight."

The other man's expression eased. "Thursday next."

Brandon grunted and dropped a few coins on the counter. "A pot of heavy wet."

He took the mug of ale and carried it to a small table. The room was busy, with men coming in for a drink before disappearing into the back, going down to see this fight or the next one. No one noticed him here, just another unlucky drayman washing down the loss of his weekly pay before staggering home. He pulled his woolen cap lower on his forehead and drew the guttering candle close before unfolding the note Phipps had passed him. Stafford didn't waste a moment, sending him to spy on someone else before this job was even concluded.

But that wasn't all the note said.

The bench scraped along the floor as he jumped to his feet, holding the note close to his face to reread it. He glanced toward the stairs to the cellar, then jammed the note into his pocket, leaving behind his barely touched ale and heading to the door. He strode through the narrow, twisting streets of St. Giles, jumping over the sewers running in the gutters and ignoring the catcalls of the whores. As he went north the buildings seemed to expand and brighten, the cramped poverty of the rookery giving way to more spacious gentility. The houses here were clean brick edifices, tightly fitted together with neatly swept steps and painted railings, their windows dark mirrors for the gas streetlamps. There were still thieves here, but they kept to the shadows.

After a few streets Brandon turned into an alley and went to the back stoop of a house near the end of a long terrace. The door was surely locked tight for the night, but he didn't bother to try it. Instead he braced one hand on the door, stepped up onto the short railing beside the steps, and reached upward to grab the ledge of the window. He pulled a knife from the sheath strapped under his upraised arm and wriggled the flat of the blade beneath the sash of the window, twisting the knife until he could fit his fingers into the opening. With one hard shove the window slid up; holding the sill with both hands, he walked up the wall until he could pull himself through the open window and into the house. Brandon glanced around as his feet hit the floor, but he'd learned to do that trick almost silently. No sound of footsteps betrayed alarm in the house—not that it would have really mattered, except to his pride. The owner of the house left that window unlocked for just this reason, so Brandon could let himself in without any servant seeing him. He closed the window and went in search of the man.

Light seeped from beneath the door of the master's study; Sir James Peterbury was still awake. Pausing only a moment to listen for voices, he turned the knob and slipped into the room.

"What the—? Bloody hell," exclaimed the man who sprang to his feet, first in alarm, then in recognition. "You nearly scared me witless, man!"

"Sorry for that," said Alec Brandon. He pulled Phipps's note from his pocket and held it up. "Did you know?"

James looked at the note, then back at Alec's face.

"I presume you mean your brother's death," he said quietly. James always had been a quick one, Alec had to give him that. "Yes, I knew. I wanted them to tell you some time ago, but they insisted you were vitally occupied."

Alec's tense anger drained away. He dropped into a chair and hung his head. "He died months ago, and no one told me." There was nothing he could have done, but he still should have been told. He rubbed one hand across his eyes, feeling the raw sting of grief in his throat. "Damn it. I should have been *told*."

James took the other chair by the fire. "My mother wrote that it was a lingering illness contracted in the winter. No one thought it was terribly serious, but he just grew worse and worse. You know Frederick never was very strong." The Peterburys no longer lived only a few miles from Alec's family, but James's mother and Alec's mother were still fast friends and wrote each other often.

Alec nodded, swallowing his emotions. He hadn't thought of his older brother in some time, but James was right. Frederick might not have been as vigorous as Alec, but he had always been wiser, more dependable, and most importantly, always there. Alec had never expected Frederick to die. "And the rest of my family?"

"Your mother and sister are well, as are Frederick's widow and children." James cleared his throat. "I understand a cousin has stepped in to manage the estate. I suppose he thinks he's inherited everything now."

He knew what James was thinking. That cousin hadn't inherited anything, because Alec was still alive. But only a handful of people knew that. To most of the world, Alexander Brandon Hayes had died a traitor to his country during the battle of Waterloo, his body ignominiously dumped into an anonymous grave. He had sworn he wouldn't return home without proving himself innocent, but neither he nor James had been able to do it. For five years James had made every effort to locate the letters from a French colonel, found in Alec's personal belongings after Waterloo, that branded him a traitor. But with Alec presumed dead—and unwilling to risk prosecution if discovered otherwise—James had had to tread with extreme caution, and had been utterly unsuccessful. Alec had become a spy, hoping his service to the Home Office would win him a reprieve, and instead he was being sent home, unmasked and still shrouded in disgrace.

But Frederick was dead and Alec was the head of the family. James would argue that that duty outweighed all others. Perhaps it did, for the sake of his mother, his sister, his brother's widow and children.

"I'm returning to Marston," Alec muttered.

His friend's face shone with fierce satisfaction. "I knew you would. It's time, you know, and I've been thinking about your situation. Wellington is Master of the Ordnance now and has politics more on his mind than old battles. If we could secure an interview with him, and perhaps have your present employer put in a word—"

"Wellington, who said he would have shot me himself if the French hadn't been good enough to do it first?" Alec shook his head. "I'm not going to Wellington without proof."

James fell silent. Both of them knew it was highly unlikely any proof of Alec's innocence would surface now. "It's still the right thing to do," he insisted. "Going home, that is."

Alec sighed. He held out the crumpled note from Phipps. "I haven't got a choice."

His friend took the note and read. Stafford was sending him home to Marston, not out of any tender compassion for Frederick's death, but to find a missing man. Sergeant George Turner had gone to see Colonel Lord Hastings, a Deputy Commissary General for the army, in London and never come home to Marston. He'd been gone for almost four months now, and his daughters had appealed to Hastings, who had asked Stafford to look into it. Just another spy's task on the surface, and a routine one at that. Only a terse line at the end—*I regret to inform you of the death of Frederick Hayes this past spring*—gave any indication Stafford was aware of the ramifications of sending Alec to that particular town, where he would be known and reviled by all.

"Bloody cold of him," remarked James. "Who is this Sergeant Turner he wants you to find?"

"I've no idea." As usual, Stafford gave very little information. He often sent Alec out almost blind, expecting him to quickly find his way and report back how things stood so Stafford could assign other agents most effectively. Alec was used to that; he had done much the same thing when he was in the army, helping guide Wellington's army around the countryside of Spain and Portugal. In this case, though, Alec thought he might have earned the courtesy of more explanation.

"What's Turner done, I wonder?" James murmured. "Hastings is a proud man. I can't see him taking up for a lowly sergeant."

He had wondered about that, too, but Stafford wasn't above doing favors for people with influence, and Hastings was certainly in a position to command Stafford's notice. By far Alec's greater interest was in why Stafford had chosen *him* for this job. There was no question of masquerading as an old army mate of the missing sergeant or a clerk from the Chelsea pensioner board, not when everyone in Marston would recognize his face and know his name. He would have to return as himself, and that would complicate things on many, many levels.

"It doesn't matter what he's done, or who he really is. Hastings wants him found for some reason, and that's enough for Stafford. I wouldn't think anything of it if Turner hadn't gone missing from my own village." Alec took the letter back. "Stafford should have the spine to explain that part at least."

"Do—Do you plan to refuse? I believe you should go, but perhaps not like this . . ."

He shrugged. James meant he shouldn't go home as Stafford's spy, and with good reason. "What choice have I got? Who else would take a chance on me like he's done?"

"Perhaps this means he's discovered something." His friend sat up straighter. "It would be like that old parsnip to keep it to himself and squeeze a few more months of service from you. But he knew your situation and promised all along to do what he could to restore your name. This"—James shook one finger at the note—"must mean he thinks the time is ripe for you to go home. He'd never expose one of his best men without good reason."

Alec said nothing. It was true that John Stafford and Phipps had known exactly who he was when they hired him as one of their agents; it was true they had pledged to do what they could to help his cause. But sending him home like this could hardly be beneficial. Part of him wondered if it might be a sign that Stafford had become convinced Alec actually was as guilty as he appeared, but he reminded himself that Stafford was far too ruthless to deal with him this way. If Stafford believed him a real traitor, he'd be dead by now, not sent on another assignment. Could Stafford have some evidence that he hadn't conspired with the French? He must have made some provision to keep Alec from being arrested the moment he was recognized. Was there any way he could know?

Probably not.

"Would you write to my mother?" he asked. "Would you tell her . . ." He hesitated. It was unfair to ask James to explain his actions. "Would you tell her to expect me?"

"Of course."

Alec flexed his hands, suffocated by apprehension. Could he do this? What would his family think of him, first for disappearing and then for returning? What had happened in their lives since he became someone else? He had dreamed for so long of going home, but not like this; he had imagined going home an exonerated man, not as a spy in truth. "Thank you. I wouldn't want the shock to kill her on the spot."

"I'll send it tomorrow," James promised. He eyed

Alec somberly. "Is there anything else I can do? You know you only have to ask."

As if he hadn't done enough already. James had believed him when he denied committing treason, helped him get out of Belgium right under the nose of the whole British army, given him clothing and money while he recovered from his wounds sustained at Waterloo, and then found him a not-quite-respectable job as a spy for the Home Office. Suddenly Alec felt the burden of that loyalty; if he could never prove his innocence, it would reflect very badly on James.

But James was all he had. Alec liked to think that his other friend from childhood, Will Lacey, would have stood by him as well, but Lacey really had died at Waterloo. Without James, Alec would have been a dead man and he knew it.

"I'll leave by the end of the week," he said, rising to his feet and extending his hand. "Thank you for everything."

James shook his hand. "Promise me one thing." Alec raised his brows in question. "When you catch the bastard who really did write those letters to the French, tell me. I should like to see him hang."

"You may depend on it," Alec vowed.

His friend didn't smile. "Won't you stay here until you go? You look a bit haggard."

"Small wonder," said Alec wryly. "Don't all dead men, before they rise again?"

Chapter 1

Penford didn't appear to have changed much. Three stories of limestone, stately but comfortable, with a pitched roof he had once skidded off on a sled when the snow was particularly deep. The grounds still ranged somewhat wildly about the house, as if the gardener had been let go, but it was all by design; his mother had always favored an almost wilderness air to her grounds, and her children had loved it, spending hours scampering through those woods when they were supposed to be at their studies.

Penford looked almost too much the way he remembered it, as if time had not passed at all. Alec shifted in the saddle, ashamed that he had unconsciously expected to see some sort of decay, some sign that he—and now Frederick—had been missed. Instead it appeared just as it always had, at least from this distance. Perhaps it was comforting that it was more ageless than he was, that it was still a safe and secure home for what remained of his family.

He hoped the next few days wouldn't shake that security too badly.

Alec gathered the reins and urged the horse forward. He had had a whole week to prepare for this day, which ought to be filled with joy. He'd only been dreaming about it for five long years. Instead he let the horse walk, and tried to quell the sudden urge to turn and go back the other way, back to the inn where he had stayed the previous night or even all the way back to London. He had sent word that he was arriving today, and Peterbury had written them as well. Even without Stafford's mission to pursue, Alec had no choice but to go forward.

When he reached the curve in the drive, a figure emerged from the house. He shaded his eyes and watched Alec for a few minutes, then strode down the graveled drive to meet him, the tails of his coat flapping behind him in his haste. Alec drew up the horse when they met, and looked into the curious, wary eyes of his cousin John.

For a long moment they just studied each other. John had grown tall and solid, his fair hair cut short and his complexion ruddy from the sun. He was dressed as any country squire might be, the image of a hardworking landowner. He had an honest face, Alec thought, though his expression was pure amazement at the moment.

"Alec? Alexander Hayes?" said John slowly. "Is it really you?"

There was no denying it now, and no going back. He swung down from the saddle. "It is good to see you, John."

John's light green eyes moved up and down, taking him in. "By God," he said softly. "It is. It really is."

Alec's hand stiffened on the horse's bridle. "Yes."

"By God," murmured John again.

He cleared his throat when the pause wore on too long. "Is my mother . . . ?"

His cousin shook himself, still seeming dazed. "Yes. We received James Peterbury's letter a few days ago, and then yours a day later. It was quite a shock, but of the happiest kind. My aunt has been beside herself awaiting this moment. You must come in to her at once." He stuck out his hand, and when Alec took it, he threw his arm around Alec's shoulder, pulling him into an awkward embrace. "Welcome home, cousin," he said in a voice muffled against Alec's shoulder.

It was far more cordial than he had expected. He hadn't seen John in nearly a dozen years, and they had never really been friends. But after a moment he returned the embrace, then stepped back and collected the reins. John fell in step beside him and they walked toward the house. "I understand you've been looking after things here," said Alec, for lack of anything better to say while John still watched him from the corner of his eye as one would watch a circus curiosity. He told himself to get used to seeing that expression.

John jerked around to face him, eyes wide, but then he laughed, a bit ruefully. "Oh—yes. Freddie invited me for the Christmas holidays, and then after he fell ill . . ." He pursed his lips and looked at the ground. "My condolences on his death."

Alec nodded once. Freddie, John called him. Clearly John had had a closer relationship with his brother than Alec had, even allowing for the void of the last years. "Thank you," he murmured. "I am pleased he was not alone or consumed by estate business."

It took a moment for his cousin to reply. "No, no, he was not burdened by it." He kicked a rock from the drive, sending it bouncing into the neatly trimmed lawn. "I shall be happy to go over the books with you at your convenience. I believe they are still kept in the same manner as your father kept them. Freddie never changed, and I . . . Well, I assumed he would return to form in due time and come thrash me if I changed his accounting."

Frederick had never been one to thrash, and they both knew it. Frederick would have frowned and pinched his lips together, then gone off and redone the books the way he wanted them. Alec felt a stab of pain that he'd never see that disappointed look again. "I'm sure everything is fine."

"I have tried to run things properly, as your father and brother would have done . . ." John's voice died abruptly as Alec stopped.

"And because you thought they were to be yours," he said quietly. "John—"

"No, no." John held up one hand, his smile grim and tight. "I thought that, yes. But it is a far greater happiness that you are still alive. Losing Frederick was very hard on your mother."

Alec looked toward the house. Other people had come out. His mother, leaning on his sister, Julia's arm. His sister-in-law, Marianne, holding a child in one arm with another child clinging to her black skirts. Abruptly he felt suffocated, hemmed in, and gripped by a mad desire to mount his horse and ride far from all of them before he could see the expressions on their faces. Frederick had died honestly; Alec had just disappeared, letting them believe him dead because it suited him, and for a brief horrible moment, he wished he'd had the decency to succumb to his injuries on the field of Waterloo.

"Come." John nodded at the welcoming party. "They are anxious to see you."

As they drew near, Alec began to focus on telling details. Marianne's children hid their faces at his approach. Marianne, more lovely and fair than ever in her widow's weeds, seemed on the verge of tears as she stared at him, her knuckles white where she held her smaller child. Julia watched him almost belligerently, her chin high and her eyes blazing, looking taller and thinner than before. But his mother . . .

"Mother," he said softly, stopping an arm's length in front of her. "I've missed you."

She reached out her hand to touch his sleeve. She was smaller than he remembered, more stooped and wrinkled. Her gaze lifted to his face in wonder, the same deep blue eyes that peered from his mirror every morning. Funny how he had forgotten until now that he had her eyes. "Alexander," she whispered. "You *have* come back." She released Julia and took two steps forward until she could lean on his outstretched arms. Her hands trembled as her fingers curled into the fabric of his coat, digging into his arms. "Oh, Alexander," she said again, tears beginning to stream down her face. "My *son*."

Alec felt the first real bite of despair as his mother laid her cheek against his chest and wept. She was his mother, as familiar as his own flesh, and yet not. A deep shame swept over him. No matter that he knew he was innocent of treason; his family could not have known, and if they had believed him innocent nonetheless, they had done so without any proof or even assurances from him that it was so. In his outrage and humiliation and even fear, he had simply vanished and left them to face the public scorn for him. "Mother," he said again, helplessly. "I am so sorry."

She raised her head to look at him. "Never," she said fiercely, through her tears. "Never apologize. Whatever grief I have endured cannot match my joy at your return. I lost both my sons, and now one has returned to me. I don't care how or why, I only care that you are alive and well and home."

"What you must think," he began, until she put up her hand, touching his cheek.

"Not now," she said gently. "Today is a day for celebration, nothing else."

Her words only made him feel worse somehow. If she had demanded to know if he truly had sold secrets to the French . . . if she had asked where he'd been for the last five years and what he'd been doing . . . If she had only asked why he hadn't sent her even a whisper of a suggestion that he was still alive . . . All those questions would have been her right to ask, and the fact that she didn't ask one, but merely gathered him into her arms as she had done so many times when he was a boy, rent Alec's heart. He was better as a spy now, alone and unfettered, when he didn't even have to pretend to any sort of honesty. Gingerly he held his mother and let her weep.

"Oh, but I've gone and turned maudlin," she said, raising her head and dabbing at her eyes with a handkerchief. "On this, the happiest day in many a month." She stepped back, and Alec saw her make a small hand motion urging Julia on.

His sister didn't appear nearly as pleased to see him. "Alec," she said, ducking her head in a stiff curtsey.

"It is good to see you again, Julia," he replied. She pressed her lips together and said nothing. "And you, Marianne."

Frederick's wife jumped as he said her name. The child she was holding clung tighter to her neck and started to whimper. "Welcome home, Alec," she said quietly. "We were overjoyed to hear of your return."

"Thank you," he murmured. Everyone was looking at him, and with such naked curiosity and emotion. It made his skin crawl to be the focus of so much attention, after years of avoiding all notice.

"Well," said his mother brightly, "shall we go inside? You must be tired, Alexander dear, and in want of a drink." Clinging to his arm, she steered him into the house. He couldn't help glancing up and around as he passed through the high arched door into the main hall. He might have left only a month ago; the house was just as he remembered it inside as well as out. The butler and housekeeper were waiting within, and from the quick patter of footsteps, the rest of the servants had also been loitering about the hall, hoping to catch a glimpse of the man come back from the dead. Alec tried to rein in his dark mood, but it all began to seem quite ghoulish.

"Farley, see to Major Hayes's things at once," his mother told the butler. "Mrs. Smythe, send tea to the drawing room, along with . . ." She glanced up at Alec. "A bottle of port, and some brandy." The servants bowed and hurried off. "Come, dear," she said to Alec. "Won't you sit with me?"

Like a funeral train, everyone filed into the sitting room. Marianne followed after sending her children upstairs with a nursemaid. The thought that he was attending his own funeral grew more pronounced; irrationally, Alec felt like saying it aloud to provoke any other reaction. Only his mother seemed oblivious, settling herself in the chair that had always been hers, beaming at Alec as he sat next to her.

But then no one seemed to know what to say. The silence grew more and more ominous as they all sat and hardly looked at one another. Alec finally forced himself to speak. "I only recently heard of Frederick's death. If I had known—"

"Then what?" Julia said under her breath.

Perhaps if they had a loud screaming row, it would air out the grievances everyone must be feeling, like ripping a bandage from a festering wound in one painful swoop. Alec turned to face his sister. "What do you want to know, Julia?"

She lifted her chin, taking up his challenge. "The same thing we all want to know, I daresay. Where you've been for five years and why the bloody hell you didn't send Mother even a single word that you were alive—"

"Julia!" cried her mother.

Julia's mouth pursed. "I was just answering his question, Mother. Didn't you say we must go on as if nothing had changed?"

Anthea Hayes flushed. "Not today, Julia," she said with steel in her voice.

"No, no," Alec replied, watching his sister's face burn red. "Let her speak. Julia and I were never coy with each other."

Julia's hands balled into fists in her lap. "Weren't we?" she retorted. "And yet you've been exceptionally coy these last five years, neglecting to tell us you still lived."

His sister was seething with fury, and oddly it made Alec feel better. This was better than sitting and being stared at with amazement and suspicion. "I wouldn't call it coy or neglectful—"

"Oh?" She sniffed. "Perhaps willfully deceitful, then."

"Julia," said Marianne softly.

His sister opened her mouth, then closed it. She lurched to her feet. "Pray excuse me, Mother. I feel a headache coming on and would like to retire to my room." She shot a furious glare at Alec before sweeping from the room.

He clenched his jaw as the door slammed shut behind her. He saw the worried look Marianne sent John, and the way John replied with a tiny shake of his head. "I am so sorry," said his mother, reaching out to put her hand on his. "Julia is . . . Well, it was a tremendous shock . . ."

"Mother, I understand." Alec shook his head. "I don't expect her to be overjoyed."

"Julia always loved you so; this has been a very hard week for her," she replied. "She was distraught after Waterloo, when we heard . . . But she will come around in time."

In time. The thought of the weeks and days ahead

made Alec's head ache. If this was the reaction from his family, how much worse would it be when he met neighbors and old friends? He might as well have come home with the word "traitor" branded on his forehead. "I'm sure it has been very hard on you as well."

"Oh, no!" His mother's face lit up. "When the Peterbury boy wrote to us, telling us you were alive and well— Alexander, you cannot know what happiness I felt, and then doubly so when your letter arrived a day later. This has been the longest week of my life, waiting to see for myself. Your father . . ." Her voice wobbled. "He would have been overjoyed as well." Tears glimmered in her eyes.

"Excuse me," John murmured, rising to his feet. "I have some things to see to . . ." He trailed off and coughed, looking ill at ease.

"And I should go to the children." Marianne rose. "You must wish to have some time together. Welcome home, Alec."

In the silence after their departure, Alec turned to his mother. "I know everyone will have questions, Mother. You mustn't tell Julia she should go on as if nothing has happened."

She pressed her lips together. "Julia should moderate her tongue."

Alec was surprised into a short laugh. His sister had always been the most outspoken of the Hayes children, for she had known she was the apple of their father's eye and would get away with anything. "Why start now?"

His mother didn't respond to it. She touched the cuff of his jacket again, smoothing her fingertips over the fabric as though to reassure herself he was real. "Never mind. Julia will get over her upset. All will be well now that you are home again."

Alec thought of all the reasons she was wrong. He suspected his mother was willfully turning a blind eye to every one of those reasons, and that it would only delay the inevitable questions and explanations. More potently than ever, he wished he had been able to refute the charges of treason; now he had come home without the vindication he needed and would be even more suspect because of it. Who would believe him innocent after he had disappeared for five years without a word to his family? Thanks to Stafford's intervention with the Home Office, he wasn't about to be arrested, but Alec hardly thought that would prove anything to the people of Marston, who had long ago accepted his guilt.

But it would be cruel to say that to her now. Let one person at least rejoice in his return. He covered her hand on his arm with his own. "I hope so, Mother."

But I doubt it.

Chapter 2

Alec strode toward the breakfast room early the next morning, still buttoning his coat. A previous assignment for Stafford had been as a footman, where he'd had to rise before dawn to start fires and begin his day's chores, and he had kept to the hours ever since. They weren't so different from army hours. Even if he hadn't been accustomed to rising early, though, Alec would have been up and dressed; he was desperately eager to leave the house.

His mother had put him in his father's chamber. Of course it must have been Frederick's until his death, but Alec remembered only his father in that room, from the stern reprimands he had received as a child to the solemn farewell he had taken of his father, by then grown old and ill and confined to bed, before leaving on that last fateful campaign in Belgium. Alec had shied away from it; he asked for his old room, but after some fretting his mother finally confessed it was now John's. All of Alec's possessions had been packed away in the attic after Waterloo. Besides, she urged him, he should have the master's suite now that he was the master. It seemed to tighten a sort of noose around his neck, hearing those words, but in the interest of peace and grace, he had just nodded and accepted it.

But by the time morning came, Alec thought he might go mad if he didn't get out of that room—out of the whole house, in fact. He intended to gulp down a cup of coffee and spare himself and his family a painful breakfast together. Perhaps a long ride about the property would restore his connection to the place and bring him some peace.

He pushed open the door and stopped short. Julia stood looking out the window, a cup of tea in her hand. At his entrance she turned with a smile that withered as soon as she saw him.

"Good morning," he said.

She sipped her tea and turned back to the window. "Good morning."

The sideboard had already been laid out with a number of dishes, a welcome sight. Still, from the blushing sky, it was very early. "Do you normally rise this early?" For the life of him he couldn't recall what Julia had done before he left.

"Yes," she muttered.

"Ah," Alec said when it was clear she meant to say no more. "It is just one of many things I have forgotten."

"Perhaps I've changed. It's been years and years, you know."

He heard the chill in her words. Even though he told himself it would take time for them to get used to each other again, it pricked his temper a little bit. "I am aware of exactly how long it's been, Julia."

She gave a quiet sniff.

Alec poured a cup of coffee. "I don't pretend nothing has changed. By all means, speak your mind."

"What can I have to say, to the prodigal son returned home at long last? To our own Lazarus, back from the dead when Mother mourned all these years not even being able to tend your grave? Why, what could I *possibly* have to say that might interest you now, when you've not cared a fig for what any of us thought or felt for the last five years?" Her light, airy tone was more biting than any sarcasm or bitterness could have been.

He took a sip of the coffee. Hot and rich, it was the best coffee he'd had in years. Once he would have met Julia on her own terms, replied in kind, and erupted in a blazing fury. As children, they were two of a kind in temperament. He had grown used to controlling himself since then, though. A spy learned to keep his thoughts and feelings to himself. "Of course. Forgive me for taking an interest."

"I am sure it will pass in short order."

"Julia, shall I apologize again?" he said curtly.

"Whatever for?" She turned to face him, eyes wide in feigned surprise.

"I didn't come home to argue with you," he snapped in spite of himself. "What do you want from me?"

"Nothing—Nothing at all!"

"I see."

"How could you?" She shook her head. "Things were so much easier when we thought you were dead." Alec froze. Julia's face turned deathly pale, but she put up her chin and glared at him. She did not retract her words. His own sister, the girl who had once adored him and teased him and written tearstained letters to him in Spain, wished he were dead.

Carefully, deliberately, Alec put down his cup and walked from the room.

He rode like the demons of hell pursued him. The horse was Frederick's, long-limbed and sedate, but under Alec's hand he stretched his stride and fairly flew over the hills and meadows of Penford. By the time Alec pulled him up on the edge of the ridge, the horse was lathered with sweat and breathing as hard as Alec himself.

He swung down from the saddle. His last few years had not included much riding, but his body remembered the rhythm well. As they'd charged up the last hill, his memory flashed vividly back to another charge up a hill, with French bullets whining past him and artillery shaking the ground. He'd had a saber in his hand and the bloodlust of battle in his heart, and no real inkling of what was to come. What a bloody fool.

Alec wound the reins around his hand and walked, cooling the tired horse after his run. He rarely thought about his army days anymore; it was a distant memory, a long-ago life that had little bearing on the present. He turned and surveyed the rolling, verdant lands of Penford, his inheritance, his home. The sight inspired nothing within him. It might have been any piece of land, in England or Belgium or the distant reaches of America for all the meaning it had to him now. For too long he had been no one, not an officer, not a gentleman, not even Alexander Hayes but Alec Brandon, imposter and spy. Now he didn't quite know who he really was.

The horse tugged against the rein, stretching his neck for a bite of grass. Alec roused himself from his thoughts and turned back to what he did know. He still had Stafford's business to attend to, and right now it was a more attractive proposition than anything that awaited him at Penford. With a pat to the horse's neck, he mounted again and turned in the direction of the Turner property.

Sergeant Turner had taken Brighampton, a modest estate just a few miles from Penford. In truth it was more of a farm than an estate, but Alec noted the fields were not well-tended as he rode past them, taking the shortest path instead of going by the main road. Nor did he see anyone working in the fields, another sign that the sergeant's absence was trouble. Who would lease a farm like Brighampton and then not farm it? And when he came in sight of the house, other signs of neglect became apparent, from the overgrown shrubberies to a shutter hanging loose.

The house sat on the edge of a small copse of trees, a cottage really. Behind it were a squat stable and a few other outbuildings, with a large vegetable garden that did look neat and tidy. From the other side of the trees spread a wide meadow dotted with grazing sheep. The sergeant appeared to have done fairly well for himself at some point. Perhaps he just didn't intend to farm the land. Alec catalogued other details about the property as he rode up, trying to form a view of the missing man and his situation before hearing from his family. But then a strange sight caught his attention, distracting him from conjectures about the Turners.

A man was sneaking out of the stable. There was no doubt of it, from the way the fellow glanced left and right every few feet. He was a big man, broad in the chest, with long arms hunched close up to his sides and a cap pulled low over his forehead. Alec couldn't see his face, but when the man sidled around the corner of the stable and took off at a run, he nudged the horse to follow. It could be a servant, shirking his duties . . . but Alec's instincts said not. Better to take a look and find nothing amiss than to let someone significant slip away.

The man had disappeared into the woods by the time Alec reached the edge of it. He pulled up at the trees, which were quite dense, and stared into the shadowy woods. Birds chattered in the branches and a rabbit darted under a fallen log, but there was no sign of the suspicious character. Alec turned and rode back to the stable, wondering what the man had been doing in there so stealthily.

It was a modest stable. There were two horses in the stalls munching on hay, but the rest of the stable was empty and apparently unused. Alec moved slowly and silently, peering into empty stalls and around corners, trying to see what could have attracted a man who ran off into the woods. It looked very ordinary, neatly kept although far from filled. He could see no signs of damage or anything maliciously done. The man couldn't have been carrying anything large. If he weren't a thief or a vandal, what could he be?

He heard the whisper of a footstep just before the question came from behind him. "May I help you, sir?"

Slowly Alec turned, put on guard by her tone of voice. Frigid with scorn, it wasn't nearly as polite as the question. Sure enough, his eyes fell first on the pistol in her raised hand, pointed right at his chest. He had faced pistols before, though, and more than one of them had fired—not usually at such close quarters, but he had learned to ignore the urge to flinch and dive for cover. It was much more prudent to be ready to strike back, should the opportunity arise . . . as well it might, he realized, finally looking the woman in the face.

She was tall and slim, and not half as old as he had expected. Her heart-shaped face was framed by long tendrils of brown hair, pulled loose from the knot on top of her head. The heavy pistol trembled almost imperceptibly in her grip, but her eyes—luscious eyes the color of cinnamon and gold and amber—were utterly calm and level. Alec's interest rose a notch; he'd never been shot by a woman.

"Perhaps," he said. "I've come looking for Sergeant George Turner."

Her chin went up. "He doesn't live in the stables. Perhaps you noticed the house on your ride in?"

His lips twitched. "Indeed. But I saw a man about the stables, and thought it might be he."

"He would still prefer to receive you in the house, I am sure."

She wasn't giving anything away without being forced to it. Alec had been deliberately vague and she had not corrected him. "No doubt. Forgive me. I will go to him there, then."

She hesitated. "He is not at home, at present."

Alec was well-aware of that, but wanted to see

what she would tell him. "When might he be at home?"

This time she bristled. "When he returns. I'm not his keeper."

Alec's eyes slid down her figure in quick appraisal. Sergeant Turner was a man in his fifties, with two daughters and his elderly mother in his household. This must be one of the daughters. She was, however, still pointing a pistol at him. "You are his wife?"

"His daughter." With a click she pulled back the hammer of the pistol. "Who the bloody hell are you?"

"Alexander Hayes, at your service." He gave a slight bow; he hadn't even noticed the pistol wasn't cocked. Damn this assignment. Damn her eyes. "We are neighbors."

Again she hesitated. She glanced past him to his horse, tied at the stable door, and then she slowly lowered her arm. "You have odd manners for a neighbor, sir."

"Forgive me," Alec said again. "I merely thought to avoid troubling the whole household." He noticed she hadn't suggested he had seen a groom or other servant. There was no sign of one, though, and the man he'd seen did not look like a stable boy. He looked like a thief, to be honest. "I apologize, Miss Turner. I shall call at a more convenient time."

She clearly didn't like him. Her mouth pressed into a hard, thin line, and she merely jerked her head in a grudging nod and stepped back, inviting him to leave. Alec hid his mild amusement and bowed. There was nearly as much information in her pose and actions as if she'd actually told him. Either she was of a highly suspicious or secretive nature, or other people had come around the farm before, looking for her father. And how interesting it was that she pulled a pistol on him before bothering to discover his name or purpose.

He could feel her eyes on his back the whole time he walked to his horse, mounted, and rode away.

Chapter 3

Cressida Turner watched until the stranger rode away, down the road this time. Then she turned back toward the house, only to meet Tom coming at a dead run.

"What's happened?" he demanded, his hair standing up every which way and his face flushed. "Your sister said you'd gone out in a hurry."

She smiled, hiding her clenched teeth. "Nothing happened. There was a man out at the stables, looking around."

Tom stiffened. "And?"

"And that's all, or all I caught him doing. He says he's a neighbor." She snorted. "Such fine neighbors we've got here, all coming around to spy on how terrible things are." It made her fume; did ordinary neighbors sneak into each others' stables and examine the horses? Of course not, as he knew full well. He hadn't been surprised at all when he looked down the barrel of her pistol. She almost wished she'd had the nerve to fire the gun, just to rattle that calm, piercing gaze of his.

Tom's face creased in a worried frown. "You can't go running off everyone who comes about."

Cressida looked at the heavy pistol in her hand and sighed. Her fingers felt stiff and cramped from gripping it so hard. "Someone's got to. You were fixing the sheep fence. Next time I'll let you run them off, if you prefer."

He didn't look mollified, but nodded and fell in step beside her. Tom Webb had been in the army with her father and was now their general man of work, and he was as protective of Cressida and her sister as a fussy old hen would be of her chicks. "Did he give a name?"

"Alexander Hayes."

Tom gave her a sharp look, and she couldn't help glancing over her shoulder just to be sure the man she spoke of was gone. "The dead one?"

Cressida shuddered. News of the resurrection of Marston's most infamous resident had swept through the town in the last few days. Major Alexander Hayes, the younger son of a very old and prominent local family, had been thought dead on the fields of Waterloo some five years ago, which everyone agreed was a good thing, since the man had turned out to be a traitor. His family had suffered terribly, according to local gossip. The elder Mr. Hayes died of despair soon after his son's treachery came to light, and just this spring the new master of Penford had also died of a lingering illness. The family had lived very quietly for some time, still respectable but widely pitied. This Major Hayes's return, if he really *was* Major Hayes, would stir up the neighborhood to no end. She wondered what on earth he could want with her father.

"The obviously *not* dead one," she said in reply to Tom's question. "He doesn't look even the slightest bit

worm-eaten." Far from it, in fact. Which was too bad.
Now even people who were supposed to be molder-
ing in their graves were coming around to pry into
their troubles. Cressida would fear demons escaping
hell to torment her next, except that she suspected
they were already upon her. If only Papa would come
home . . .

They had reached the house. The door stood open,
begging a cool breeze to drift through, to no avail. It
was as hot inside the house as it was outside. Cressida
knew the heat was shortening her temper as much as
her other worries were, and she dragged the back of
her hand across her forehead, feeling her sleeve stick
to her arm. She wished they hadn't moved here. If
they still lived in Portsmouth, she could have sneaked
down to the sea after dark and gone for a swim to
cool down. How she missed Portsmouth.

"George? George darling, is that you?"

Cressida paused, glancing up at Tom. Her grandmother's voice was so bright and hopeful, as if she
truly believed Papa might just stroll into the house.
Tom, looking grim again, opened his mouth, but
she pressed a finger to her lips and handed him the
pistol. Tucking a loose strand of hair behind her
ear, she straightened her shoulders and walked into
the drawing room as if she hadn't just confronted a
stranger at gunpoint while he studied her horses with
an eye to buying them at auction.

"No, Granny, it's just I," she said, going back to
her seat. They had been having tea when her ears
picked up the sound of hoofbeats behind the house.
She had slipped out with some murmured excuse
to her grandmother, who was a little hard of hear-

ing and hadn't noticed the approaching horse. Her older sister, Callie, shot her a questioning glance, but Cressida just smiled.

"I was sure it would be your father," Granny said fretfully, her gaze lingering on the doorway. "Your step sounds so like his, my dear. And he is due home any day now."

Cressida picked up her tea. Her father had been due home any day now for four months. He had gone missing before—or rather, he had left and not told them where he went or when to expect him back, but they had always known it before. Papa would wink and pinch her cheek and say he was off, and he'd be back "in a fair while." "A fair while" had lasted anywhere from a fortnight to three months, but he had always come back just before the money ran out. Papa seemed to have a knack for knowing when the money was about to run out. Not this time, though. This time they were staring complete and utter ruin in the face, and there was still no sign of her father.

"I'm sure he'll be home soon," she said for her grandmother's benefit.

"Of course he will." Granny put down her tea and turned to stare out the front window, the one that faced the road. "Any day."

He'd better, Cressida thought, staring into her tea, now stone cold in the expensive new teacups Papa had ordered when they moved to Marston. Otherwise they were all sunk.

After tea, when Granny had dozed off in her chair and they had cleared away the tea, Callie followed her to the kitchen. "What was wrong?" she wanted to know, setting down the tray of dirty dishes as

Cressida put on her apron. Papa had hired a cook and a pair of maids, but they were all gone now. How fortunate that Cressida and her sister were quite used to having no servants at all. "You just jumped up and ran from the room, and then were gone a quarter hour. Granny remarked on it."

"Did she?" Cressida poured out the dregs of the tea from the pot. "What did she say?"

Callie sighed. "She thought you might have heard Papa approaching. She's certain he'll walk through the door at any moment."

"If only he would," she muttered. "I begin to wonder . . ."

Her sister went still. "To wonder what?"

"To doubt," Cressida admitted. She picked up a teacup and began to wash it. "He's never been gone this long without some sort of word, not unless there was a war going on. And then we certainly knew where he was."

Callie bit her lip and said nothing.

"I heard a horse," she said bluntly. "Out behind the house. I thought it might be another creditor, so I went out to see. A man was walking around the stables, and I thought he had come to take the horses."

"Cressida, you shouldn't go out there by yourself! You should send Mr. Webb—"

"He was busy mending the fence, and there wasn't time to fetch him. We'll be even worse off if the sheep get loose. Don't worry," she added, seeing Callie's dismayed expression. "I took Papa's pistol, just in case."

Callie gasped. "You pulled a pistol on him?"

She flushed. "I didn't shoot him, if that's what you're worried about. Even Granny would have heard that." The door creaked open, and Tom came in. At the sight of Callie he stopped short, ducking his head in a hasty bow.

"Mr. Webb, my sister says there was a man on the property, looking at the horses," Callie said.

He glanced at Cressida, who kept her eyes on the teacup she was wiping. "There was."

"What are we to do?" When no one answered, Callie threw up her hands. "What aren't you telling me? Did he take the horses? Did he set fire to the stables? What happened?"

Tom just looked at Cressida, who took her time washing every last crevice of the delicate cup. It would be worth more unchipped, when she had to sell it. "It was our neighbor," she said.

Callie looked puzzled. "Which one?"

"Major Alexander Hayes," Tom answered for her. Cressida shot him a dark look.

Callie gasped, her hand flying to her throat. "Oh dear—the dead one?"

"He's definitely not dead anymore." Cressida handed the cup to Callie to dry. "And he was looking for Papa."

There was a long moment of silence in the kitchen, broken only by the splash of water as Cressida washed a plate. The three of them were conspirators, keeping the bad news from Granny that Papa was gone and apparently not coming back. Cressida hated to think that, but every day that he was gone was another day of doubt that he would ever come striding back through the door in his exuberant way, roaring with laughter and bearing gifts for them all. Every day that he was gone, they sank deeper into debt, since Papa had left only a few weeks' worth of funds. Among the three of them standing silently in the kitchen, they had managed to feed themselves and the animals, but they'd had to let go all the servants and quietly return most of the more frivolous things Papa had bought. They were getting by, but only just, and Cressida knew they were perilously close to slipping beyond that into true difficulty.

"Perhaps I should go after the sergeant," said Tom at last. "He's been gone a long time."

Callie made a soft noise of distress and Cressida shook her head. "I think we'd rather you stay, Tom. Papa . . ." She paused, steadying her voice. "Papa can look after himself." *I hope . . .*

"Thank you, Mr. Webb," Callie added in a heartfelt tone. "But I—yes, we would much rather you not go."

Tom flushed. "Of course, Mrs. Phillips," he mumbled. He and Callie kept up a formality in address that Cressida had long since discarded. Tom was like a member of the family after all these years. He'd come home with her father from the wars, and with no family of his own to go to, he'd stayed. He had become a man of work around their house in Portsmouth and now the farm, with a much more practical bent than Papa had. Papa could charm an extra pint of ale from even the most hard-hearted innkeeper, but Tom could fix the fence around the sheep pen and start a fire with new wood—infinitely more useful talents, particularly in their present situation.

"Well, the good news is that he wasn't here to collect on a debt Papa owed him," said Cressida.

"He said that?"

She frowned at her sister. "No, but how could Papa owe a man who was dead and buried five years ago?"

"Obviously he was not really dead and buried five years ago," snapped Callie. "He's had just enough time to find debt markers in the late Mr. Hayes's things."

That was true. Papa might have owed money to Frederick Hayes, and his brother could have discovered the note. Cressida sighed. "Perhaps. Tom, could we get by without the horses? They cost a fortune to feed."

Tom folded his arms and thought a moment. "That'd be the end of farming. Oxen cost just as much and can't pull a carriage. And you'd have to tell your grandmother."

With great care Cressida set down the last clean teacup. She didn't want to tell Granny, who had lived so frugally and even meanly to raise two motherless granddaughters while their father was at war, that they were destitute again. Granny had been happier than any of them to move to Marston almost a year ago, delighted beyond words that Papa's grand plans had finally paid off and bought them a life of relative comfort and ease. Leaving this country cottage would be hard on Granny, even had it not been a tacit admission that Papa was not coming back any time soon.

"We'll worry about that if he comes again seeking repayment," she said softly. "For now, we'll just . . . keep on as we are."

Chapter 4

Cressida's plans had progressed no further than that when they were abruptly ruined the next morning. In the middle of her morning chores a knock sounded at the front door. Pausing only to pull off her apron—Granny would ring a peal over her head for opening the door in her apron, even if everyone knew the Turners had no more servants and must do the cleaning themselves—she opened the door and inhaled sharply. Standing on the front step was the man who had been in the stable the previous day, the dead man who was not dead.

"Good morning," he said, doffing his hat with a courteous bow to reveal close-cropped dark hair. Cressida could only stare at him in mute horror.

"Is there someone—? Oh!" Callie had come up behind her. Cressida couldn't seem to look away from the visitor, even when she felt her sister's gaze on her. He looked different in the sunlight: taller, cleaner, more commanding. Richer, too; unbidden, the fear that he had come for money owed him clutched at her. They had no money to pay anyone. And he was still looking directly at her with searing blue eyes that seemed to have frozen her mind and tongue.

"Good day, sir," Callie said after an awkward pause. She poked Cressida in the back as she bobbed a brief curtsey. "May we help you?"

He finally turned that gaze on Callie. "Forgive me for calling unannounced. Alexander Hayes, at your service. I have come on a somewhat delicate matter, involving Sergeant George Turner. This is his home, is it not?"

Cressida's knees locked. Oh dear God. A delicate matter. He had come about money. She gripped the dust cloth in her hand until her fingers shook.

"Of course," Callie said hesitantly. "Please come in. I am Mrs. Phillips, and this is my sister, Miss Cressida Turner. Sergeant Turner is our father."

Major Hayes bowed again, without looking in Cressida's direction. Her face feeling like wood, she followed Callie's example and bobbed a curtsey. A fine sort of gentleman he turned out to be. Vulture, she thought wildly, even though she knew it was unjust. If the Hayes family had lent Papa money, they deserved to be repaid. She just didn't know how she would do it.

She followed Callie and Major Hayes into the parlor, which thankfully she had already dusted. In fact, the dust cloth was still in her hand, and she hastily dropped it on her chair and sat on it, trying to calm her thundering pulse. Perhaps she should have told him to just take the horses the other day . . .

"I have come at the request of Colonel Lord Augustus Hastings," said the major when he had taken a seat. "I believe you wrote to him inquiring after your father." Callie shot a worried look at Cressida, but slowly nodded. Major Hayes smiled a little, a kind, reassuring smile. Not at all like a vulture. "He has asked me to look into your father's disappearance, and to see if I might be of assistance to your family."

"Why didn't you say this earlier?" Cressida said before she could stop herself. He had come to help them, not to beggar them—oh, if only she had known that yesterday! She had pointed the pistol at him before he could explain anything, it was true, but if he had mentioned his connection to Hastings or his intentions, she certainly wouldn't have kept pointing it at him.

He turned those deep blue eyes on her, and she wished she hadn't spoken. "I was somewhat discomposed when we met previously, Miss Turner. Forgive me."

"Of course," she muttered. If he had been discomposed, what would describe her feeling now? Regret, that she had almost shot a man who came in response to her letter? She could hardly apologize for that now, with Callie glancing curiously between the two of them. Cressida dug her fingernails into her palms. No, it wasn't regret; more like red-faced embarrassment. Had she really called him a vulture, even if only in her mind? She resolved to let Callie, the more temperate sister, speak from now on.

"That is very good of you, sir," her sister said when Cressida sat in resolute silence. "Lord Hastings sent us only a brief note that he knew nothing of what my father might have done after their meeting, and that he would make inquiries."

Major Hayes nodded. "I was informed of your situation and asked to make those inquiries. I know only the bare facts, though, and anything you can tell me would be a great help."

Callie cleared her throat and looked down. "Yes. Thank you. I— We— That is, my father left four months ago. He had gone to meet Lord Hastings in London, and we expected him to return within a fortnight."

"Did he send any word after his meeting with Lord Hastings that he would be delayed or planned to stay longer?"

"No."

The major's piercing eyes flashed toward Cressida for just a second. "And you did not write to Lord Hastings until a fortnight ago."

This time Callie turned toward Cressida, silently appealing for help. She wet her lips and reminded herself to be calm and polite. "Our father is not in the habit of telling us his every plan. We did expect him home sooner, but it would not be unusual for him to do . . . other things."

"Might those other things delay him three months?"

"Yes," she said. It didn't reflect very well on Papa, and she hated telling this stranger that he regularly took off on unexplained larks, but there was no point in hiding it, and she was beginning to run out of patience with her father anyway. "Sometimes."

"Ah." He was still looking at her. "And do you usually worry?"

Cressida felt the blood rush to her cheeks. Did they often write to senior military officers and ask for helping finding him, was what the major meant. "Not normally, no."

"If I may be so bold, what has alarmed you this time?"

He knew, she thought; he knew it was because they were running out of money. "He has never been gone this long," said Callie, diplomatically stepping into the breach. "We've had no word from him, and he did say he would return soon. We wrote to Lord Hastings in the hope Papa might have mentioned something to indicate where he had gone."

"Of course. I hope I may be of assistance in locating him soon. As I've no acquaintance with your father, it would be most helpful if you could describe him, sketch his character for me, to give me an idea where to begin."

Cressida bristled, although she tried to hide it. How was this man going to find Papa when he didn't know the first thing about him? "He's my height," she began in a flat voice. "Dark, like my sister, and very fit. If there is a gathering in the pub sharing ale, my father will be in the center of it, laughing and talking with everyone. He's clever and very amiable, the sort of fellow everyone likes."

Alec listened closely as she spoke, absorbing every detail available. The two sisters were nervous, although the taller one, whom he had met the other day across her pistol, was also angry—at whom, he wasn't certain, although from the way her eyes flashed when she looked his way, he was sure her opinion of *him* had not improved overnight. The other lady, Mrs. Phillips, was the prettier sister, with wide dark eyes and a delicate face. Her hands were slender and graceful, and the pile of curls atop her head gave her the appearance of a willowy flower.

Miss Turner, though, was more interesting. From her clenched hands to her rigid posture, he saw more of interest in her than in anything about her sister. Aside from the fact that she was not pleased to see him—perhaps out of instinctive dislike, perhaps out of embarrassment for her behavior the previous day—he could tell she was holding herself tightly in check. That alone made her intriguing, but Alec knew it was more than that.

He had to work at keeping his eyes away from her, in fact. She wasn't beautiful, but rather striking—not just for her height, which was quite tall for a woman, but for the fire in those extraordinary eyes. There was no name for that color, he thought, because it wasn't just one color but a changeable swirl of gold and brown, like a kaleidoscope. He had a feeling her eyes mirrored her thoughts, maybe more than she knew. She and her sister were both hiding something, of course. It could have been as mundane as a lack of money, but for all the fire in Miss Turner's gaze, Alec didn't think she was rash or foolish. Something had made her take a pistol into the stable and point it at him without even asking what he was about. He wondered what they weren't telling him about their father, or themselves, or their situation.

"Is there anyone else who might know Sergeant Turner and his habits?" he asked. So far neither woman had said anything he hadn't already known or guessed. Turner was a bit of a scoundrel, but a lovable one.

They shared a glance. "Our mother died many

years ago," said Mrs. Phillips. "Our grandmother lives with us, but she is not well."

"I am sorry to hear it. Perhaps when she is recovered—"

"She is not physically ill," said Miss Turner. "She is just . . . not herself. I don't think she'll be able to tell you anything useful about Papa."

"Ah." Perhaps the old lady's mind was not strong. Perhaps something had occurred to unhinge her. Alec tucked the thought away for future investigation. "Then I shan't disturb you any longer."

"What do you plan to do?"

He smiled briefly at Miss Turner's terse question. "Ask about. It's been a while since Sergeant Turner was in Marston, so it may take some time."

Mrs. Phillips shot to her feet. "Thank you, sir," she said in a rush. "It was very kind of Lord Hastings to send you."

"It is my pleasure," he replied, still looking at Miss Turner even as he rose. She had pursed her lips in unveiled skepticism. "Good day, Mrs. Phillips. Miss Turner." He bowed and left, trying to shake the image of those golden brown eyes.

"So." Callie folded her arms and gave Cressida a stern look when he was gone. "You threatened to shoot him."

She ignored that look and occupied herself with running the dust cloth along the already-clean table. "Obviously I was wrong. But what else was I to do? He certainly didn't tell me all . . ." She waved one hand. "All that!"

There was a long pause. "You also did not mention he was so handsome."

Cressida shrugged. "Do you really think so? He's awfully . . . tall."

"I have never seen eyes so blue. And yes, he looks very well indeed for a man who was, as you said, dead and buried five years ago."

"I thought he had come to take our horses." Guilt pinched her again; had she really threatened a man on such a quick assumption? *That* man?

"If he did take a horse, at least it would save us the expense of keeping it. And now someone will be out looking for Papa. Perhaps we shall pull through after all."

Cressida heard the fearful hope in her sister's voice and closed her eyes. "It seems very odd for Lord Hastings to send *him*."

"Well, perhaps," Callie slowly agreed. "But surely Lord Hastings wouldn't send someone unsuitable . . ."

Cressida snorted. "No, he sent a man thought dead these last few years—dead, and a traitor as well. What would be odd about that?"

"Do you not want his help?" Her sister sounded frightened. "What choice do we have?"

She didn't answer, just shrugged again. Perhaps there was no choice, but something about the major set her on edge. Cressida didn't like feeling flustered or slow-witted, and he made her feel both.

After a moment, Callie tilted her head and looked thoughtfully into space. "Too tall? I should think you liked being able to look a man in the eye for once."

"If you fancy him so much," she retorted, "by all means, try to attach his interest."

"I am done with men," Callie said with quiet dignity. "But you—"

"Oh, stop! I would rather have Tom any day!"

The humor, and the light, vanished from her sister's face. "I'm sorry, Cressida. I should not have teased you so. Forgive me."

Cressida felt utterly wretched as Callie walked from the room, as composed as ever but avoiding her pleading gaze. *Stop*, she wanted to cry to her sister, *I didn't mean it!* But Callie was gone, and Cressida listened as her footsteps crossed the hall, echoing now that the rugs were gone, then climbed the stairs before fading away altogether. She closed her eyes and drew in a deep breath, praying for patience and more moderation in her speech. How hard would it have been to go along with Callie's mild teasing, to admit that Major Hayes was almost sinfully handsome in addition to being the possible answer to their prayers? And even worse, to taunt her sister about her interest in him after Callie had already been married to a son of Lucifer and barely survived it?

With a curse that belied the earnestness of her prayer, Cressida flung the dust cloth across the room. She strode into the hall and seized the broom, sweeping vigorously for several minutes in an attempt to work off her frustration with physical activity. When she threw open the front door to sweep out the dirt, though, an unpleasant sight met her eyes.

The visitor, Major Hayes, was talking to Tom down the lane by the end of the fence, where the sheep had gotten through the broken gate. Tom leaned against the gate, nodding now and then but saying little. His posture was stiff and uncomfortable. Cressida put down the broom and started forward, worry and outrage quickening her step until she was almost running down the lane.

He saw her when she had covered half the distance. She was too far away to see his expression—or those damnably blue eyes—under the brim of his hat, but he bowed his head and raised one hand before swinging onto his horse's back. He said something else to Tom, who nodded, then Major Hayes rode off, cantering around the bend in the road without a glance back.

Cressida slowed to a walk, holding one hand against the stitch in her side. She was still staring after him when she reached Tom. "What did he want, Tom?"

Tom looked troubled. "He said he's come to look for the sergeant. Asked if I had anything to offer, any suggestion to make."

"Yes, that's about what he told us."

"Hmmph," was Tom's only reply.

Uncertain, Cressida looked down the road where Major Hayes had disappeared. "Callie thinks it is the answer to our prayers. Lord Hastings sent him, it seems." She turned back to Tom. "I wonder why he was sent to us. One might think coming back from the dead would require all a man's attention, even if he weren't a suspected traitor."

Tom shrugged. He had gone back to the gate and had a nail between his teeth as he hefted a rail into place.

"What did you tell him?" Cressida knew she was pestering him but couldn't stop herself.

Hammer in hand, Tom stabbed the nail into the rail. "Nothing," he mumbled.

"Well, of course you had nothing to tell, since we don't know anything. I don't know what on earth he's going to do that we haven't thought of." Tom began hammering the nail, sharp blows that shook the gate. Cressida sighed. "All right. Thank you, Tom."

The sound of his hammering followed her back to the house. Cressida was still worrying over the major's visit when she almost ran head-on into her grandmother.

"Granny," she exclaimed, stopping short. "What are you doing downstairs?"

Granny beamed up at her, wobbling a bit on her feet even though she clutched her cane. "Did I hear a gentleman's voice in the house, dear?"

Cressida's face heated, to her disgust. "Yes, Granny." She hesitated; mention of Papa was often enough to upset Granny to no end, and send her into a fretful decline. But not explaining the major's true purpose would let Granny think the intolerable—which her next question confirmed.

"Was he here to see you, or your sister?" Granny had such a twinkling smile.

"Er—both, really." There was no way around the truth. Cressida put one arm around her grandmother's frail shoulders and gently steered her toward the sitting room. Granny had become so thin lately, her skin like worn cotton over her bones. "Do you remember that I wrote to Lord Hastings, to see if Papa might have mentioned something about his plans?"

"You did?" Granny was trying to crane her neck and peer around Cressida's arm, out the open front door. "Well, yes, your father had better come home soon, if there are young men coming to call. It wouldn't do at all, dear, to consider a suitor without your father's permission. Was he a handsome fellow?"

Cressida repressed a sigh. First Callie, now Granny. "He wasn't a suitor. He came because Lord Hastings sent him to find Papa."

The instant she spoke, she knew it had been the wrong way to say it. Granny's smile turned into a frown in the blink of an eye, and she drew herself up to her full, diminutive height before turning on Cressida with her sternest voice. "Your father is not *lost*, young lady. I am sure he is off doing something very important—he must be, or he would have returned by now. He'll be home any day, you wait and see. Such a good man, and a good father, too. Hasn't he brought us to this lovely home? All those years away, he couldn't wait to be home. And now you dare suggest he's lost?"

This time she couldn't hold back the sigh. "Of course not," she replied, wishing Callie were here to soothe their grandmother. She had too much temper for the task. She wanted to burst out and ask Granny just where Papa was if he was so anxious to be home with them, and why he couldn't have let them know where he was, or at the very least sent money. He must know they didn't have enough to live on. But that would be enough to send Granny into a high-tempered scold, which would leave her winded and weaker than ever. "We were . . . worried about him.

And we miss him so, just as you do. What if he were injured somewhere and had no way to send word to us?"

"He always finds a way," said Granny firmly, letting Cressida help her into a wing chair near the window. Cressida grabbed a light throw from the settee, and knelt to tuck it over Granny's feet and legs. It was still fiercely hot, but Granny was somehow always cold.

"I am sure he will," she said. "Would you—?"

"Now this young man," Granny interrupted her. "Who was he?"

"Not a suitor," Cressida muttered.

"Was he handsome?"

She sat back on her heels and pushed the tendrils of damp hair from her forehead. "Handsome enough, I suppose." God would forgive her that little lie.

"Oh, my dear!" Her grandmother giggled like a young girl, clapping her hands together. "How exciting! I remember when Mr. Turner, your grandfather, came to call on me. You must wear your best dress next time, Cressida dear, and try to do something with your hair . . ." She reached out to smooth Cressida's wayward hair.

Cressida dodged. "I'll try." It was easier to agree to her grandmother's fanciful suggestions and ideas than to argue any sort of sense to her. She would be very happy never to deal with Major Hayes again, just as she had long since despaired of taming her hair into anything like Callie's smooth curls. Wear her best dress, indeed; for a man she had almost shot as a horse thief?

"Well, I do hope he's a charming fellow, like your

father. And prosperous, too. How lovely it would be if you could live nearby! I am sure your father will be pleased by that, to see his daughter so well-provided for."

Cressida gave a halfhearted smile and let her grandmother's words roll over her. Certainly it would be lovely to have a prosperous, handsome suitor, or even just a prosperous one. She sighed, almost amused by her wandering thoughts. Any suitor at all would be enough to please Granny, who still harbored hopes of seeing her married someday. Callie had at least been a wife, even if a desperately unhappy one. Cressida had once been engaged herself, but after it ended in humiliation, she had decided the Turner girls were better off without husbands, no matter how much Granny might long for them to find some.

Still . . . Her eyes strayed to the window, looking down the road that stretched hot and dry into the beech trees. It wasn't that she wanted to be a spinster all her life. When she passed a mother carrying her child, or saw a man smile at the woman on his arm, the longing to experience the same grew almost painful. But in cooler moments she could admit it wasn't likely. She had only ever had one suitor, and that had been when she was much younger and had been almost pretty. Ten years later, she probably had a better chance of unearthing diamonds from the vegetable garden than of finding a husband. She was cursed with being too tall, too plain, and too blunt-spoken. It was a rare man who didn't recoil in distaste from something she said or did, even if all she did was smile politely down at him.

Except for Major Hayes. When he sat in this parlor and looked at her with those unreadable blue eyes, she couldn't deny that some tiny part of her had felt a thrill of appreciation. He hadn't looked intimidated or affronted even when she pointed a gun at him, which was certainly worse than anything she had done to other men. And she didn't have to look down at him at all.

But that meant nothing. Cressida gave herself a mental shake. No, it didn't mean *nothing*; if anything, it probably meant the major had far more serious defects, if he didn't mind conversing across the barrel of a gun and never took the chance to reprove her for it. As if she needed another reason to be wary of him, after his shocking return from the dead and then his startling announcement that Lord Hastings had sent him to find Papa. No one needed to tell Cressida what all that meant: Major Hayes was best dealt with carefully, and only when absolutely necessary.

Chapter 5

The moment Alec had been dreading arrived all too soon.

John was waiting for him the next morning. "I've got the books ready for you," he said. "I'm sure you've been wanting to see them."

Alec had been wanting no such thing. In the few days since his return, he had done everything in his power to avoid taking the reins of Penford. It appeared to have prospered under John's care, and Alec had no idea how to keep it on the same track. He had been a soldier for almost ten years, then a spy; he hadn't spent more than a few months at Penford in all that time, and certainly didn't feel qualified to run it. But it was unreasonable to expect John to keep doing everything now. He saw no way around it, and so nodded and went off with John to the estate office.

"Edward Pitt is the estate manager," John said as they tramped down the path to the outbuildings. "He's a good man, been here for several years now. You'll be able to rely on him."

"Excellent."

"I'll stay a few weeks," John went on. "Or as long

as you would have me. Just in case . . . well, yes. Just in case."

Alec muttered something vaguely agreeable, then stopped. "This is bloody awkward. Can we be honest?"

John faced him warily. "Of course," he said, his tone as guarded as his expression.

Alec struggled to find the words he wanted, then cursed and blew out a sigh. "You're welcome at Penford as long as you want to remain."

John looked at him expectantly, then finally spoke, but slowly. "I think it best if I go. It will make things . . . easier."

Alec laughed, short and bitter. "There's little chance of that, no matter what you do." John looked away. "I regret upending all your expectations."

"Can't be helped," said his cousin with a philosophical shrug. "And truly, I am glad. My aunt has been transported with joy since learning you still lived and were coming home."

And with that, Alec felt the weight of Penford and all its dependants slide onto his shoulders. "I'm not a farmer," he said. "Never was inclined to be one. I went into the army to get away from it, for God's sake." He hated admitting inadequacy, but there was little point in denying it. John would realize it soon enough on his own, if he hadn't already.

Something like sympathy drifted across his cousin's face. "Pitt will handle most of it, if you direct him to. This—Penford—is in your blood. Don't be so quick to deny it. 'Tis a good estate with fine, fertile land, well-organized, and not too encumbered by debt. Freddie and your father were responsible men, and I believe you'll be the same." He grinned. "You never did like to come up short. Freddie and I would marvel how you'd damned near kill yourself to do what you said you'd do."

Alec blinked, then the memory came. "Black Bess."

"The meanest animal I ever saw. I've still got a scar on my arse where that bloody horse bit me. And you rode her from here to Marston and back."

"She bit me, too," Alec reminded him.

John snorted. "Aye, before you even got in the saddle. But still you climbed up there, swearing for all you were worth. Freddie was sure you'd have a broken arm or two for your trouble."

"Father whipped me hard enough to break his arm." Alec grinned, but it faded soon enough. Riding a nag, even a vicious one, was hardly the same as running Penford. He squared his shoulders, knowing John was right about his determination to succeed even as he suspected the urge to wander would well up again in time, stronger than ever. He was a nomad by nature, but he would have to subdue it for a while to see to his family duties. "Let's to it, then."

Finances were growing extremely tight in the Turner household.

After Major Hayes's surprising visit, a flood of bills seemed to descend on the house. The largest one was for feed for the horses. Tom handed it to Cressida without meeting her gaze, knowing as well as she did what it would mean.

"Does he want payment now?" she asked anyway, hoping against hope she might be able to put it off.

Most of the others could not be; apparently Papa had already delayed payment, and they were firm about being paid this time. But a shake of Tom's head indicated that he had already tried, and failed.

Cressida sighed and pressed the back of her wrist to her forehead. She should have done this weeks ago, in all likelihood. "Take the horses into town and sell them, Tom. I'll explain to Granny."

Tom nodded and ducked from the room. Cressida hoped he could get a good price; the horses were decent animals, and they were certainly well-fed, as her depleted purse could prove. The funds from selling the horses, though, would allow the rest of them to eat well for several months.

But when Tom returned later, the news was not good. "I need to speak to you," he muttered as he tromped through the hall.

Cressida hurried after him, her heart thumping. "What happened?" she demanded as soon as she closed the door of Papa's study behind her.

Tom folded his arms. "The horses were hired."

For a moment she couldn't breathe. Hired? But no; Papa had said . . . "What do you mean?" She sank into the room's only chair.

"Bickford showed me the paper. The sergeant signed it, right and proper. Two carriage horses, hired from his stable, paid six months."

"Papa said he bought them," she said through numb lips. All this time she had been scraping to feed two beasts that didn't even belong to her.

"Perhaps he did, at a later date, and Bickford thought to fool me." Tom looked around the small room. "Perhaps we can find a bill of sale."

Her heart had stopped thumping. It might have stopped altogether. A black, cold pit seemed to have opened up inside her. "I don't think so," she whispered. "I looked through all the papers in here and didn't find it. It didn't even occur to me there ought to be one."

The silence was overwhelming. Then Tom squatted in front of her and patted her hand. "There, don't fret. We'll manage."

Cressida closed her eyes and gulped in deep breaths. What other choice did they have but to manage? She just didn't know how. "Did you take the horses back at least? Is Mr. Bickford going to be coming to collect money owed him?"

"No, he said it had been paid in advance. I gather he took the impression your father didn't want it widely known the horses weren't his."

That was no surprise. Cressida thought bitterly of how proud her father had been, a gentleman keeping his own team and carriage. How he had laughed when she asked about the cost and told her they were well-situated now, and he meant to live like it. No one could overrule Papa when he set his mind on something, although she'd certainly tried on some occasions. Mostly everyone got caught up in his infectious enthusiasm and promises of having it all in hand. Cressida admitted to herself that she, perhaps most of all, had wanted to believe it was so, that Papa had come home from the war with connections and funds and would lift the burden of endless economy from them all.

Apparently not. She scrubbed her hands over her face and tried to think. "We'll have to take them back anyway, and see if Mr. Bickford will refund any part of what Papa paid. It will save on feed if nothing else." Tom nodded, and let himself out.

Cressida stayed in her seat for several minutes after Tom left, nearly paralyzed by the enormity of their problems. There was no money to be had from the horses; the lease was coming due; they had lost several sheep; even the vegetable garden wouldn't be putting out a bounty, thanks to the incessant hot weather. They were worse off than in their most pinched days in Portsmouth, and there was still no sign of her father. "Where the bloody hell are you, Papa?" she said to the still, stuffy room.

Slowly she pushed herself to her feet. Desperate times called for desperate measures. She had tried to nibble at the problem, selling all the fancy new things Papa had bought. Unfortunately, he had purchased so much on credit, she hadn't realized much money. Now Cressida saw few choices open to her. They had the house for a few more weeks. That gave her just enough time to unload as many of their unneeded possessions as possible and find a suitable new lodging. Returning to Portsmouth was out of the question, much too far away. Cressida still missed the ocean, but Marston was a nice town as well. She and Callie had made friends here. Still . . .

With heavy feet she climbed the stairs, catching Callie just as her sister emerged from Granny's room with a tray. Callie put one finger to her lips and closed the door.

"She didn't eat much." Cressida noted the nearly full bowl of stew with dismay. Granny was wasting away.

Callie bit her lip. "I tried, but she says she's just not hungry. Tea is all she'll take."

Another worry. Cressida sighed. "Later I'll make some scones. Perhaps that will tempt her appetite."

"Perhaps." But there was no conviction in the word.

"We have another problem." Callie's face grew even graver, and she set down her tray to follow Cressida into her bedchamber across the hall. "The horses aren't ours."

"What do you mean?"

"Papa hired them. He didn't buy them."

Callie's lips parted in understanding. "But that means . . . Oh dear."

"Oh dear," Cressida echoed grimly. "I told Tom to take them back—we'll save on feed at least—but what are we to do now?"

Callie sank into the chair, her forehead creased in worry. "I don't know," she murmured. "There's nothing left?"

"Not much." Cressida sat on the end of the bed. The two sisters looked at each other in silent comprehension. "We can't stay here," she said at last.

"Where will we go?" Callie gave a sharp, wild laugh as she jumped back to her feet. "This was supposed to be home—better than Portsmouth, Papa said. Secure and comfortable. When is the lease up?"

"A fortnight."

"I can draw on my funds," Callie began. Mr. Phillips had left her almost a thousand pounds, all currently invested in the four percents. It was a small income, but they needed it.

Cressida flipped one hand. "We'd have nothing

when it was gone. At least with that income and Granny's annuity we have something."

Her sister sighed. "Perhaps Major Hayes will locate Papa soon."

Cressida said nothing. She rolled a bit of her skirt between her fingers and studied it.

"You aren't still considering refusing him, are you?"

Cressida shrugged.

"Give me one reason why," exclaimed Callie, hands on hips. "Who else has offered to help us?"

"I don't know about him," she muttered. "He makes me . . . uneasy."

"He makes me uneasy, too, but we are not in a position to be particular."

"I know," Cressida admitted. It did make her feel better to hear that Callie was uneasy about him, but her sister had clearly gotten over it enough to accept his help. Cressida wished she could shake off her own wariness; she wished even more that her unease weren't so tied to the way her nerves jangled like a shopkeeper's bell when he looked at her.

"Granny's tonic is gone," said Callie in a subdued voice. "I'll walk into town and get more."

"No, I'll go." Cressida leaped to her feet. Heaven knew she could use the exercise. Perhaps something would come to her on the way, some grand scheme to extricate them from this difficulty. A modest proposal to shore up their finances. Even a small plan would be nice. But nothing came to her as she put on her bonnet and counted out some of their few remaining coins before starting off for town.

Chapter 6

Alec's next encounter with Miss Turner happened purely by chance.

He was driving down the road from Penford toward Marston when he came upon her walking the same direction, a basket swinging from her arm. Even without glimpsing her face, Alec recognized her. There was no mistaking her brisk stride, or her height, or the slender slope of her neck beneath the plain straw bonnet. She stepped to the side to let his gig pass, and before he could reconsider, Alec brought the horse to a stop.

"Good day, Miss Turner."

She whirled to face him, her golden eyes opening wide in surprise. "Oh," she said, obviously flustered. "Good day, sir."

Alec smiled. "Do you go into Marston?" She stared at him, and nodded. "May I offer you a ride?"

"Er . . ." She hesitated, tugging on one of her bonnet ribbons. The ribbons were bright cherry red, a striking contrast to her plain gray dress. Somehow that bright bit of color charmed him.

"I am sent to fetch my sister, Julia, home, and would be very glad for some company," he said. He

had planned to call on her later anyway; he told himself it would save a trip to Brighampton to offer her
a ride, even if she did stand there biting her lower lip
in a way that caught his interest unlike anything John
Stafford had ever charged him with.

Finally she smiled politely. "Thank you, that would
be lovely."

He jumped down from the gig and held out
one hand, helping her up into the gig. She tucked
her skirts around her as he circled the carriage and
climbed up beside her. The seat was wide enough
for both, but just barely. His arm brushed hers as he
lifted the reins, and her skirts spilled over his boots
despite her best efforts to contain them. She sat very
still and primly upright, eyes straight ahead and her
hands wrapped tightly around the handle of her
basket. Every time the gig hit the tiniest rut in the
road, her figure seemed to strain away from him.

Alec began to regret his impulse; he was far too
aware of her every movement to persuade himself it
was mere courtesy or part of his job to take her up.
He just had an irrational fascination with the curve
of her neck, and the color of her eyes, and the swell
of her—

"I do hope the rain doesn't come and ruin your trip
into town," he said, quelling his wayward thoughts.

She glanced at him warily. "I have my cloak. It was
very kind of you to take me up."

"It is my pleasure. It's quite a long walk into town
from Brighampton."

Her mouth compressed. "It's not so very long. I'm
very fond of walking, in any event."

She must be; it was at least four miles, and she

would have to walk home with a heavy basket while clouds multiplied in the sky. The air was thick and humid, and rain would be welcome after the heat. Alec remembered the two sturdy horses in her stable, and wondered again about the Turner finances. "As am I," he replied. "Although not in the rain."

She said nothing, and they drove in silence for some time. Silence, Alec knew, could work wonders. More often than not, saying nothing was a good way to prompt someone to say something, especially women, especially when they had something on their minds. The glances he stole at her from time to time indicated that she did have something on her mind, from the way she kept rolling her lower lip between her teeth. The action left her lips deep pink and glistening, and far too intriguing. His eyes seemed drawn to her mouth every time he looked at her. He silently cursed himself as a sad, lonely wretch, sneaking peeks at a woman's mouth and fantasizing about the curve of her neck.

"Major Hayes," she blurted out at last, "I must apologize for the other day, when you first called at Brighampton. I reacted in haste and very much regret my actions."

"Which actions, Miss Turner?"

She might be grinding her teeth, from the set of her jaw. "All of them," she muttered.

The road made a sweeping turn to the west, following the River Lea. Alec didn't slow the horse at all, and she almost leaned over the side of the gig to keep from touching him. He wondered if it was intense dislike, or something else, that made her do that, and then he wondered why he cared. "I took no offense."

"I had a fear of horse thieves," she said. "But I would not have shot you."

"Don't raise a gun unless you are prepared to fire it."

"I only meant to frighten you—or rather, a horse thief—away."

"You didn't cock the pistol and you stood close enough that I could have taken the pistol from you if I wanted to. A real thief wouldn't have been frightened."

She was watching him from the corner of her eyes, looking slightly amazed. "You weren't alarmed at all?"

"No." Her interest, even mixed with caution and suspicion, was tantalizing. Alec kept his eyes fixed on the road, although he could feel the warmth of her body near his.

"Do you have pistols pointed at you often?"

"I was in the cavalry, Miss Turner. Pistols, rifles, heavy artillery—and most of them firing at the time."

"Yes, of course," she murmured. "I forgot."

"Why should you have known?" He couldn't resist turning to look at her. She had cocked her head at an angle to see him without having to turn and face him. A fine line divided her brows, and wisps of golden brown hair drifted around the brim of her bonnet. Alec knew he was being sized up. If she told him they didn't want his help, he would really have no more excuse to stare at her. Not that it would change his mission from Stafford to find the sergeant, but he would have to do it without the intriguing Miss Turner's cooperation. The job would be more difficult, and far, far less entertaining. That ought to be reason enough for him to stop provoking her, but instead he was behaving like a man gorging himself in anticipation of a coming famine.

She blinked and jerked her eyes away from his. "I didn't know," she said, staring straight ahead again. "I only knew your rank. I never thought officers cared much for being under fire."

Alec smiled wryly at the subtle insult. That was a regular soldier's view, and certainly true of some officers, but not true of him. Perhaps it would improve Miss Turner's opinion of his character if he told her how many times he had led a charge directly into French fire. "May I ask why you were so quick to assume I was a horse thief?"

"Well . . . You were in the stable."

"Right. Well, I did see a man leaving the stable, in a very suspicious manner. Perhaps he was your horse thief."

Her expression grew uneasy. "Was there really another man?" she said, then blushed. She thought he had lied to her.

He let it go with a nod. "Yes. A big fellow, creeping rather furtively about before running into the woods. I presume he doesn't work for you."

"No," she murmured. "I—I expect it was a creditor, or someone from Mr. Bickford's stables."

Creditors normally came to the front door and demanded their money. Alec added that mysterious figure to the list of things he must look into.

"I doubt he was a horse thief. It was broad daylight, after all; an odd time to steal a horse, don't you think?"

"Having never stolen a horse," she said, "I wouldn't know the best time to do it."

"I recommend after dark. Or in a pouring rainstorm, for no one wishes to chase after you then. Of course, you should take care to choose a placid horse in that event, who won't take fright at the storm."

She glanced at him in alarm. "You seem well-versed in the matter."

He met her eyes. "Such knowledge comes in handy from time to time."

She shifted away from him in her seat. "I wonder why Lord Hastings sent you to help us, then. Since we don't, in fact, need any horses stolen."

"I wonder why you are so reluctant to accept a well-meant offer of help. Perhaps you have reconsidered your desire to locate your father."

Her mouth dropped open. "I have not! How could you think that?"

He pulled up the horse, stopping the carriage with a jerk that made her clutch at the seat cushion, and turned to face her. "According to your account, he left four months ago. You waited more than three months to contact Hastings, and when Hastings sent someone—me—to your aid, you gave every appearance of being unpleasantly surprised instead of delighted." She opened her mouth to protest, but he draped one arm along the back of the carriage and leaned toward her. Just a bit, but she shrank away from him, clutching the basket protectively against her chest. "A suspicious man might wonder if perhaps it was just for show, that your father's disappearance suits you very well after all and you're merely going through the motions of searching to avoid revealing just how satisfied you are without him. Or perhaps you know exactly where he is . . . buried." He whispered the last word, tempting her—no, goading her—to lose her temper and tell him something he didn't know.

"What—What kind of man would ask that?" she stammered. "It's dreadful!"

His gaze wandered over her face until he could almost feel her skin against his fingertips. He had to squeeze the reins in his fist to keep from reaching up to touch her. This had been a very bad idea, inviting her to sit so close beside him. He should have known to keep his distance the moment he saw her. "A very thorough one," he replied. "All too often the more dreadful a possibility, the truer it is."

She wet her lips. "It's not true in this case, and I am appalled you would think so."

He raised one eyebrow and straightened on the seat. "Did I say I thought so? I never assume the answer to questions like that."

"Then why did you bring it up?" she demanded furiously. "My family certainly doesn't need the help of someone who would leap to that sort of conclusion!"

"No, but you need the help of someone who will ask that sort of question."

"I don't think we do!"

He could tell she wasn't so certain of that by the tone of her voice—not softening in doubt, but ringing with outraged defiance. She didn't trust him, didn't like him, and Alec had worn through his limited supply of diplomacy anyway. "Miss Turner, clearly you have run out of patience that your father will return on his own. If you still believed that, you wouldn't have written to Hastings. I was sent to act on his behalf, fulfilling *your* request. Now, either you don't wish to find your father after all for some reason, or you simply don't want me to do it." He knew it was a gamble to be so blunt with her. Normally he acted in the shadows, listening here and prying a little there. It felt odd to be so open and brazen about his purpose, but there was no way around it. Everyone knew who he was now; no more hiding in the anonymity of a footman's livery. There was little doubt in his mind that she had heard the stories about him, and his aggressive tactic would be enough to send most ladies into an outraged fit—or into a dead faint.

But this lady . . . he thought not. Between the pistol and the fact that she had accepted his offer of a ride into town, Alec sensed that Cressida Turner was made of sterner stuff. In fact, although she was obviously shocked by his suggestions, her reaction appeared to be more anger than anything else. A flush of fine color had come into her face, and her glorious eyes were positively smoldering. He realized his shoulders had tensed in anticipation of being struck, and that the possibility was more intriguing than irritating.

"What the devil do you want from me?" she said, biting off each word. "What am I supposed to say to that?"

Alec smiled thinly, gathering the reins. "The truth, Miss Turner. That is all I am after." He snapped the reins and the gig jolted forward.

"What if the truth is that I don't want to speak to you ever again?" she said over the rumble of the wheels. She had clapped one hand to her bonnet, and held tight to her basket with the other. She no longer held herself so stiffly away from him.

"You don't have to."

That stopped her. "Oh?"

He looked at her. Her chin was raised, her eyebrows were arched slightly, and her full mouth was soft with astonishment. She was almost pretty with that flush on her cheeks. "Of course not. I should be very glad for your assistance, though."

She licked her lips again. Damn, he was like a boy, entranced by the sight of a woman's mouth. "Then you would still look for my father, even if . . . ?"

"Yes." He leaned forward and peered past her, checking that the way was clear. They had reached the main road into Marston, and he turned the horse onto it. "I gave my word."

"But Lord Hastings . . ."

"He never said I must secure your approval. Perhaps he assumed you would grant it without question, since you asked for help and he sent it." He wasn't sure what Hastings presumed, but he was taking too much pleasure in needling her.

Cressida clenched her teeth. He was deliberately misunderstanding her. Arguing with Major Hayes was like chasing a cat. Everything she said, he twisted and turned until she wanted to scream. She should have declined his offer, even if it meant walking twice

as far into town. "I don't want to appear ungrateful
to Lord Hastings."

He flashed a darkly amused glance at her. "No."

She decided to be blunt. Heaven knew he hadn't
shied away from it. "Three days," she said. "I would
like three days to consider your offer to try to find
my father."

"What will happen in three days?"

"I—I have to talk to my sister," she said, taken aback
by his swift riposte. "And to my grandmother."

"What will you tell them?"

It was almost as if he was daring her to accuse
him of all the horrible things the gossips said about
him. Cressida set her jaw and made herself smile. "I
will ask their opinion of the matter. We might prefer
someone more familiar with our family."

"Your man Webb, I suppose. Of course, you haven't
sent him on it yet."

"We like our privacy," she snapped. "I don't have
to tell you anything. We are used to doing for our-
selves, and if I prefer not to tell you all my father's private doings and secret habits, I don't see how *you* of
all people could possibly fault me for it!" She stopped,
horrified. Her temper had gotten the better of her in
spite of her resolve not to let it.

It had a better effect on the major than she had expected, though. He turned to her, no longer quizzing
and poking, but almost . . . pleased. "Thank you, Miss
Turner, for your honesty. I certainly can respect that
reason, and I will. Three days, you say?"

"Er . . . yes." She nodded once. Had he done all
that just to get her to lash out at him? It seemed so
. . . but why?

He looked away, but she still caught the trace of a smile on his mouth. "If we are to cooperate in this, you should know that I prize honesty and truth above all else. The truth may be ugly at times, but it always comes out in the end, and often appears even uglier after being hidden. But I also value discretion. Nothing you tell me about your father shall ever be repeated except in pursuit of the truth, and then only with as much care as possible."

"Thank you," she murmured. Perhaps he had been trying to do that, fluster and disarm her. Perhaps he wanted her to lose her temper and say what she meant to conceal. She stole a glance at him as he drove, and wondered if perhaps he had a better idea what he was about than she thought. Honesty and truth above all else . . .

"Where may I set you down?" He reined in the horse, slowing to a walk.

She jerked her eyes to the front and realized they had reached town. "Oh—anywhere. Thank you for the ride."

He stopped the gig in front of the millinery. Cressida grabbed her skirts and jumped down before he could help her. She hesitated, then turned back. "Thank you also for what you said about truth and honesty. I do not treat Papa's disappearance lightly or carelessly, I assure you. It's just that . . . Well, Papa has a penchant for going off without leaving word, and I am reasonably sure this will prove just another of those times if we simply wait."

He had listened in silence, propping his elbow on his knee to lean down to her. "Are you prepared to wait it out?"

She fiddled with the ribbon of her bonnet. "No. Not any longer." She looked up at him. He had the most inscrutable face, and a way of looking at her that made her feel utterly exposed, as if he was determined to discover every last thing about her. It was alarming and, she was appalled to acknowledge, a little thrilling. Men did not look at her that way. "But it is a tremendous service to ask of a complete stranger, who must have cares and concerns of his own . . ." Nervously she stopped. He had to know what she meant.

"But the service is sincerely offered, and any debt you owe is to Hastings, not to me. Remember that as you consider. Three days?" She jerked her head yes. Major Hayes smiled at her, his eyes lit with an unsettling light as he tipped his hat. "Until then, Miss Turner."

"Yes," she whispered as he drove away. She gulped in a deep breath and pressed a trembling hand to her cheek. Three days. She had three days to decide if she could endure more of his presence, or if she dared refuse it. Cressida had no idea how she was going to decide. He rattled her . . . but she felt like a fool turning down any help, particularly from someone who appeared quite capable. He had managed to make everyone think him dead for five years, and avoided being hanged for treason even though everyone knew he was guilty, which must have taken some cunning. Apparently he knew how to steal horses, and he was quite brilliant at making her lose her temper. Compared to all that, finding one missing man would be like child's play to him.

She sighed and started toward the apothecary. A week ago she would have said it didn't matter, that she would accept help from the devil himself if it brought back her father and saved them all from ruin. She just hadn't thought the devil would take her up on it.

Chapter 7

"**C**ressida!" She jumped, startled out of her thoughts, and looked up to see Julia Hayes hurrying toward her. A smile bloomed on her face at the sight of her friend, and she turned to meet her. "What were you doing with *him*?"

Julia's tone took her by surprise. "Major Hayes? He passed me on the road and offered me a ride."

Julia took her arm and turned away, casting a dark glance in the direction her brother had disappeared. "I thought he would have the sense—" She sniffed, and started down the street, pulling Cressida with her. "If only he'd go back to wherever he's been hiding these last five years."

Even though she might have wished the same thing, Cressida was shocked to hear it from Julia. She hadn't seen her since word of the major's return had spread, but she had assumed Julia would be pleased by her brother's reappearance—by the fact that he wasn't actually dead, at the very least. "Why do you say that? Aren't you pleased he's returned?"

Julia shook her head. "It would be better for everyone if he had not."

"But he's your brother . . ."

Julia closed her eyes and took a deep breath. "Yes. I'm sorry to be so short-tempered." She made a visible effort to shake off her ire, and smiled. "I should have said I am so pleased to see you. How are your sister and your grandmother?"

"They are both well, thank you." Cressida looked over her shoulder; the major was long gone. It occurred to her that this was a golden opportunity to ask someone she knew and trusted about the major. "I am very glad to meet you," she went on. "I wanted to ask you about Major Hayes—"

Julia's smile faded. "Whatever for?"

"He came to call on us the other day," Cressida replied, leaving out any mention of his first visit. No one else needed to know about that, if she could help it. "He said he had come to help search for my father."

Julia stopped dead and gaped at her. "What? Why? Does he know your father?"

"No, not at all. But he said he was asked by Lord Hastings, whom Papa had gone to see, to offer his aid in looking for Papa."

This was clearly news to Julia. "Lord Hastings?" she repeated. "Who is he? How would Alec know him?"

"Lord Hastings was a commissary officer Papa knew in the war. Papa was very hopeful Lord Hastings might recommend him for a position he wanted."

"Oh. The army." Julia still looked puzzled, but then her expression grew grimmer. "Then that's why Alec's come home. Has the army known all along where he was, I wonder? And after the things they told my mother . . ." She broke off and pressed her lips together.

Cressida hesitated. "Should I not trust him, then? Callie thinks I'm mad to hesitate, no matter what . . . Well, it is what we wanted, having someone sent by Lord Hastings to discover where Papa has gone." It was unsettling to realize how much she had hoped Julia would put her worries to rest, and declare Major Hayes trustworthy and the victim of terrible lies and injustice. The notion of someone riding to their rescue and locating her errant father was appealing, even if the person of Major Hayes shredded her nerves. If Julia defended him, her decision in three days would be that much clearer.

Looking troubled, Julia shook her head. "I don't know." She lifted her shoulders helplessly. "I simply don't know him anymore. Before . . ." She glanced around and lowered her voice, and they resumed walking, leaning their heads close together. "Well, he was as wild as any young man, I suppose, although I was a girl at the time and thought him simply brilliant. He was so dashing and so daring, always in the thick of trouble but so much fun. He was in love with Marianne, you know, and we all thought she would marry him; every girl in Marston was mad in love with him." Cressida's eyes widened. "But he had joined the army by then, and while he was gone, Frederick fell in love with her and she with him. When Alec came home, there was a horrible row; he said awful things. Freddie of course just listened quietly, as he always did, and then Alec went back to the army. Before—Before Waterloo, we always heard such grand reports of him as an officer, how fearless and capable he was. Twice he was mentioned in Wellington's dispatches for his bravery, to my father's immense pride. But then of course that all changed, and now . . . I just don't know. How could a man disappear for five years and let his family think him dead—and worse?" The bitterness was creeping back into her voice. "It killed my father. He was ill when Alec left, and the news that Alec was missing and presumed dead was devastating enough. But then, to hear he had been a traitor . . . The shame killed Father, I know it. And now Alec's just reappeared, without one word of explanation or contrition, and I cannot forgive him for it. He seems to think we've all been waiting for him to come home and will go on as if nothing has changed."

"He must have a reason," said Cressida slowly. She wasn't precisely defending the major, but put that way, the major's disappearance sounded uncomfortably like her own father's "expeditions." Except for the bit Julia had left out, the part about treason. Surely that demanded some sort of explanation.

"Not one he's condescended to tell us. He's upended everything, and only Mother is happy about it. The rest of us don't know what to say or do around him, and he seems not to notice or care."

"Perhaps if you tell him . . ." Cressida thought of her father again, who never seemed to understand how much his absences upset the family routine. Of course, her grandmother *was* just waiting for him to reappear, and she *would* act as if nothing had changed. More than once Cressida had been obliged to swallow her own impertinent remarks after one of Papa's expeditions. "Perhaps he hasn't yet realized how his return affected everyone."

"It would pain my mother if I said anything. She's been revived since we received word he was still alive and well, and would banish me to live in the stables if I ruined her joy and happiness." Julia smiled ruefully. "I'm sorry. You shouldn't have to listen to me ramble on about sordid family matters."

Cressida flipped one hand. "As if you haven't listened to me complain in my turn! Who can one complain to, if not to one's friends?"

Julia laughed. "Indeed! But you asked me a question, and I fear I cannot answer. Once upon a time, there was no one like Alec for achieving the impossible. He thrived on it, in fact; let Freddie or Will Lacey say a shot could not be made or a horse could not be ridden, and Alec would risk his neck to do it. Father used to say he was indestructible. Five years ago I would have sworn he could do anything he undertook, and that you could wager your life on his word. But can you trust him now? I don't know, Cressida."

Cressida sighed. This was certainly complicating her view of the major. "Thank you anyway, Julia."

"If you find you cannot trust him, why, you could always write to Lord Hastings again and express your disappointment." Julia looked grim again. "No doubt Lord Hastings will be able to guess why."

Cressida managed another weak smile, knowing she wouldn't dare do that.

"Oh. I nearly forgot." Julia sighed. "Or rather, I wanted to forget. Mother is having a party. Not a ball, because of Freddie, but a small party, because of Alec.

She's desperate to reestablish him in Marston's eyes, after all the scandal broth brewed here over him. Do say you'll come."

Her face burned. A party, at the beautiful Penford estate? Even if she had a gown worth wearing, she wasn't certain she was ready to face the major again. She would move to the workhouse before she submitted herself to his probing gaze in her plain blue calico. "Oh, no. I don't know your brother at all, and would be completely out of place."

"Nonsense." Julia squeezed her hand. "It has nothing to do with who knew him then, or now. Mother won't be inviting certain people who were cold to her after he went missing, you may depend on that—and there are plenty of them, no doubt all perishing of curiosity now that he's returned. She'll only have people who bear him no ill will, and I told her to add your family to the list." Still Cressida hesitated, and Julia added, "Perhaps it will give you a chance to decide if you want his help or not. Please say you'll come. It's to be this Saturday evening."

Cressida bit her lip. Julia must not realize how poor they had become. She meant the invitation kindly and sincerely, and ordinarily Cressida would have accepted with pleasure. Still . . . "I'll consider it," she said, clinging to the scraps of pride she had left.

Julia beamed. "Excellent! I will see you then." She said farewell and walked in the direction Major Hayes had gone. Cressida turned slowly back toward the apothecary shop for Granny's tonic. Her frail little grandmother was fading away. Perhaps for that reason alone she should accept the major's help: seeing Papa return home would be good for Granny, who fretted over his absence daily. For Granny's sake, she could endure the major's presence, couldn't she?

She shook herself. Three days—and perhaps an evening at Penford.

Alec felt the notice of the townspeople as he drove through town. Marston was tiny, and by the time he reached the stationer's shop where his mother had told him to look for Julia, it seemed the entire populace was watching him either openly or covertly. He ignored it, tying up the horse and removing his hat as he went into the shop.

Old Darnley's was the same as he remembered it, smelling of clean paper and ink. Alec remembered being sent here as a boy to fetch things for his mother, more as a way to occupy him than because of his mother's pressing need for ink. Now, as then, Darnley was perched on his high stool at the back of the shop. He looked up at the bell, his round pink face beaming, until he saw Alec. Then the smile froze, just for a moment, but long enough to set Alec's teeth on edge. He forced a polite expression to his face and stepped forward.

"Good day, sir. I am looking for my sister, Miss Hayes."

Relief flashed in Darnley's eyes. "Oh yes, bless me, she was here not too long ago. I expect she's just gone around the corner or next door."

"Thank you." Alec glanced around the shop. "Your shop is exactly as I remember it, Mr. Darnley. I feel as though I should ask for some ink and a new nib, for my mother."

Mr. Darnley chuckled, his expression easing a bit.

"Why yes, she did send you here quite frequently. I had to wrap those bottles of ink very well, if I recall correctly."

Alec smiled. He had climbed trees and walked along stone walls on the way home, and more than one bottle of ink had cracked open in his pocket in the process. "Yes, I remember. Many a pair of trousers and stockings had to be thrown out after I fetched ink from you. My mother said it was often not worth the effort of sending me."

Darnley laughed, his face creasing into well-worn lines as he pressed his palms to his apron. He hesitated. "May I welcome you home, sir."

The lighthearted memory faded. Alec inclined his head. "Thank you. Next door, you say?"

"Yes, yes, she was here only moments ago." Darnley hurried to open the door for him, still smiling and nodding, but Alec felt the man's relief like a wisp of cold air. He stepped back into the street and looked left and right. Darnley hadn't said which direction Julia might have gone. He scanned the faces, not seeing his sister's, until his gaze snagged on a plain straw bonnet with a bright scarlet ribbon.

Alec admitted he was quite curious to see what three days would add to Miss Turner's opinion of him. He wondered what she expected to learn in that time. Of his past in Marston, there was plenty to hear; he had been a hellion as a lad, and even into his army career. Of his alleged betrayal at Waterloo, there was also no doubt plenty to hear, but Alec suspected she had already heard most of it. Of the last five years, and what sort of man he was now . . . of that there was precious little anyone in Marston or anywhere else could tell her. And sadly, that had far more bearing on what he could do for her now than anything she might discover about the hellion or the traitor.

He started down the street, intending to look into each shop as he passed in search of Julia. Miss Turner's bonnet was still visible, thanks to her height. She was slowly strolling down the street with another lady, leaning her head down to her shorter companion's. Perhaps that was part of his fascination with her; she could almost look him in the eye, something few women could do. He smiled a little, thinking of looking into her glorious eyes again, and then he finally recognized the lady at her side.

Now what could Julia be telling her? It was unlikely to improve him in Miss Turner's eyes, given his sister's animosity. Perhaps it was something wholly unrelated to him, although Alec found that unlikely. It was unfortunately obvious that his return was the most momentous event of some time in Marston. Even now, as he walked down the street, people drew away from his path, darting curious but nervous glance at each other and avoiding his gaze. He hated it. He hated feeling like an oddity. He hated the fact that everyone wanted to stare at him, but no one would speak to him unless forced to do so. And he truly hated the fact that for some unknown reason, he cared what Miss Turner thought of him, and hoped that Julia was chattering about fashion instead of venting her spleen against him.

He just caught a glimpse of Miss Turner's bonnet again as she went into the apothecary shop. Julia had turned his way, and seen him. Her face set, she was striding toward him, a package from Darnley in her arms. Alec stopped and waited, bowing his head as she approached.

"I suppose Mother sent you," she said.

"She worried you would be caught in the rain."

Julia cast her eyes upward. The sky had been overcast all day, but not one raindrop had fallen. "Of course," she said dryly. "Well, let's be off."

Alec kept his face clean of expression and followed her to the gig. Julia climbed in without waiting for him to give her a hand up, and he made no comment. He untied the horse and swung up beside her.

Neither spoke until they were out of town, bowling down the same road he had just traveled with Miss Turner. Alec thought again of her face, of those expressive eyes and the way they flashed at him when he questioned her motives. Whatever else she thought of him, Miss Turner wasn't afraid to look at him or talk to him. Three days . . .

"I could have walked, you know," Julia announced. She still stared straight ahead.

"Mother thought it better if you didn't."

"Odd," she replied. "She hasn't minded for the last several years."

Alec said nothing. He knew very well his mother had sent him in hopes that this forced companionship would revive his and Julia's affectionate relationship of old. Personally, he doubted anything would. Not because Julia had made no secret of her anger at him, but because he had changed so much in five years, he didn't know how to respond to it. He and Julia had always been much alike, both hot-tempered and impulsive, given to speaking their minds and apologizing later. There had been no reserve between them, for good or for ill.

Alec recognized all that still in his sister, even as he knew it had been hammered out of him. On his first mission for Stafford, he had lost his temper and been drawn into a brawl. When it was over, a man was dead—the man Alec had been assigned to befriend for information about a group plotting an armed uprising. After the brawl Alec was too notorious in that town to continue; all his work had been for naught, and Stafford's deputy, Phipps, had cursed a blue streak at him and threatened to give him the sack.

Chastened and furious, he had vowed never again to lose control of himself that way. All his daring and courage mattered little if he couldn't mind his tongue and temper. Ruthlessly he repressed that part of himself, becoming a silent, unnoticeable watcher instead of a brazen imposter mingling with the targets of his mission. Other agents took those parts, and Alec faded into the background as a servant or a beggar or a common tradesman, nobody worthy of note. He was used to that now; he was comfortable with it. And so he said nothing in response to Julia's icy remark.

His silence seemed to increase his sister's anger. Her expression grew stormy. "I wish you would speak to Mother," she said suddenly.

"About what?"

"The party she's planning."

Alec had barely listened to his mother's hopeful plans. "And what should I say to her about it?"

"You can't tell me you want her to throw a party in your honor!" Julia exclaimed.

"I never asked her to, no."

Her face was bright pink. "I don't understand."

"It was entirely her idea, and she didn't ask my opinion of it, if that's what you mean."

"No, that's not what I mean." She twisted in her seat to face him, making the gig rock. "I don't understand anything about you anymore."

Alec thought of all the ways he could answer that plea. He wondered what his sister would think if he told her he had been a spy, guilty of deceit and impersonation. He wondered what she would think of his reasons for wanting to be supposed dead for so long, or his reasons for coming back as he did. Most of all he wondered what she wanted him to be. "Perhaps it's best that way," he murmured at last.

Julia inhaled loudly, then turned forward again. "You can make sure of that. You can keep your secrets and leave the rest of us to wonder and be forced to offer excuses for you, and there's nothing we can do to compel you. Such a pleasure it is to have you home again."

"So I should tell Mother to cancel her party?" he retorted. "I should tell her that I don't want her to be happy? I don't care tuppence for the happiness or good opinion of her guests, but I see no reason to crush her own joy."

"Oh, this will be a marvelous party," Julia replied. "The host glowering at everyone in sullen silence, and the poor hostess pitied by everyone else because of it."

Alec pulled up the horse before he lost his temper. He handed the reins to his sister and jumped down.

It was a quiet horse, she would have no trouble with him.

"What are you doing?" she cried as he started off down the road.

"I think I'd better walk."

"Why?" She started the horse. The gig drew alongside him and kept to his pace. "Why won't you tell me anything? What are you hiding, Alec? I assure you, it can't be worse than what everyone thinks you've done."

"Do you?" He kept his eyes forward. "Do you believe it?"

"You give me nothing else to believe!"

He stopped and looked at her. Julia was practically hanging out of the gig, her face screwed up in frustration. For a moment he was buoyed by it. Perhaps he should explain everything, and she would be reassured . . .

He couldn't. He wanted to; Alec saw the hope in his sister's eyes and knew she wanted to believe him. But Julia was expecting him to tell her something honorable, or at least pardonable. That he had become entangled with a woman who incriminated him, perhaps, and then fled England in shame. That he had committed some error on the battlefield and been made a scapegoat by his superiors. Something, anything that would explain why he had disappeared for so long. What would she think of the truth, especially when even *he* didn't know the complete truth?

Alec sighed. That was the trouble. Without the complete truth, his story didn't sound much better than the rumors. He could all too easily picture Julia flying into a temper at someone in town, responding to someone's sly comments about him, and bursting out that he *had* been a spy, but for England. The gossips would pounce on it. It would only make things worse, for his family and for him. He was still Stafford's man, in fact if no longer in full, and he knew exactly how well the general public would take that news. Another of Stafford's agents had taken a terrible beating just a fortnight ago after being discovered working as a serving wench in a tavern in Cheapside, and barely survived. Announcing himself a spy for the Home Office wouldn't have the exculpatory affect Julia might expect.

"I can't, Julia," he said quietly. "Not yet. There are too many things I don't know myself. I swear to you I never dealt with the French. But the rest of it . . ." He lifted one hand and let it fall. "It might not comfort you as much as you think."

Her face grew wooden. "No," she said, her voice tight and clipped. "I see that now. Forgive me for prying into your affairs." She snapped the reins and the horse leaped forward.

Alec watched her go. Perhaps that had been the wrong decision. He felt as though he had been boxed into several of them lately. Or perhaps there were no more right decisions for him anymore. Perhaps it was no longer possible for him to be anything but a spy, keeping his troubles to himself and fading from sight when his job was done. But Stafford had sent him home, thrusting his true name and old disgrace back upon him, and he no longer had the luxury of fading from sight.

With a sigh he started after Julia and the gig. There was no other direction to go.

Chapter 8

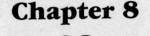

June 1816
London, England

The man he had come to meet was late.

Alec Brandon took a swallow of ale and let his eyes wander around the room. This fellow, Mr. Phipps, was supposed to be here by seven o'clock. Alec had arrived half an hour before that, and waited close to an hour now. If he hadn't been reduced to desperate measures, he would have been gone before the clock finished striking the hour.

He sighed and gazed into his tankard. That was a lie. If he weren't in this position, he wouldn't have come here at all, let alone still be waiting for a man who might have nothing to offer him. He didn't even know what the offer would be, since James Peterbury had told him little when he arranged this meeting.

"Just listen to him," James had urged. "I think he could help us."

Alec hadn't really believed it then, and he still didn't. The anniversary of Waterloo, as the battle was now dubbed, had passed with a great fanfare of patriotic pride just last week. A year had gone by. A year in which Alec had learned precious little about his fall from grace, and all of it was bad. There were incriminating letters, found in his belongings and sent up the chain of command until Wellington himself saw them. The general had lost his famously sharp temper and declared Alec far better dead than alive. James Peterbury had tried to locate those letters, but without success; his every move, Alec realized, was hamstrung by the fact that no one else knew Alec had survived the battle. Everyone considered the matter closed, the less said about it the better.

But it was better that way, for now, although it made Alec a man without a name or a country. To some that would be an invitation to disappear for real. Many casualties in any battle were simply lost, their bodies dumped in unmarked graves and forgotten, particularly when looters had picked the corpse clean of identification. It would be all too easy to take advantage of that and leave the army and England and accusations of treason far behind, immigrate to the American wilderness and begin a new life.

But Alec couldn't bring himself to do it, even though staying in England under this cloud of suspicion risked a date with the hangman. He preferred to remain, but to remain presumed dead. Leaving the country would appear an admission of guilt. And Alec would go to his grave in truth before he gave in to that.

So he had spent the year in hiding, recuperating from his wounds, working odd jobs and moving around every few weeks. With Peterbury's help he came back to England, and finally to London. As the peace settled on the land, the army contracted, disbanding regiments and furloughing officers. He was just one of many unemployed army men filling England's towns and cities, all at loose ends now that their training was no longer needed. Alec felt their despair and anger and helplessness, both as one of them and as a gentleman who, in the normal scheme of things, might have made a small difference. He had promised to look after Will Lacey's widow and child, but could not. He might have offered work on his family estate to some of his men, but could not return home. He couldn't even contribute to the Compassionate Fund for widows and orphans, because he had no money. It had been a year of infuriating frustration.

The door slammed shut, and Alec took a quick glance. A bland, doughy little man stood there, a nobody of a fellow whose eyes flickered around the room in a second. Without hesitating he came directly toward the small corner table where Alec slouched.

"Brandon?" It was barely a question, but Alec nodded once. The colorless fellow pulled out the chair across the table and sat down, leaning forward on his elbows. "Phipps here. You know what I've come about?"

"Not precisely. Peterbury said you might have something of interest to offer me."

"Perhaps."

Alec shrugged. "Perhaps not."

Mr. Phipps's mouth pulled into a thin, straight line. "All I can offer is an opportunity. Should you accept, it would be up to you to distinguish yourself."

"Is it legal?"

Phipps paused, his eyes narrowing.

"Never mind," muttered Alec. "Go on."

"It will require a great deal of discretion. Our first concern is success, and with as much honor as possible . . . but sometimes honor has no place in this business, as we are well-aware."

"Morality is permitted. How refreshing."

Phipps sat back. "Do I bore you? I begin to think this wastes my time and yours."

Alec reined in his temper and forced himself to remember that James Peterbury had thought this a good offer, and that being churlish and impatient was never the way to accomplish anything. Who was he to talk of honor and morality anyway? "No," he said. "Go on."

Mr. Phipps tapped his fingers on the table. "Peterbury indicated you had . . . requirements."

Alec leaned against the wall, tired of being coy. "What I need, you cannot give."

"Perhaps not." Phipps leaned forward. "I cannot give you back your good name, no; but I have it in my power to lend you another's."

"Oh?" Alec smiled faintly. "Whose would that be?"

"Lord Sidmouth's." The other man's eyes gleamed as Alec's face went slack with surprise in spite of himself. The Home Secretary's name was possibly the last one he expected to hear. Who was this man Phipps? How had Peterbury come across him? And what exactly had Peterbury said about him? "His lordship is most appreciative, when he has cause to be," Phipps added. "Do well for him, and he'll do well for you."

A squirrelly fellow, cagey and secretive, but with powerful connections and willing to take chances—that was how Peterbury had described Phipps. Alec dipped his head, thinking hard. "How well?"

Phipps's smile was cold and calculated. Mephistopheles must have smiled just so when he struck his infamous bargain with Faust. "Very well."

Very well. Sidmouth had power, even though he was far from popular among the people. He was a member of the Cabinet, certainly well-placed and well-connected enough to get what Alec wanted—if he chose to do so. "What does he require?"

He listened expressionlessly as the other man outlined what would be required. Disguise. Subterfuge. Lies. A willingness to set aside, or at least overlook, certain laws and morals in pursuit of his objectives. Although neither said the word aloud, Alec was under no illusion about what he was being asked to become. How cruelly ironic that his only chance at restoring his honor was to become wholly dishonorable, that to prove he hadn't been a spy, he would become one in truth. If he failed, he would lose whatever shred of protest he had that he had never done anything wrong. But if he succeeded . . . If Phipps really could secure him a reference from the Home Secretary . . . If Phipps could locate those letters and deliver them into Alec's hands . . . He felt strangely distant from the rancid little pub, as if he merely watched and heard the scene instead of being part of it. He could almost feel the specter of Faust at his side, as he contemplated selling his soul to this cold-eyed fellow for an ephemeral chance at regaining his name.

"I'll consider it," he said at the end.

"Consider it well." Phipps leaned back in his seat.

"You'd still be serving your King, you know. We've need of intelligent, capable men here at home. Having defended England so well overseas, I'm sure you'll see the necessity of defending her in her own cities."

Alec ran one hand along the table's edge, studying the grain of the wood. It was dark and smooth, even the gouges worn to a satiny sheen. Every indignity this table had suffered had been ground down and smoothed over until the casual observer would almost think it crafted that way. "Why would you take a chance on a turncoat?"

"Peterbury says you are not." Phipps cocked one eyebrow. "Is he wrong?"

"No. But no one else believes it." And it was telling that Phipps was taking Peterbury's word for it, against the word of the whole English army, including its immensely popular and politically ambitious hero. "You'd run counter to Wellington's own opinion on the matter."

"But I do not come on behalf of Wellington." He lowered his voice again. "You'll be paid, of course—"

The mugs of ale rattled as Alec slammed his palm down on the table. "I don't want *money*," he bit out. "I am not a mercenary."

This seemed to please Phipps. His flat smile spread once more across his face. "Good. The payment will not be much. We prefer to deal in other compensation. Let me know your decision by noon on the morrow." He got to his feet and dropped a card on the table. "Good eve to you, Mr. Brandon."

Alec finished his ale before he touched the card. He didn't know what Peterbury might have told this man about him to make Phipps so confident in his offer, and he wasn't sure he wanted to know. Could he become a spy? A black smile crossed his face; hadn't he already done so, changing his name and altering his appearance, moving around from place to place without staying anywhere for long, always listening, always watching . . . But if he took this position, all that might come to something useful. He had a feeling Phipps would be very pleased to have a dead man working for him. That way, if Alec erred too badly, it would be no trouble to get rid of him. Dead men had no rights—and made no protests.

John Stafford, Magistrates Court, Number 4, Bow Street. Alec turned the card over and over in his hand. It went against everything he thought right. Spies were rabble, not gentlemen. Some would view turning spy as an admission of guilt, a continuance of past sins. In other circumstances, Alec would believe the same. But what choice did he have? Peterbury had discovered nothing in almost a year. The documents that proved his guilt might exist, or not, and Alec had no way of knowing. If he didn't know, he could hardly refute them, and if he couldn't refute them, his best option was to take this job. If such damning documents existed, Sidmouth would be able to find them. All Alec asked was a chance to see them, to defend himself against them, and this might be the price of that chance.

And if it led to a noose around his neck . . . he was hardly any worse off.

He slipped the card into his pocket and walked out of the pub.

Chapter 9

July 1820

The invitation to Penford arrived the next morning. Cressida held it a moment, admiring Mrs. Hayes's elegant script. She still hadn't decided if she wanted to go, but it was very lovely to be invited.

"What is that?" Callie had heard the servant at the door. She paused on her way through the hall to look. "Oh my."

"Julia told me about it," she said, ignoring the curiosity in her sister's tone.

"We've never been invited to such an event at Penford before."

"Er . . . no." She handed the invitation to Callie and picked up her basket. Callie followed her out into the garden.

"What sort of party is it?"

"I think it's to celebrate the major's return home." Cressida bent over the herb garden. She cut some lavender, breathing the soft scent with a sigh of pleasure.

"Oh." Callie fingered Mrs. Hayes's note. "We haven't anything grand enough to wear."

"Not nearly."

"And you still don't like him."

Cressida concentrated on cutting some sage, laying each velvety sprig carefully in the basket.

"Well, shall we go?" Callie kicked her foot lightly.

"I don't know." She cut some mint for Granny's tea. Perhaps it would settle her digestion. The expensive tonic had made little difference.

"You don't have long to think about it."

"I know!" For a moment she considered telling Callie what the major had said yesterday, that they might not really want to find Papa after all, and his advice on horse stealing. They didn't know anything about that man, and she was not wrong to be cautious, she wasn't . . . Except that he had been right, curse him, about everything. She hated it when going against her instinct was the sensible thing to do. "We'll talk about it later," she said. "At dinner."

Callie brought up the Hayes party as soon as they sat down to eat. For once Cressida was relieved Granny had taken to her bed; her grandmother would be so pleased to hear they were invited to the best house in the neighborhood, she would have no choice but to go. More and more Granny seemed to live in her own world where worries about money and proper clothing didn't intrude. As it was, she and Callie talked the matter over while Tom ate in silence, his head lowered over his plate. But they couldn't reach a conclusion

"I'm sure it will be a lovely evening," said Callie wistfully as they cleared the table. "But we've really nothing to wear."

"No." Cressida felt a mixture of relief and resignation. Relief that she wouldn't be required to face the major any sooner than three days hence, resignation because . . . Well, because she hated being poor and shabby and it would have been nice to go to a fine party. But, like much else in life, it couldn't be helped. She told herself she would send a polite refusal in the morning.

But she still hadn't written it by midday, when Tom came into the kitchen and handed her a package.

"What is this?" She pulled the string. She hadn't asked him to purchase anything, not when they didn't have any money. The package was round and soft, like a cushion, and wrapped in a generous length of linen. Tom didn't answer, and was halfway to the door by the time she got the string off and unfolded the linen to reveal a bundle of silk the color of spring roses.

"Oh, Tom!" She was almost speechless. The silk spilling out of the linen wrapping was far finer than anything Papa had ever bought them. "What on earth . . . ?"

"You and Mrs. Phillips need nice dresses."

"But— Tom, wait!" Hand on the doorknob, he stopped and turned back, eyebrows raised. Cressida stroked the silk, unable to repress a sigh at the cool softness of it. Underneath the rose she saw a shimmer of blue-green, like water captured in fabric form. "I can't pay for this," she blurted out.

"Do you not like the colors?"

"Yes! No! It's beyond beautiful, but—"

" 'Tis my gift to you both," he said. "For the party. I

wanted you to have enough time to make something nice."

"Tom . . ." She shook her head to clear the haze of delight, and carefully folded the linen back around the shimmering fabric. "It's too much."

"That's my decision," he answered gruffly. "I sold a few of my consuls and had some coins in my pocket when I saw the bolts in the shop, and thought it would become you well. I've still got my pension," he said at her expression. "Don't worry about me. You told me I've been like a brother to you, aye? Can't a brother give his sister a gift?"

Not when the gift cost this much. And she had called him a brother years ago, when she was still a girl. Cressida realized this was more than a brotherly gift. Tom knew how tight their finances were. He hadn't sold his consuls to buy silk for her and Callie, but to help feed them. In that light, this expense was even more outrageous, but the gift was so touching she couldn't bear to argue with him about it. She bit her lip and nodded. "Thank you, Tom."

The corner of his mouth crooked upward, then he slipped through the door. Cressida caressed the bundle of silk, already thinking of the dresses they could make. The rose would look best on Callie, of course, with her darker hair and eyes, but the blue-green was the most beautiful color she'd ever seen. For one night, at least, they wouldn't look like the poorest people in town.

It also sealed her fate regarding the party. There was no way she could refuse to go now—and if she was very honest with herself, she was not sorry the decision had been made for her. She hugged the package close to her chest and ran up the stairs in search of Callie, who was mending in her room.

Her sister's eyes widened in amazement when Cressida showed her the silk. "Where did you get it?" She stroked it lightly.

Cressida hesitated. "Tom gave it to me—to us."

Callie's hand froze. "How on earth?"

"I think he would be gravely insulted if we refused. He knows how things stand. He said it was a gift, like from a brother to a sister." Callie put her hand back in her lap, looking troubled. Cressida sank onto the opposite chair. "He said we should go to the Hayes party, and needed something to look nice."

"That was his reason?"

Cressida nodded.

Callie chewed her lip. "We are not Mr. Webb's sisters. Granny would not approve of us accepting such a gift from him."

"Granny won't know," Cressida said bluntly. "If that's your only basis for objection . . ."

"Then you want to go to the party at Penford. I know you, Cressida; if you were set on not going, you would have told Mr. Webb in no uncertain terms, and he wouldn't have bought this."

Again she hesitated. Cressida wasn't immune to the lure of the blue-green silk, nor to the thought of looking elegant and even lovely in a dress made of it. And if the enigmatic Major Hayes were to see her in it . . . "Julia is my friend," she said. "She particularly asked me to go, and Penford is lovely. We've little enough to do at nights, except mend and read. Why shouldn't we have a night out?" Callie's eyes narrowed at her. Cressida felt the heat rising in her face, but somehow couldn't stop herself from blundering on. "And perhaps it will help us form a better opinion of Major Hayes and decide if we wish to accept his help in finding Papa."

"You are the only one hesitant to accept his help," Callie pointed out. "What do you have against him?"

She didn't even entirely know, beyond the fact that she seemed unable to act sensibly and rationally in his presence. "Don't you think it odd, that a man who had been thought dead for five years, whom everyone thought to be a traitor, should suddenly reappear? And not just that, but come straight to us and offer to help find Papa? Why would Lord Hastings send him, a man who is likely to be mistrusted by everyone and who must have a great many other things to tend to?"

"Lord Hastings must have had a good reason . . ." Callie's voice trailed off.

"Well, no one knows what it is." Cressida sighed, drumming her fingers on the package that lay across her lap. "Even Julia said she doesn't know if we can trust him."

Callie touched the silk again. "I think we have little choice. You yourself said we have no idea where Papa might have gone, or why. Major Hayes is the only person who has offered help, and we need it. The rent is due in a fortnight, we're about to lose our horses, we still owe half the merchants in town, and we have only a small income. We'll be cast on the parish if Papa doesn't return soon."

"I know." Cressida shook her head, shoving aside

her reservations. "Very well. I promise to either present a good argument against him, or graciously accept his help, by the day after the party. Because we're going to go and have a splendid time."

"We'll have to sew through the night." Callie's eyes sparkled as she set aside the drab brown dress she had been mending.

"Get your scissors," Cressida replied with a grin. "We're going to look marvelous!"

For two days they sewed, early in the morning after chores and late into the evening after dinner. Callie, with her eye for fashion, cut the shining silk for two gowns, and Cressida ripped lace from her old best gown for trim. Cressida, who could whip a fine straight seam in no time, did most of the construction work, while Callie turned rosettes on the skirt hems and corded the sleeves with tiny bands of silk. Working with such fine cloth, anticipating the evening awaiting them, their spirits rose above all the worries about money, Papa's absence, and Granny's health. Granny sat with them during the day, smiling and laughing with them both, just as they used to do in Portsmouth. Tom sat with them at night, smoking his pipe in the corner and blushing whenever Callie would hold up a sleeve or a skirt and ask his opinion. For two days Cressida didn't worry about anything but the undeniably exciting prospect of being well-dressed, well-fed, and carefree for an evening.

When the night arrived, Brighampton was a flurry of activity. Cressida shivered as she pulled the sinfully soft silk over her head, marveling at her appearance. The aquamarine color looked very well against her skin and hair, and the line of the gown flattered even her gangly figure. She turned from side to side, admiring the swing of the skirt and the feel of the silk against her skin, and for a moment she felt beautiful.

"Hold still, you can bask in your glory in a moment," said Callie, who was trying to fasten the buttons on the back of her gown.

Cressida stopped turning and laughed. "Glory! Next to you, I'm still the plain one." Callie looked stunning tonight, with her dark curls pinned atop her head and Granny's gold earrings in her ears. The matching locket was around Cressida's neck.

Her sister finished the buttons and gave her a quick pat. Cressida shifted aside and they shared a moment looking at themselves together in the mirror. Both gowns were on the simple side, with little ornamentation, but still fashionable and so gloriously luxurious it almost made her moan in delight. "It's lovely not to look poor for one night," said Callie softly, echoing Cressida's thoughts. "Even if we are."

"I think we look utterly smashing," Cressida declared. "Rich gentlemen will faint dead away at the sight of us, and we shan't be poor for long."

Callie burst out laughing. "We'd better go, then!"

Tom was waiting with the carriage. Granny, dozing in her chair by the fireplace in the sitting room, woke up to exclaim over how lovely they looked and kiss them both. Granny didn't want to go with them, and was staying home instead with a neighbor from down the road. But she was still standing in the doorway waving good-bye as Tom drove them down the lane.

Penford was ablaze with lights. Julia had said it

was to be a small party, but Mrs. Hayes still brought the full resources of her estate to bear on the arrangements. Cressida relinquished her light cloak at the door, trying not to gape as she looked around. She had been a guest at Penford before, but never when it looked like this. The wide hallway glowed with candlelight and smelled of the freshly picked roses that graced the marble-topped table in the center of the hall. Penford's garden was famed throughout Hertfordshire. Mrs. Hayes was there, greeting her guests with a gracious smile. And beside her, tall and dark and almost broodingly somber, stood the major.

Cressida's breath seemed to have solidified in her throat. He looked . . . powerful, as he had never looked before, and at the same time almost dangerously attractive. The dark severity of his evening clothes suited the hard lines of his face and his unfashionably short hair. There was nothing soft or light about him, just a pure masculine appeal that rooted her feet to the floor. He did not look at all like a man to be trifled with—and yet so far she had been rude, abrupt, and querulous to his face. Now she apparently was trying to be stupid as well, as he looked up from shaking the curate's hand, right into her eyes, and her brain completely stopped. She couldn't move, speak, or even think as his bright blue eyes held hers. Callie nudged her, and she jolted forward.

"Are you ill?" whispered her sister.

"No," Cressida muttered, flushing at her own awkwardness. She pasted a smile on her face and followed Callie.

Mrs. Hayes greeted them cordially before turning

to her son, standing at her side. "You have already met my son Alexander, I believe," she said with a smile.

"Indeed, sir. It is a pleasure to see you again." Callie curtsied as he bowed over her hand.

"Mrs. Phillips. Welcome to Penford." Cressida braced herself. "And Miss Turner." This time there was a slight curve to his mouth. "Welcome to Penford."

"Thank you," she managed to say as he took her hand.

"I trust you had a pleasant walk home the other day."

He was still holding her hand, still watching her with that secretive gleam in his eye. Callie was speaking to Mrs. Hayes. She had to save herself. Cressida stiffened her spine, flashed her widest smile at him, and said, "Superb, thank you."

It worked. His eyebrows went up a fraction of an inch and he straightened, which seemed to let a rush of fresh air between them. Or perhaps it was because she was holding her breath every time he came near her. She hated that feeling, the way her heart seemed to seize and then jump into her throat when he fixed his attention on her. It just wasn't fair that he could unsettle her so easily.

"Cressida!" With perfect timing, Julia swooped down on them. "How wonderful to see you," she cried gaily, clasping Cressida's hand. The major had released her as soon as Julia called out her name. "Excuse us," Julia said to her brother as she pulled Cressida away. "Thank heavens you've come," she whispered. She linked her arm around Cressida's and headed toward the drawing room. "I've been expecting you for ages."

"We're not but a quarter hour late," said Cressida with a shaky laugh. Now that she was away from the major, her heart—and tongue—seemed to work again. "What horror have you had to endure in that time?"

Julia sighed. "The whole party is a horror. Everyone is being so careful not to say a thing about the last few years, but no one can think of anything else. And Alec! He's not helping things by being so grim and silent."

He hadn't looked very grim in the hall, when he teased her and held her hand too long. Cressida tried to banish the memory of his long fingers around hers. "What would you have him do?"

"He could explain himself properly."

"What, just stand up in front of everyone and tell all?" She looked around the room, not recognizing most of the guests. After five years, quite likely the major didn't, either. "That doesn't seem likely."

Julia dipped her head, acknowledging the point. "You don't know Alec. He has no trouble speaking his mind."

Cressida remembered him walking so stealthily and watchfully through her stable, then not saying a word as she aimed her pistol at him. He might not have trouble speaking his mind, but he also had no trouble holding his tongue. In fact, he seemed almost nothing like the man Julia described, and she wondered who was mistaken. "Nor do I," she said instead. "And I say this is a lovely party, and I thank you for inviting us."

"Yes, indeed! Thank you very much, Julia." Callie had come up beside them, her eyes sparkling and her cheeks flushed. Julia's expression brightened, and they talked of other things.

Alec never thought he would miss the French sharpshooters, but as he strolled through the drawing room with his mother, he would far rather have faced a field of Bonaparte's finest than the thinly veiled curiosity of their guests.

His mother was intent on telling him all about everyone. "Mr. Edwards, the new curate," she would murmur. "Perfectly acceptable, but his wife is a little too full of Christian piety. I do believe she beats her children, they are so quiet and still." And the curate's wife would curtsey to him with her mouth primly pursed, condescending tolerance writ large on her face. Alec knew this party was really for his mother, to reassert her own pride in him to the world at large, so he simply smiled and bowed until his mother reached the only interesting guests in attendance.

"Mrs. Phillips and Miss Turner." Mother clucked her tongue softly. "Very sad."

"Oh?" said Alec, his attention caught at last. "How so?"

"I believe they have been living above their means and are about to suffer a fall. I don't think it's been entirely their fault. Their father is quite a spendthrift, and now he's gone and abandoned them. Julia is well-acquainted with Miss Turner, and she fears the family might lose their home soon."

Now that she had given him the excuse, Alec took a long look at Miss Turner. She looked lovely tonight in a shimmering gown of sea green, a golden locket gleaming right above the swells of her breasts. The soft light from the chandelier darkened her hair to the color of chestnuts, but when she turned her head it shone like fresh honey. She was with Julia, listening to his sister with a mischievous little smile that made his stomach tighten. "How unfortunate," he murmured.

"Indeed. Still, they are both very amiable ladies." Mother paused. "Mrs. Phillips in particular."

Alec shifted his gaze to look at Mrs. Phillips. She was beautiful in a deep rose gown, but his eyes strayed back to Miss Turner. Not a beauty, that one, but something more. "Yes. I had the pleasure of meeting them both the other day."

"Did you?" Her voice rose with interest. "Is that where you go off to? I wondered why you are never about. I should have known, an attractive lady in the neighborhood—"

"Don't start matchmaking, Mother," he said evenly. "I called to offer my assistance in locating Sergeant Turner."

She stopped and looked at him in amazement. "Good heavens, I never knew that. Are you acquainted with Sergeant Turner?"

"No." She waited expectantly, her wide blue eyes fixed on him. Reluctantly, Alec added, "As a favor for someone in London."

"Oh!" She looked delighted, as though she'd been anticipating this moment since he came home. To be fair, she probably had been. "Then you have been in London? Alexander . . ." She touched his arm. "I have wondered, dear, what to tell people. Everyone has been so . . . so *curious*, you see, how you have been and what adventures you might have had . . ."

Alec felt a pang of shame and unease. His mother had been waiting so patiently for him to explain everything to her, and he hadn't said a word. Of course people were talking about him; he certainly knew it. The convenient response would be to make up something out of whole cloth, to tell a story of injury, hard luck, perhaps a bit of secret romance or memory loss, anything to answer the question of where he had been for the last five years. Twice already he'd had to stop himself from inventing details of his recent past, as had become his habit. Say anything, Stafford had always instructed him, except the truth. Never the truth. Somehow, at some time, the truth had become dangerous.

But that was to strangers. Alec didn't want to lie to his mother unless he absolutely must. "I've been to London," he answered vaguely. "It was a favor for someone from the army. Miss Turner wrote to him asking for assistance, and he asked me to look into things."

"Oh." Mother looked nonplussed. "The army. I see."

He hoped not. "I want to be discreet about it, for the family's sake. They do seem like amiable ladies, and I would hate to bring any more distress to them." Too late he remembered Miss Turner had not yet given him her blessing, and that he might end up making his inquiries on his own. But she was here to-night—surely a sign that she was considering giving her approval—and he wasn't waiting on her blessing in any event. He realized he had been watching her for several minutes, and turned away.

"Of course." A shadow had fallen over her face. "And that is why you've come home, isn't it. Because the army sent you."

The faint sadness in her statement pierced him. *Never the truth.* Alec bowed his head. "No," he said quietly. "I came home because of Frederick."

Chapter 10

Cressida found herself having a lovely time as the evening wore on. Most of the guests were pleasant, undemanding people, all polite enough not to comment on the main purpose of the gathering and willing to enjoy the evening. By the time Julia excused herself to go check on the refreshments, Cressida was surprised to realize almost two hours had passed.

"I'm so glad we came," Callie said softly beside her.

"I am, too," she admitted.

"And not just to feel pretty again, although that is wonderful." She moved, setting her rose skirts aflutter as they both admired the glow of candlelight ripple across the silk. "It's so nice to be out in company."

"I'm sure the gentlemen in attendance are thinking the same thing. You really do look beautiful tonight."

Her sister had a way of wrinkling her nose just a little, managing to look fetching instead of gruesome. "They are not all looking at me." She paused. "Major Hayes certainly looks at you a great deal, though."

Cressida jerked in surprise. "He does not."

"You don't think so?" Callie was watching him across the room. Cressida glanced at him from under her eyelashes, just in time to realize he was looking her way. He stood by his mother, and as they watched he leaned down and murmured something to her before walking out the back of the room. "I vow, every time I happen to catch a glimpse of him, he's looking at you in that contemplative way."

"Rubbish," Cressida said with a small, uncomfortable laugh.

"You look very nice tonight. Perhaps that's it."

"Perhaps he's contemplating where I might have my pistol hidden." Callie laughed and Cressida grinned, although she would perish of embarrassment if anyone else knew she had pointed a gun at their host.

"You always make fun when I suggest a man might be admiring you."

She went rigid. "I am sure that is *not* why he's looking at me. The very idea is ridiculous." Ridiculous and dangerous. Just the thought of those piercing eyes turned on her like *that* . . . Cressida shivered, then gave her sister a frown to reinforce her statement that it was ridiculous. Even if he did seem to look at her mouth fairly often.

"I doubt it's ridiculous, but of course I have no idea," Callie conceded. "But any time I say such a thing, about anyone, you turn it into a joke."

Cressida turned and walked toward the open doors. Callie followed her into the empty hall. "It *is* a joke. Gentlemen look at you that way, not at me. I don't mind," she said as her sister looked at her in reproach. "Truly I don't."

"You must."

She shook her head, running her fingers along the edge of the marble table. The hall was quiet and cool, scented with roses. She loved the genteel comfort of this house. Penford managed to be grand without being ostentatious, elegant without being cold, and above all a home, where children were allowed to skip in the corridors and there was always some bit of greenery brightening the rooms. "Not much. You've always been prettier than I, and everyone knows it. And you're also more even-tempered, with a sweeter disposition and a gentler nature, so there's never much reason for anyone to look at me at all when you're about."

"I don't think much of that is true, but even if so, it doesn't stand to reason that every man would prefer me to you." Cressida snorted, and Callie poked her in the arm with her fan. "Nor should they! And you should not assume they do."

Cressida snorted again. She didn't like this conversation. It wasn't Callie's fault she had a knack for turning men away. It was just easier to make sport of them all than to admit out loud that she would in fact not mind being married, if only she could find someone who didn't treat her like an oddity. She should find a prosperous innkeeper who would be too busy to mind her plain looks and might even welcome her sharp tongue and practical manner.

"Don't you want to marry? Ever?"

The smart retort was on her lips. Cressida swallowed it and forced herself to be honest. "I suppose I wouldn't mind, if the right man . . ." She glanced at Callie and sighed. "Why do you ask?"

"Because I have been thinking about our problems and how we might solve them. If one of us were to marry—"

Cressida felt a flicker of panic, but gave Callie a withering glare to hide it. "You've been listening to Granny again."

"No," said her sister quietly. "I arrived at this myself. Cressida, what are we going to do? If one of us married a well-situated man, we would be provided for. Granny would be provided for." That was true; they had Granny to think of as well, Granny with her wandering mind and failing body. "I confess, it is a daunting thought"—Callie's voice faltered—"but I'm selfish not to consider it."

"But to whom?" They were whispering now, huddled close to each other. Cressida clasped her sister's hands. "Is there someone you admire?"

Callie blushed. "N-No, not in particular, but I think—I think I must look. And you must as well. We neither of us want to end as poor spinsters, I think."

Except that Callie was already a widow. Cressida was the spinster, and she hadn't Callie's reason to be skittish about marriage. "I intend to speak to Mrs. Blatchford in Marston about taking in work."

"Taking in sewing isn't going to support all of us," Callie pointed out. Cressida fell silent. For a moment they just stood in somber contemplation of their future.

"Well, this needn't ruin our evening." Cressida shook herself and squeezed her sister's hand. "We can't change anything tonight, so we might as well be merry."

"No." Callie glanced around the hall. "This is an odd place to discuss such a thing, I suppose."

"Very," Cressida agreed dryly.

"Well. Shall we go back?"

She shook her head. "I want to see the garden at night. I'll return in a moment." Callie smiled and went back into the drawing room. Cressida slid her fingers once more along the marble table, catching up a few rose petals that had fallen. She brought them to her face and breathed in the soft, wild scent as she went through the back of the hall to the door to the terrace.

"Would you like one?"

She froze, petals clutched guiltily in her fist. She dared a glance behind her, but the major was no-where to be seen, even though his voice had sounded very near. Then she saw him just around the corner at the foot of the back stairs, down on one knee with a small plate in his outstretched hand. Two tiny pairs of slippers scrambled out of sight, and a little girl's voice said, "Mama said we mustn't."

"Hmm." As Cressida watched, he selected a tiny cake, little larger than a thimble, from the plate and popped it into his mouth. "Did she also say you must stay in bed?" The little girls, who must be his nieces, said nothing. "These are very good," the major added. "I wouldn't blame anyone who wanted just one."

She should go. She was eavesdropping, and spying, and Granny would be horrified at her. Cressida knew all this even as she stayed where she was. There was something in the major's voice that entranced her and kept her silent and still.

A small hand crept out and took one of the cakes, then another one. The major ate another delicacy from his plate, a smile on his lips. Cressida wet her lips and swallowed. She had grudgingly admitted he was handsome even when he was somber and doing his best to provoke her temper. Now he was at ease and at home, and Cressida thought she would be in serious danger if he ever looked at her that way. Not that it was likely, but her conversation with Callie had fixed her thoughts on men and marriage and made her wonder, *what if* . . . It was bad luck the major happened to be the first handsome, unmarried, smiling man she saw, Cressida told herself. She didn't even like him . . . just the way he smiled that small, secret smile for two little girls sneaking out of bed.

"Do you like the party so far?" he asked them. One pair of slippers slid back into view as the owner leaned forward to take another treat. Major Hayes silently extended the plate, and she took another. Cressida saw the gleam of blond curls; that was Patience, the older girl.

"Not much," she said. "We like to see dancing, and no one is dancing."

"No." He looked down for a second. "I don't think Grandmama meant it to be that sort of party."

"I thought all parties had dancing." Patience reached for the plate again, her prior reluctance fading quickly. "They used to, before Papa died."

The major inhaled audibly. "I am sure there will be dancing again soon. Your papa would want you to be happy and see dancing, and someday dance yourself."

"I don't know how to dance!" She giggled.

"You will learn," he told her. "And you, too, Grace."

There was a rush of whispering in high, sweet childish voices. A second, smaller, pair of feet slipped into view. Grace, Marianne's younger daughter, reached out and took a cake from the plate.

"Don't tell Mama we said so," said Patience. "We aren't to bother you, Mama said." She stopped abruptly.

"And you are not bothering me." Major Hayes put the depleted plate of cakes on the floor. "But you made me think of dancing, and now I want to dance more than anything. Will you dance with me, Miss Patience?"

She giggled again. "No!"

He drew back. "No?"

"No!" she said again, happily.

He sighed, then turned to her sister. "Will you dance with me, Miss Grace?"

To Cressida's surprise, the tiny girl slid off the stair and put up her arms. He got to his feet and took her little hands in his, twirling her in circles and making her white nightgown bell out around her. A wide, nervous smile brightened her face, and then Patience jumped in, clapping her hands until her uncle gave her one hand and twirled her around, too. Both little girls stayed quiet, as if mindful they would be sent to bed if their mother discovered them, although their giggles grew louder as the major spun them in wider circles and finally scooped up Patience and swung her off her feet. Then he swung Grace, and Cressida felt her heart wobble at the open grin he wore. This was a side of the major she had never seen, and didn't expect.

After he had swung them each a few times, he set them back down. "You had best run along to bed now," he said. "Dancing wears a fellow out."

"It was fun!" said Patience, hopping up and down in excitement. "You won't tell Mama we were out of bed, will you?"

"Not unless she asks me directly. Now go, before she finds out on her own."

"Oh! Come, Grace," she said, taking her little sister's hand. "Good night, Uncle!" With more giggling and some thumping, the girls disappeared up the stairs.

Cressida belatedly realized she should slip away, but before she could take a step, the major had turned in her direction.

"Would you also like to dance, Miss Turner?"

Her face burned. "Oh, n-no," she stammered. "I—I am sorry, I did *not* mean to spy. I was just in search of a breath of fresh air . . ."

He smiled, and made no mention of the fact that she could have gotten to the garden directly from the drawing room. "Ah. I should hate to keep you from it." He swept out one hand in wordless invitation, and she ducked her head and hurried past him, to the back of the house and out the door there. It would be better if he didn't follow her; it would certainly be easier for her. But she knew he would, and wasn't at all surprised when his footsteps sounded behind her on the flagstones.

"So, have you made up your mind yet about me?"

She gave a guilty start. Alec prowled a step closer.

He found he could bear the scorn and distrust well enough from almost everyone else, but for some reason he felt compelled to press her on the issue. Perhaps it was the way that, despite the guilty start, she was still standing her ground, looking up at him with her chin raised and her eyes glowing. Everyone else glanced away to avoid his gaze or looked in fear of their lives if he spoke to them. His own nieces had first looked at him as if he were an ogre come to eat them, until he offered the plate of sweets. At least Miss Turner wasn't afraid of him.

"I am still considering," was her pert reply.

Alec clasped his hands behind him and hid a smile. He definitely liked this woman—beyond reason, most likely. "I see. Tonight you have me at your mercy. What are your reservations?"

Her eyes darted past him to the bright windows of the drawing room. The murmur of conversation and laughter spilled into the dark night. "You are not at my mercy. You don't have to speak to me at all."

"Perhaps I would like to speak to you." More than she might guess, and far more than he would ever let on.

She rolled that lower lip between her teeth. Alec, who had watched her do it again and again when he drove her into town, almost held his breath as he watched. "Perhaps you're just hiding here to avoid the other guests."

"As you are?" As hoped, her lips parted at the counterattack, rosy pink and glistening. Perfect. He moved a step closer.

"Well . . . yes."

He grinned. He liked her all the more for admitting it. "Then we are bound together in secrecy by our guilty consciences."

She pressed her lips into a line, then stopped fighting it and gave him a sheepish smile. "I suppose we are."

Alec turned to face the garden and put his head back to look at the night sky—anything to keep from staring at her mouth. "What makes you dread the guests inside?" He could almost hear her stiffen. "I dislike being watched so closely, as if people expect a violent outburst at any moment. The curate's wife looked as though she was making a list of sins I might commit this very evening."

There was only silence beside him. Alec didn't glance her way, so he had no idea of her expression, but perhaps that ploy hadn't worked. He did want Miss Turner's cooperation. He wanted to be done with this assignment as soon as possible, and her assistance would make things much easier. And if she came to like him a little better . . . Alec couldn't deny an unwarranted desire for that. So instead of just asking questions, he volunteered information. Nothing she couldn't guess on her own, but a peace offering of sorts, after the way he had quizzed her the other day.

But she didn't reply. Alec gave a silent sigh. "I had forgotten how beautiful these gardens are at night," he murmured. "My mother always let it run a bit wild, and as a boy I imagined it an enchanted forest." The silence endured. He started to leave. "I shan't disturb your enjoyment of them."

"An enchanted forest?" she said softly, stepping up beside him. "Enchanted by whom?"

He smiled ruefully. "An evil witch, I'm afraid. The vines there"—he gestured toward a towering wisteria, silver-spangled in the moonlight—"I imagined an angry monster, like a hydra. The roses in the center were a Scylla, and in the pond lurked a Leviathan, ready to slither out and drag me down if I went too close. I, of course, was a valiant hero come to battle them all."

She darted a guarded glance at him. "That was very good of you, to protect the household from such dangers."

"I always thought so. Once I went fishing for the Leviathan. I pictured myself hauling it into the house like a hunting trophy. But just as I lowered my line into the water, a frog jumped in, right where I had cast the hook and was leaning over to check my progress. I fell headfirst into the pond, then bolted into the house dripping wet and covered with moss." This time she did laugh, though quietly and stifled.

"The poor frog." She was definitely entertained by this. Alec caught the beginnings of a smile on her lips.

"Perhaps, but those roses truly are a Scylla. I fell into their vicious grasp many times, and was thoroughly scratched."

She drew in a deep breath. "Rather like the guests inside."

"I suppose one could look at it that way," he replied in the same easy tone. "Though the scratches run somewhat deeper."

For another several minutes they stood in silence. "I hate that everyone knows we've fallen into debt," she finally said, very softly. "I hate being poor, and I hate everyone pitying us because Papa's disappeared. I know some think he's just abandoned us."

Alec pictured the curate's wife, with her primly pursed mouth and sanctimonious eyes. "You don't believe he has."

She shook her head. "No. Whatever failings Papa has, he wouldn't abandon us. I don't believe so, at any rate." She paused. "What do you think has happened to him?"

It was a thorny question. "I was not told much," he said carefully. "Only what you wrote Hastings, in fact. You and your sister told me more than he did, and even with that . . . I shouldn't like to form an idea that may prove wrong. I can only assure you that I have no other object than to discover the truth, and I would not have agreed to that if I didn't fully intend to succeed."

Cressida studied him, tall and imposing despite his neutral expression and even tone of voice. He had a way of holding so still, he seemed a shadow himself. If not for the white of his cravat and waistcoat, he would be entirely dark. He was still an enigma, but she couldn't shake the image of him swinging his young nieces and smiling so openly. She wet her lips again. "What do you plan to do? I cannot think how you will proceed when we, who know Papa and his habits, have been unable to get word of him."

His mouth curled again. "So it is my abilities you doubt."

She blushed, damn it all. Hopefully he couldn't

notice in the dark. "No! Not at all. I am sure you are very able, I just . . . that is . . ."

He watched her, his head cocked to one side and that curious light in his eyes. As if he had seen her blush and liked it. As if he was thinking of something other than finding Papa. As if he found her intriguing. "Hastings must have thought my talents well-suited to the job."

Cressida closed her mouth to avoid making a fool of herself. She was being very foolish tonight, spurred on by her sister's ridiculous suggestion that he . . . She looked at her feet. The major hadn't moved or done anything that might justify her leaping pulse; he'd walked out with her, told a few amusing stories about his youth, and been perfectly polite. Poor man. If he ever knew what she was attributing to him, he'd be horrified.

She took a fortifying breath and faced him, squaring her shoulders. "Thank you," she said, "for offering to help. We would be very grateful for your assistance."

He bowed his head. "I shall do my best not to disappoint."

The man had a dangerous smile, dark and knowing, as if they shared some secret. Cressida felt again that he would tease all her secrets out of her, if given enough time. And she shuddered to think how little time that might be, given that just standing in the dark with him had made her mind run wild and her knees wobble. "I shall do my best to help."

His smile grew. "I look forward to it," he murmured. "Shall we begin tomorrow?"

"I . . ." She swallowed. What abilities, she wondered inanely, were well-suited to this task? Did he just corner people against a wall and look at them until they burst out in confession? It would bloody well work on her. "Yes."

He held her gaze a moment longer. "Excellent. Until the morrow, Miss Turner."

He turned and walked away. Cressida pressed a hand to her bosom, wondering exactly what she had just agreed to. And why she felt such a hot surge of anticipation for his visit.

Chapter 11

He took her at her word, and arrived early the next morning.

"How shall we begin?" Cressida wanted to be involved in whatever he did. What was he going to do that would miraculously locate Papa? Or was there some obvious thing she ought to have done weeks ago? She was still wildly curious to know why he of all people had been sent to them, but like many other things, that seemed to be something he kept to himself.

"Tell me everything about your father's trip. Even the smallest detail may have significance."

She sighed, but related everything she could remember regarding Papa's journey to London. The major listened closely, asking only a few questions. Cressida waited to hear something insightful, but instead he appeared to abandon the topic altogether.

"Where would your father keep his private papers?"

She frowned. "Why? What has that got to do with anything?"

"It might reveal another destination, or another interest he might have had in London," Alec explained.

This, he had to admit, was easier when there was no subterfuge. Being able to ask a question openly was far quicker than his usual methods. He could see Miss Turner still wasn't completely won over, but she was cooperating, and somehow her sharp, watchful gaze was even more attractive than her suspicious gaze.

For a moment she didn't reply, folding her arms. With her chin tipped down and her head cocked, she regarded him with unmistakable doubt. It also exposed the lovely long line of her neck, wreathed as ever with escaping wisps of hair. For some reason Alec always wanted to sweep his hand up the curve of her shoulder and smooth those loose hairs back into the heavy mass pinned atop her head. It was annoying that he was so distracted by her neck, and he clasped his hands behind his back to stifle the urge to touch any part of her.

"What do you expect to find?" she said at last.

"Anything that offers an avenue of possibility." At her continued silence, he added, "I regret the invasion of your family's privacy, but I am doing my duty. If you have any other suggestions, by all means share them, and I shall endeavor to follow them."

She drew breath as if to argue, then let it out. She unfolded her arms and held out one hand. "Of course. You are right. I apologize, sir."

Alec hesitated just a moment before clasping her hand in his. Like the rest of her, her fingers were long and slender, but she returned his grip as firmly as any man might. He let go at once, calling himself a fool for finding this woman so intriguing.

"Papa made his study down here," she said, turn-

ing to lead the way from the room. As she moved past
the parlor windows, the sunlight streamed across the
nape of her neck, turning her skin to glowing ivory
and setting those tempting wisps of hair agleam
with hidden highlights, not just brown but gold and
chestnut and honey. Alec blinked, disoriented at his
inexplicable fascination.

"What do you hope to find?" she asked, interrupt-
ing his thoughts.

"Er . . . a diary, indicating private plans, bills from
merchants he might have gone to see, even letters
from acquaintances indicating plans to call. Anything that might give some idea where to turn next."
He gave himself a mental shake and followed her,
scrupulously keeping his gaze away from her neck.

She led the way down a narrow hallway into a
small room at the back of the house. Bookshelves
lined two walls, but they were mostly bare. A scarred
wooden desk stood beneath the room's only window
and a narrow wooden bench sat opposite it. The walls
were faded, and the tiny fireplace was cold. Overall
it was a sad, dingy little room, and Alec's instincts
pricked up.

"Why did he choose this room?"

Miss Turner opened the wooden shutters, letting
in more light. Even so, it was still dark in the room
on a sunny day. Alec could see a corner of the stable
through the window. "He likes the privacy and quiet
of it. My grandmother never comes back here." She
turned to face him, her back to the window. "His
papers are in the desk."

"Right." Alec crossed the room and sat at the desk,
opening drawers and sifting through the contents

with practiced speed. It was almost child's play to search a room in daylight, even if he was all too conscious of the woman standing in front of the daylight. Women like her shouldn't be allowed to stand in front of windows, where their figures were so well-outlined and the sun could catch every highlight in their hair.

He sorted through bills, bills, and more bills. There were a few letters, mostly from former army superiors responding to Sergeant Turner's inquiries about employment opportunities. Turner had ambition, Alec realized, noting what sort of positions the man had sought. No hard labor for him; Turner asked about clerkships to governing boards and plum posts in the scaled-down army. Those seemed a bit out of reach for a sergeant, even a distinguished one, but the replies were all apologetic in their refusal, even deferential. It struck Alec as odd that Turner would think himself fit for these posts, and be refused with so much solicitude. He was sure mid-ranked officers would have been refused these patronage positions, which were highly sought for the combination of comfortable pay, modest status, and low work requirements. He tucked that thought away, adding to his still-forming picture of Sergeant Turner.

The bills were more interesting, but still told him little. Turner seemed to play things out just to the point of becoming unpleasant before he paid. He bought on credit almost exclusively, and apparently had no trouble getting it anywhere from Marston to London. Alec looked through the desk, but there was no ledger to verify the bills' payments. "Would your father keep an account ledger?"

Cressida started at the question. He had been so quiet for so long. The way he went straight to work, sorting through the mess of Papa's papers, was almost preternaturally silent and efficient. She had peeked at those papers herself, when Papa had been gone a month with no word, and knew they were in a horrible mess. She had given up trying to sort the bills into order—an exceptionally depressing task, given how many of them there were—when her grandmother scolded her for interfering in Papa's affairs and shooed her out of the room. So far Major Hayes had flipped through every one of them and made three neat stacks on the desk, and now he was looking at her with that piercingly direct gaze. It was so unnerving, and so blue, she completely missed his question. "What?"

"An account ledger, to keep track of payments. I don't see one."

"Oh—yes. He does."

He waved one hand across the desk top. "It's not here."

Cressida bit the inside of her lip. She knew it wasn't there from the time she had tried to look through Papa's things. It had bothered her then, too, for she knew he kept one; she had seen him making entries in it. But she had brushed it aside as inconsequential; Papa might have left it anywhere or even taken it with him. Perhaps that had been a mistake . . . She thought of all Callie had said, and what Major Hayes had said, and realized she must honor her decision to cooperate. She had accepted his help and must freely give him her cooperation. Otherwise she might as well be guilty of the horrible things he had suggested when he drove her into Marston. "I don't know where it is," she admitted. "I know he kept one, but I couldn't find it when I looked."

The major seemed to sit up a little straighter. "Might he have kept it somewhere else?"

"I don't think so. This was his room. We weren't to enter it, under normal circumstances."

He was on his feet before she finished, turning in a slow circle and taking in the entire room. "But you did?"

"He kept his strongbox here. I had to come in and get money, after he left." She didn't mention that she'd had to pick the lock to get it open, nor that it had been nearly empty. It was highly unlikely Major Hayes hadn't already deduced that much.

He stepped closer to the wall and ran one hand over the wainscoting. "Where was the strongbox?"

"In the lower desk drawer." She watched in astonishment as he knelt on the floor and began tapping on the panels. "What are you looking for?"

"A hiding place." He pulled off his coat and tossed it on the chair, then returned to the floor and leaned his ear against the wall before rapping on it with his knuckles.

Cressida gaped at his broad back. "Why?"

He rapped some more. "This is an odd room to choose for his study. It has no light. It's more like an estate manager's office than a gentleman's study." Another rap. He moved along the floor, smoothing his hand over the wall as he went, stopping to feel every crack and edge. "And if he kept his strongbox here, quite likely he kept the ledger with it. Unless you found it in his bedchamber?" He swung around so quickly Cressida jumped back, banging her elbow on the desk. She had followed his progress without realizing.

"N-No." She rubbed her elbow as he nodded. There was a curious light in his eyes, almost elation, as though he had a plan.

"Many of these old houses have hidden cupboards. Not terribly secure, just an out-of-the-way place to keep something private." He turned back to the wall and spread his hands over the wood. "I could be wrong, of course."

Cressida watched, askance, as he leaned into the wall. That made sense, she supposed, even though he didn't know Papa at all and couldn't know how close-mouthed her father was about certain things. "No," she said slowly. "I think you may well be correct."

She moved to the opposite wall and began rapping on the panels herself, but stopped after a few tries. She didn't know what she was doing, and was probably just making it harder for him to hear whatever he was listening for. Again she retreated to the window and waited, with nothing to do but watch as he systematically rapped at every square inch of wall. Intent on his task, he said nothing, which unfortunately only left her mind free to wander to inappropriate subjects.

The shape of his hands, for instance.

When he laid his palm flat against the wall and spread his fingers wide, Cressida couldn't help noticing how strong and capable his hands were. He paused and ran his fingertips lightly over the edge of one panel, his cheek laid right against the wall as he scrutinized every stroke of his fingers. A funny feeling stirred in her belly as she watched him caress the old wooden panel, stained dark from age and smoke. A cavalryman's hands, she thought, ought not to be capable of such delicate motion.

"Ah," he sighed in satisfaction. A slow smile curved his mouth and Cressida's breath stopped in her chest for just a moment. She had better go scrub floors or pick vegetables or—

"I was about to suggest we look in the bedchamber," he said, "but I think there's no need."

It took her brain a moment to function again. "Oh," she said, then: "Oh!" Under those strong, capable fingers, a panel in the wall was sliding inward. He pressed harder, until the wood squealed a little and then gave way, revealing a dark space about a foot square behind the wall just to the left of the fireplace.

"It's warped," the major said, pushing it fully open. "There's a tiny nail hole here, as if someone tried to seal it shut. That may have alerted your father to its presence."

"Oh," she said for the third time. She never would have noticed such a thing. Was the major this observant about everything? "Of course."

He grinned at her and reached into the space to pull out two books, one the ledger Cressida had seen her father write in, and another, smaller one. He brought them to the window, beside her. "Let's see what we have here," he muttered, opening the larger book in a ray of sunshine.

"That's the ledger," she said stupidly. Of course it was a ledger, the pages lined with long columns of neat numbers; a man who would notice a pinprick of a nail hole in the wall didn't need to be told that.

"Indeed it is." His eyes were flitting rapidly over the page, and he turned through a few more before closing it and setting it on the desk. "And what is this?" He flipped open the smaller book.

"I have no idea," she said after a moment. "It looks like Papa's hand, but . . ."

"It looks like a journal." He touched one page. "Dates."

It was. But aside from the dates, everything was nonsense. The words looked like ordinary words from a distance, but were composed of random assortments of letters that didn't spell anything in English. "It's a code," she said in amazement.

He glanced at her in surprise, then paged through the rest of the book. Everything was the same odd jumble of letters. "I believe you're right. Did your father tell you he used codes?"

She shook her head. "He's always been fond of puzzles and secrets. I—I suppose that's what led him to hide the books. I never saw this one, though."

"It's old. The dates go back over ten years, although they end only six months past." He looked up, meeting her gaze. "Then you probably don't know the key."

Cressida pursed her lips. "No, but . . . I should like to take a turn at deciphering it."

"You like codes?" His eyes lit up, and she felt absurdly pleased at having delighted him. "By all means. I'll take this"—he tapped the ledger—"and you have a go at this."

She took the journal. The leather was stiff and creased, and the pages crackled when she turned them. But it smelled of Papa's tobacco, and she held it close to her heart. "I will."

He turned away and began stacking the sorted bills on top of the ledger. "I'll go through this and match up the bills with the payments, to see if he owes anyone. He might have made a quiet trip to discuss a debt. It will be quite tedious, I'm afraid, or we could do it here. I know you wish to stay informed of all I do."

Cressida blushed at his matter-of-fact statement. "I do, but I don't wish to interfere." He gave her a wry look that indicated he knew exactly how much she wanted to interfere, and she blushed harder. He would think her face permanently red, the way things were going. "I hope you find something helpful."

"And I you." He placed one hand on the ledger and the other on his hip. With the window at his back, in his dazzling white shirtsleeves, he seemed large and powerful and very male. "How shall we go on?"

"Go . . ." She cleared her throat—difficult to do with her head tipped back to see him. "Go on?"

"Yes. You did say you wanted to remain involved. Shall I work until I discover something, or shall I call every day even if I have no news?"

Every day. She cleared her throat again. "As often as you see fit, Major."

He looked at her. "Alec," he said. "Please."

"Oh." She tried to laugh and ended up making a strange coughing sound. They were very close together here by the window and the desk. Cressida didn't remember the last time she had been so close to a man who was not Tom or her father, let alone

one who looked at her like this. "I don't think . . . That is . . . If you wish."

"We'll be thrown together a fair amount, I expect." Finally he looked away. "I'm not in the army any longer. I haven't used the rank in some time." He raised one brow and cast a significant glance over her shoulder, to where his coat lay on the chair. Cressida hurriedly stepped aside, and he moved past her, his boots brushing her skirts. She stood clutching Papa's journal to her chest as he put on his coat and collected the ledger and bills. They walked into the hall, where she murmured a good-bye and he bowed and left with a promise to return soon.

Alec. He swung onto his horse's back and touched the brim of his hat to her. *We'll be thrown together . . .* Did that mean he wanted to call her Cressida? He hadn't asked. She hadn't invited him, either, but that was more because her tongue seemed tied up in a knot. What would her name sound like on his lips? And just how often would he call?

"Cressida." She started, and turned to see Tom standing in the hall behind her, twisting his cap in his hands. "Might I have a moment?"

"Of course, Tom. What is it?"

He glanced over her shoulder. Cressida could still hear hoofbeats, and her mind called up the image of Major Hayes—Alec, she reminded herself with a nervous tingle—with his perfect cavalry posture, riding away, guiding the horse with the smallest touch of a heel or a knee, his hands as calm and gentle as they were steady and commanding.

"He's been around a lot lately," Tom muttered.

"Er—" Cressida plastered a smile on her face to hide her wandering thoughts. "He's going to help us find Papa." She held up the journal in illustration. "And see, today we've found something."

Tom stared at the dusty old journal, and the color drained from his ruddy face. "Where'd you find that?" he asked in a thin voice.

Cressida narrowed her eyes at him in surprise. Tom had obviously seen it before. What did Tom know that he hadn't told her? she wondered suddenly. "In the study."

Tom's eyes were riveted on the book. "Did you find anything else?"

"Yes," she replied slowly. "A ledger. Major Hayes has taken it to see if it will reveal anything useful."

"Should you have let him take it?"

"Why not?"

Instead of answering, Tom sighed and pushed one hand through his hair, standing it on end. "What do you hope to find?" he asked her, sounding weary and almost despairing.

"The truth. I want to know where Papa is, and why he hasn't come home."

He closed his eyes and hung his head. For the first time Cressida noticed there was a small bald patch at the crown of his head, and that his sandy hair had threads of gray. "Truly? What if it is ugly or unpleasant?"

"What do you mean? How could it be worse than not knowing?" He didn't answer. "I want to know what happened to my father," she exclaimed. "Do you fault me for that?"

He sighed again. "No. I just fear . . . I fear you might

not find the answers as comforting as you expect."

"Do you know what happened to him?" Cressida was shocked by the possibility, but then, she was just realizing that never once had she heard Tom say he hoped Papa came back. He was always ready to lend a helping hand or a comforting word on almost any other subject, but not that one. When he had offered to go look for Papa, and she and Callie had refused, he never pressed the issue—as if he wasn't sorry his offer had been rejected. But Tom had been with her father for years, over a decade. If he didn't have any affection for Papa, why had he stayed so long?

Tom shook his head. "As God is my witness, I have no idea. I know as much as you do, that he went to London to see Lord Hastings and planned to return within a fortnight."

"But you *have* seen this before." She held up the journal.

Tom glanced at it before dropping his eyes to the floor. "Yes, that's the sergeant's journal. He kept it for years."

Cressida flipped it open and paged through it. The writing was small but precise; Papa did write a very gentlemanly hand, something he took great pride in. But it was clearly in code, an odd thing for a private journal. "Do you know what code he used?"

"No," Tom mumbled. "He started that in Spain, after hearing about French letters being in code. He liked the idea tremendously."

Cressida believed that. For all that she loved her papa, she knew he had a secretive bent and a fondness for mysteries and drama. When she was a child and he would come home on furlough, he would make puzzles for her and Callie to solve, usually revealing the location of a bag of sweets he'd brought them. She never knew how he managed to hide the sweets before he got home, but they would always be right where the puzzle indicated. Callie had been frustrated and then bored with the puzzles, but Cressida loved them. She loved the euphoria of solving one, and the twinkle in her father's eye when he would pinch her cheek and say she had a quick brain behind her pretty face. And this promised to be the biggest, most challenging—and perhaps most important—puzzle he ever gave her. Already her fingers were itching to start making notes, looking for patterns and clues.

But there was something wrong about Tom's reaction to the sight of the journal, as if he knew—or suspected—Papa had dangerous secrets hidden inside it. But dangerous to whom? And if Tom had known about it for years, why did he never say anything sooner?

"Tom," she asked slowly, tracing one finger down the edge of one page, "do you want Papa to come home?"

"I don't want you and your sister to be hurt."

"That's not the same thing—or is it?" She closed the journal and took a step toward him. "How could Papa's return harm us?"

He shrugged. "Don't know."

"I know he wasn't the noble saint my grandmother describes. I suspect he was . . . *is* . . . a bit of a scoundrel at times. I'm not blind. But I want to know; he's my father."

Tom looked at the book in her hand again. There

was no mistaking the anguish in his face. "I know you love your father, and it does you great credit. But that book will only lead to heartache. Trust me, Cressida."

"You don't want to see him again, do you?" she said in blank amazement.

After a long moment of silence, Tom sighed. "No."

"Why?" She was shocked. "You've been with him for so long! You might have left us at any time. We cannot pay you for the work you do, and—"

"I don't want money," he snapped. "Not your money, at any rate. It's not that. It's just that . . . Well, have you not noticed that things run smoother when the sergeant's not around?"

Cressida pressed one hand to her forehead and paced away. "I know. I know, Tom! But what can I do? He's my father." She chastised herself daily with those words. If not for the lack of money, her wicked, selfish mind thought, they would get on quite fine without Papa. There would be no quarrels over silly things. Callie had completely lost the cowed expression she'd come to wear in Papa's presence. There was peace in the household, and Cressida couldn't deny, to herself, that it was nicer than the boisterous strife Papa spawned wherever he went.

"I know." Tom came up behind her. "You're doing a fine job keeping things together, but perhaps we could get on better if we stop waiting for him to return and go on as if he might, in fact, never come home."

"You think he's left for good this time," she replied in a flat tone.

"He might have done, yes."

"You're wrong." She opened her eyes and looked out, down the winding drive to the road. "He didn't take every last penny in the house. Granny still has her locket and earrings, and if he meant to abandon us, he would have taken them."

Tom's hand touched her arm, then fell away. "Perhaps it was a sudden decision."

"When he'd had a promising interview for a position he wanted?" She shook her head. The road was empty. Major Hayes was long gone, and so, still, was Papa. "He meant to come back. I know it, Tom. And therefore, since he hasn't, it's likely something has happened to him."

"Aye," he agreed on a sigh. "I suppose it is. But that book—" He frowned at the journal she had tucked under one arm. "That book won't bring you peace. Take my advice and put it back where you found it."

As his footsteps echoed and faded away, Cressida continued to stare out at the deserted road. There was no help from that direction, as usual; not yet, anyway. The journal was important. She was sure of it. But unfortunately, she was just as sure that Tom was keeping something from her.

Chapter 12

It was, as Alec had expected, a tedious job. For two days he painstakingly matched bills to the ledger items, shaking his head from time to time at the way Turner spent money. No humble soldier's life for this fellow, with receipts for fine handkerchiefs, china, and wines. Turner bought like a man with a healthy income and no worries about the morrow. The only thing missing from the ledger was proof of his income. Alec added up almost three hundred pounds' worth of outstanding debt, but several times that amount had gone out over the last three years. Where was Turner getting money?

He turned his attention to the entries for money received. They were far fewer than the entries for payments made, but after a while Alec thought he had them sorted out pretty well. Turner collected a modest investment income on behalf of his widowed daughter, as well as his army pension and a small annuity of his mother's. In the last two years there were frequent but not regular payments from "W. Pren.," with no other description except the word "Ludgate" written in tiny script under the last of those entries.

Even added together, all this income didn't balance the expenditures, but he had to start somewhere. It took only a little effort to discover that a printer named Willard Prenner operated out of a small shop in London off Ludgate Hill. Alec had a guess why a London print shop might be paying Turner, but when he told Miss Turner he was going to London to see Prenner, he didn't tell her what it was.

"I shall come with you," she said at once.

"You shouldn't trouble yourself. I expect it will be a rather dull trip."

"But my father hasn't been seen since he went to London. What if we should discover something that would lead right to him?" She moved to the edge of her seat, her golden eyes alight with determination and eagerness.

"It seems unlikely," Alec said, again keeping his thoughts to himself. He couldn't shake the growing feeling that George Turner had disappeared for reasons that might be best left unknown. The debts, the inexplicable income, the odd letters seeking plum positions . . . they all added up to a man not quite as honorable and unassuming as his family obviously thought him. Miss Turner no doubt pictured them rescuing her father from unjust imprisonment or a sick house; Alec was beginning to suspect they would find Turner, if they found him at all, holed up in a pub with a new name and a sad tale to win him some flush new friends. Alec had no patience for that sort of man, and thought his family might even be better off without him. But he had been charged by Stafford to find the man, and find him he would, if at all possible. And if he could find Turner without a witness, Alec wouldn't hesitate to remind the man, forcefully, of his familial obligations.

"But it might. I want to come with you."

Not for the first time, Alec wished he could suppress his interest in her. Just the thought of taking her to London with him was planting wicked thoughts in his head. She said she wanted to know, and he couldn't lie to her. "You should know there's always a chance we would discover something unpleasant," he warned her, making one last effort to persuade her to stay.

Her bosom rose and fell as she took a deep breath. "I understand," she said quietly. "I am prepared. But I want to know what has happened to Papa."

Alec gave in, telling himself it was totally unrelated to the surge of triumph at the prospect of being alone with her for two entire days. "Very well. I shall call for you in the morning."

After he left, Cressida went to pack her valise, only realizing then that she would have to explain to Callie. And true to expectations, her sister was alarmed at the prospect.

"Do you really need to go?"

"Yes." Cressida didn't mention that the major had said she needn't. "We're leaving in the morning."

"Just the two of you?" Callie nibbled her lip. "Perhaps Mr. Webb should go as well."

"Tom should stay here. We'll only be gone overnight, but if something should happen, you might need him." She placed clean garments in the valise and hesitated. "Besides, I'm old enough no one will care. And it's not as if Major Hayes will be tempted to ravish me."

"I don't know," Callie murmured. "He did look at you most attentively at the party . . ."

Cressida snorted, but turned away all the same so no embarrassing blush could betray her pleasure at that thought. "Nonsense."

"And you are not too old," Callie persisted. "Granny will care."

"Callie, you're only thinking that because of our talk the other night. He's not going to ravish me, even if I were the most enchanting woman alive, and I most certainly am not."

"But you look very well next to him." She turned on her sister in shock, but Callie put up her chin and nodded. "You do, both so tall. You look very ladylike next to him, and I think he admires you."

"Callie!"

"Admires your spirit, then. And you admitted to Granny he's a handsome man."

"Go away," she growled. Callie just shrugged and left, thankfully. Cressida fussed with the strap on the valise, unable to block her sister's words out of her mind. Did they look well together? Had he noticed such a thing—or would he even care? "Of course not," she said under her breath, and went out to pull weeds from the garden to make herself forget everything Callie had said.

They left early the next morning, and made good time to the city. It was only twenty miles, but seemed half that on a fine day in a well-sprung carriage with a good horse. As they drew near to the city, the major began pointing out sights, to her increasing interest. They passed the magnificent St. Paul's cathedral, and maneuvered through the bustle of Fleet Street. A large, austere building loomed to one side, and when she asked, he told her it was Fleet Prison. That sobered her thoughts considerably, and when they turned into an inn courtyard a short distance away, she couldn't help glancing back at it.

"Papa couldn't be in there, could he?"

"He wasn't when I last checked." He jumped down from the carriage and handed the reins to the stable hand who came running.

"You checked?" She gathered her skirt and took the hand he held out to help her down. "When?"

"The day after Hastings spoke to me, Miss Turner." He flipped the boy a coin and offered his arm to her.

"I didn't know that."

"He wasn't there, so I saw no reason to alarm you by mentioning it."

Cressida took his arm and let him lead her into the inn, silenced by his calm reply. The day he drove her into Marston he had said she needed someone who would ask the terrible questions; apparently he asked them of everyone, not just of her, and she found this strangely comforting.

Inside the inn, he engaged two rooms for the night and arranged for dinner later. Cressida sat in the taproom and had a cup of tea while he saw to the baggage, then they set off on foot for the print shop, just a few streets away. This time she avoided looking toward the prison, and tried not to think what other dreadful possibilities Major Hayes might have already considered and investigated.

The shop was a small one, squeezed between

a florist and a hatter along the bustling street. The windows were filled to shoulder height with various prints for sale. They were mostly the satirical prints popular now, many mocking the new King or lauding Queen Caroline, who had become something of a heroine since her return to England. Major Hayes opened the door for her, and she went in, her heart accelerating in anxious hope.

"Can I help you, madam?" An obsequious little clerk smiled up at her, rubbing his hands.

"I would like a word with Mr. Prenner," Cressida said with a polite smile. The major had stayed a step behind her, as silent as a servant. They had arranged between them that he would act that part while she inquired, since it was her father.

The clerk's eyes darted up and down her. "Of course, of course. I will let him know you wish to see him." He hurried off to the rear of the shop and disappeared. Cressida barely had time to exchange a look with Major Hayes before the clerk returned, ushering them into the back room.

It was a tiny room, crowded with a desk shoved under the window and a bookcase groaning with books and papers. An armchair prevented the door from opening fully, but she squeezed through, the major close behind her, and the clerk shut the door.

"Good day, madam." Willard Prenner was of middle age, with thinning hair and a simpering smile. He wiped his hands on his ink-stained apron and clasped them before him. "You wish to see me?"

"Yes." She waited until the man's eyes lifted from her bosom to her face again. "My name is Cressida

Turner. I've come to discover what you might know of my father, George Turner."

The smile vanished. "What do you mean?" Prenner asked, his eyebrows flying up in exaggerated confusion. "Mr. Turner is your father, you say? I am sure you know far more about him than I do."

"He has gone missing, and your name was in his ledger. I know he visited you shortly before he disappeared, and hoped you might have an idea where he could have gone."

Prenner hesitated. Cressida had the feeling he was thinking furiously. His smile reappeared, colder and dismissive. "He's disappeared? Well, I know nothing of that. We concluded our business some time ago. I didn't expect to have further dealings with him, in fact."

"What was that business?" she pressed him. "Might he have gone to another printer on similar business?"

Prenner gave a patronizing chuckle. "I don't think he would want you to trouble your pretty head about it."

Cressida wanted to curse in frustration. "You paid him over a hundred pounds in the last two years; there must be a good reason."

"Yes, and I don't have to tell you," he replied with a sniff. "It's my business, too, and you've no right to that."

"I am just trying to locate my father," she began, but the printer heaved a noisy sigh.

"Try the Dove's Nest, if you're so keen to find him."

Behind her, Major Hayes muttered something in

a disgusted tone, then stepped around her, striding right up to Mr. Prenner. The printer's squinty eyes opened wide as the major towered over him.

"When did you last see Sergeant Turner?" he asked, all the more intimidating for speaking so quietly and evenly.

Prenner curled his lip even as he tipped his head back to see him. "I can't recall."

With a sharp twist, the major seized the front of Prenner's shirt, right under his chin, and yanked, pulling the smaller man up onto his toes. Prenner's sallow face turned brick red. He swung his fist and cursed, but the major didn't seem to notice.

"When did you last see him?" he repeated.

"Piss off," spat Prenner. He opened his mouth as if to yell.

Major Hayes gave him a sharp shake, and Cressida heard the man's teeth knock together. "Has Turner been here since April? You're wearing out my patience."

Prenner just glared at him. Cressida noticed his hand groping behind him, searching for something on the desk. A penknife glittered in the dusty sunlight. "Watch," she managed to say, pointing. "He's got a—"

Major Hayes had seen. He drew back his free hand and drove it into Mr. Prenner's stomach. The printer's body jerked backward from the force of the blow. He looked like he would be sick. "Bloody thief," he choked. "Have you . . . arrested . . ."

"Then I might as well be hanged for a sheep as for a lamb," replied the major. He twisted his arm, driving his elbow into the underside of Prenner's chin and knocking the man's head back. Then he followed that blow with a neat punch from his left hand, and Mr. Prenner went limp. Major Hayes caught him under the arms and dragged his limp form over to the armchair, dropping him into it. He turned back to her.

"Come, look in that desk. Quickly," he added in quiet command when she just stood gawking at him.

Cressida closed her mouth and jumped to follow his directions. Her heart raced and her hands shook as she scrabbled through the haphazard collection of books, ledgers, bills, letters, and various other papers stuffed into the desk. Good heavens. The major had just knocked Mr. Prenner unconscious, with very little difficulty and even less hesitation. She stole a shocked glance at him from under her eyelashes. He was rifling through the bookcase by the window, frowning as he sorted through that mess. The sunlight coming through the dusty window picked out the lines of his face, including a faint scar on his cheek she had never noticed before. Unlike her, he looked as though he knew exactly what he was doing. What sort of man was he really? First his single-minded search of her father's study, now this. Cressida was increasingly sure there was much more to the major than he was telling any of them, and she could only be glad that—for the moment—he was on her side.

He looked up, meeting her gaze. The sun slanting through the dusty window lit his eyes to the color of the sky. "Something wrong?" he asked in the same muted voice.

"Ah . . . It's stuck," she whispered, pulling at a

random drawer to cover her lapse. Must he catch her staring at him every single time she did it? She half expected the drawer to fly open and catch her in the lie, but it remained firmly closed. She tugged at the handle and rattled it, hoping it was just stuck and not locked.

"Shh." With two soundless steps he crossed the room to her. Cressida quivered as he reached around her, his arm almost embracing her. She would have moved away to let him at the desk, but he was right behind her, and the room was small and crowded. She was stuck in place, caught between him, the desk, and the wall. She couldn't help glancing at his hands, so large and strong. He gave a firm pull at the drawer, then put his other hand at her waist. "Let me," he whispered, easing around her. She looked up at him as they awkwardly traded places. He barely glanced at her, his attention wholly on the desk. Cressida retreated to the bookcase he had been searching, watching from the corner of her eyes as he went down on his knees and reached into his coat pocket. He took out what looked like two long thick needles, and inserted them into the lock.

A snort from Mr. Prenner broke into her thoughts. She jumped, darting a worried glance at him, but he slept on. Major Hayes slid open the stuck drawer with only a faint murmur of wood on wood, but it sounded loud in the quiet room. What would they do if the assistant came back? A trickle of perspiration slid down between her breasts. Cressida sucked in a shaky breath. She was not born for sneaking around like this. Uncertainly she turned to the shelves and started poking through the books, no longer sure of what she was looking for, when the major whispered to her.

He had a large book open on the desk. When he beckoned to her with one hand, she hurried back to his side in relief. He leaned his head close to hers and murmured, "Say something."

"What?" She had trouble speaking. His lips had almost brushed her skin, his words skimming her cheek like a lover's murmur.

"Keep talking as if to him." He jerked his head in Mr. Prenner's direction. "The long silence will be suspicious if anyone comes by the door."

"Oh." Cressida wet her lips. "Mr. Prenner," she began in her normal voice, "it really is imperative that you tell me anything you know about my father. Not only have we been quite worried about his absence, but the people in the government have begun asking questions . . ." She was babbling, saying anything that crossed her mind while she watched the major's finger skim down a column of names and payments. "Turner" leaped out at her, then again. The major didn't say anything, just tapped his fingertip on the entries to call them to her attention. Cressida nodded each time he did so, noting the date and the sum beside the name. Mr. Prenner had paid Papa a good amount of money, at regular intervals, even more than indicated in Papa's ledger. But it didn't say why . . . until the major turned back a page to previous entries, dated more than two years ago. One line contained a single extra word: lithos.

Lithographs, Cressida mouthed. What lithographs?

The major, looking intently at her, gave a slight shrug. He turned a few more pages, but no more entries with Papa's name turned up. With a glance at the door, he closed the ledger and put it away, silently sliding the drawer closed once more. "Time to go."

Cressida nodded immediately. "Then good day to you, sir!" she said loudly to the unconscious Mr. Prenner. The major, already by the door, opened it for her and she rushed out, feeling as though every eye in the shop must be trained her way.

Perhaps it was. The clerk who had showed them in appeared in front of her with a smile that looked menacing to Cressida's nervous eyes. "May I show you out, madam?"

She could feel the color in her face. The major, hovering at her side just in her range of vision, bowed his head slightly. She was supposed to say yes, even though the man's eyes made her skin crawl and the thick air of the print shop was suffocating her. "Yes, please. I feel a little faint."

"This way." He swept out his arm and Cressida followed, pressing her handkerchief to her face. The major didn't make a sound behind her. They were drawing the man away from Mr. Prenner's office, so he didn't go inside at once and find Mr. Prenner knocked out cold. She understood, and appreciated why, but when they stepped into the street and the door was closed behind them, she drew in a long, shaky breath.

"Bloody hell!"

Chapter 13

Her curse amused him. She could see the curve of his mouth as they walked, and she didn't care. She was more shaken than she cared to admit by the visit, and took refuge in fury. "Of all the insufferable—" She stopped and rounded on him. "Did you know?" she demanded. "Did you *know* he would be so—so awful?"

"No." His smile grew a little wider. "I did suspect."

"Oh—oh!" She could hardly speak. "That rat! That weasel!"

"Both at the same time?" He took her arm to propel her through the street. She let him, still seething.

"Yes! If I had a torch, I'd set his hateful little shop ablaze."

"We could light it on our way out of town," Alec said mildly.

"I am very tempted. I wish I had never laid eyes on that place."

He grinned. "What a turnaround. I should go back and thank Mr. Prenner for convincing you of that when I failed so completely."

"Oh, stop!"

He just laughed. Cressida knew he had earned that laugh at her expense, but she was still shaking with temper and nerves so she just strode on. He was so calm, so unruffled; he had assaulted a man! And very neatly, too. Cressida could only glance at him from time to time in mingled shock and admiration and a tiny bit of envy. She certainly would have liked to punch Mr. Prenner herself.

He caught her looking at him and raised one eyebrow. "All right?"

She jerked her eyes to the front. "Fine." From the corner of her eye she could see he was still grinning.

He left her at the inn, saying he had an errand to run before dinner. Cressida went up to her room and stared out her window at the busy London scenery for a long time. She hardly knew what to think about this. Papa had been in business with that wretched Prenner, selling lithographs of some sort. She could see why he hadn't told them, especially if the lithographs in question looked anything like the other prints in Prenner's shop. Perhaps it shouldn't surprise her. Papa had a habit of drawing little cartoons on the rare letter he sent home, all rendered with a sharp eye for humor. When he came home, he would always draw miniatures of her and Callie to take with him on campaign. She didn't think Mr. Prenner was paying for sketches of rabbits and birds, though, nor of her and Callie.

Cressida sighed. Perhaps nothing she learned about Papa should surprise her. He had been more absent than home in her life; until he'd left the army three years ago, he hadn't spent more than a few consecutive weeks at home with them since Cressida was a small child. Most of her perception of him had been born of her grandmother's stories, and Granny thought Papa the cleverest, noblest, most amiable man on earth. On furlough Papa was jovial and kind, always laughing and full of ideas, with sweets in his pockets for his little girls and a gift for his mother. Cressida had adored her father as a princely figure who whirled through her life from time to time, but she could hardly say she knew him.

The last few years had shaded her adoration somewhat, or else she had seen him with new eyes once she was grown. She still saw Papa's charm, but also his quick temper and extravagance. He was bluff and brash, and couldn't seem to understand why Callie was quiet and reserved. Perhaps they were just as strange to him as he was to them, she thought. It was easy to retain the affections of two little girls, especially with Granny singing his praises every night he was gone, but two grown women were apt to be more critical and difficult to please. Callie had survived a bitter marriage and come home quieter than ever, and Cressida had grown into the practical head of the household as Granny's mind began to slip. Papa came home as charming and energetic as ever, but they were not the same, not waiting with clasped hands and bated breath for him to swagger down the lane to their tiny house with his pack on one shoulder. Just as Papa was not used to being at home, they were not used to having him home.

Somewhere in the city a bell tolled the hour. The shadows in the street below had slanted until everything was tinged with gray, although the sky was still bright. It was near dinnertime. The major had engaged a private parlor, and would be waiting for her.

Cressida washed her face and hands. There was another man she couldn't make out, although at least in this instance she had the excuse of not knowing him for long. By some accounts he was a traitor and a liar, a man who went missing for five years and then just returned without a word of explanation. Gossip in Marston held that he must have been engaged in illegal activity during that time, with everything from piracy to swindling to murder mentioned, and that he was being quiet to avoid being sent to the gallows for it. There was certainly something dark about him, but Cressida didn't think that it was dangerous. She couldn't forget how he had stood his ground at the muzzle of a pistol, nor how he returned the next day and said not a word of confrontation or reproof. The major, she thought, was very sure of himself and had clearly mastered his emotions. It made his actions today all the more surprising—had he simply lost patience with Mr. Prenner's rude manner, or was it calculated? From the calm way he went about searching the office, even telling her to keep talking to avoid raising the clerk's suspicion, she suspected it had been entirely calculated. And she could only imagine what he might have done had she not been there.

Cressida felt very conscious of him when she went down to the private parlor. A hearty dinner was laid on the table, and the innkeeper smiled and bowed to her as he herded the serving maid out of the room ahead of him. The door closed, leaving her alone with him. She pressed her palms to her skirt and cleared her throat. Out of nowhere she remembered that he had asked her to call him Alec, but she had never done so yet.

He sat on a bench beside the fireplace, a stack of papers on the floor at his feet. He was frowning at one in his hands. "I believe I've found the lithographs," he said without looking up. "They are signed 'GT,' at any rate, and were published not long after the payments."

"How on earth did you locate them?" She crossed the room to take the print he held out.

"I asked about," he said vaguely, sliding over to make room for her. The bench was short, and even though she sat primly on the end, his knee still brushed hers. He had washed; she could smell his soap and see his close-cropped hair glistening damply. She bent her head over the print studiously and told herself not to think of it, or him, or how intoxicating this strange intimacy was.

"Good heavens," was all she could say. "Are they all like this?"

"You needn't look," he said, reaching for the print.

"Are they?" She clung to it, feeling slightly nauseous. She had seen outrageous prints before, but surely it was dangerous to draw such things—and she was uneasily certain her father had drawn this image. The King was portrayed as a fat sow, and the piglets suckling at his teats had the faces of Cabinet ministers. A gaunt John Bull figure slopped the pig with a bucket of coins. For the first time since her father had gone missing, Cressida was seriously frightened. Could Papa go to prison for this?

"I doubt it," he said, and she realized she had

blurted out her last question. "It's no worse than what some are selling, although he'd be wise not to boast of it in certain parts of town."

"The rest are just as bad, aren't they?" She let him take the sheet from her lax fingers. "What was Papa thinking?"

"Money." He leaned down to collect all the prints from the floor. She caught sight of another one with the King, again corpulent and drunken-looking, surrounded by nearly naked, equally fat women, dancing and vomiting on a carpet woven of men in army uniforms. She looked away, chewing the inside of her cheek in worry.

"What might happen to him?"

"Libel is difficult to prosecute, and going after one man would only draw excess attention to his lithographs. The government has been mocked more harshly than this and done nothing except bribe the printer not to sell the offending prints." He put the prints into a leather satchel and set it aside.

"Then what have we discovered?" she asked bitterly. "That my father despises the government? That he dealt with a shifty, mean little printer to profit from his dislike? But none of that would endanger him, you say, so what has this gained us? We still don't know where he went or where he is!"

"It's a piece of the puzzle," he said quietly. "One small mystery solved. I have learned not to overlook any piece, no matter how small, just because I can't see what it means."

She dashed the angry tears from her eyes before they could fall. Of course he was right. "I hoped so desperately Mr. Prenner would know something, but that was silly, wasn't it? I should have known this trip wasn't vital, and not insisted on coming along."

"Nonsense," he said. "No one knew what it would yield."

"You did. You told me I needn't come and it would be dull. You even warned me we might discover something unpleasant." Her gaze slid over to the portfolio of lithographs. Her fingers itched to throw the whole collection into the fire; a pointless impulse, but a strong one.

"You are too harsh on yourself."

"I am trying to admit I was wrong, and you were correct," she said dryly. "My sister would advise you to revel in my humble admission, because I do not make them often."

He laughed. "I doubt right and wrong are so clearly divided. It might just as well have turned out the other way round."

She doubted that. She knew he doubted it, too, and was just being kind. Today's events had demonstrated quite clearly that the major knew what he was doing far better than she did. "What is the Dove's Nest?"

He sobered. "A brothel."

Cressida shuddered. "I feared as much." She remembered his remark about the prison. "Have you already . . . ?"

"No. I will go inquire, if you would like—"

"No!" She blushed again. "But thank you for telling me honestly. I do appreciate it, Major."

"Alec." He turned his head to look at her. They were still sitting on the narrow bench, so close she could see every flicker of firelight reflected in the deep blue pools of his eyes. "Don't call me Major."

"Oh," she said, flustered. "I don't know . . ."

"Please," he murmured, in the same voice he had used in the printer's office when his lips had almost touched her cheek as he whispered in her ear. His gaze flicked to her mouth for a moment, and Cressida's heart nearly stopped at the sudden wish, strong and sharp, that he would lean forward the last few inches and kiss her. She sat, paralyzed by shock at her own longings and quaking with apprehension. Just because he looked at her like that didn't mean . . . anything, she told herself frantically. But if it did mean something, whispered a little voice in her heart, and if he did kiss her . . . she would enjoy it very much.

"All right," she whispered, barely able to form the words. "If you wish . . . Alec."

Alec inhaled at the husky way she said his name. Perhaps he shouldn't kiss her, but he most certainly *could*, and she would kiss him back. Her glorious eyes were dark with desire and yearning; she wanted him to kiss her. They were alone together, not just in London or in this room but in this short respite from their cares and duties at home. Tonight he could forget his responsibilities, and he could make Cressida forget hers. He *wanted* to forget everything tonight—except her. She was everything he was not, the antithesis of all he had become. She wasn't used to sneaking around, and when he'd rattled up Prenner, she'd gone as white as a sheet. But she hadn't screamed or fainted or made a word of protest, and when she erupted in a temper as they walked away, he'd found it entrancing. Arousing, even. And now . . . She sat waiting, poised in expectation. He felt his body bend toward hers; he saw her mouth soften, heard her breathing accelerate, and Alec's blood surged in anticipation.

A knock sounded on the door. She jerked backward, a blush flooding her cheeks. Alec silently cursed. "Yes?" he called out, resigned.

The innkeeper put his head around the door. "Beg pardon, sir, the girl forgot to bring the wine you ordered. I've brought it right up."

"Excellent," he said wryly. "Thank you." He turned to Cressida as the innkeeper brought in the wine and then hurried back out. "Shall we have dinner?"

"Yes." She gave him a rueful smile, her color still high. She had remembered herself; they both had. But awareness of that moment, when they had stood on the brink of forgetting, still echoed in the air like the fading vibration of a plucked string. Alec could feel it on his skin as he pulled out a chair at the table for her. She sat stiffly, holding her body away from any contact with his, and he knew she felt it, too.

The food was plain but still warm, and they ate in silence for a while. Alec guessed from Cressida's expression that her thoughts had turned back to their reason for being in London. He almost regretted that; as much as he knew her family was depending on George Turner's return, he hated to see the worry and cold disillusionment creep back into her eyes, banishing the hot glow of longing. He wanted to see that glow again, and not in some chance, reckless moment.

"Why did you knock out Mr. Prenner?" she finally asked.

"Ought I not to have done so?"

"Oh no, you were very right to have done so. He's a rat."

"And a weasel," he murmured.

She tried and failed to hide her smile. "He *is*. And I'm not sorry you struck him, I just wondered why you resorted to that so quickly."

"I thought of doing it the moment I saw him. My restraint in waiting as long as I did is quite admirable, in my opinion."

"I've long wondered why Lord Hastings sent you to help us." She laid down her fork and knife to regard him levelly. "You said it must be due to your particular talents—I presume you meant punching people unconscious and stealing horses."

Alec chuckled. She was sharp as a pin, this one. "Do you remember every last word I've ever said to you, with the hope of someday using it against me?"

"No!" Indignation made her blush. But then, much did, and she had the fair complexion to show off the color in her cheeks to its best advantage. He liked watching the wave of pink roll up her face, and couldn't help thinking of other ways to make the color bloom under her skin. "You have asked me to explain and relate everything about my father, yet told me very little about yourself and how you plan to proceed. One day you say you've come to search through Papa's papers, then to say we're off to London to see a printer."

"I never said you must come with me," he corrected her, avoiding the thrust of her question. "There was really no need for you to meet the rat."

"I want to help," she protested. "He's my father."

"Your sister doesn't ask to come along."

"No." She looked down at her lap. "Callie wouldn't."

She hadn't eaten more than a few bites, and now looked rather woebegone. Alec thought of the lithographs—nothing he hadn't seen a hundred times before, but it wasn't his beloved father making them. She was doing her best, answering his questions and going along with his actions even when she didn't understand and he wouldn't explain. He sighed and poured more wine into both their glasses. "When I was in the army, I gathered intelligence. It's not quite the same, but one learns tactics for discovering important information. Prenner wasn't giving me answers, so I decided to search for them myself."

"Gathering intelligence," she repeated. "Like a spy?"

Alec choked on a mouthful of wine, then laughed ruefully as he set the glass down. "No. Well, yes, I suppose in some ways. I mostly spent my time riding about the countryside, asking people if they'd seen any Frenchmen go by." She raised her eyebrows, waiting for more. "Sometimes they wouldn't tell me, and I had to persuade them."

"With your fist?"

"With my great charm," he said, and finally she laughed. Alec grinned. "The rules of fair play do not apply in love and war, Miss Turner."

"Your sister tells me you had a knack for achieving the impossible," she said. "All this is forming a very colorful image of you, sir, quite unlike the one you have given me yourself."

"Oh?" He leaned back in his chair. "What is the image you had formed?"

She became absorbed in tilting her glass back and forth, watching the wine swirl. "Not very colorful.

Quite dark, in fact. You frightened me."

"I could tell," he said dryly. "I'd never been shot by a woman before."

"You still haven't been, to my knowledge." But she smiled again. "Are you certain nothing would happen to Papa for those drawings?"

He considered a moment before replying. "Can I swear it? No. I don't think he would be sent to prison or tried for libel, but if he offended the wrong person . . ." He stopped as her expression grew tense. "It's highly unlikely."

"But he disappeared after coming to London," she said. "He might have come to see Mr. Prenner as well as Lord Hastings."

"He might have done. But there's no record in Prenner's ledger of a payment around that time." She looked at him steadily. They both knew that meant nothing. Alec sat forward in his chair, trying to change the subject. He wasn't used to light conversation, especially not with women. "A colorful image, you say. Dare I ask?"

Her eyes dropped, and she sipped her wine. "Better not. I daresay much of it is exaggerated."

"Really. You tease my curiosity unbearably."

"You?" She raised her eyebrow. "I find that hard to believe."

"That I have curiosity, or that you tease me?"

The color was rising in her cheeks again. "I do not tease you." He just tilted his head to one side and studied her. The pink deepened to dusky rose. "I do *not.*"

"Right." He poured more wine. "Now I shall be awake all night, worrying about your opinion of me."

"Oh, really," she exclaimed. "By now you must have such an opinion of me that it could hardly matter what I say to you."

"My opinion of you," he repeated thoughtfully. "Would you like to know it? I think you are the head of your family, even when your father is about. It must be wearing, to feel such responsibility. But you're practical, and willing to do what needs doing. Loyal to those you love, ready to defend them against all harm, and wary of outsiders. But you're not intractable in either instance and will listen to reason." He paused; there was more to his opinion of her, but he sensed this was the main point. "I suspect you want to be more trusting, but have been burned by it in the past."

"Who hasn't?" she said with a forced smile.

"I understand."

She shook her head. "No, you couldn't. My sister . . . She was married to an absolute devil. He was older, handsome and respectable and rich—rich in our eyes, at least. Callie was only eighteen, and the most beautiful girl in town. When Mr. Phillips came calling on her, we were all so delighted; Papa was very pleased, and Granny was beside herself at the thought of Callie snaring such a fine gentleman. He spoke to Papa and they were married almost immediately, but then . . ." She paused, then went on in a flat voice, "I think he beat her. She never would admit it, but I saw the marks on her arms and shoulders. Papa had gone back to his regiment and Granny refused to believe it, for Mr. Phillips was always very charming to her. But my sister stopped laughing and looked ten years older than she was, and there was nothing I could do for her."

Ah. Alec felt another piece of the puzzle slip into place. Not the puzzle of George Turner's disappearance, but of Cressida herself. Somehow he found himself far more interested in investigating that one tonight.

She drained her wineglass, as if telling him her sister's dark secret had finished her. "And now that Papa's gone, someone has to look out for my family. Callie is too gentle, and Granny is too delicate."

"What of Mr. Webb?"

"Tom?" Her voice rose in surprise. "Tom was in the army with my father. He came home with Papa on furlough . . . oh, many years ago, and has just been here ever since. He said he hasn't got a family of his own to go home to, so he's adopted us."

"Then he and your father are friends?"

"Not . . . Not precisely," she said slowly. "Papa doesn't really have friends. He has companions and admirers. He's the sort of man who can readily charm people into buying him a round at the pub, and have them all roaring with laughter late into the night. Tom is a quieter sort."

"May I ask why Tom never went searching for your father before you wrote to Hastings? You must have worried much sooner."

She hesitated again. "He offered, once. We didn't want him to go."

Alec added Tom Webb to the list of people who had reason to wish George Turner gone. How very curious that Miss Turner would describe her father so, admitting it wasn't a personal bond between two soldiers that kept Webb at Brighampton. Perhaps his motives were innocent enough, but Turner had two attractive daughters. Alec wondered which one Webb fancied, guessing it was Mrs. Phillips and then reining in that thought. If Webb fancied Miss Turner, he probably wouldn't have seen the two of them off to London without protest, but the man hadn't said a word. Perhaps Turner didn't think Webb good enough for his daughters, or perhaps Webb grew desperate and wanted to make the lady more in need of a husband. And there was likely more to the story than Cressida had just told him. He tucked the thought away for future investigation.

"Thank you," she said. "For coming to our aid."

Alec felt that echo of awareness vibrate across his skin again as he met her open, unguarded gaze. Cressida Turner had the oddest effect on him. She smiled at him and his blood raced. She frowned at him and his stomach tightened. She thanked him for doing his job and he wanted to lay her down before the fire and do all manner of wicked things to raise that fine pink flush over all her skin. He was a bloody fool, and suspected he would be a bigger one before he was done with her, but he blessed John Stafford all the same for sending him into her life. "It was my pleasure," he replied.

More than you'll ever know.

Chapter 14

After the trip into London, there seemed to be little trace of Papa anywhere. The major—Alec—said he would begin asking in Marston. Cressida doubted he would learn much there but kept it to herself; hadn't he already done more than she expected just in locating Papa's journal and ledger?

She started tinkering with the journal in earnest. Alec had asked her about it on the way home from London, and she was ashamed to admit she hadn't made much progress. Now she got it out every day and covered page after page with notes. Papa had written the dates in English, which at first frustrated her. It would have helped to have a code whose translation she could easily guess, or at least narrow down to twelve possibilities. She tried the usual trick of counting the most frequent letters, which made little headway. But she worked on, looking for common characters and codes and comparing them to places of battles and persons mentioned in Papa's letters home. Often it took just a few words solved to make the rest start to fall.

She didn't know what the journal would lead to. It might be a complete waste of time when she had more immediately pressing concerns, like paying the bills. Tom sold most of the sheep to pay their debts, and she was quietly looking for a new place to live. The horses would go back to Mr. Bickford's stable as soon as they had moved house. With a little time, they might make it through this tight spot well enough after all. And if she solved the journal, they might even locate Papa as well.

She was scribbling more notes when she heard a horse in the lane a few days after the London excursion. Thinking it might be Alec, she hurried into the hall. The visitor was just lifting his hand to knock when she opened the door.

The stranger doffed his hat. "Miss Turner?"

"Yes," she said warily. A terrible chill skittered down her spine. This was not a social call.

"Walter Clarke, ma'am." He bowed, but his expression was not cheerful. It was businesslike and firm. Cressida bobbed a slight curtsey, bracing herself. "Is Sergeant Turner at home?"

"No, I'm afraid he is not. I am his daughter."

"Ah." He didn't even offer to wait until Papa returned. Cressida knew what was coming before he said it. "Then I must inform you in his stead. I am the agent for the owner of this property, and he has leased it to new tenants. Your removal is desired by no later than tomorrow noon."

"What?" she gasped. "The rent was due but yesterday!"

"Yes, and you did not pay it."

"No, but—"

"I am afraid your lease would not have been renewed in any event. It expires tomorrow, and the owner has already, as I have said, taken new tenants." He smiled politely.

Cressida pressed one trembling hand to her heart, which was pounding painfully. She had known they must move soon, but in a few hours' time? "Without even a chance to renew? My father . . ."

"Sergeant Turner did not pay the rent. I am sorry, Miss Turner, but I am only doing as my employer asked."

Vividly but silently, she cursed her father. If only he were here, surely he would be able to persuade this unctuous fellow to let them stay another week. Or perhaps he might have even paid the rent when it was due. "This is very little warning," she protested. "I am not sure we will be ready."

"I have orders to see the house is cleared by to-morrow at noon. I am sorry, Miss Turner." He said it gravely, but Cressida thought bitterly that it was very easy for him. He had a home to return to.

She went numbly into the house before Mr. Clarke was even down the lane. They must pack at once—and go where? "Callie? Callie!"

Her sister came running, but stopped when she saw Cressida's face. "Oh dear. What is it?"

"We must pack," she said in a hollow voice. "We must be out of the house tomorrow."

Callie's eyes grew wide. She ran to the door and evidently saw Mr. Clarke departing. "Oh dear," she breathed again. "Where shall we go?"

Cressida pressed the heels of her hands to her temples. "Marston, I suppose. We have little other choice."

Her sister's face paled. Without another word

they hurried in search of Tom, to fetch the boxes and crates.

By mid-morning next day they had packed as much as they could. Granny was growing hysterical, fretting that Papa would never know where to find them, and he would be so upset at them for leaving Brighampton without his permission. Granny's grasp of the reality of their situation was tenuous at best, thought Cressida, replacing another box that her grandmother had tried to take from the carriage before Callie led her back into the house.

Julia Hayes came cantering up the lane. "Are you really turned out?" she cried as she leaped from the horse's back. "So suddenly?"

A flush of humiliation burned Cressida's cheeks. "Yes."

Julia's eyes flashed. "How draconian. How unchristian. How—" She stopped. "I have come to take you to Penford. You must stay with us until you take a new house."

"Oh . . ." It was a godsend, and yet . . . "Julia, that is too generous. But your family will not want us—"

"They don't want you to be cast out into the lane like vagabonds. My mother is fond of you and your sister, and she is in full agreement that I invite you. Mrs. Turner," she said, turning to Granny, who had wandered out of the house again. "Won't you be our guests until you take another house?"

"Well, that is very kind of you, but I don't know, my dear." Granny cast a reproachful glance at Cressida. "We are expecting Sergeant Turner at any moment. He may have other plans."

"All the more reason to stay close to Brighampton.

And you must not worry about a thing; I shall have Farley send someone with a wagon for your things within the hour. Oh, how nice it will be to have you all at Penford!" Julia beamed at Granny, who brightened up and smiled back. Apparently being invited to Penford canceled her objections to moving without Papa's permission.

Cressida breathed a sigh of relief. It was humiliating to have Julia see them evicted so abruptly, but the tense fear that had gripped her heart since yesterday loosened. It was charity, but from a friend, and honestly given. It didn't matter that Alec would be there. She had gotten over her worst discomfort at his presence, and surely with a little more time, her pulse would stop leaping whenever he crossed her path. She sent Granny back to tell Callie, and drew Julia aside.

"Thank you, Julia. We would be very grateful to stay at Penford."

Her friend laughed. "It will be a delight to have you!"

"It is especially kind of Major Hayes, after he has already done so much for us." Julia's mouth puckered, but then she just smiled again and turned to lead her horse to the block. "Your brother does know, doesn't he?"

Julia patted her arm with one hand as she gathered her skirt to mount her horse. "Alec isn't even at home most of the time. There's nothing to worry about."

"He—He does know you invited us, doesn't he?" she asked again, more anxiously. Julia stepped onto the block and swung into her saddle. Cressida automatically helped tug her skirt into position. "Julia?"

"Good-bye, Mrs. Turner," Julia called, raising one hand to Granny and completely ignoring Cressida's question. She wheeled the mare around and grinned down at Cressida. "Good-bye for now. I will see you soon!"

Cressida sighed as Julia cantered away. She closed her eyes and said a quick prayer for patience. Penford belonged to Alec, and Julia wouldn't dare invite them without knowing he would approve. Surely not. And she had already gone and accepted; they had no real choice, anyway. She would just be very careful not to trouble him much, and look for another lodging as fast as she possibly could.

And God save her until then.

From his bedchamber window, Alec saw Julia ride back up the drive, looking victorious. Quietly he strolled down the corridor to the top of the stairs, in time to overhear her talking with the housekeeper, directing Mrs. Smythe to prepare rooms for the Turner ladies. Then Julia hurried off, calling to their mother. Her voice rang with confidence and delight. They were coming.

He didn't want to think too closely about what had happened. Alec was not sure his actions, let alone his motives, would stand up to any sort of scrutiny. It was mere chance that he'd overheard a man in Marston mention the new tenants of Brighampton arriving soon, displacing the poor, indebted Turners. It was simple indignation that he'd felt on behalf of a family about to be tossed from their home when they quite likely had no other place to go. But it was something less noble that led to his mentioning those facts in his sister's hearing, guessing what her reaction would be, and it was something entirely unthinkable that fed the fire in his blood at the thought of Cressida Turner in his house, smiling at him across the dinner table and wrinkling her nose at him in the garden. He might see her a dozen times every day . . . and night.

But not for nothing had he learned to control his impulses. She would be a guest in his home, and he would treat her as such. It would make his work easier, in fact, if she was close by to help his search and answer his queries. He spent most of his days away from Penford as it was. She would no doubt be looking to take another house soon, and the sooner he located her father, the easier that would be for her.

But God help him until then.

Chapter 15

~~~⟨⟨~~~

Visiting Penford and living at Penford were very different.

Once Granny was all settled in a lovely room overlooking the woods, Cressida found herself at loose ends. There was nothing for her to do now, no chores, no cleaning, no cooking. Servants came to unpack her things in the spacious room she would share with Callie, accomplishing the task with speed and precision. She went once more to thank Julia, who just laughed and brushed aside any mention of gratitude, and perversely this only made Cressida feel more out of place.

Dinner, although delicious and elegant, was awkward. Tom, who had always eaten with them, elected to take his meal below stairs, which just felt wrong. They were no better than Tom, yet she and Callie were at the dining table set with china and silver while Tom ate with the Penford servants and Granny ate in her room with a servant attending her. It put off her appetite, and from the way Callie picked at her dinner, her sister suffered the same. She could almost hear Granny reminding her to be careful what she wished for; she might someday get it. Cressida had admired Penford, had dreamed of living in such a place. Now she did, for a short time anyway, and it didn't appear she would enjoy a minute of it.

She couldn't sleep at night, despite the exhausting day. Cressida lay on the soft feather mattress under the cool, crisp linens and stared at the ceiling for what felt like hours. This was only a reprieve from her troubles, not a solution. Tomorrow she would have to talk very seriously with Callie and Tom to determine what they would do next. Now not even the prospect of finding Papa gave her hope. Papa would be annoyed they had lost the house, and Cressida knew she would be so annoyed at him for leaving them, there would be a dreadful argument. She thought again of what Tom had said, that things went on much more smoothly without Papa, and felt even worse for admitting, deep in her heart, that she might be changing her mind about Papa returning home, no matter what she insisted to Alec.

Alec. Thoughts of him had plagued her since the moment Julia left Brighampton that afternoon. Ever since Tom drove them around the bend of the gravel drive and Penford came into view, she had been bracing herself against seeing him, preparing herself for their first meeting, and then it never happened. He hadn't been with Julia and her mother to greet them, nor at dinner, nor in the drawing room afterward. It was fraying her nerves, this constant expectation—anticipation, even—of seeing him at any moment. It was almost as bad as the disappointment of not seeing him even once.

She sat up in bed and swung her feet to the floor. Callie murmured in her sleep from the other side of the bed as Cressida slipped her feet into slippers and pulled on her dressing gown. She shouldn't roam about someone else's house at night, but she thought better on her feet and desperately needed to walk off some nervous energy. The clock had already chimed two in the morning, and everyone would be asleep. Without lighting a candle, Cressida opened the door.

The house was quiet. She wandered through the corridors and down the stairs, feeling a bit like a spy as she marveled again at the beauty of Penford. She walked through the long, shadowy gallery, squinting at the portraits shrouded in shadows. She peered into the conservatory, where Mrs. Hayes had created a wonderland of delicate plants, and found the music room, where the pianoforte and harp stood waiting for musicians. She let herself into the large drawing room at the back of the house, and went to the tall windows, admiring the view of the garden. Even in the darkness, with all its vibrant color dimmed to silver and shadow, it was a beautiful, peaceful scene, and Cressida thought that despite Penford's grandeur, she could grow accustomed to living here if only for the gardens.

"Good evening."

She started violently, clapping one hand to her chest as she whirled around to see Alec Hayes sprawled in a chair, watching her. A bottle stood on the table next to him, with a glass half full of wine. He looked idle, even debauched, but the gleam of his eyes was still brilliantly watchful.

"I beg your pardon," she said breathlessly. He had discarded his waistcoat and cravat, and his shirt was pulled open at the neck, exposing a long slice of skin down his chest. A shiver ran up her spine.

He waved one hand in negligent dismissal. "None is needed. Or perhaps I should beg yours, for disturbing your midnight ramble."

"Oh, no, no, the fault is mine alone, for rambling about a house not my own. I just couldn't sleep, you see, and thought I might as well get up and walk about . . ." For some reason he smiled at that, a dark, bitter smile. She wondered why. But he said nothing, and she hesitated; she ought to say good night and go back to her room, forget this image of him, and go to sleep. Or rather, try to go to sleep. It took great effort to keep her eyes away from the bare column of his throat, all the way down his chest. "I certainly did not think anyone else would be awake so late," she added with a small, nervous laugh. "I never meant to disturb you."

"You didn't." He rolled his head to one side, contemplating her.

"Oh." Tonight his ever-present air of focused energy was gone. He sat in the chair as though someone had draped his body over it, one leg extended and the other tucked almost beneath the seat, one hand dangling over the chair arm and the other curled around a small wooden horse propped on his knee. He ran his fingers over its roughly hewn surface as if trying to memorize it, but she sensed his thoughts were elsewhere. Sitting here alone in the dark, in the middle of the night with only a bottle for company, he seemed . . . lonely. Broodingly, sadly lonely. She wet her lips. "It's a fine carving. Did you do it?"

"No." He turned it over. His brow dipped. "A

friend did. I had forgotten all about it until I saw it on the shelf over there." His chest rose and fell in a silent sigh. "He was my closest friend, from the time we were boys. He carved this in Spain, outside Burgos. We had besieged the town and there was little to do most of the time. Damned waste, as it turned out. Never took that town." He held up the horse, angling it from side to side and squinting one eye to study it. "Fine job he did," he murmured.

"Yes," she said quietly. "Very nice." She wondered if he still knew that friend; if the friend were still a friend, even after . . . In that moment Cressida passionately hoped he was.

"He died," Alec went on in the same distant tone. "Waterloo. A hero's death, they said; very honorable."

"I'm sorry."

At her whisper he flinched. "So am I," he said bleakly. "I never thought he would be the one . . ." His mouth twisted. "Lacey was aide-de-camp to General Ponsonby. He ought to have been behind the lines, not leading a cavalry charge at the French. A clever chap, Will was; knew when to hold his tongue and when to speak. He should have been a politician, for the way he could talk a man into anything and make him think it the finest idea ever conceived."

"Lacey?" Cressida asked when he stopped and fell silent. "Of The Grange?" The Grange was an estate a few miles away, owned by Mr. Angus Lacey. Lacey was an elderly man in ill health who rarely went out, but was known in Marston for his short temper and his sullen servant, a large man named Morris. Cressida always gave Morris a wide berth whenever she crossed his path. She had imputed the same cold, vaguely menacing manner to his master, but now felt a pang of sympathy, if Mr. Lacey had lost his son at Waterloo.

"Yes. Will was old Lacey's only son and heir, and painfully conscious of it." Finally Alec's eyes lifted to hers. "You've met the old man?"

"Oh no," she said quickly. "Not really. I only know of him."

The corner of his mouth curled. "I can imagine what. He was rude and short-tempered years ago, and I am sure his manner has not improved."

"But if he has lost his son . . ." She shrugged, wrapping her arms around herself. "It's hard to lose someone you love."

His hand closed on the horse until she thought he would break it. Cressida's eyes grew wide with alarm, and she even opened her mouth to say something, his expression had grown so savage. "Yes," he said grimly. "It is." With great care he stood the horse on the table, then refilled the wineglass. Instead of lifting it to his lips, he held it out to her.

She hesitated only a moment before taking the glass from his outstretched hand. It was good wine, rich and warm on her tongue. She took another sip, watching him over the rim. His heavy-lidded gaze seemed fixed on her mouth as she drank. Cressida lowered the glass, unconsciously licking the last drop from her lower lip. His jaw tightened, and something dangerous glittered in his eyes.

It seemed the whole world had shrunk to just the two of them, alone in a pool of moonlight. Cressida had admitted Alec Hayes was a handsome man.

She knew him to be intelligent and determined but possessed of a bit of gentleness as well, as when he twirled his young nieces around until they shook with giggles. But even if it made him more attractive, as a man, that alone meant nothing. She had known other men who were handsome and kind, the sort of man a girl dreamed of, and they had never looked at her the way Alec was looking at her now.

Slowly she held out the glass, her hand shaking a little. He raised his gaze to hers, and she felt the full force of the wild, hungry longing there. Oh dear God. That look stirred something deep inside her that she had kept tightly leashed for years. Those sorts of desires only led to ruin and heartbreak, as she well knew. Once before a man had made her feel that way, and she had thrown herself into the blaze of lust between them. But the blaze subsided, sooner for him than for her, and she had been left behind, sadder and wiser. Giving in to desire again would be unforgivable; hadn't she already learned her lesson the hard way?

He took the glass and glanced away. Whatever he felt, whatever he desired from her, he kept caged within himself. She should learn from that example, Cressida told herself. She opened her mouth to excuse herself before hurrying back to bed.

"Sit." He raised the glass to his mouth and drank as he swept one hand toward the other chair, on the other side of the little table.

It would be a mistake. She wanted to stay, and she knew it was because she wanted to see that look again, to see the heat of a man's desire—of *Alec's* desire—for her. It was easy to tell herself she was being foolish to think about him when he had never done more than look at her with unreadable calm, the way one might look at a hideous painting and try to think what to say to avoid hurting the painter's feelings. But this look, the one she craved, held nothing of that. It coaxed forth that lonely ember of desire in her own breast, fed it and fueled it until she no longer wanted to put it out. And instead of saying good night and going back to bed, Cressida sat.

"He carved this in Spain?" She touched the small horse. For all that it was a rough carving, the vitality of the animal came through clearly. The mane blew on the wind, the ears were pricked up, and one foot was delicately poised in mid-step. And it was so small, just the size to fit in one's hand. "It's remarkable."

"Yes. I sent it home to Julia, thinking she might like it. Will had no brothers or sisters, and by then his father had cut him off."

She looked up in surprise. "His only son? Why?"

Alec stared at her long, slender fingers rubbing lightly along the arch of the horse's neck. His skin prickled and tightened at the thought of those fingers running over him, curling around him, stroking, squeezing . . . He should not have invited her to sit, but the wine had dissolved his noble intentions even before she walked into the room, drifting like a ghostly temptress to stand in front of the window in her nightdress with her hair cascading down her back. Somehow it seemed significant that she had been restless, too, roaming the house on a night when he couldn't sleep, either. Something about the way she angled her head as she gazed out the window made him think that she, too, longed to be out there, not trapped in the house, confined by her family's expectations and needs. Something about her called out to him, and he couldn't ignore it tonight.

"He didn't approve of Will's choice of wife," he said, belatedly answering her question. "She was a Spanish girl of good family, sympathetic to our cause in Spain, but still not English. I expect Lacey thought Will would set her aside if he were harsh enough, come home and marry Darrowby's eldest or some other girl from Hertfordshire. He waited years to have a son, and by the time Will came along, Lacey had his whole life planned for him. Unfortunately for him, his son was just as strong-willed as he was, and put up quite a fight." It still made Alec angry to think of how Lacey tried to control Will. His friend's back and legs had been scarred from Lacey's discipline. He gulped the last of the wine in the glass and reached for the bottle.

"Good for him," she murmured.

Alec paused. "To fight his father?"

She put up her chin. Even in the dim light he could see the glitter of her eyes. "For standing by his love. For honoring his promises to her."

Therein lay a tale, Alec thought. The wine loosened his tongue before he could think better of it. "Someone broke your heart." She quivered as if struck but gave him only an angry glare in response. His hand curled into a fist; someone had. But that was not his business. Alec eased his fingers open and held out the refilled wineglass, and she took it almost defiantly and drank.

"Marianne broke my heart," he said, unconsciously reverting to his spy's bag of tricks, telling his own story as a way to coax her into telling hers. Of course, this story happened to be true, unlike the lies he had spun as a spy. "I was madly in love and thought she was, too—until I came home from Spain and she told me she preferred a more stable sort of fellow. Like my brother, in fact, who proposed to her while I was gone."

She gasped. Alec grimaced, even though all the bitterness had faded from the memory now. It was an old wound, long since healed. "Yes, my own brother courted the girl I wanted to marry. Unsporting thing to do to a brother, don't you think? I damned well could have killed him for it, if only he'd had the courtesy to fight back. Frederick would just stand there and insist he loved her too much not to marry her, and then offer to step aside—as if she would have had me then, or I her."

"Did you really love her?"

He sighed. "Yes, but not the way she wanted to be loved. It was a young man's love, rash and reckless and unrestrained. And utterly unfounded in any mutual passion or sympathy of temperament, either. My father told me we would make each other miserable—which, naturally, only increased my determination to have her. I did so hate it when he was right and I was wrong. Marianne wanted poetry and delicacy, and she made a far better match with Frederick." He shifted, settling more comfortably in the chair and at the same time giving himself a better view of her. "So in the end it was better that she threw me over, although it took me some time to admit that."

She was quiet for a long while. Alec waited, sensing again that she wanted to tell him. Then he cursed himself; no, he was waiting because he wanted her to tell him, to trust him and confide in him. It wasn't the confession he craved, but rather the trust and respect that went with confiding in someone. He was tired of being a liar and imposter, always on guard against letting some small bit of truth slip. The wooden horse had been the last straw tonight, and now he'd gone and told her his most embarrassing disappointment: being jilted for his own brother.

"His name was Edward," came her voice at last. "He was a lieutenant of the navy, and due for his own command soon. It was right after my sister had married, and I was left a bit more on my own. He said he would show me the world, that we would sail together when he had his own ship. But he changed his mind when his superior officer pointed out that my family would be no help to his career."

"The bastard," he muttered.

Her mouth flattened. "Indeed. I have hated the navy ever since."

"Quite rightly so."

She leaned forward and set the glass back on the table. "But as you say, it was better in the end. I don't think about him anymore."

Alec nodded, hiding his pleasure at her answer. Anyone who would do that to her didn't deserve to be remembered. "Enough of old heartache. What keeps you up so late this night?"

She shrugged, twisting a fold of her dressing gown between her fingers. "Nothing of consequence."

He raised one eyebrow. "Nothing?" He picked up the bottle to refill the glass, but it was empty. He set it down again. "Then what leads you to wander?"

"I really did not think anyone would be awake," she said. "If I had known you would be here . . ."

"Then what?" he murmured. She looked away. "Would you have stayed away, Miss Turner? Do I still frighten you?"

Her head whipped around, and she glared at him as if insulted. "No."

His gaze wandered over her. Cressida felt it through her plain, worn wrapper and nightdress as if he touched her bare skin. Again she had the sense that, even half drunk, Alec could see right through her. Now, though, instead of unnerving her, his gaze had a different effect. Her skin tingled with goose-flesh, and her nipples pulled into tight, hard buds as his eyes lingered there. By the time he met her eyes, she felt choked with confusion. She couldn't give in to the feeling, but, oh . . . oh, how she wanted to.

"Good," he whispered.

She nodded once, too afraid of what might burst out of her lips if she tried to speak. She got to her feet and turned to go. "Miss Turner." She stopped and looked back in question. "Thank you for the conversation."

Cressida cleared her throat. "It was a pleasure." She hesitated. "Good night, Alec."

"Good night," he replied, his voice a low rumble that drifted off as though he was about to fall asleep the next moment. She made her steps quick and quiet as she left. Just as she closed the door, though, so softly she wasn't even sure she heard it, she heard him speak again:

"Good night . . . Cressida."

Chapter 16

That Sunday Alec agreed to accompany the family to church for the first time since his return home. His mother beamed at him in delight. Miss Turner gave him a thoughtful look that became a small smile when he tipped his hat to her. Just that hint of warmth was enough to lift his spirits even as he steeled himself.

Aside from a few trips into town, he had avoided most of Marston. Today would be the first time many of the townspeople had actually seen him, and their reaction was everything he had expected. A flurry of whispers swept the church as they walked to the family pew. From the corner of his eye Alec saw Miss Turner sit stiffly between her sister and Julia. He helped his mother, then sat beside her to face the curate, who was smiling nervously at everyone but Alec as he waited to begin the service.

There was a rumble behind them, even as the whispers died down. Shuffling steps came up the aisle. Beside him, Mother glanced up at the late arrival and went still just as the footsteps stopped abruptly right behind him.

"You," gasped a voice, all too familiar. Alec's stomach knotted but he kept his face expressionless. He had been prepared for this. The entire church was as silent as a grave now. Slowly he turned and faced his father's dearest friend, and his dearest friend's father.

Angus Lacey had grown stooped and lame since Alec last saw him. His narrow face was more wrinkled and gray, but his pale blue eyes were as alert as ever, and they were fixed on Alec with unmistakable shock and hatred. "You," he croaked again.

Alec met that horrified gaze evenly. "Sir."

Lacey's chin quivered. The hand clutching his cane shook, and he wobbled on his feet. The large servant behind him reached forward to steady him, but Lacey shook off his hands. "You dare to show your face," he said with quiet venom.

"Mr. Lacey," Alec's mother said sternly, "we are in church."

Lacey didn't even look at her. "Traitor," he spat, then turned and shuffled right back out of the church, his servant lumbering after him.

Mr. Edwards the curate leaped forward as the excited hiss of whispers filled the church again. "Let us pray," he said somewhat desperately. With a thunderous clang, the door of the church swung shut.

When the service was over, an eternity later, Alec helped his mother back into the carriage. He swung onto his horse, avoiding everyone's eye but John's, to whom he gave a curt nod before heading south, out of town and away from Penford. The moment they cleared the town, Alec urged the horse into a canter and didn't look back.

He rode for a long time. At first the desire to keep

heading south, back to London, was almost impossible to fight. Not to hide, but to break into the War Office and search for those damned incriminating letters. What had patience and caution gained him—a five-year delay in being convicted of treason? He was used to it for himself now, but his mother had been steadfast in her loyalty and love for him, as any mother might be for her son. When Lacey had snarled that last vicious word, Alec had felt her flinch beside him. She'd sat like a stone throughout the service, and his thoughts had run on very unchristian paths regarding Lacey.

It certainly was no surprise to him that Lacey hated him. When he and Will were lads, Mr. Lacey had blamed most of Will's misbehavior and disobedience on Alec's bad influence. It must seem the worst sort of cruelty to him that his son had died while fighting valiantly for his country, while Alec had survived after apparently betraying it. As Cressida had said the other night, it was crushing to lose someone so beloved, and Lacey had settled all his hopes and affection—whatever that amounted to for him—on Will. Alec understood that.

But the man went too far by insulting his mother, in front of all Marston, while they were ostensibly gathered for prayer. Why was Lacey entitled to blind affection for his son, but Alec's mother was not?

When the road crested a rise, he halted the horse. A few more miles away lay the turnpike into London. In a few hours he could be in town; he could go to Stafford and demand an inquiry, even a trial. His years as a spy had been very instructive, and Alec was almost ready to take his chances in the dock.

At least it would provide an end to the matter, and if the government must make a case against him, he would at last know just what had cast suspicion on him. And if he was found guilty anyway, then the hangman would be all too willing to put him out of this miserable existence.

The horse snorted and tossed his head. Alec realized he was holding the reins too tightly, and let them go slack. He took one more look down the road toward the city, and knew he couldn't ask his mother to endure a trial, not now. If he were going to put his family through that, he should have done it five years ago. He turned and started for home.

At Penford he went straight to the library. The best brandy was still kept in there, in the rosewood chiffonier. He poured a generous glass and took a long sip.

"There you are," said Julia from the doorway. "Where did you disappear to?"

"Just out riding."

She came into the room. "Mother was worried. You should go to her. She's been imagining all sorts of horrid things. I think she feared you would do yourself harm."

"No." He squeezed the back of his neck. The glass was already over half empty, and the more Julia talked, the more he thought about pouring more.

"Or perhaps do harm to sour-faced old Lacey. That man hates you."

Alec inhaled. "Do you really think so? Imagine."

"He's been very cool to Mother, but I never thought he'd cut her directly. In church, too."

Alec swallowed the rest of his brandy. "Is there something you wanted, Julia?"

"Yes, now that you ask." She came to stand in front of him, hands on her hips. "I wanted you to stand up and tell him differently when he called you a traitor."

"In the middle of the church?"

"What better place to tell the truth?"

Alec finally realized what made his sister so angry with him. She wanted him to explain, to tell her where he had been and why he had let them believe him dead. She wanted a rejoinder to fling against the slurs and insults that must have dogged her as his sister. But mostly she wanted him to fight, with passion and fearlessness and ruthless disregard for the casualties. She saw the truth as a cannon, obliterating everything in its path. Alec knew it was more like a finely honed saber, capable of decapitating one opponent with a stroke but insignificant against a hydra of rumors and gossip. He put down his glass. "Julia, it isn't that simple."

"*Why*, Alec?"

"I can't prove it," he growled. "Not any of it. I did nothing wrong, but I can't prove one bloody word of it!"

She stared at him incredulously. "I didn't ask for proof!"

"But Lacey would," he retorted. "It's my word against his, against popular opinion, against Wellington's condemnation. Think for one moment what people will say if I declare I committed no crime and never conspired with the French. 'Where is your proof?' they will cry."

"Only because you were missing for so long—"

"Do you think I don't realize that?"

Julia stamped her foot. "Oh! Damn you, Alec! You *did* do something wrong. You let us believe you were dead for five long years! Do you know what that did to Father—to Mother? To Frederick and to me?"

"I don't need a scolding about that."

"And why not?" she flung back at him, her voice quivering. "What have you been doing since you vanished? Since we received that short, grave letter saying you were dead, not gloriously or bravely but lost on the battlefield? Since we heard you had not only died, but died a traitor? Have you been happy without us, or did you even bother to think that we might be suffering without you?"

Alec's temper finally gave way under the lash of her tongue. Julia, his beloved younger sister—a woman now, a stranger—cut him more deeply than he ever could himself. Before he knew what he was doing, his jacket was on the floor, then his waistcoat. With shaking hands he ripped off his cravat and yanked open the collar of his shirt. "Was I happy?" he rasped, and pulled the shirt over his head. "I was almost *dead*, Julia—left for dead by my mates, named a traitor to my country by men I fought and bled beside, unable to show my face or say my own name. Do not think I have suffered less than you or Mother or anyone at Penford when I wear the scars of those five years and feel them with every breath I take!"

His sister's eyes flitted over the scars, the long puckered tracks of French swords that crossed his chest and side where a Flemish farmwoman had stitched him back together as he lay unconscious on her hearth, without finesse or skill but just well enough to save his life. The scars twisted around his back, over his shoulder, stopping less than an inch short of his collarbone. Alec knew from the breadth of them that those wounds had nearly killed him, and the fever that had left him unconscious for a week ought to have finished the job. Only through some happenstance—and at times Alec thought it had been a pitilessly cruel one—had he lived, to bear the scars and the disgrace for the rest of his life.

Julia must have guessed as much; her face crumpled, and she turned on her heel and fled, her footsteps dying with the slam of the door.

Alec's anger faded into embers as quickly as it had flamed to life. What he had done? It accomplished nothing to shout at Julia, when she couldn't have known what he'd endured—precisely because he had not told her or anyone. It was his private shame, concealed as much as possible and yet always there, contaminating every fiber of his being. Alec felt lost again. Penford held all he thought he wanted, all he thought he was fighting to reclaim. Why did he feel so alien? He bent to retrieve his discarded shirt and wondered for a moment if Stafford would take him back and send him to France, to the Continent, anywhere he could be unknown again.

A noise behind him made him glance over his shoulder. Cressida Turner stood just inside the doorway from the small drawing room, one hand still on the knob. There was a book in her other hand, as if she had come to return it to the shelf. She was staring at him with her lips parted in shock, her eyes roaming over his exposed back.

But it wasn't horror in her face. When she raised her gaze to his, for one everlasting moment, Alec saw his own longing and desire mirrored there.

"I'm so sorry," she said, her voice a thin whisper of sound. "I didn't mean— Please excuse me—" She took two steps forward, laid the book on a table, and quickly turned back to the door.

Alec lunged. "Wait." He caught her wrist. She pulled, turning her face away from him in a vain attempt to hide her blush. "Wait." With one hand he pushed the door shut, wanting to keep her, to hold her, to feel her desire him, even if all he could say was an inarticulate "Wait."

She twisted in his grip. "I should have knocked," she said, breathing rapidly. Her golden eyes flickered down his bare arm, his bare chest, and lower before jerking back up to meet his gaze. Her lips glistened when she licked them. A dozen things ran through Alec's mind as he stood looking down at her, mesmerized by the flutter of her eyelashes and the pulse in her throat. She tugged once more against his grip, but without effort; Alec shuddered, and reached for her.

She gasped and closed her eyes. He moved toward her at the same time she turned toward the door, and the momentum of those actions brought them to the closed door. Alec exhaled a silent moan as their bodies collided full-length against the wood, her back against his chest and his arms on either side of her. Her hands came up to brace herself, but she didn't protest or wriggle away. She smelled of fresh air and, faintly, of gardenias from his mother's garden. Alec laid his cheek against the silky coil of her hair. Good God, he wanted her, more than he could ever remember wanting another woman.

Cressida leaned her forehead against the door, breathing so hard she trembled. He was holding her, his bare arms almost around her. His hands slid up the door, his forearms taut and flexed beside her shoulders. She could feel his breath on the nape of her neck, and couldn't stop thinking what they must look like, pressed together like lovers. If she had had any notion, any suspicion he would be standing in the library bare from the waist up, she would never have opened the door . . . or so she told herself. The truth, Cressida shivered to think, was probably somewhat different. The truth was that when she unwittingly stepped into the library to replace her book, she had been rooted to the floor by the sight of him standing there, naked to the waist and head bent as if in penitence. Not until Alec saw her did it occur to her to stop looking. He was magnificent, lean smooth muscle and sinew despite the blemishing scars. She had seen scars before, although not of the breadth and length of Alec's. One went over his shoulder and across his back, as if the enemy had tried to cut him in two. They must be years old, yet still stood out against his skin in stark lines as if they hadn't healed very cleanly.

She curled her fingers into fists against the door to keep from turning in his arms and touching those scars that must have caused him so much pain. She wanted to hold him and console him and ease whatever darkness lingered in his soul. Julia was wrong, *wrong* about him, she thought fiercely. He wasn't grim and arrogant; a man with those scars had lived through something horrible. Whatever secrets he kept were his own terrible burden.

"Wait," he whispered again. His lips were at the back of her neck, stirring the wisps of hair that had pulled free of the braid. "Please . . . wait."

Cressida waited. She waited to see what he would do, now that he held her, and she waited to see what she would do in response. She would have waited a year, here in his arms. He held her not as a captive but as a man might hold something dear, a treasure he had been searching desperately for and finally found. No more could she tell herself she was being foolish or silly—or rather, she might very well be both, but she couldn't deny the reason any longer. She was falling for Alec Hayes.

He touched the back of her neck, his fingers tangling in her hair. Cressida swallowed a moan of pleasure, letting her head drop forward until her temple pressed against the wood of the door. His palm flattened against her skin and swept up her spine, and his mouth pressed hard and hot against her neck. Cressida stopped breathing, then sucked in a long, shivering breath that was almost a sob of want. He murmured against her flesh, his lips moving to the tender spot behind her ear.

Her fingers flexed, trying to dig into the wood as he kissed her there, a lingering gentle kiss that pulled at her soul and poured heat into her body. Her nipples tightened and her knees softened. She wanted his arms around her, his mouth on her everywhere. She wanted to turn around and touch him and kiss his skin. She wanted him to know she wanted him.

"Alec," she whispered as he nuzzled the soft skin at the curve of her shoulder, his hair brushing her cheek. "Alec . . ."

He stilled, and abruptly released her. Cressida swayed on her feet as she turned, her body still melting from his touch. Anything he wanted of her was his, and she was almost shaking with eagerness. But as she faced him, ready to surrender her heart and body, he cursed and took another step back. The flame-bright desire burning in his eyes faded into bleakness that made her almost ill to see.

For a moment they faced each other, both breathing hard. Just as she was about to reach for him he drew back a step. "I'm sorry," he muttered. "Very sorry." He hung his head and cursed again under his breath. "Forgive me."

Cressida watched in astonishment as he turned and strode away, snatching up his shirt from the floor. She just glimpsed what appeared to be dozens of small marks on his back before he yanked the shirt over his head. Without stopping or looking back, he walked straight out of the room, pulling the door shut behind him with a boom that echoed in the still library.

Slowly she crossed the room. His coat, waistcoat, and cravat were scattered across the rug, as if he had ripped them off and flung them every which way. Perhaps he had. She picked up the coat and folded it, laying it neatly across the sofa. She wondered what tormented him, and how he managed to keep it bottled inside him so tightly. She held up the waistcoat. It was new and made of very fine—and expensive— cloth, but he had undone the buttons so forcefully one had been ripped right off. She looked around and found it on the carpet some feet away. Soberly she tucked it into a pocket of the waistcoat and laid it on top of his coat. A bit of handkerchief peeked from the pocket, and she found herself staring at it as she folded the cravat. Before she could think better of it, she whisked it from the pocket and tucked it into her sleeve, then hurried from the room before anyone could discover her.

In her room she took out her stolen prize. It, too, was new, freshly laundered. "ABH" was embroidered in one corner. When she held it to her face, it smelled only of soap and the slightly toasted scent of pressed linen. It might have been anyone's. Cressida laid it against her cheek.

Who was he, really? The hellion, the officer, the traitor, the prodigal son, the man who looked at her with desire and despair in his eyes and wore a cloak of scars. She rubbed her cheek against the smooth linen. Perhaps he was all that, and more. But she was falling in love with him just the same.

Chapter 17

26 June 1815
Forest of the Soignes, Belgium

Do you hear me?" The voice sounded strange, guttural and foreign. He wondered who it was, and why he could hear that voice as he floated in a vast sea of darkness.

"Eh, soldier. You'd better wake up one of these days."

One of these days. Alec let that thought roll around in his brain for a while. Wake up. Soldier. Now that she mentioned it, he realized it did feel as though he had been asleep for a while. *Soldier. Wake up. Soldier.* Ah . . .

He flinched, as if a French artillery shell had gone off nearby. But no; there was no rain of fragments and debris, no screams of wounded men, and he realized it was memory that had startled him. The French had shelled his dragoons horribly, decimating the unit. Men were cut down in mid-word, falling with the shock fixed on their faces. The French lancers came out of nowhere, the sun gleaming on their long, deadly lances, and sent half the men fleeing in a dead panic. Alec had gone after them, trying to rally them back into position, but they seemed to scatter on the wind.

You'd better wake up one of these days . . .

He forced open his eyes, just a little. "Why?" he croaked.

The old woman looked up from her knitting. Her face was like a dried apple, with shiny little eyes and a broad nose. "Englishman," she said, and Alec realized then that she had spoken some sort of bastardized French before. She rose from her chair and came to lay her warm hand on his head. "No fever," she said. "Good."

"What has happened?" he asked, struggling with his French. "The battle?"

She shrugged. "The English duke held the field. The emperor fled."

They held the field. Even in his utter weakness, Alec felt a surge of euphoria. It passed quickly as he pictured the battlefield, littered with dead and dying. "What is this place?"

"My farm." She nodded. "Safer than out there."

No doubt. Alec remembered the look and sound of a field in the aftermath of battle. The woman moved around the little cabin, adding a pillow behind his head and pressing a cup of clean, cool water to his lips. "How long?"

She thought a moment. "Seven days. If you had not woken by tomorrow, I would have taken you to the surgeons."

There had been no surgeon? Alec's heart jolted in alarm, and he began trying to move his arms and legs, vainly hoping he still possessed his limbs. He struggled to raise his head. "No surgeon? None was sent for? Was I bled?"

The old woman shrugged. "Why? It did not appear you had much blood left for the leeches. I left it in God's hands."

He couldn't hold his head up for even a minute. Exhausted, he fell back onto the narrow cot. "Thank you," he murmured. One by one, he flexed each finger and each toe. The tinges of pain that traveled up his arms and legs reassured him that he had apparently survived intact.

"Rest now," she said. "I won't throw you to the butchers yet."

Over the next few days, Alec learned more. Widow Gustave, as she was called, had found him on the battlefield, stripped to his skin and bleeding from saber cuts that crossed his back and chest, as well as a lance wound to his side. He suspected she had been out looting the bodies with other industrious local peasants and been about to pass him by, seeing that he had nothing left to steal. Many corpses were picked clean by battlefield looters; it made identifying the dead virtually impossible, even when they weren't disfigured by wounds and decay. It could take a week or more to bury the casualties from a major army action, and Alec judged there were few larger or more deadly than the one just fought.

But Widow Gustave hadn't left him. She had seen Alec's face, miraculously unscathed beneath the spatters of blood, and been reminded of her son, who had been lost at sea some years ago. In a fit of maternal pity she loaded him into her handcart—along with a few more practical relics of the battle—and brought him back to her tiny farm near the forest. She stitched up his wounds and wrapped him in a blanket before her hearth, and waited to see if he would survive.

Even after he woke, it seemed at times he might not. One long saber gash, slicing down his shoulder and deep into his side, turned red and rancid. The widow calmly took a dagger and split it open again, digging out putrefied flesh with the tip of her knife until Alec blacked out from the agony of it. Widow Gustave gave him her hard apple cider, in the absence of stronger liquors, and within two days the long, angry wound had started to close again. It took him a week to manage sitting up, and another week before he could stand, but slowly he was mending.

"I must go to Brussels," he told her one evening.

She said nothing, just cast a skeptical eye on his bandages. She had given him her son's old clothing, but there was so much linen wrapped around his chest, it barely fit.

"No one knows where I am," he said. "I've likely been reported missing or dead. I should like to at least send word to my family that I'm neither."

The widow shrugged. Despite her nobility in bringing him home and caring for him, she was a taciturn old lady, clearly more comfortable with her solitary life than with a restless invalid. "If you want," she muttered. "It's a long walk to Brussels."

Alec looked at the dented tin cup in his hand, a cup that looked very like the ones used on campaign by his cavalry brigade. To the widow it was just a cup, saved from being wasted and put to good use. To him it was a gruesome reminder that the soldier who used it last was likely lying in a shallow grave,

blown to pieces by artillery fire and trampled by fleeing horses. The urge to rejoin the army and send reassuring word to his family grew more strident by
the day. "I shall manage."

She shrugged again and said nothing. The next day
she brought him a sturdy branch. He carved it into a
makeshift crutch, and then rose at dawn and looked
down the road that wound into the forest. In a few
miles, Widow Gustave told him, it would meet the
Brussels road, and then he would walk another few
miles to the town. Alec took the sack of bread and
jug of cider she gave him, tucked the crutch under
his arm, and set out.

It took hours. Before long it was only raw determination making him put one foot in front of the
other, as the long wounds in his side pulsed with
agony. Sweat was rolling down his neck before he
even saw the Brussels road. After taking a break to sit
and eat, Alec forced himself back into motion, resort-
ing to fantasies of fresh beef and good wine waiting
in Brussels to keep himself moving. By the time he
reached the city, it was growing dark, and he was
so sore and tired he contemplated falling down to
sleep beside the road until morning. He called up the
image of his lodgings in town, comfortable and clean,
and somehow kept moving.

The town was one giant army camp. Men in
uniform were everywhere, and many houses bore
marks on the door indicating wounded were quar-
tered within. Whatever hospitals the surgeons set up
would be overwhelmed. Alec hobbled through the
streets, trying to find his way. His best hope was to
run into a friendly face, another officer who could

direct him and help him. The journey had severely taxed his strength, and he didn't want to join the ill and maimed left to fend for themselves in the streets.

By luck a familiar figure crossed his path before long. Hurrying down the street, some loaves of bread under his arm, came James Peterbury, a junior officer who hailed from Hertfordshire like himself. They had been in the same division under Uxbridge. There was a bright pink weal across his cheek, but otherwise he seemed in good health, walking unaided and without visible bandages. Alec's spirits lifted. He hated the aftermath of battle, learning which of his mates and friends had died. At least Peterbury was well.

"Peterbury," he managed to call out, his voice hoarse from exertion. "James."

The young officer stopped and turned, his gaze sweeping the street. Alec raised one hand. Peterbury froze. His mouth dropped open and he stood goggling.

"Good to see you again," Alec added with a weary smile.

Peterbury came across the street, eyes still popping from his head. "Hayes?" he whispered in astonishment. "Is—Is it really you? Alec Hayes?"

He nodded. "More or less. I suppose—"

James jumped as if prodded from behind, dropping his bread, then seized Alec's arm and began pulling him off the street into a nearby narrow alley. Alec sucked in his breath at the pain that shot through his arm and down his side at the rough handling, and started to curse when Peterbury shocked him by slapping a hand over his mouth.

"Shh, man, hush!" he ordered. He glanced around nervously. "Keep your voice down, for the love of God!"

"Why?" Alec frowned but lowered his voice. "What has happened?"

But Peterbury paid no attention. He peered closely at Alec's face, craning his neck from side to side to see every angle, much to Alec's bemusement. "I survived, as you can see," he finally said. "Is it so very shocking?"

Peterbury made another shushing motion with his hands. "Quiet," he said, almost harshly this time. He bowed his head and pressed his fists to his forehead. "Oh, Lord . . ."

This was not what he had expected from a friend, even one taken utterly off guard. Alec shifted his weight on the crutch and waited, an ominous feeling flooding him. What could be so wrong?

At last Peterbury looked up. "You're dead," he informed Alec, sounding as though he disapproved mightily that it was not so. "Your name was on the casualty lists."

"But I'm not. Obviously. A farmwoman picked me out of a pile of corpses and took me home out of pity." Alec cocked his head and forced a halfhearted grin. "You don't seem quite as overjoyed by the news as I might have hoped. Has my brother already promised you my hunter?"

The other man just shook his head. "No. No, no, no, no, no. But now . . ." His voice trailed off. "Not that I was happy when I thought—but this— Oh Lord."

"James," said Alec, growing annoyed, "what the devil are you blathering about?"

"You're better off dead," his friend said then. "I hate to shock you by saying that, but . . . the papers. They found the papers in your effects. My God, man; I don't want to believe it, but how could you?"

James's shock seemed to be wearing off, exposing an anger Alec didn't understand. Better off dead—this, from one of his oldest mates, a man who had been his friend since they were mischievous lads? "How could I what? You're making no sense. And what is the news? I heard Bonaparte fled the field, but what of the Royal Dragoons? What of Lacey, Ponsonby, and Uxbridge?"

In the dim light, James's face hardened. "Uxbridge has lost his leg. Ponsonby is dead, and so is Lacey. And you'll wish that farmwoman had left you where you lay, if anyone else should see you. Why the hell have you come back?"

"It is my duty," said Alec through dry lips. Ponsonby and Will Lacey, dead. It felt like a physical blow to his chest.

"You'll be shot, you know. If you leave now, I won't tell anyone, out of respect for your family, but if you ever return—"

"I've no idea what you're talking about," Alec interrupted. "I've been lying in a farmhouse for more than a fortnight, incapable of walking, and have heard no news at all, let alone why I might be shot for returning to my regiment as I ought to!"

"The letters." Peterbury clenched his jaw. "To the French. You should have burned them."

For a moment he just stared. "Letters?"

Some of his ignorance must have impressed Peterbury. He hesitated, and a frown creased his forehead. "You know what I mean."

Woodenly Alec shook his head. His arm had gone numb from leaning so long on the crutch, and when he tried to shift his weight he almost lost his balance and fell. With one hand he groped for the grimy brick wall behind him, and leaned heavily against it. "I've no idea what letters you mean—to the *French*? Are you accusing me of . . . treason?" He whispered the last word as the implications crashed in on him. His breath felt short as he waited, prayed, for Peterbury to contradict it.

"Yes."

"And you believe it?" Alec was appalled. If he hadn't felt light-headed from the long walk, he would have thrown his fist into Peterbury's face. Except that there seemed to be two of Peterbury at the moment.

Peterbury hesitated. "I didn't want to."

"It's not true!" His legs were shaking. With a curse Alec gave up and collapsed, sliding down the wall to fall on his knees. The makeshift crutch clattered to the ground. "Bloody Christ, James. How could you?" He pressed one hand to his side, and felt the familiar warmth of blood seeping through his shirt.

Peterbury squatted beside him. "It's not true? You didn't correspond with the French and reveal how many men Wellington had and where they were camped?"

"Never!" He was losing his voice. He coughed, and his whole body seemed to spasm. Warm blood welled beneath his fingers and needles of pain jabbed at his side. He had forgotten how sharp that pain was, how it stole his breath away and made sweat roll down his back.

"Never?" Peterbury grabbed the front of his woolen shirt and hauled him upright with a firm shake. Alec hadn't even felt himself slip to the side. "Do you swear?"

"On my father's honor," he said, before coughing again. Now there appeared to be three of Peterbury, all staring at him with thunderous scowls. "If you— *you*, of all people—don't believe me, just walk away. I'd rather be left to die than branded a traitor."

For a moment it seemed Peterbury would take him up on that. Alec closed his eyes; his brain felt slow, as if it had been muffled in that one word, "treason." He would rather die here in an alley than be condemned for that. But then he felt an arm around his back. "I can't let you die," his friend muttered. "But you mustn't stay here." He shoved the crutch back into Alec's hand, and began trying to push him onto his feet. "Come. We'll puzzle it out somehow."

Chapter 18

1820

At the end of the week John Hayes's mother and sister came to visit. They were going to stay a week, then John would go home with them. Cressida watched Mr. Hayes welcome his family to Penford, and remembered that only a few weeks ago he had been the master here, and perhaps his mother and sister had expected to be here permanently. Julia had told her that branch of the Hayes family had a much more modest home near Tring. Mrs. Hayes and her daughter Emily, a lively young girl of about sixteen years, were pleasant and friendly, much like Mr. Hayes himself. One would never suspect from his open, amiable countenance that he had suddenly lost a large and prosperous estate to a cousin who was not as dead as everyone thought.

As for that man . . . He was gone from the house before breakfast every day; estate concerns, his mother explained to her and Callie—as though she needed to excuse him. He was only at dinner one night, and from a snatch of overheard conversation between servants, Cressida deduced that he was rarely expected at that meal. She had hardly seen him at all since that agonizing, exhilarating day in the library. It was almost exactly what she had hoped for when she accepted Julia's invitation to stay at Penford, and it was driving her to distraction.

Mrs. Hayes had arranged a dinner to welcome her guests, and since there were now so many ladies in the house, she had invited a few gentlemen from the area to balance the table. Even Tom had been persuaded to join the party. Cressida and Callie put on their silk gowns and tried not to gossip too much.

Callie was ready first, while Cressida couldn't seem to decide how to fix her hair. "I declare, you normally don't have this much care for your toilette," said her sister with a smile.

Cressida blushed. "Go on down," she said. "I'll just be another moment." Her sister laughed, then left. Callie had spent much of their time at Penford tending to Granny, who clung to her bed and pined for Papa. Cressida wanted to help, but her presence only made Granny fretful; twice she had scolded Cressida for moving them out of Brighampton without her father's consent, and finally the sisters agreed that Callie would see to Granny for now, and Cressida would be responsible for finding them a new place to live. That hadn't been going smoothly, as there were plenty of people in reduced circumstances looking for places to lease, and rents had crept alarmingly high. They would almost surely have to take Callie's money out of the funds, no matter how much Tom argued against it.

And in between worrying about money and places to live, she was left to wonder about Alec.

He had held her and kissed her as if he wanted her desperately, but then he had all but disappeared. Did he regret it? Or was he avoiding her because of something else?

She scowled at her reflection. As if he had nothing else to worry about in his life but her feelings. She pinched a wisp of hair from her temple and wound it around one finger, wishing her hair would shine and curl like Callie's instead of needing tight braids and pins to stay put. The wisp of hair uncurled from her finger to hang limply beside her cheek, and she gave up and went downstairs.

It was a fine dinner. Callie was seated next to a Mr. Davis, and he appeared quite taken with her. Cressida was between Tom and Sir Edmund Leslie, an old friend of the family. Sir Edmund was charming and talkative, unlike Tom, who grew quieter as the evening went on. Alec was nowhere to be seen, and after a brief hesitation, John stepped into the role of the host. There was an odd glance between him and his mother, but Alec's mother just smiled graciously and thanked John.

After dinner they retired to the large drawing room, and Emily Hayes played the pianoforte before card tables were set up. Cressida watched her sister agree to partner Mr. Davis. Callie's eyes shone as he escorted her to the table and seated her, then fetched her a glass of sherry. Callie, she realized, looked happy with a man for the first time in years. Since her dreadful marriage, Callie had shied away from men; Tom was the only one she was at ease with. It broke Cressida's heart to think of her generous, kind-hearted sister spending the rest of her life alone. But as Callie grew more confident and easy, gentlemen noticed her. Mr. Davis, for certain, seemed enchanted. Granny would be so pleased.

She turned and caught sight of Tom, standing by himself just inside the door. He had excused himself after dinner, and she hadn't seen him come back. He was so quiet and somber, and wore an odd expression as he gazed across the room. Cressida took a step toward him, thinking he must be looking for her, when she realized where his eyes were fixed.

Not on searching for her. On Callie, now laughing at something Mr. Davis had said.

Cressida sucked in her breath in dismay. Oh dear. Now she saw, with painful clarity, why Tom had sold his consuls to buy the fabric for the dresses she and Callie wore tonight. Tom was in love with her sister. And Callie, to judge from her pleasure at Mr. Davis's attentions, either had no idea or didn't return the feeling.

He caught her staring at him then. His face changed and he turned and slipped out of the room. Cressida murmured an excuse to Julia, seated beside her, and hurried after him, following all the way to the stables.

"Tom!"

He stopped, squared his shoulders, and turned. "Aye?"

"I wanted to thank you again," she told him. "For the silk."

He gave an embarrassed grin. "It was my pleasure, Cressida. And you look so lovely, too."

"Thanks to you." She couldn't stop stroking the soft fabric that flowed over her body like a cool, bright stream of water. "Such a choice of colors! Callie's dress is just perfect for her."

His face softened even more. "Aye," he murmured.

"How long have you been in love with her?" Cressida asked in the same matter-of-fact tone. For a moment Tom didn't react, and then he just turned on his heel and walked away. Cressida went right after him. "I saw how you looked at her just now, and realized I was a fool not to have guessed earlier. Does she know?"

Tom's face twisted but he made no effort to deny it. "Ah, blessed Lord, I don't think so."

"Why not?" He looked miserable, but Cressida pressed on. "Why have you not told her? What if she returns your feelings?"

He jerked so hard she thought he would fall to his knees. "She couldn't. Feel the same, I mean. You won't— I beg you—"

"I think you might be wrong," she told him softly. "I think Callie cares for you very much. But after the way Mr. Phillips . . . well, after being married to him—"

"He was a coldhearted devil," growled Tom. "I knew it from the moment I met him, but your father wanted—"

He stopped so suddenly Cressida blinked. Her father had approved the match, even though he hardly knew Julian Phillips, but then he had gone back to his regiment. In fact, none of them really knew Mr. Phillips before he offered for Callie, but he was a well-to-do local merchant, and very eligible for a soldier's daughter. "What, Tom?"

He shrugged and turned away. "Nothing."

Cressida picked up her skirts and ran after him as he walked off again. "What did you start to say? Tom!"

Tom stopped but didn't face her. His hands clenched and unclenched at his sides. "Phillips offered him two hundred pounds for her hand," he said, his voice echoing in the carriage bay. "The sergeant needed the money. And if—if she married Phillips, then she could never . . ." His voice quivered a moment. "Never marry someone like me."

Cressida closed her eyes and exhaled, as if part of her spirit had deserted her. *Oh, Papa . . .*

"That's what the sergeant didn't want," Tom added. "Not ever. Not even after Phillips got his rightful reward."

"That's why you stayed with us," she whispered. Not for Papa's sake; for *Callie's.* "You've been in love with her for years. Oh, Tom . . ."

"I don't want pity," he said. "It's not her fault. I tried to go, Cressida. I just . . ." His shoulders slumped. "I just can't."

She didn't know what to do, or say, or even think. Her heart quailed from believing her father would so callously deny one man and reward another. Callie's marriage to Mr. Phillips had been disastrous and wretched, but Cressida had always thought Papa acted in Callie's interest, to find her a well-situated husband and a secure home. He had encouraged her to receive Mr. Phillips, pointed out how advantageous a match it would be, and given Phillips permission to marry Callie in barely a month's time. Had he done that for money—and to deny Tom?

Traitorously, she suspected he had. She recalled all the times Papa had made sport of Tom, laughing at his steady temper and humble dreams. Papa's dreams had never been humble, and nothing about him was steady. Tom had always absorbed it with a halfhearted smile or a shrug and never seemed much to mind it. But in denying him Callie's hand, Papa had still succeeded in tying Tom—steadfast, devoted Tom—to their family for years.

"I've got to clean the tack," Tom mumbled as she stood there, too aghast to say anything. "Need to make myself useful around this fancy house. Good night." He disappeared into the back of the stable, leaving Cressida alone with the horrible knowledge that her father was not merely less noble than her grandmother had always claimed, but that he might in fact have been an utter fraud.

Chapter 19

∞

Cressida took her time returning to the house. She couldn't go back to the drawing room, where the rest of the company was chatting and laughing. She sat outside on a bench in the garden for a long while, trying to reconcile this new view of her father with her long-held affection for him. It was not easy to admit that the man she had always loved, if not revered, could have been so cold—but as she had realized in London, she hadn't known him as well as she thought. It was Granny who worshipped him, and she had taught her granddaughters to do the same.

Now that Papa was gone, it seemed she was learning ever more unsavory things about him. Cressida had been working on the journal and made some progress, but it was years old and probably wouldn't tell her anything about where he now is. Perhaps that was best. She would continue working on it, because she couldn't bring herself to leave a puzzle undone, but only for enlightenment on who her father really was. If he truly was gone for good, it might be her only chance to know.

The cold of the stone gradually seeped through her skirts, and she rose to go back inside. The house was quieter when she did, the servants no longer standing at attention in the hall. The gentlemen who lived nearby must have gone home, and it was past the hour when Mrs. Hayes usually retired. From the drawing room she could still hear Julia and her cousin Emily, talking with John and Callie. She hesitated, not wanting to be rude but also not wanting to join them.

"Cressida."

Her heart lurched. She swung around to see Alec, in his greatcoat and hat. He must have come in from the side door, closer to the stables, and missed crossing her path outdoors. He looked tired and dirty, but the sight of him unleashed a sudden burst of happiness within her.

"Yes?" she said, a little breathlessly.

Laughter drifted from the nearby drawing room, Julia's voice and Emily's. His eyes moved to the doors, then back to her face. "I trust you enjoyed the evening?" She nodded. He sighed, peeling off his riding gloves and stuffing them into his pocket. "Excellent. Might I . . . might I have a moment to speak to you?" Again she nodded, and walked with him in silence to his study.

A fire was already burning, and the lamps lit. A servant appeared to take away his coat and hat. Alec had to look away from Cressida until the footman left. She was temptation itself in that ocean green gown, with her hair pinned high on her crown and one long wisp curling down her cheek. It made him think of the other day, when he had held her up against the library door and her hair had tumbled loose as he dragged his fingers through it. He gestured toward the settee, and then sat as far from her as possible. "I must beg your pardon. I've spent this week looking into your father's disappearance, and have found no trace of him."

"Why must you beg pardon for that?"

Because he had thrown himself into that effort to avoid the house—and her. If he could locate her father, she would be able to leave his house before he lost whatever remained of his honor and seduced her, which had been on his mind almost every minute since he held her in his arms and tasted the soft skin at the nape of her neck. He didn't *want* her to leave; quite the contrary. But he adamantly wanted her to have the freedom to leave. He knew all too well how it felt to be hemmed in and powerless in life. The best thing he could do for her—aside from controlling his private desires—was give her back what she had lost. So he traced every connection and possibility, riding out early in the morning and coming home late at night, making no secret of his object and paying generously for information. Stafford would have an apoplexy when he heard how much money Alec had spent in pursuit of this one sergeant. "Because I promised to keep you better informed of my actions," he said. "In my defense, I can only say that it was tedious and tiring, and involved roaming about the country asking a great many people very dull questions."

She nodded soberly. "I see."

"I have looked from here to London and back, at every town on the main road and some off to the sides, and no one has seen him or heard from him since he vanished." He paused. "I'm sorry."

"Thank you."

Alec didn't feel compelled to tell her the uglier details, how many bills George Turner had left unpaid, nor how many of those publicans and merchants had expressed an interest in getting their hands around Turner's neck, if not his purse. He didn't tell her about the retired soldiers and officers who seemed oddly relieved Turner had gone missing, nor about the well-to-do widow who claimed he had been engaged to her even as she spat on the ground at the mention of his name. None of that changed the fact that all his inquiries had come to nothing. He would wait a bit longer, in case his questioning flushed out information later, but for once Alec was at a loss. The man had simply disappeared, along with his horse and whatever baggage he had taken to London. He didn't want to discuss any of that with Cressida.

There was, however, the encounter in the library between them. She was a guest in his mother's home, for pity's sake, and he had trapped her and held her and kissed her. But when he tried to form an apology, it wouldn't come; he knew he should regret his actions even as he thought about repeating them every day. Avoiding her hadn't dimmed the desire at all, and now she was here beside him, more tempting than ever and not looking reproachful in the slightest. It was a siren call to the beast inside him, tempting him to close the distance between them and take up where he had left off that day, when she had been aroused and seductive and his for the taking.

But he was not that beast. Cressida Turner had a loyal but wary heart, and it had been broken once before. How could he ask her to risk that again? He wasn't the sort of man she needed, a decent honorable man who could give her a proper home. He was a man adrift, disgusting to his own family and unwanted by his neighbors. Even if he offered her marriage, she would be a fool to accept. Alec focused on his hands, clasped on his knee, and reminded himself of that last fact. If he looked at her too long, it might just slip his mind.

"Unless there is something in his journal, I fear we have few avenues left to explore."

She started at the word "journal." "Oh! Yes, I have been working on it, but haven't solved the code yet."

He nodded. "Perhaps that will reveal something."

She nodded, smoothing her palms over her lap. "Yes, perhaps." After a moment of awkward silence she got to her feet. "Thank you for telling me. Good night."

He drew a harsh breath as she crossed the room. "Cressida." She paused at the door without looking back. "The other day, in the library . . ." Slowly she turned her head, not quite facing him. Her eyelashes veiled her gaze. "I apologize."

Her eyelashes trembled. "For what?"

"For—" Not for kissing her. Not for touching her. "For keeping you when you wished to go."

"And for the rest?"

Finally she looked at him, that direct, open gaze that had first caught his attention. Alec couldn't have lied to her now to save his soul. "I am only sorry for that if you are."

The color rose in her face and heat flared in her eyes. He would probably spend the rest of his life trying to find a name for that color. "Good," she whispered. "Neither am I." She opened the door and went out, closing it softly behind her.

* * *

Cressida went to her room, hardly able to believe she had said that to him. She might as well have said out loud that she wanted him, which made her smile nervously as she climbed the stairs. The flash of desire in his eyes was everything she could have hoped for. She just didn't know what it could lead to.

Callie was unpinning her hair, humming quietly. There was color in her face and a sparkle in her eye that Cressida hadn't seen in a long time. The rose silk dress was hanging over the wardrobe door, as if spread out for continued admiration and enjoyment. The sight brought back her conversation with Tom, and shook her out of her haze of longing. Silently she picked up the brush and went to work on Callie's curls.

"What a lovely evening," Callie said. She smiled at her reflection, tilting her head a little to the side and looking almost coquettish. "Did you enjoy it?"

"Yes."

Her sister glanced at her. "You disappeared quite early. Where did you go?"

"I didn't have your queue of admirers waiting on me. I'm surprised you noticed I was gone."

"Hardly a queue. One gentleman who was kind."

Cressida raked the brush hard through Callie's hair, making her sister squeak. "Very kind, it looked to me. No, I walked out and talked with Tom instead. Sometimes it seems we take him for granted, since he's been with us for so many years."

"I suppose," said Callie on a gasp. She was holding tightly to the edge of the table as Cressida yanked on her tangled hair. Cressida relented and gentled her strokes until her sister's fingers eased their grip and slid into her lap.

"I think we've all underestimated Tom. He is one of the most wholly decent men I know, a gentleman in deed if not by birth. Just think of where we'd be now if he hadn't stayed with us all these weeks since Papa left. I cannot imagine life without Tom, can you?"

"Of course not." Callie looked surprised by the question.

"And it struck me, as I was watching Mr. Davis hang on your every word, that I've known Tom for years. We get on quite well together." She had Callie's undivided attention now. Cressida hid her satisfaction and continued sweeping the brush through her sister's long dark curls as she talked. "Perhaps I've been overlooking something, or someone, right before my eyes."

"Cressida." Callie seemed to have trouble speaking. "Are you—are you saying—or trying to say—is he—*Tom*—does he—?"

"Well, setting my cap for Tom would be sensible, wouldn't it? We would neither of us be deceived in the other's character. Granny would always have a home, and you, too, if you wished."

"Well . . . perhaps, but—"

"And he has his pension. He told me, when he bought the silk for the dresses. Now that we've lost Brighampton, we might go anywhere. In Portsmouth there would be more work for him, and we could take one of those cozy houses down by the quay, the ones you and I used to admire so much."

"So you—you are in love with him?"

Cressida heaved a sigh. "No, not *in* love, although

I am very fond of him. Didn't Papa always say that would be more than enough? I suppose I'm too old to be particular about that anymore."

"Papa said—" Callie's voice rose into a high squeak. She stopped, then spoke in her normal tone. "Papa disapproved of Tom. Mr. Webb, I mean."

That was twice Callie had slipped and called him Tom. Cressida would have smiled, except that she heard the feeling not in those utterances, but when Callie called him Mr. Webb. "Papa's no longer here, and I cannot help thinking he doesn't mean to come back. And in any event, I'm hardly a young girl who has to do my father's bidding. I daresay if Tom will have me, I couldn't find a better match."

Callie sat silently.

"Do you not approve of my idea?" Cressida prodded.

Her sister stared at her reflection with wide, dismayed eyes. Cressida sank down and sat on the back of the dressing table bench. "Unless, that is, you fancy him," she said quietly. "And think he might return your affection."

"Perhaps," whispered Callie, meeting Cressida's gaze in the mirror.

"Did Papa . . . ?"

Callie blinked, and gave a slight nod. Cressida tamped down the burst of anger at her father. She put her arm around her sister's shoulders. "Then you should—"

"Cressida, you don't understand!" Callie sprang to her feet and almost tripped over the bench in her haste to scramble away. "You can stand up to Papa. He—He terrifies me. When he looks at me with that stern air, like he expects me to say or do just the right thing or lose his regard forever, I seem to freeze inside. And when I disappoint him, it's dreadful; just the look on his face makes me want to cry."

"That's why Papa bullies you. He likes having command after being in the army, I suppose, and he's not much used to having daughters around." Even as she said it, Cressida knew it was no excuse. She thought again of Alec swinging his nieces in the air at his mother's party, grinning at their squeals of delight. He could hardly be used to little girls, either, but his affection was obvious.

Callie shook her head, looking helpless. "It doesn't matter. I crumble inside when he scolds me."

"But he's not here now, is he?" Callie bit her lip and looked at the floor. "Tom wants to leave." Her sister's gaze shot up. "And why not? We have no money, and just lost our home. A man would have to be a bit slow not to realize his chances were better elsewhere. But for some reason, he's still here." She got up and took her sister's hands. "Do you care for Tom?"

Color flooded Callie's face. "Yes," she whispered.

Cressida squeezed her fingers. "You might let the poor man know of your regard. I fear Papa made his disapproval known to Tom as well, and now he doesn't dare look at you the way he did tonight, when he thought no one was watching."

Callie's blush deepened. "How did he look at me?"

She thought for a minute. "As though he would be happy never to look away."

"But Papa—when he returns—"

"Carpe diem, Callandra Phillips," said Cressida firmly. "Together you and Tom can tell Papa to bugger off." Callie started, then burst out laughing. Cressida joined her, until the two of them were laughing so hard they had to hold each other up.

"What would I do without you?" gasped Callie.

"You'd have to brush your own hair."

"Oh, name the one thing that would make me better off." Cressida caught a pillow from the bed and smacked her with it. Callie threw up her hands. "Stop! Unfair!"

Cressida stuck out her tongue. "Unfair that you got Mama's lovely curls!"

Callie flung the pillow back at her. "Unfair that you got Papa's courage!"

Cressida caught the pillow with one hand and tossed it back onto the bed. "I did, and I'm giving some to you now." She shook her finger at her sister. "I mean it. Or I will tell Tom myself."

"You wouldn't!"

She smirked. "Do you really want to take that chance?"

Callie glared at her, but more in exasperation than anger. "Good night."

Cressida laughed, and began getting ready for bed herself. Her fury at Papa's actions was significantly tempered by the thought of Callie finding happiness—and with Tom, of all people. If Papa really had left them for good, it might at least lead to something good.

It was almost enough to distract her from wondering what might happen the next time she saw Alec.

Chapter 20

Callie found her an hour after luncheon the next day, her eyes shining and her face flushed. "I have something to tell you."

"What is it?" Cressida laughed. "It must be very happy news."

"It is." Callie took both her hands, her fingers trembling. "Mr. Webb—Tom has asked me to marry him. And I have said yes."

Cressida's mouth fell open. "He—— You— So soon? But you only just knew!"

"Don't look so surprised," her sister cried. "You yourself told me he has been like family for so long you were considering marrying him!"

"Well, I never did! I knew he loved you, not me, and I wanted to make you see it, too." Cressida felt a flicker of alarm, but Callie burst out laughing.

"You must know I'm teasing you. He . . . he told me of your conversation last night. How it gave him hope. How it gave him the boldness to speak to me when he never would have dared before." Callie's eyes were moist. "Cressida, I am forever in your debt. Without you, I might have never believed he cared for me, and I never would have had the courage to tell him I cared for him so, knowing how Papa—"

"Papa won't dare interfere," she said when Callie stopped abruptly. "I won't let him."

Her sister drew a deep breath and squared her shoulders. "No. *I* won't," she said firmly. "Not anymore."

"Good." She gave a stout nod. "And I am very happy for you and Tom both."

Callie's smile bloomed again, so bright with joy Cressida couldn't help smiling back even though her heart was pounding. "We're returning to Portsmouth," Callie said. "We both felt more at home there, and want to return. Now that Brighampton is gone, we neither of us want to burden the Hayes family any longer than necessary. And we want you and Granny to come with us. I shall ask Major Hayes to tell Papa, if—when—he locates him, to send word to us there."

"Oh. Of—Of course."

Callie looked at her closely, but Cressida smiled quickly, and her sister let it go. "I am going to Granny now. I do hope she'll be happy—oh, Cressida, do you think she'll fret that he's . . . ?" Callie fluttered her hands nervously.

"That he's a soldier like Papa? A decent man? Madly in love with you? Why on earth would she?"

Her sister flushed. "She always wanted us to marry well."

"Callie," said Cressida quietly, "if you marry Tom, you will marry very well indeed."

"I know." Callie seemed unable to contain herself any longer, and she embraced Cressida before hurrying off to tell Granny the news.

Cressida pushed aside Papa's journal and the sketch pad where she'd been making her notes on it. Back to Portsmouth . . . Her eyes flitted around the conservatory. Away from Penford. She got up and walked slowly through the house. Her mind reeled. Callie and Tom, to be married! It was wonderful that two people so dear to her could find happiness together; it was everything she had hoped for . . . but it was also a thunderous crack in her world. For so long they had all been together as a family, but now they really would be family—and Cressida knew with a creeping discomfort that it would be strange to see Tom married to her sister. They would set up house together. They might have children. They would sit by the fire at nights together, and then they would go to bed together. And Cressida, the spinster sister, would be left sitting by the fire with Granny.

She was not jealous. She was *not*. Cressida refused to be jealous when she really was truly happy. It was demeaning to herself and unfair to Callie, who deserved love and happiness, and to Tom, who had loved her so long and so patiently without hope. Her fingernails dug into her palms as she wrestled with her wildly irrational emotions, and before she knew it she was standing in front of Alec's study door.

John Hayes opened the door when she knocked. Cressida wet her lips. "I beg pardon. I didn't wish to interrupt—"

"We were finished," Mr. Hayes said. He glanced over his shoulder at Alec, who stood behind his desk. "Were we not?"

"We were. Please, come in." Alec beckoned with one hand for her to enter. Mr. Hayes bowed his head politely as he held the door for her, then let himself out.

Suddenly she felt like a fool, running to unburden herself to Alec when he clearly had worries of his own, and had shouldered some of hers as well in his search for Papa. What was she to say? That her sister was getting married and it made her heart writhe with longing to be the one someone loved beyond all reason? It was jealousy, small and petty, and Cressida hated herself for feeling it. But he came around the desk and held out one hand to the sofa. "You look distressed," he said. "Has something happened?"

"Yes." She shook her head, sitting at one end of the sofa. "But a very happy thing. Mr. Webb has proposed to my sister and she has accepted."

"Ah." His gaze swept her face. "I wish them both very happy. I suspected he harbored hopes in that direction."

She gave an embarrassed laugh. Of course Alec would have noticed even what she had not seen in years of living with Tom and Callie both. "Yes, I think he has done for some time. My father . . . I think Papa would not approve . . ." She stopped, concentrating on stilling her hands in her lap. "No, I must be honest with you," she said in a low voice. "Papa knew Tom loved her, and he warned Tom away. He even . . . he even married Callie to that horrid Mr. Phillips to prevent Tom from marrying her." Alec said nothing. Cressida swallowed. "So Callie truly deserves to be loved, and I think Tom will make her happy. I cannot imagine a finer man."

"Indeed," he murmured.

For a moment it was silent as Cressida sat picking at a loose thread at the edge of her apron and not looking at him. What had she expected him to say? "They plan to return to Portsmouth," she said to fill the void. "Granny will go with them, I am sure. She was born and raised in Portsmouth, and now that we've lost Brighampton, there's no reason for her to stay here." The loose thread had begun to unravel in earnest under her restless fingers. She forced herself to stop and clasped her hands.

"I will speak to Webb, then," he said. "He'll want wagons for the journey."

Cressida nodded once. "That is very kind of you." But not what she longed to hear. Had he assumed she was going with them as well? What *had* she hoped he would say? That he wanted her to stay, to argue with him more and question his every move and insist on being included in his trips to find her father when her presence only complicated his efforts? That he wanted to hold her up against the wall as he had done that day in the library and press his lips to the back of her neck in earnest, and discover how little it would take to melt her reserve?

"And do you go with them?"

She looked up and met his gaze. Her heart thudded and her white-knuckled fingers trembled. She should say yes, because Callie had invited her to live with them and she had no reason or excuse not to go with her family. She wanted to say no, because she didn't want to leave Penford and him and the uncommon connection she felt between them. Instead she sat there staring into Alec's fathomless blue eyes and said nothing at all.

An eternity seemed to pass. Cressida knew her only thought must be written on her face, but she was helpless to hide it. Perhaps she shouldn't even try. Perhaps he would make the decision for her. He was too honorable to trifle with her. Surely he would be merciful and wish her well with her family in Portsmouth if he cared nothing for her, or knew there was no future for them. Because Cressida, who always had a smart answer and who never shied from speaking bluntly, was completely tongue-tied by the realization that she did want him to ask her to stay, for any reason at all.

Abruptly he surged to his feet. "Would you walk with me?"

Dumbly she nodded. She stood and went out the door when he opened it, walked with him through the house and out into the garden. Past the gardenias and the roses, past the wildflowers that carpeted the lawn just behind the garden, across the grass, and on and on they walked. Cressida didn't know what he intended, but she realized that it didn't matter; she trusted him. And she would be happy to walk with him like this all day.

"I never missed Penford much while I was away," he said suddenly. "I strained toward adventure, and did my best to find it at every opportunity. I was the terror of Marston, along with Will Lacey, as anyone will tell you. When I was seventeen my father was only too happy to purchase a commission in the army for me and pack me off to all the adventure one could have fighting Bonaparte, and I was only too happy to go. I packed my trunk and didn't look back."

He came to a stop on a slight rise overlooking sloping fields, with the river sparkling in the distance like a fine silver thread. The house was behind them, nestled in the verdant gardens. It was warm and bright and beautiful, and again Cressida felt gripped by the sense that she would rather be here than anywhere. How could he leave without looking back, without growing sick for home at some point, when *this* was home? But Alec's eyes seemed to be focused somewhere else entirely as he narrowed his eyes against the sunshine.

"I never thought Penford would be mine, or that I would have such a duty to it. If I had suspected . . ." He paused, and spoke more slowly, choosing each word with care. "If I had suspected, I might have acted differently. Or perhaps not.

"A battle is unimaginable. No one who hasn't survived one can truly understand the confusion, the frantic efforts to control men and horses and guns and get them into anything resembling what the commanding officers ordered, the blind panic that drives men to abandon their positions and run when the tide of battle changes. It is terrifying and yet, at the same time, exhilarating. One's blood runs hot and fast, one's mind works at a feverish pace. At moments you feel capable of inhuman feats, and perhaps you are. There are long stretches of waiting, or forming up, or trying to maneuver into position, and then all hell breaks loose and you have less than a second to react, or be killed."

He fell silent again. Cressida gazed out at the gentle swells of peaceful green grass and tried to picture them swarming with men, bloody and wounded and charging forward with murder in their eyes. Papa had never said much about actual battles, and the dispatches printed in the newspapers always painted such a glorious picture of gallant officers leading their men into the fray, of steadfast British infantry standing firm under withering enemy fire. She knew men died in war, or came back mangled and scarred, but she had really only known Tom and Papa, who both returned home whole and healthy. *And Alec*, whispered a little voice in her head, reminding her again of the scars that crossed his back and chest. *You know him . . .*

"What comes after the battle, though, is worse—far worse." His voice had grown soft and hollow. "Everything is chaos, as regiments are scattered far and wide, or perhaps so decimated they can never be found. Men you loved as brothers are gone, blown to pieces or shot up badly enough the surgeons must cut apart what's left. The waste of life, both human and animal, is astounding, and yet one's mind dulls to it. After a while you can look over a battlefield rotting in the sun and simply not feel much of anything. Relief, perhaps, that you are one of the survivors, or regret that you lost good men, or failed to hold your position, or failed to completely crush the enemy. But there is always another battle to come; there will always be war, and death, and treachery."

"Why are you telling me this?" she whispered. She knew before he said it what he was going to tell her next.

His eyes drifted shut. "I know rumor holds I left Waterloo for piracy in the West Indies, or fled to America in disgrace with a pile of French gold. The truth . . . The truth . . ."

After a long moment of silence, she said, "The truth is that you came home five years later to help a complete stranger, even after she pointed a pistol at you and questioned your intentions. You asked uncomfortable questions that needed to be asked, and told uncomfortable truths." She glanced sideways at him from under her eyelashes. "Those are not the actions of a coward—nor, I think, of a scoundrel."

"You had—have—no reason to trust me," he replied. "And indeed you did not, initially."

Cressida thought about that a moment. "No," she said slowly. "I had no reason to trust you. But I do, all the same." She paused. "I suppose it wouldn't be trust if it had to be proved, would it?"

Alec filled his lungs, the fresh air almost painfully sharp in his chest. There was that. How odd that she alone wouldn't jump at the chance to know the truth when he knew everyone else in Marston would have. "The truth is that I became a spy," he said before he could reconsider. "For the Home Office. I posed as servants and tradesmen to spy on rabble who muttered discontent with the government. It was the only chance I could see to restore my good name, eventually. And it failed. I never meant to come home without my honor, but here I am, with a history as clouded and obscure as the day I woke up to discover I was accused of treason. I would rather have remained dead, for all intents and purposes, than come back now, like this, and yet . . ." He made himself breathe. Carefully he straightened his fingers, which had curled into fists as the familiar helpless fury stole through him again. It had been months, even years, since that feeling had gotten the better of him.

Her eyes had grown large and round during his

outburst. She stared at him, white-faced, for what seemed an eternity. "Oh," she murmured. "I see."

Did she? He gave a bleak smile. "I wanted you to know."

Those wide golden eyes didn't waver. "Why?"

"Because . . ." He shook his head and looked away. "I did."

She was quiet. He couldn't be surprised if she turned and walked—or ran—away. "And that—that's why you were sent to find my father? You said your talents were well-suited to it, and I always wondered what you meant."

Alec let out his breath in surprise. "Yes. Hastings asked my employer, and he sent me."

She blinked a few times in quick succession, and swallowed, fixing his attention on the slim column of her throat. "Then . . . The Home Office is interested in my father's whereabouts? Why?"

"I don't know." He had a few suspicions, but that was all. Alec couldn't bring himself to share those suspicions, biased as they no doubt were by his years of living among liars and cheats and every other stripe of villain. The most likely excuse for Turner's disappearance was still misadventure or abandonment. If any of his suspicions proved correct, he wouldn't hesitate to tell her, but in the absence of proof . . . he didn't see the necessity.

Her shoulders sagged. "I wonder if we'll ever know what happened to him. Or much else about him, really. It seems so much of my perception has been wrong."

"I have not given up," he said. "Not yet."

She looked at him as a tremulous smile curved her

lips. "Thank you," she whispered. "Your confidence gives me comfort."

Alec knew what she meant. In the days after Waterloo, only James Peterbury had known he was alive and had believed him innocent. Having one defender, just one, had mattered a great deal, even if Peterbury had had to proceed painfully slowly and with such caution it seemed nothing would ever improve. For months Alec had lived a grim, dark existence, with Peterbury's steadfast support one of the few rays of light. And now Cressida Turner was standing beside him, trusting him, comforted by his presence and looking up at him with glowing eyes. It was strange for Alec to think himself a comfort to anyone, but the feeling it inspired inside him was not pride or unease, but a fearsome swell of satisfaction that he *could* comfort her.

He extended one hand and she grasped it at once, still wearing that shaky little smile. He took a step toward her. "You are welcome to stay," he said. "When your sister goes. If you wish to stay."

Her lips parted. The pulse in her throat was a flutter of motion. She looked at him, half yearning, half uncertain.

"I would like you to stay," he added. She ran the tip of her tongue over her lower lip, his undoing. He took the last step, until there was nothing more separating them. Her head fell back and she swayed toward him in invitation. Alec lowered his head until his lips almost brushed hers. "Stay," he breathed. What would he do if she left? "Please."

"Yes," she whispered, and he kissed her.

Cressida hardly dared breathe as his lips met hers.

Every muscle she had felt stiff and taut as she tried not to shiver apart into a thousand pieces while he kissed her, gently, reverently. He still held her hand lightly in his, the only other contact between them, but something far stronger than that held her in place. It wasn't certainty; Cressida had no idea what lay ahead. She might be galloping headlong toward another broken heart, even more shattering than the last. But as his lips moved on hers, she could only think of Papa's dearest maxim, usually reserved for cards but strangely applicable to her mood today:

Nothing ventured, nothing gained.

Chapter 21

July 1815
Forest of the Soignes, Belgium

It took Alec a few days to recover from the set-back his trip into Brussels had cost him. James Peterbury hired a cart to drive him back to the farm, and left with a promise to come back as soon as he learned anything. He seemed to be reserving judgment, at least for the moment, and was still willing to help. It was small comfort, but better than none.

Alec's wound had reopened, and Widow Gustave shook her head over him, muttering unintelligibly as she wrapped him up tighter than before. He was sure the widow was ready for him to heal and be gone as much as he was ready to go, but there was nowhere for him to go now. Instead of being on his way back to England, or even lodged in Brussels to recuperate, he couldn't leave the forest for fear of being recognized by the wrong person—namely, anyone but Peterbury. He had little to do except ruminate on the shocking news that he was considered a traitor to England. All James had mentioned in the way of proof was some papers, allegedly found in Alec's baggage after the battle. Either it was all a terrible mistake and would be sorted out as soon as someone read the papers and realized they were not his, or someone had put them in his things with this intent. His thoughts ran dark and murderous as he contemplated who must have planted them there, and why. It was the only explanation he could see, and it would be easy enough to do in the chaos after the battle.

He knew he was known as a bit of a hell-raiser in the Dragoons, with a certain fearlessness in battle that endeared him to his men and generally impressed his superiors. But the army had its own hierarchy, and no shortage of vanity or short tempers. The path to advancement was paved with the good opinion of commanding officers; a note of praise in the dispatches was invaluable. And even then a man could not be promoted until an opening appeared in the ranks above him. Alec didn't think any of his junior officers would go so far to secure a majority, but as the days marched on and James didn't return, he began to wonder.

Finally, James Peterbury came back, a full week later. Alec was stacking cordwood a neighboring farmer had split for the widow in return for her spinning his wool. It was hard work, but Alec was determined to make himself well. The French saber had slid up his ribs before catching on his collarbone. The muscles burned with pain every time he raised his arm, but he forced himself to lift another log, and another. He refused to be left an invalid by this. But when he heard the horse approaching, he stopped stacking logs with as much relief for the rest as he had hope for the tidings.

Peterbury tied his horse to a tree, taking just long enough that Alec knew the news was bad. He turned away, ducking his head to wipe the sweat from his face with the tail of his shirt. Good God. He had really believed James would find the mistake, easily discovered and promptly believed. If not—if it couldn't be proven or, worse, was simply not believed—what would he do?

Footsteps sounded behind him. "How goes it?" he asked without turning.

There was a pause. "Not as well as we hoped, I'm afraid."

Alec nodded. "I suspected as much."

"The papers . . ." James paused again, as if picking each word carefully. "They are apparently quite an extensive correspondence with a French colonel, over some years' time."

"Is there anything at all to identify the recipient?"

"I don't know," came James's low answer. "I didn't read them." Alec jerked around then, incredulous. James held up his hands. "I tried—repeatedly. It took a devilishly long time to find someone who had actually seen the letters himself, and even longer to get anything but vitriol from him. Everyone thinks it does not matter now, as you are supposed dead." He tried a weak smile, more gruesome than reassuring. "That is the good news. Since everyone thinks you're dead, no one is looking for you or making a great fuss over the charges. There are whispers, but nothing more. The victory has crowded out most other talk."

"That's the good news," Alec repeated. He lowered

himself onto the woodpile. "At least there is some."

James looked at the ground. "It's more valuable than you think."

"Believe me, I know." Alec ran one hand over his face. "You said Will Lacey is dead." He had hardly been able to think about his oldest, dearest friend lying cold and broken on the field, never again to flash his wry grin over a commanding officer's tantrum or quietly lend a hand to a wounded soldier. Alec's heart twisted with grief for the loss, not just to himself but to Will's family, his proud, strict father and his newly widowed wife, not to mention the child who would never know him.

James sat on the woodpile beside him. "He died heroically. Ponsonby sent him to direct a squadron of dragoons to charge, and just as he was relaying the order, an artillery shell made a direct hit on the commander, cleaving him in two. They say Lacey seized the sword from the commander's hand and led the charge himself, into deadly French fire. The fighting was fierce, but he pushed onward, and captured the enemy's colors before being cut down."

A true hero's death. Alec bowed his head for a moment. "His wife? She was in Brussels."

"I do not know. There are many widows in Brussels."

He shoved himself to his feet. "Find her, if she's still there. Do all that you can for her. I gave Lacey my word I would see to her security, but now . . ."

Peterbury understood. He jumped up and saluted crisply. "I will, sir." Then he blinked and looked uncertain. "What will you do?"

Alec glanced around the little clearing about the house. Widow Gustave was ready for him to leave, and he would go mad if he had to stay much longer. "I can't stay here."

"Where will you go?"

That was a damned good question. Where, indeed? He stared at his hands, flexing his fingers until his knuckles strained white. "I will disprove this," he said instead of answering James. "I will." His hands curled into fists. "Somehow."

After a moment James extended his hand, palm open. "I know," he said. "You have my help."

Alec laughed grimly. "You don't need to promise me anything. Aiding a traitor isn't in your best interest."

"I'm not aiding a traitor, I am aiding a friend in need." His hand hadn't wavered. "And I pledge my help whether you shake my hand or not. I'll find those letters and track down the true recipient, and expose this man as both a traitor and a liar. No one is served by the wrong man being punished; it makes a fool of the entire army."

He took a deep breath. James was younger than he, but no green boy. He was a staff officer, albeit a very junior one, and he had always had a knack for talking people into seeing things his way. And now, he was the only friend Alec had. He clasped James's hand in his. "Thank you."

"Well, there's something," James said with a short chuckle. "The hard-charging Major Hayes has accepted my advice and aid."

Alec held up one hand. He supposed this possibility had been fermenting at the back of his mind all along, that he would need a second plan of action if the allegations couldn't be easily dismissed, because now there was no hesitation when he spoke. "Not Major Hayes. From now on I shall be Alec Brandon." The name just appeared on his lips, his nickname and his mother's family name. "Alexander Hayes is dead."

Chapter 22

1820

If Alec had feared his confession would cause even more upheaval, he was happily disappointed. In fact, the household seemed to grow more peaceful—although perhaps that was due to his own apprehensions being eased by Cressida's compassion. He had dreaded anyone knowing; no matter who employed him, no matter what he hoped to achieve in return, Alec couldn't shake the thought that a spy was a spy, and he had a particular reason for abhorring the very word.

But Cressida didn't. A spy's talents had come to her aid, and then she had looked past them to see him. That went deeper to his heart than anything had in years. He might never be able to prove his innocence, but she didn't ask him to.

He explained to Mrs. Phillips what he had told Cressida, that he could find no trace of her father. Mrs. Phillips's new fiancé, Tom Webb, hovered unsmiling and protective in the background as he spoke, but Alec set the thought aside. He also saw how Webb looked at Mrs. Phillips, and remembered what Cressida had told him. Webb had a powerful motive to want Turner to vanish, but even had Alec had evidence or proof of that, he wasn't so sure bringing it to light would benefit anyone. In fact, as the newly engaged couple made plans for their wedding and removal to Portsmouth, there seemed a quiet acceptance that George Turner was gone forever.

His cousin John was preparing to leave, and Alec finally began taking on his estate responsibilities. He might never feel truly comfortable with the mantle, but as he rode with John, it managed to drift down onto his shoulders more lightly than expected. He began to feel the love for Penford that his father and Frederick had had creep into his soul. And after roaming the land—his land—it felt natural to return to the house. To his family. To Cressida. To the realization that the rolling lands of Penford might not be the only love growing in his heart.

For the first time, Alec could envision a life here. He had a duty to Penford, and he had his family to look after, but most of these visions came to involve Cressida Turner. Since the day he invited—asked—her to stay, he had only become more intrigued. When he first met her, Alec had thought her striking, but not beautiful; now he found it hard to take his eyes off her, especially when she wrinkled up her nose to laugh at something her sister said, or sucked on her lower lip as she concentrated on something, or just turned her face up to the sun, eyes closed in a peaceful expression. He wanted more than a chaste kiss from her. He wanted to see her with her hair down in the moonlight again, her nightdress soft and thin in his hands as he slid it over her shoulders and down her hips. He wanted her eyes to burn when he touched her. He wanted *her*—and now that his assignment from Stafford had drawn to an end, he finally might be free to pursue her.

But of course nothing ever ended that easily. One hazy afternoon, he was returning from the estate manager's office when a smart phaeton turned in the drive, followed by a cloud of dust from the dry road. He paused, and watched for a moment before realizing what had caught his eye. The woman in the carriage was Angelique Martand, another of Stafford's agents.

He crossed the gravel to meet her as the carriage drew up to the house. "Angelique," he said, helping her down and taking her hand to his lips. "Ian." The driver, also Stafford's man, tipped his hat and winked. "What brings you to Hertfordshire?"

Ian Wallace laughed. "The fine weather," he said in his broad Scots accent. "Doesn't everyone flee the city when it's hot?"

Alec smiled, but kept one eye on Angelique. He had never really got on well with Ian, a tall, lanky fellow with lusty appetites and a booming laugh, both of which tended to attract too many women and too much trouble. He also had a deft touch with horses and was absolutely deadly in a fight, traits that made him invaluable to Stafford's schemes despite the women and trouble. "I'm not sure you've come to the right place," he said. "It's bloody hot here, too."

Ian laughed again before snapping the reins and driving on where a stable boy was waving to him. Alec turned back to Angelique.

She smiled her dimpled smile. Alec had marveled

out loud the first time he realized she could smile either with or without dimples. *"Alors, we have come to see you,"* she said, "to see how you get on in the fresh country air. Major Hayes, *non*? I shall have to remember not to call you Brandon." She sank into a curtsey.

Alec dropped her hand. "Stop."

"I do not mean to tease you." She clasped her hands in front of her. "Not too much, that is. We have come to see how you progress with Stafford's work, of course. He grows curious without word."

His eyes swept over the grounds, the limestone house, the well-kept lawns, the neat gravel drive, and knew how it would all look to Angelique. "I've made some progress, but not much worth reporting."

"Are you in need of help?"

"No."

Angelique arched an eyebrow. "Either you make progress, or you require help. It is not like you to muddle along."

He thought about what to tell her; what did he want Stafford to know? Nothing much, he admitted. But Angelique was no fool, and she had worked with him before. The urge to talk through the problem with someone else was extremely tempting. "What did Stafford tell you about this assignment?" he asked abruptly.

She fluttered her fingers. "A missing man. A favor for a politician. He has dozens of these little favors that need doing."

"Do you recall our last job?"

Her face grew tight. "All too well. What of it?"

Alec hesitated. His theory about George Turner,

still somewhat nebulous, was only that: a theory. He, of all people, balked at staining the name of an honest man. Saying the words out loud seemed an irreversible condemnation, even if he only said it to Angelique. But the mere fact that he suspected as much gave him pause. He had worked four years now for Stafford and never once questioned his employer's motives. Been on his guard, yes; watched his own back, always; but never doubted the basic information he had been given. But Stafford hadn't always repaid him well. Not two months past he had been caught in a scheme that was not what Stafford had told him, and it could have killed him. Lying in a narrow servant's cot, waiting for his wounds to heal, he had reflected on one basic truth: Stafford had lied to them all and sent them into a dangerous situation without being honest about the most likely source of the trouble. And no doubt that was due to one of those little favors for a politician Angelique mentioned. Stafford worked for the Home Secretary, Lord Sidmouth, and the last thing Sidmouth would want was Stafford's agents poking around the affairs of other politicians—or at least, getting caught at it. Anything Stafford meant to hide would be dangerous to expose. He had better be sure before he drew Angelique into the web.

He sighed. "We should talk later. What am I supposed to tell everyone about your sudden appearance—with Ian, no less?"

She still watched him thoughtfully. "He is my husband. We are dear friends of yours from London, stopping by for a short visit on our way north."

That should make for an entertaining evening. Not just Angelique, with her foreign looks and secretive manner, but Ian as well. Marianne might faint at the sight of him. "Your husband, eh? And why are you being punished?"

Angelique laughed. "It is not so unbearable. I shall be able to keep him in line."

There was no doubt of that. Alec shook his head. "You have walked into a hornet's nest here." She laughed again and he put up his hand. "You should let me explain before you laugh. I presume your, er, husband will be seeing to the carriage?"

She raised her eyes to the sky and made a soft noise of despair. "Of course. If there is a choice between a horse and a woman, Ian will choose the horse every time."

He chuckled and escorted her into the house. The housekeeper seemed mesmerized by Angelique, staring at her with unveiled astonishment before hurrying off to prepare rooms. Ian came in from the stable yard, and after they assured him they would rather talk before resting or refreshing themselves, Alec led them both to his study.

"Done right well, Brandon," said Ian, looking around. "Far sight better than your last quarters, I must say."

Alec repressed his annoyance. "Thank you," he said evenly. He rang for tea, and bade his guests sit.

He walked to the fireplace. Someone had relocated Will Lacey's carved wooden horse to the mantelpiece there. Somehow it had become a lodestar to him, a relic of the friend he had lost. Will would have known how to have this conversation, while Alec didn't look forward to it in the least. Not only did it draw him back into Stafford's web, it would force him to name things he was not *sure* of. Alec hated not being sure, especially in serious matters.

"So," said Angelique behind him. "You have found nothing worth reporting." Angelique was the true leader here, not Ian. Ian, he suspected, was here because it pleased her more than because Stafford wanted Ian to be here.

Alec fiddled with the carved horse a moment before putting it firmly aside. He took the seat opposite her, and she turned an expectant face toward him. She might smile and tease, but Angelique's mind was never far from her work. "There is something odd about this assignment," he began. "I can hardly put my finger on what, precisely, is wrong, but there is something. And after the Doncaster affair, I find it hard to ignore the feeling."

"What did he tell you?" As usual, she cut straight to the point.

Alec flipped one hand in irritation. "That a man was missing. His family was worried, and someone in the government asked Stafford to look into it. I asked who the man really was; Stafford said he was just an ordinary sergeant on half pay. Fine. Perhaps the man got involved in a pub brawl on his way home and met an ignominious end. Perhaps he got caught in the arms of a woman between London and here. Perhaps he ran off to escape debts. There are a hundred ways an ordinary man can go missing."

"Is this an explanation of why you have made no progress?"

He growled at her. "His family was not expecting me; they did not know someone would come. Another minor point, but again, if Hastings took such trouble to set Stafford on the case, why not write and inform the family?"

"Hastings . . ." Ian repeated, an arrested look creeping over his face. "Augustus Hastings?"

"Yes." He leaned forward. "Why?"

Ian shrugged. "Perhaps nothing. Eh, go on—I'll tell you after."

Another little mystery. Alec didn't like the way they were accumulating. He went on with his tale. "Turner's daughters told me he often goes off—expeditions, he calls them, and normally he comes back in a few weeks or even months, often with no other word. The man sounds a veritable vagabond, but he's always come home to his family, and flush with funds when he does.

"This time he expressly said he would return in a fortnight, and he left them no money. Whatever else he's done, so far he has provided for them, including moving house here to Marston a year ago, into a modest cottage with some good farmland attached. And here's where the story grows interesting."

Angelique's expression sharpened. Ian frowned again.

"There was no ledger in his things. We finally located one, hidden behind a wall panel."

"Ah," said Ian quietly.

Alec nodded. "It took some deciphering, but he's received payments from a printer in London. A little investigation turned up a good bit of money from the printer, most likely for drawings mocking the King and his ministers."

"You think Stafford wants him found for these drawings?" Angelique asked.

He shrugged. "Perhaps. But why didn't he set me on the printer from the beginning? It's much easier to trace a printer than an anonymous artist."

She acknowledged that with a quick nod.

"With the ledger there was a journal, written in code. Cressida tells me her father was in Spain with Wellington and heard about Bonaparte's diplomatic cipher, so decided to create his own. The entire journal is written in it. What sort of simple sergeant takes the time and effort to create his own cipher for a private journal?"

The ringing silence was answer enough. Angelique sat forward in her chair. "What is it you think of this simple sergeant?" she asked, ignoring the rest without a word.

"I think he's not so simple. Even with the printer's money, his income isn't enough to support his family in the style he preferred. The man's got debts all over town, and more in other towns. Cressida admitted he does that; she says he's got the devil's own charm and manages to talk his way around everyone. But the ledger indicates the debts were usually paid, eventually. The money just seemed to . . . appear. There are no entries indicating how he got it, just that he paid it out."

"I see you have talked your way around this daughter," Angelique said slyly. "Perhaps you have other motives for finding this sergeant, perhaps an important question you desire to ask him."

Alec stiffened. "That would be none of your concern, if it was true, and either way it has no bearing on anything I've told you."

She retreated at once, although a wicked smile still curved her lips. "Of course, of course! I only meant to tease. You are always so serious. One must find amusement in this business from time to time."

Alec waved it away. He hadn't seen much amusing in this assignment, and he did not want to be teased about his intentions toward Cressida. He leaned back in his seat and drummed his fingers on his knee. He wouldn't mention this possibility to Cressida, but he needed to tell someone. It was beginning to eat at him, for a multitude of reasons, but perhaps Angelique could see a flaw in the idea. He devoutly wished she would. "I wonder if Turner might be blackmailing people," he said abruptly.

The smile vanished from Angelique's face. She tilted her head, studying him closely. "Have you proof?"

"No."

Her eyebrow arched. "It is a large accusation to make."

"I know." Alec dug his fingers into the tight muscles at the back of his neck. "I would have suspected bribes, but Turner has no authority or power that would invite them. I suppose it could be theft, undertaken on his various expeditions, or forgery. He seems too memorable a personage to manage those, though; by all accounts he stands out in a crowd."

Angelique was tapping one finger against her lower lip. "What is in this journal? Have you found any evidence that would support your idea?"

"Cressida's begun working on it." Alec smiled ruefully. "I haven't the patience for ciphering. Never had.

But still, it's not the sort of thing you'd leave proof of, would you? Not unless you were a bloody idiot or the most arrogant fool alive."

She lifted her shoulders. "One must have proof in order to extort a good sum, so if you are correct, it must lie somewhere. You have searched the house, of course."

"Not a thorough search," he admitted. "They've lost the lease for lack of funds and . . . well . . . Julia's gone and invited them to stay here."

The knowing look she gave him made Alec want to scowl and scold her. It had been Julia who invited the Turners . . . even if he had deliberately mentioned their distress in front of Julia. Even if he had already kissed Cressida and invited her to stay at Penford. Even if his heart quickened and his blood heated at the thought of Cressida potentially around every corner he approached. He was drawn to her, no matter how he fought it, and he feared his restraint was crumbling against the constant press of that desire. It had been so long since he truly cared about a woman, Alec had almost forgotten it was possible.

But Angelique seemed to understand that this was not the moment to make sport of him. She simply smiled. "See what is in the journal," she said instead. "Perhaps it will explain the money."

"Of course." It would also give him an excuse for closer proximity to Cressida. Alec tried to quell the fierce surge of exultation at the prospect.

"Is that all?"

He closed his eyes. "No," he muttered, hating the word. "There is a possibility that Turner is dead."

"'Tis always a possibility," said Ian. "The man's been gone—what?—five months? It doesn't take but a minute to put a knife in someone's back."

"You have a suspect," said Angelique softly. "Who? And why?"

Alec hesitated again. He wished they had not come, not yet. "Turner's eldest daughter is newly engaged to his man, Thomas Webb. Webb came home from the army with Turner and has been with the family ever since. The daughter was married once before, to a man who beat her. Cressida said . . . she told me her father blessed that marriage because it would keep Webb from having her sister. And that Webb knew it."

"That is suspicion, nothing more."

"Of course not," Alec snapped. "But it is a possibility. Webb has never seemed particularly keen to find Turner. Every time I spoke to him about the man, he put me off or said he knew nothing."

"Would you be eager, in his place?" Angelique shrugged. "Perhaps he views it as Divine Providence. You said they were recently engaged, but the lady has no fortune and no great breeding; perhaps it is nothing other than desperate love. If he has been waiting for years while she was married to another man—"

"I realize all that!" Alec inhaled a deep, even breath. "I fervently hope that is so, Angelique. I don't believe Webb is pretending to love her. In truth, I think he adores her."

For a moment she was quiet. "Love is a powerful motivator," she murmured at last. "But if you have evidence . . ."

"No, I don't," he said in relief. "Not a scrap."

She smiled gently. "Then I think we cannot do anything."

Alec shook his head. He hadn't planned to do anything about it, but Angelique's agreement reassured him. She wouldn't hesitate to tell him if something changed her opinion. He recalled one other point that niggled at him. "What did you mean to say earlier about Hastings, Wallace?"

Angelique paused in the act of rising from her chair. Ian cleared his throat. "Ah. Not so much—more an impression, I suppose. He's been to the den, see." Ian usually called Stafford an old fox, and referred to his offices in Bow Street as the fox's den. "Bit of an odd one, if you take my meaning. Pompous and cold, but with nervous eyes."

"He's a Deputy Commissary General of the army," Alec said.

Ian's smile was flat and humorless. "All the more reason to suspect something's not right, if you ask me. But like you, I've got no proof, just that I've seen him at Bow Street. Angelique must know more. Old Staff's set his cap for her, has her round for tea all the time."

A delicate flush rose in Angelique's cheeks. "Nonsense," she said in her usual cool manner. "I know nothing about this Hastings."

Somehow Alec didn't quite believe her, but if she didn't want him to know, he would never learn it from her. Angelique had all the reticence of a sphinx when it suited her. He got to his feet as Ian did the same, now that Angelique was standing. "I hope you will stay for a few days," he said, more to be polite than because he wanted them to stay. He didn't like to see his two lives brought face to face like this. If he could have bundled Angelique and Ian off the property at once, he would have been very tempted to do so.

Angelique's smile hinted that she knew that. "*Oui,* a very few," she said. "Might I have the tea in my room?"

"Of course," Alec said. The maid was just tapping at the door with the tea tray. He went and opened it, instructing her to serve it in his guests' room.

"Do not worry, Alec." Angelique laid one hand on his arm as she passed him. "Not every puzzle can be solved."

He just gave a slight bow as she left with Ian, leaving unspoken his next thought: *Nor* should *every puzzle be solved.*

Chapter 23

Cressida almost missed dinner. She had spent the afternoon poring over Papa's journal and its infuriating code until her head ached. She knew it probably would amount to little, but pure stubbornness kept her at it for hours.

After Alec laid out the results of his efforts, she, Callie, and Tom had agreed together that Papa was probably gone for good, or at least until he wanted to be found. Even if something ill had befallen him, the result was the same. They also agreed it was unfair to ask Alec to keep searching, particularly with such thoroughness. Cressida had been slightly shocked when he explained all that he had done, all the places he had gone, and the avenues he had pursued. He truly had devoted an enormous amount of time— and, she suspected, money—to it. Tom and Callie were anxious to find a house in Portsmouth, and Granny's health had declined even more. She rarely left her bed now. If they waited too long, she might be too weak to make the trip, even though she had been overcome with happiness, and somewhat revived in spirits, at the news that Callie was to be married.

So while Tom went ahead to Portsmouth in search

of a house and Callie sat with Granny to sew her wedding dress, Cressida returned to the journal. She hadn't exactly told her sister she intended to stay at Penford, although she wondered if Callie might have begun to suspect something. Callie seemed to glance her way an inordinate number of times whenever she spoke to Alec—and, to Cressida's private exhilaration, he came to speak to her a great deal. Now even she couldn't deny that he looked at her often. She didn't want to. She wanted him to look as much as he might like.

And she didn't want to miss dinner. Since Alec was no longer riding far and wide in search of her father, he had dined with the family almost every night. She bundled her notes away, rushed through her dressing, and then hurried down the stairs.

Guests had arrived. Not neighbors, but a couple Cressida had never seen before. The man was a brawny, redheaded Scot with a ready laugh. The woman was petite and exotically beautiful, with sleek black hair and dark eyes. No one else seemed to know what to make of them, leaving only Mrs. Hayes and John to talk to them.

"Friends of Alec's," Julia murmured, coming up beside her. "They arrived unexpectedly a few hours ago."

"Oh." Cressida watched as Alec strode into the room. He glanced around, his eye catching and lingering a moment on her. He gave her a tiny, almost imperceptible smile before going to his mother's side and greeting the new guests.

"They came from London. Mother has been in a frenzy of curiosity to know how he knows them, but she'll never ask. Alec can do no wrong in her eyes."

"Julia," murmured Cressida.

She put up one hand. "I'm not angry, Cressida. I just don't know what to think about him anymore—and I believe he prefers it that way. He's decided to keep his secrets, and there is nothing I can do to change that." She looked at her brother as she spoke. The anger that had once heated her words about Alec was gone, replaced by something more like resignation.

Cressida shifted uncomfortably. She alone knew Alec's secret, it seemed. She longed to defend him, to justify and explain to Julia why he had been so silent. She longed to tell Julia that whatever his family had suffered, Alec had endured far, far worse, not just from the wounds that scarred his chest but from the damage to his character that still followed him, damage he had tried but been unable to repair. And most of all she longed to tell Julia that it was her duty as his sister to accept him anyway, whether he told her his secret or not. Cressida knew that if her father were to stroll into the room this moment, even after all she had learned about him and his actions, she would still run to embrace him and her heart would leap with gladness that he was well, because he was her father. For all Papa's faults, she couldn't help loving him. How much might it have meant to Alec if his sister had been able to set aside her hurt and anger, and do the same?

The guests were Mr. and Mrs. Wallace from London, stopping in for a few days on their journey north. Mr. Wallace was brashly charming, easily failing into conversation with everyone. His wife was quieter, but unsheathed a sharp wit when she did speak, her voice inflected with a lilting French accent.

Mrs. Wallace was seated next to Alec, and whenever she spoke, he paid strict attention to her every word. Mr. Wallace spared them no mind; at the other end of the table he was busy regaling the two Mrs. Hayeses and their daughters with tales of his native Scotland.

Cressida found herself watching Mrs. Wallace after dinner. There was something quietly watchful and alert about her, quite unlike her husband. That gentleman seemed to have a hundred tales and humorous stories, and he kept them all laughing. Although, for all Mr. Wallace's loquaciousness, neither he nor his wife had revealed much about themselves. Rather like Alec had done when he first returned to Marston . . .

The thought stopped her. Could they be, like Alec . . . ? But no; surely spies did not pay social calls on other spies. She glanced at Mrs. Wallace again, so darkly beautiful and polite as she listened to Mrs. Hayes. Could that delicate lady be a spy? Cressida tried to picture her in the part, then smiled at her own imagination. As if she even knew what spies did, let alone how the typical spy looked.

Thankfully the company retired early. The Wallaces had spent the day traveling, and John and his family were to depart on the morrow. After stopping to say good night to Granny, Cressida and Callie returned to their room.

"You're not planning to work on that now, are you?" Callie wrinkled her nose as Cressida took out the journal again after getting ready for bed.

She shrugged. "For a little while. I think I'm about to solve it. I can feel it."

Her sister sighed. "You and puzzles! Well, don't let me disturb you." She got into bed and opened a book.

Cressida pulled the chair up close to the writing desk and opened the journal. In a few minutes she had picked up where she left off earlier.

The code was frustrating her to no end. It appeared to be simple, and it surely was; more than once, she thought she had it solved only to see things fall apart as she applied her key to larger sections of the journal. If Papa's code had changed over the years, she wryly acknowledged, she might never get it. But she pressed on, tinkering with different passages and trying to fit the information into one encompassing model.

She had learned about codes from her father. Papa had an ear for languages, and whenever he came home he would try to teach her and Callie what he had picked up. Instead of telling them what he was saying, though, he would just speak to them in a Spanish dialect or Flemish. She learned to map some words by their proximity to other words, deducing "sister" by how often it occurred before or after Callie's name. This, she decided, was much the same. She had drawn up a list of battles and places to correspond to the dates, and had thus picked out a number of words, mainly places in the Peninsula that shed little light on the rest of the journal. But those small successes did reveal a few letters, and she had covered pages and pages with tentative translations that all ground to a halt eventually.

With a sigh, she picked up the journal and tried to look at it as a whole. It had its own language; perhaps she just needed to listen to its flow a bit more, and stop concentrating on the individual words. She let her eyes drift across the lines as if she were reading. One word kept snagging her eye, "sg." There were quite a few instances of it, and she thought it meant "an." She couldn't think of another two-letter word in English that occurred so often. But that implied some things about the words that followed it, and she hadn't been able to make that work. Cressida huffed in impatience, and rolled her head from side to side to stretch her neck. If only it were three letters. Then she would think it represented "the," which would eliminate so many of the problems she was having with vowels . . .

She raised her head as the thought sank in. What if . . . ? Her hand shaking with excitement, she tore another page from her sketchbook and tried it. Once she quit trying to force "an" from "sg," things fell into place. She counted letters again and realigned her mapping of them. And when she applied her new key to a paragraph chosen at random, the whole thing made sense. She made some corrections to her code—it seemed "sg" didn't always translate directly to "the," but only when it stood alone—and tried another paragraph. With a thrill, she realized that one also made sense, and she slapped her hands down on the desk and exclaimed in triumph.

Now all thought of sleep vanished. She opened to the beginning of the journal and began translating. In front of her eyes, the curtain lifted on her father's life in the army. He described the dirt and the heat, the drenching rainstorms and the paucity of good food. He wrote of the horrific slaughter of thousands of horses at Corunna as the British navy whisked the army away from being crushed by the pursuing French. He wrote of his fellow soldiers and the officers who sometimes led them, and sometimes sent them to certain deaths through sheer stupidity. He wrote of pomegranates and port wine and long brown Portuguese cigarettes, and the startling carnage created by Shrapnel shells. Every so often she had to make another small addition to her key, but overall the code was broken. When Cressida's hand cramped and she had to put down her pen, she was shocked to realize hours had gone by since she sat down to work.

Callie had blown out her lamp and was fast asleep. The house was quiet. Cressida simply had to tell someone, though. She pulled on her dressing gown, snatched up her papers and the journal, and slipped from the room, heading straight for Alec's study.

To her immense relief a line of light glowed under the door. She tapped gently, then pushed the door open at his muffled summons.

He rose from the wide mahogany desk, his hair rumpled and his cravat pulled askew. The desk was covered with papers and open books. "Come in," he said at once. "Is something wrong?"

She came into the room and closed the door behind her. "No, nothing is wrong. I've just made some progress in solving this code, and . . . well, I wanted to tell someone," she said with an embarrassed little laugh, catching sight of the clock. It was very late. He would think her demented over this journal. "I didn't realize it was so late. I don't want to be a bother."

"No, no, of course not. Since John is leaving, there's just more to be done." He pushed aside some of the clutter on his desk and motioned for her to come over. Cressida hurried forward to lay the book in front of him, eagerness banishing her hesitation.

"I realized it's a fairly simple rearrangement cipher," she said, leaning down to show him her notes. "At first I tried to match the letters to those that appear most often in English, but that always got snarled in the end. Just tonight I discovered a twist: not all these words map exactly. For instance, 'sg' represents 'the.' I've checked it through several pages and it seems to hold true unless the letters 't-h-e' are part of a larger word, like 'other,' and then it reverts to the rearrangement scheme. But I was able to translate two separate passages into sensible English, and then began in earnest. I think this is the correct key." She laid her much-annotated key on top.

Alec was frowning at the scribbled notes. "You mean the letters are simply out of order?"

She shook her head. "No, not quite. Think of it instead as a reassignment; an 'e' now means a 'k,' for example. Well, not always, but usually. I can see that he got better at it as time went on. In the beginning of the book"—she flipped open to a page near the front—"every letter is formed individually, as if he had to keep checking the key. But later, the words are written almost as if he knew this different alphabet by heart and didn't need to think before writing." She turned to the middle to show him.

He leaned forward, cocking his head as he studied the page. "What does he write of?"

Cressida pulled out the sheets where she had begun translating. "Army matters, and any other thing that interested him. Who has been promoted, rumors, battles, who has been killed. An argument between officers, and a soldier whipped for desertion. But I have only just begun, on entries from years ago. He talks of Corunna and Oporto."

"A decade ago." He sighed and propped an elbow on the desk. "How relevant is that?"

Cressida fell silent. In her excitement at solving the code, she had lost sight of the real purpose of the task. How could an army diary a decade old help find her father now? And, to be truthful, did she really want to anymore? What she did not tell Alec was the deeper implications in Papa's writings. He hadn't just kept a journal, he had kept notes on others. She couldn't help noticing that his remarks seemed to center on dishonorable activities, scandals and failures and incompetence. And one little note, so brief she hardly knew what to make of it, even appeared to hint that Papa might have been paid to keep quiet about those things.

It was possible that happened only once, when Papa interrupted some soldiers abusing a pair of local women and stealing from their farm. He had noted the penalty for their actions would be a fierce lashing, but then added, "they secured my discretion quite reasonably." She had first thought nothing of that, assuming the men were friends of Papa's whom he didn't want to see punished. But as she worked her way into the book, Cressida got the uncomfortable feeling that Papa's discretion had been secured more than once with money, and for larger and larger sums. And when it became a habit rather than a single instance, there was only one word for the person selling his discretion: blackmailer.

She hated even to think that word. He was her father, for heaven's sake, who loved her and her sister and sent them money every quarter and brought them sweets when he came home on furlough. If the money he sent them had come from . . . this activity, did that make her culpable as well?

But none of that was proven, and she didn't want to shame her father for things he might have done only a few times, years ago. When she had translated more of the journal . . . well, then she would decide what she had to do, depending on what she read.

"I don't know," she murmured in reply to Alec's question. "But I have only just begun translating."

"Perhaps as you move ahead in the book something more useful will come to light."

"Perhaps." She gathered up her notes. She knew his suggestion had merit but it was sobering nonetheless. No matter how hard she tried to ignore it, Tom's voice echoed in her head: *That book won't bring you peace.* Cressida had been telling herself she wanted the truth, peaceful or not. Could she keep this terrible a secret about her father, though? And did she want to? Would the knowledge that Papa might have been a blackmailer eat at her inside if she tried to conceal it? She headed toward the door, all her elation gone.

"Cressida."

She turned. Alec had risen to his feet. The lamp-light cast severe shadows on his face, drawing him in sharp angles and hollows. He looked tired. "Good work," he said with a slight smile. "It looked pure gibberish to me."

Her cheeks warmed in spite of herself at the compliment. "Oh no. It wasn't that difficult, but just took time."

His smile widened ruefully. "For you. I never had the patience to solve puzzles like that. Frederick would sit and work out problems and I . . . I would be off climbing trees and racing horses."

She smiled back. How odd it was to hear a man say, with admiration, that she had done something he couldn't have done—how odd, and how pleasant. "I have always liked a good puzzle."

"There seems to be no shortage of those." He sighed and turned back to his desk. Cressida looked at him, standing there so honorably, so decently, and felt something inside her shift. "Here," he said. "Don't forget this."

She blinked and tore her eyes from his. The journal. He was holding out the journal to her, the book she had hoped would answer her questions, and feared would confirm her father a scoundrel. She went back around the desk and reached for it. "Thank you," she said impulsively. "For everything."

"I've not accomplished what I promised you."

You have done far more, and I love you for it. The force of that thought shook her a little. "You have been my . . . friend," she said softly, hesitating a little over the word. "I appreciate that."

His eyes flashed her way, hot and focused. Cressida's heart almost tripped over itself at the naked desire burning in that gaze. "Friend" had been the wrong word, after all.

It rattled her. It exhilarated her. It burned away all her good sense about guarding her heart around him, and completely drove away any thought of going quietly back up to bed. *Nothing ventured, nothing gained.* All the yearning Cressida felt for someone who understood her, who valued her and admired her, for someone who made her heart leap and made her laugh even in her foulest mood, couldn't be contained anymore. Slowly she dropped the book back on the desk. With hands that were unnaturally steady, she reached up, turned his face back to her, then went up on her toes and kissed him.

His mouth was firm under hers, but soft at the same time. He returned her kiss, as gently as the day they had walked to the ridge, but never deepened it. His restraint made her feel bold; she wanted more, so she ran her hands up his chest to wrap her arms around his neck. The muscles of his shoulders tensed, and Cressida shivered as she realized how tightly leashed his strength was. How restrained he was.

Too restrained.

She ended the kiss and stared into his azure eyes. The desire she had seen there earlier was undimmed—he wanted her, she was sure of it. But then . . .

"What are you trying to do?" he whispered. The vein in his temple pulsed, but otherwise he seemed as calm as ever.

She tried to flash a coy smile, but it faltered on her lips. "I'm trying to seduce you."

He inhaled deeply. "Why?"

The blush burned her face. "Because I want to."

He raised one hand and touched her cheek, just barely, before his fingers slid around and up the back of her neck, cupping her nape. His grip tightened, drawing her close. Cressida swayed toward him, her eyes drifting closed as he leaned down and pressed his lips to her cheek, right at the corner of her mouth. "You should go to bed," he murmured against her skin.

She arched her neck, stretching against his hand. "Alone?"

He kissed the other corner of her mouth, his lips lingering over hers. "That would be best."

"It will be harder to seduce you that way."

His chest shook with silent laughter. "Don't you know you already have?"

She opened her eyes. He was smiling at her, a funny little rueful smile, and his thumb stroked her cheek. Cressida's stomach lurched as she realized how much she craved that smile and that touch. He didn't smile enough—and she thought she would never get tired of his touch.

"Prove it," she whispered.

His smile dimmed. "I shouldn't—"

She pulled on his shirt and kissed him, before he could say that she should go to bed, alone, again. He sucked in his breath and put his hands on her waist, as if to move her aside, but Cressida pressed against the firm wall of his chest and instead his arms went around her. She shuddered as their bodies fit together like two halves of a whole, and finally his control broke.

Up her back his hands went, a firm, sweeping stroke drawing her even closer. He caught the end of her braid and tugged. Cressida gasped, lifting her chin, and he brushed his lips against her neck, right at the base of her throat where her pulse beat wildly against her skin. Her head swam. This was intoxicating—and he was only kissing her neck and playing with her hair. His fingers were combing out her braid, and in a few moments her hair hung in a wild mess down her back, growing more tangled by the second as he plunged his hands into it, cradling her head and holding her face up to his.

Abruptly he scooped her up, boosting her to sit on the desk behind her. Her fingers tangled with his as they both pulled at the fastenings of her dressing gown, and then he stripped it from her arms. He kissed the curve where her neck met her shoulder, sucking at her skin until she shivered. He popped loose the buttons that held her nightdress closed, undoing them until he could push the worn fabric over her shoulders to her elbows. Then Alec pulled back until she opened her eyes and blinked at him, gloriously disheveled and aroused.

He was just looking at her, his gaze roving over her. Her skin pebbled into gooseflesh, from the chill of the air and the heat in his gaze. "Beautiful," he murmured, skating just the tips of his fingers over her collarbone. Cressida moaned, her body quivering at the whisper-light contact, and yanked at the constraining fabric, trying to free her arms to reach for him. Alec put his hands over hers, holding her palms flat on the desk. "Wait," he breathed, leaning in to kiss her lightly on the mouth. "Just wait . . ."

She felt acutely exposed as she was, sitting on his desk naked from the waist up. Every breath seemed to draw her skin tighter and tighter until she thought she might snap and break at the next touch. But he didn't touch her. His hands stayed on hers, trapping them in place while he lowered his head and began to taste her skin.

Cressida had never felt beautiful in her life. She was too tall, too plain, her hair neither blond nor brown, her eyes an odd shade of brown so light they sometimes looked almost yellow. Her figure was neither curvaceous nor willowy slim, and her feet were dreadfully large. But as Alec bent his head reverently to her shoulder, she felt, if not exactly beautiful, then desirable. Very desirable. And she liked it. That look on his face, taut and dark with desire for *her*, sent a tremendous rush of excitement through her. Granny had always told her and Callie never to trust a man when he was wild with lust, but this was not any man; this was Alec. She felt treasured and safe and even . . . yes . . . beautiful with him.

Suddenly he shoved himself up, away from her. "Oh God," he said, half in disgust, half in mortification. "Not on a desk." He turned to her almost desperately. "Will you come upstairs with me?"

Cressida's heart was beating so hard her whole body shook, and she wasn't sure her legs would support her. But she looked up at Alec, his expression almost fierce with desire as he waited for her answer. His short hair stood up where she'd run her hands through it, his chest heaved with every breath, and Cressida felt a heady mix of love and lust scald her veins. "I'd go with you anywhere," she whispered.

His eyes blazed. He seized her hand and pressed his lips to the inside of her wrist in a kiss so hot her eyes started to close. Then he pulled her off the desk and out of the room.

Chapter 24

Later, Cressida would be very thankful it had been so late at night. She and Alec hurrying through the house, hand in hand with clothing in disarray, must have made quite a sight. Twice Alec stopped abruptly to pull her into his arms for another deep, hungry kiss. By the time he shoved open the door of his chamber and led her inside, both were out of breath.

He let go of her hand and closed the door. "Are you certain?" he said quietly. His voice vibrated with barely leashed tension.

Cressida managed a small nod. "Yes."

With a soft click, he turned the key in the lock behind him. The key flashed in the dim light from the fire as he tossed it aside, but Cressida barely noticed that. Her hands curled and uncurled as he came toward her, unhurried but deliberate. She didn't move except to raise her chin and look him boldly in the face.

He touched her cheek, caressing her jaw. Cressida made no effort to hide the tremor that went through her; she loved the feel of his hands on her skin. She shrugged off her dressing gown, letting it fall to the floor. His breath hissed between his teeth. She tugged one sleeve of her nightdress, baring her shoulder right below his hand. He traced her collarbone and glanced at her with a rakish smile hovering about his mouth.

"I quite like being seduced," he murmured. Cressida had just a moment to blush at her own forwardness before he hooked one finger in the neckline of her nightdress and tugged the whole thing down over her shoulders.

Her breasts seemed to tighten and swell as his eyes traveled over her. Her skin tingled until she was wild for him to touch her. But Alec stepped back instead of falling on her, and stripped off his cravat and waistcoat though he never looked away from her. Cressida devoured him with her eyes even as she wanted to scream in frustration. When he reached for her again, she retreated a step, letting her hips sway and flashing him a coy smile. She quite liked seducing him, actually. The nightdress slid down to her hips, but she caught fistfuls of the fabric to keep it from falling further. He took another step, and so did she, away from him again. Then she bumped against the post of the bed, and he lunged.

Together they tumbled onto the bed. Cressida let go of her nightdress and began pulling at his shirt. He bent his head and kissed her right beneath her ear. The shirt came free of his trousers and she slid her hands underneath over his skin, so warm and alive as his muscles flexed and quivered. Dimly she registered the faint tracks of the scars she had seen that day in the library, but she barely thought of them.

It was Alec she loved, scarred or not, and he was proceeding far too slowly to satisfy her.

Alec's control was fast slipping. He didn't know why Cressida wanted to seduce him tonight; he didn't care. He was going mad over her, with her pert tongue and soft eyes and that contemplative way she looked at him with one corner of her mouth crooked upward and her head tilted to one side to tease him with the sight of her bare neck. Perhaps she had been contemplating . . . this, he thought, burying his hands in the silky fall of her hair. Lord knew he had thought about it long enough to be in danger of completely losing his head as she clung to him and ran her own hands over him. He wanted to make love to her tenderly, with all the decency and delicacy she deserved, and he wanted to rip the blasted nightdress away and ride her until they both expired from bliss. He suspected she wasn't a virgin, but he didn't *know*, and therefore he should be more restrained, if not call a halt to things altogether—

"I want to feel you inside me," she said in a throaty whisper that made him even harder and completely wiped away the thought of stopping. Her hands moved down and cupped him through his trousers, and Alec had to hold his breath to keep from coming right then. With a muttered curse he pushed her nightdress out of the way. Her knees rose beside him as he finally slid his fingers through the damp curls between her legs, right into the wet heat of her body. She arched her neck and her eyes rolled back in her head, and Alec was lost.

He wrenched off his boots and shed his trousers

and undergarments. She sat up and pulled the shirt over his head, and then she was in his arms again, her smooth, soft skin against his. He touched her again, but she was already wet, lifting her hips and pushing against his fingers.

"Please," she begged. She licked her fingertip and ran her hand over the plane of her belly to touch herself. Alec shuddered; the sight of her pleasuring herself was almost unbearable. He slid one finger, then two, inside her, stroking in and out while watching her swirl her finger over that secret, feminine spot until it seemed his eyes were burning. A fine sweat broke out on his brow and his hands shook. Abruptly he caught her hand, sucking her finger between his lips to taste her for a moment. She reached for him with her other hand, and he caught both her wrists, pinning her hands above her head as he finally took his erection in hand and thrust deep inside her.

Cressida gasped. Her arms tensed, but not enough to break his grip. He raised his head and paused, but she shook her head wildly. That gasp had been one of pure carnal pleasure. Incapable of speech, she hooked one leg around his waist and raised her hips to meet his next thrust.

It was needy and hungry, as if neither could hold back. He let go of her hands so he could cup her breast, flicking his thumb across the nipple before lowering his head to take it into his mouth. Cressida ran her hands over his shoulders and arms, scraping her nails along the muscles that bunched and stretched as he moved above her, inside her, filling her body and her heart.

She felt her climax begin to collect in her belly as her nerves strained taut. She gripped Alec's arms until she must have hurt him but instead he just kissed her deeply, and changed his rhythm, angling his hips to drive into her differently. She returned his kiss and felt tears slide down her cheeks as release crashed through her in a wave of heat. Alec's back went rigid under her fists and he shuddered in his own climax.

Neither moved for a while. Cressida kept her eyes tightly closed, clinging to the feeling of utter contentment and happiness. She didn't want to leave his arms, or this bed. It had been a risk—still was a risk—to make love with Alec, but it was one she wouldn't hesitate to take again. Again and again and again, if possible, and as often as necessary to secure his heart as he had secured hers. Cressida knew she was so deeply in love, she was willing to risk ruin and heartbreak for him.

Alec dragged up his head and looked down at her. Flushed with passion, smiling up at him as she held him in her arms, Cressida Turner was the most beautiful woman he had ever seen. He had been attracted to her from the moment she pointed a pistol at him in her stable. He had come to respect her strength, to admire her honesty and decency, to find her dry humor entertaining, to value her trust. Now he knew it was more than attraction and admiration. He was fascinated and charmed, unable to imagine life without her. Alec had never been a romantic, sentimental man, but when she smiled at him like this, his heart swelled with more happiness than he could ever recall feeling in his life.

"This is not over," he said through ragged breathing. "This is not enough. I want you—not just tonight—"

"I know," she murmured, smoothing her fingers through his hair. "I know, love." That word was balm on his soul. He wasn't making any sense anyway. With a deep sigh, he rested his cheek against her breast, listening to the rapid beat of her heart, and felt complete peace for the first time in years.

He came awake suddenly, with the sense that someone was watching him. From long habit Alec lay perfectly still, listening, only to realize within a minute who must be breathing beside him, watching him intently enough to wake him.

She had rolled onto her side and propped her head on one arm. Her hair fell in a glorious wild tangle around her bare shoulders and breasts. In the soft glow of dawn she was beautiful, and Alec's heart took an unexpected leap at the sight of her in his bed. He could quickly become accustomed to waking up to this sight.

But her eyes were somber, and her lush mouth turned down. Belatedly he realized she was staring at the long scars that crossed his chest. It had been too dark to see them when she pulled off his shirt.

"They don't hurt," he said. "Not anymore."

"They must have, once."

That was obvious. "Long ago."

Finally she raised her eyes to his. "You suffered much more than you want anyone here to know, didn't you?"

Alec shook his head. "Not from these." He touched the longest scar, the one that ran from his collarbone down over his ribs. "Not even this one."

"I don't believe you." She reached out. His muscles tensed as she touched him, running her fingers down the same scar.

"I was unconscious most of the time that one was at its worst."

Her face crinkled up a little, and even though she smiled he sensed her hurt. "You won't tell me, will you? You don't have to tell me; everyone has their secrets, and we're not even all that well-acquainted—"

Alec had to laugh then. "You can say that, as we lie here in bed naked together?" He turned onto his side, facing her, and brushed her hair back over her shoulder to expose her small, plump breasts. His hand lingered at her cheek, and her eyes half closed with pleasure. His body, already primed in the usual morning way, sprang to full arousal. God, how he could get used to this. He cupped the back of her alluring neck and rubbed slow, gentle circles. "I should say we've become rather intimately acquainted."

She looked away, blushing. "Yes, in that way. But that's not the same as knowing each other. Believe me, I know the difference."

He dropped his hand from her neck. "Of course," he murmured. "You're right." He took her hand in his and placed it on his hip, where the oldest scar began. "This one came in Portugal, after Vimeira. I came upon a French foot soldier who had stayed behind his regiment to loot. It's hard to say which of us was more surprised to see the other, but he panicked first, leaping at me like a madman and slashing out with his sword. I was too dumbstruck to do more than yell, and the scoundrel got away." He carried her hand to the long, faint line down his left forearm. "This was courtesy of a Spanish guerrilla whose aim wasn't all it ought to have been. He was most likely drunk as a lord, but he didn't even hit my shooting arm."

"Did you shoot him then?"

He shrugged. "Had to. The ball went off my arm into my horse's neck and killed the poor beast. I wasn't sure I could outrun even a drunk Spaniard with blood dripping down my arm."

She gave a shocked little gasp. "No!"

Alec grinned, a little shamefaced. "It's dreadful, isn't it? I didn't even kill the fellow. My hand was shaking so hard—from anger that he'd killed my horse, mind you—it was all I could do to pull the trigger. Fortunately for me, just returning fire was enough to send him running."

Her fingers ran along the track the ball had left. "Good," she said in a low voice. She touched the star-shaped mark above his hip. "And this?"

"Waterloo. A French lance." He looked at it. "I don't remember getting it."

"And this is also Waterloo, isn't it?" Slowly, she drew her finger along the longest slash, the one that probably would have taken off his head if the sword hadn't hit his collarbone. Alec knew how ugly it was. The flesh had knit, but not smoothly at all. Still, the light pressure of her finger over each bump and pucker seemed to send sparks across his skin.

He hadn't been a monk, certainly not in the army and not even in the last five years, but he had never been to bed with a woman who seemed so intrigued by every scarred, battered inch of him. In fact, after Waterloo, he'd never taken off his shirt to make love to a woman. But then, he had never really wanted to be acquainted with them; it had been a hunger to slake, nothing more. This was something more, and he found he wanted to tell Cressida about his deformities.

She had traced the scar to its end. "Yes," he said in answer to her question. "Nearly the last thing I remember about the battle itself. By then I had command of a brigade of dragoons under Uxbridge. We took them utterly by surprise when we charged; Bonaparte's men threw down their guns and fled in front of us. The charge was so successful many dragoons overshot the objective and wound up directly under the French guns. I was attempting to turn my men back into position when a cuirassier caught up to me." And for just a moment, he could feel again the icy burn of steel slicing his flesh and see the contorted face of the French cuirassier who slashed him. He had thought it might be the last face he ever saw, and remembered cursing that it had to be an ugly Frenchman instead of a pretty woman.

"It must have been dreadful," she whispered, feeling his involuntary flinch.

"It was," he agreed flatly. "Everything about Waterloo was dreadful."

"I'm so sorry."

"There's no reason to be. It's done and over with."

Alec shook off the memory, sinking back into the soft seduction of her touch and interest. "Although I never dreamed it would so fascinate you."

She smiled slowly—almost shyly. "*You* fascinate me." She shifted, somehow inching nearer. "What else?"

"Bloodthirsty wench," he said with a chuckle. "That's the worst of it."

"What about your back?" He blinked, and she slipped one arm over him to stroke his shoulder. Alec winced as her palm crossed the marks left by the splinters of an earl's town coach blown apart by a powder keg. He'd almost forgotten about those scars, which somehow were even more disgusting to him. He was glad the marks of his spying were on his back, where he never had to see them even if he could still feel them.

Cressida snatched her hand away at his expression. "I'm sorry," she said hastily. "I shouldn't have—"

"No." He sat up and twisted to turn his back to her. Even in the weak early light, she saw dozens of tiny scars spattered over his broad back. Unlike the others, none of these looked lethal or dangerous, but there were so many of them . . . "In London," he said, watching her over his shoulder. "Just several weeks ago."

She gasped. "In London! But how—?"

"Spying is little better than the army, in that regard." He put his hands on his thighs and shrugged. "I had supposed there was less chance of being blown up, but then I was caught in the middle of an assassination attempt, and nearly didn't escape it. If not for another agent shouting a warning to me,

I would have been standing right next to the powder keg when it exploded."

"What happened?"

"I was assigned as a footman to an earl's household. Some rabble wanted to kill him—and they nearly did so, not fifty yards from Carlton House." She gaped at him. Alec smiled grimly. "So you see, perhaps you have not been sent the most successful agent. They ought to have sent Sinclair to help you. He unraveled the whole plot, and saved the earl's daughter in the bargain."

"But the earl?"

He shrugged again. "I dragged him down the street as far as I could and then fell on top of him when the keg exploded. There's a bloody lot of wood in a coach; I thought it would never stop falling, and finally a bit of it caught me just right on the head. Or so they told me later. I seem to have a knack for getting in the way of anything dangerous."

She rose up on her knees and put her arms around his shoulders before pressing a long, soft kiss at the back of his neck. "I'm glad they sent you," she whispered. "I would have shot that Sinclair man on sight in my stable."

Alec smiled. He shook his head. Then he broke into real laughter. "I doubt it. Harry's a better-looking chap, and he's got the devil's own charm with ladies—although now that he's to be married, I'm sure his wife will be very pleased you never had the chance to shoot him at all. But enough about my misadventures." He twisted suddenly, and the next thing Cressida knew she was flat on her back with him looming over her. Her heart kicked hard against her ribs as his brilliant blue gaze moved over her. "Do you have any scars?"

"No," she said. "I thought I did, here"—she touched her breast, right above her heart—"but it's small and old."

His absorbed gaze moved from where her hand lay to her face. "The navy lieutenant."

"Yes." Even now she felt a twinge of humiliation. "His name was Edward," she said. "He was very dashing, and so charming. My sister had just married, and I was left much to my own devices. When he asked me to marry him . . ." She paused to gather herself. "Well, it was the first time a man paid me any attention and it went to my head. I was very foolish."

Something in her voice must have given her away, for his expression grew still and dangerous. She forced a smile. "By the time he told me we couldn't be married after all, I feared I was with child. Granny had warned us and warned us about girls who let gentlemen have their way, and there I was, about to disgrace myself and her."

The muscles of his arms and shoulders flexed. Something changed in his face, subtly but ominously. "Any man who leaves a woman in that condition," he said quietly, "should be shot."

Her heart fluttered. "That *is* when I learned to use a pistol," she told him. "But a week later, when I knew I was not expecting his child, I was glad he had gone. I was a fool, and I learned a hard lesson, but I didn't have to pay for years and years . . ."

"Like your sister did," he finished for her.

She gave a tiny nod. "Yes."

He touched the spot above her heart, his hand sliding naturally around her breast as he stroked her skin, almost as if to rub away the hurt. Her breath caught. "I can't feel the scar there at all anymore," she murmured.

He smiled, a wolfish, predatory smile. "That's the way of it, when they heal." He molded his fingers to her flesh, pinching up her nipple between his thumb and forefinger and sending a ripple of shudders down her spine. "Has it healed?"

Cressida arched into his caress. "Yes," she said breathlessly.

"Are you certain? Perhaps I should check." He lowered his head, and her hands fisted in the sheets as he kissed her there, his breath hot on her skin. *It's healed*, she thought as his mouth moved over her breast with tantalizing slowness. *Completely, now that you're here.* She cupped her hands over his shoulders, holding him to her. Already warmth was spreading through her as he licked her nipple, then caught it between his teeth lightly.

He rose up on his knees and sat back. For a moment he paused, surveying her spread before him with unmistakable male appreciation. Of course they had already made love and his hands had been all over her—even inside her—but it had been dark then; Cressida blushed and squirmed, self-conscious at being so bare before him.

"Don't," he said, catching her hand when she made a motion to cover herself. "I want to see you."

"I'm not much of a beauty," she said, then wished she had kept her mouth closed. Why would she want to point that out to him now?

He raised his eyebrows. His hands were running down the insides of her thighs in a very distracting manner. "I beg to disagree. No—that is insufficient. You are absolutely, utterly wrong to say that when I find every inch of you beautiful."

"Every inch?" She couldn't help laughing.

"Indeed." He took hold of her ankle. "Lovely ankles, trim and neat." He stroked her calf. "Slim, strong legs, well-turned with exercise." She laughed as he palmed her hips in his hands. "Lovely hips," he said fervently. "A perfect waist." She tried to push his hand away, and he brought her fingers to his lips. "Elegant hands, but strong and capable. Also very steady, which is helpful when aiming a pistol." Cressida cringed, and he grinned. "Arms, the perfect length and diameter. Beautiful breasts . . ." He cupped one lightly. "More than beautiful, now that I consider the point." Still fondling her, he cocked his head. "Stunningly beautiful."

Cressida smiled, knowing her face must be four shades of red. She was not used to being admired, let alone so brazenly. It was arousing and awkward at the same time, but he stole another piece of her heart with his playfulness.

"And I could look at your face for the rest of my life and never grow tired of it." She gaped at him, and he leaned down to press a kiss on her mouth. "Even if you will persist in looking at me as if I've just gone mad."

"Perhaps you have," she exclaimed.

"Ah." His eyes twinkled at her. "If this is madness, there is method in it." Now he lowered himself until they were face to face, her breasts pressed into his chest, his arms tucking around her shoulders to hold her snugly under him. She felt cocooned in his strength, and the warmth in his eyes made her heart stutter. "But the most beautiful part of you," he murmured, "is here." He laid one finger on her lips.

"My mouth?"

"Your spirit." He kissed her. "Your wit." He kissed her again. "And yes, your mouth, which drives me to distraction daily." This kiss was deep and long, and fairly melted her bones. She ran her hands over him, exploring his body with no less enthusiasm than he explored hers until they were both short of breath.

He grabbed a pillow and pushed it under her hips. Cressida started to sit up, not knowing what he intended, but Alec pressed her back into the mattress, his face harsh. He sat back on his heels and caught her knee in one hand, taking a quick, nibbling kiss of the soft skin at the inside before hooking it over his elbow and dragging her closer to him.

Cressida watched, hardly daring to breathe, tensed in anticipation as he licked his thumb and then brought it to that tender, throbbing place between her legs. At the first touch, her hips jerked up and she gasped. Alec held her knee in an iron grip, refusing to let her wiggle away from his maddeningly soft touch. Cressida whimpered in ecstasy, trying to push against him, but he held her still.

Heat began to course through her. She tossed her head from side to side and writhed on the sheets, clutching at them since she couldn't reach him. And every time she looked at him his electric blue eyes were trained on her, fierce with want.

Then he moved, sliding forward and slowly entering her. She was almost sobbing now, waiting for him to plunge into her and ease the ache, but he didn't. He rocked in and out, slow and hard, and the whole while his fingers stoked the fire in her blood until she felt herself coming apart. He must have felt it, too, for he drove deep inside her then, holding himself tightly against her as her climax broke.

He released her knee, and she curled her trembling legs around his waist as he lowered himself to ride her with deep, powerful thrusts. He sucked in his breath and she felt him surge and swell within her, sparking a few lingering contractions of her own release. The tension went out of his back, but he moved once, twice, three times more before settling on top of her with a drained, sated sigh.

"Pure beauty," he mumbled, nuzzling her neck.

Cressida smiled, stretching like the well-satisfied woman she was. "Pure madness."

His chuckle was a rumble in his chest. "Perhaps, but I said there was a method in it."

"Oh?"

"Yes, indeed." She waited, but he said no more. Some of the blissful daze cleared from her mind. What did he mean?

But she was afraid to ask. And when she opened her eyes, she realized the sun was rising. It would be day soon, and she was still lying naked and wanton in his bed.

"I—I had better go," she whispered. "My sister will wake soon."

He raised his head and squinted at the window. "Ah."

In silence he moved, letting her get up. She had to hunt for her nightdress, finally locating it under his boots. Alec said nothing as she pulled it on; he lay back on the pillows and watched her with that stare that had once so unnerved her. Now she just smiled at him and pulled on her dressing gown as she went to the door.

But it was locked, and the key was not in the lock. She looked around, but it was not on the floor by the door, or anywhere else she could see.

"What is it?"

"The key," she whispered.

The bed ropes creaked as he got out of bed. Cressida peered anxiously under a table, and then the key appeared in front of her, lying on his outstretched palm. "Thank you," she said softly, reaching for it.

"Until later," he said, holding tight to the key. "Will you walk with me this afternoon?"

She wet her lips. "Didn't I tell you last night? I would go anywhere with you."

His mouth curved. "Thank you." He leaned in to kiss her as he dropped the key into her hand.

Cressida could only smile dreamily back at him. She had never realized love could make a person so happy about the slightest thing. "Thank you," she said, "for the most beautiful night of my life." She turned the key in the lock and slipped out of the room, before she forgot herself once more.

Later, after he had washed and shaved, Alec left his room, feeling as though he had opened a door to a new life. The scars of his past still marked him, but not as before. It wasn't the physical wounds that had pained him as much as the wounds on his soul, and Cressida's understanding and acceptance spread salve on those. He would never be the same man he was before Waterloo, but that was beside the point. He had been chasing a ghost, telling himself that if he could only prove his innocence, everything would be restored as it was before. Finally, at long last, he realized—and acknowledged—it was a lie. *He* knew he had not spied for the French, Cressida believed him, and that would be enough. A long life stretched in front of him, hopefully a happy one. He would be a fool to ruin that chance by clinging to anger and despair about a fact he could not change.

He met his mother at the bottom of the stairs. "Good morning, Mother." He kissed her cheek.

She blinked in astonishment at such a warm greeting. He resolved to be a better son, one she deserved. "Good morning, Alexander. May we have a word?"

"Of course." He extended his arm and they went into his study.

Mother clasped her hands and drew herself up. "I am very sorry to have to say this to you," she said gravely, "but I must. One of the maids said she saw Miss Turner leaving your chambers early this morning, in her nightclothes. I do not wish to interfere in your affairs, but Miss Turner is still an unmarried woman, and our guest. It pains me to reprove you, dear—"

Alex grinned. "Then don't. Mother, rest easy; I hold Miss Turner and her reputation in the highest possible regard."

She looked uneasy. "The servants will gossip. I scolded the girl at once for spreading tales, but I am not sure I can stop them from whispering about it among themselves . . ."

"They won't for long," he told her, still grinning like a schoolboy. "I intend to marry her."

Chapter 25

That day was one of upheaval, as John and his family left. Even Marianne, who spent most of her time in the nursery with her children, came to bid them farewell. Alec shook his cousin's hand, recognizing how much he owed the man. Without John, Penford would have been sorely neglected for the last several months, and no man could have been more gracious in the face of such crushing disappointment.

"Thank you," he said.

John's grin was wry. "Think nothing of it. I could do no less for my aunt."

"I am forever in your debt, and for far more than the comfort you gave my mother."

"I am sure you would have done the same, had our positions been reversed." Too late John realized what he said; his face flushed, and his eyes veered away.

Oddly, Alec didn't feel the sting this time. In fact, it might have been the greatest compliment John could have paid him, presuming Alec's honor equal to his own. "Of course. I hope you still consider Penford partly your home. Your family will always be welcome here."

John cleared his throat, still awkward. "We do, thank you. Good-bye, Alec."

Alec walked with him to the waiting carriage. He helped his aunt inside, then stood back to wish them all safe journey, and the coach was off. His mother and Marianne went back into the house, but Julia waved her handkerchief until they had turned at the end of the long drive.

"The house will be so quiet now," she remarked when all that remained was a cloud of dust to mark the passing of the coach. "First John, Aunt Hayes, and Emily, and soon Cressida and her sister and grand-mother will be gone."

Alec smiled to himself. "Oh?" he murmured. "Will that bother you?"

She sighed. "Yes. Perhaps it would bother you as well, were you ever here." She turned and went back into the house.

Alec let her go; he planned to be around much more in the future, but not, he hoped, to be bothered by Cressida's absence. He stood in the sunshine for several minutes, just admiring Penford. It was his home again, where he would bring his bride, and, God willing, raise his children. He had never thought of all that. Penford had not been his house, and he hadn't thought of marriage until now. The prospect was a very pleasing one. He took a full breath, and set off to hurry through the daily business before meeting Cressida.

Callie was just rising when Cressida slipped back into their room. She looked shocked for a moment, but said nothing. Cressida was sure every sinful pleasure had left some sort of mark on her, but when she looked in the mirror it was more a glow of happiness. In fact, she looked remarkably well for such a wicked woman.

"Will you come see Granny this morning?" Callie asked her.

"I do every morning," Cressida exclaimed.

Her sister pursed her lips. "I thought you might have other plans today."

She gaped at her sister in hurt, then looked down. "You can tell, can't you," she said quietly. "What I've done."

"No," said Callie after a moment. "I have a strong suspicion, though . . ."

Cressida rubbed her toe over a vine woven in the carpet. "I've gone and fallen in love." Callie gasped. "And I spent the night with him."

"Are—Are you—? Cressida, do you know what you're doing?"

She bit her lip, still concentrating on the vine. Callie alone knew the extent of her indiscretion years ago with Edward, and Cressida heard the worry in her sister's voice. No doubt this appeared much the same as that circumstance to Callie, but then, Callie didn't know Alec and how completely unlike Edward he was. "We are to go for a walk this afternoon."

"For what purpose?"

Cressida shrugged sheepishly. "I don't know."

Callie closed her eyes and said nothing for a long minute. "Then I shall reserve judgment until you return." She drew herself up. "I must know whether I should hate him with every fiber of my being and send Mr. Webb to fight him, or love him as my brother."

Cressida blushed, then she laughed. "I certainly hope it is the latter!"

Her sister smiled wryly. "So do I. For your sake, so do I."

After breakfast with Granny, Cressida couldn't sit still. She and Callie had agreed they would say nothing to Granny, who was still enraptured over Callie's engagement and didn't notice Cressida's quiet manner. What *did* Alec want to say to her on this walk? She wasn't so bold as to expect a marriage proposal, and he had already invited her to stay at Penford. She would rather go to Portsmouth with Callie than stay with fanciful hopes that had no firm basis. Then she thought of leaving, and wanted no part of that, either, but after that the alternatives grew sparse. What would he say to her?

To keep her mind from running over and over it until she drove herself mad, she turned back to Papa's journal, carrying it to the warm, bright conservatory to work. Her speed in translating steadily increased, even as her dismay mounted. There was no doubt now in her mind that Papa had been a sly opportunist, at best. He still wrote of the conditions of the army in Spain, but more and more described crimes and sins. He never used proper names, but referred to people by various nicknames, like the Scottish officer he called Owl and another man he named Hedgehog. Papa had discovered Owl abusing a Spanish boy, and Hedgehog had been stealing from the payroll funds—a portion of which ended up in Papa's pocket for his silence. Her stomach turned as she read on; Papa was quite unconcerned about his venality. More than once he wrote of his disgust for their activities, a sentiment Cressida shared. But it made her sick to her stomach to read how blithely he received money to keep other men's secrets despite that.

Callie came to share tea with her at some point, and asked how she was progressing with the journal. Cressida knew her sister asked more out of politeness than because she was truly curious about the journal, but she wouldn't have wanted to tell Callie anyway. Since her engagement to Tom, Callie had been so happy. This news about Papa would only upset her and make her worry. Now Cressida realized how right Tom had been about it not bringing her peace, and when Callie had gone, she even considered putting it aside. Unfortunately, it had become a splinter in her mind, nagging to be exposed no matter how much pain it caused. She kept at it, but resolved to burn every translated page when she had finished.

It wasn't until she reached the autumn of 1812 and Burgos, though, that she read the worst. That year the British army had marched through Spain in pursuit of the French army, and Wellington had set his sights on Burgos, a fortress in French hands. The army laid siege to the town, but only lost men by the dozen as every attempt at storming it failed. Cressida remembered Alec calling it a complete waste. Now here was her father, laboring to dig trenches that only brought them under the range of French sharpshooters. Papa cursed the general who put them there, and then one night he made only a small note.

"Met an interesting man today," he recorded. "Charming fellow from the other side."

Cressida frowned at that. What other side? Surely not the French side . . . She worked on, in deepening dismay. By the time Alec tapped on the door, she felt physically sickened by her father's actions, no matter how long ago. But when she looked up at Alec and saw the warmth of his smile, she managed to smile back.

"I came to claim our walk, but I fear the rain may spoil it," he said, coming in to sit beside her.

"Oh?" She turned to the tall windows. The sky had grown dark, as if evening had fallen early. "I didn't even notice."

He grinned. "Caught up in ciphering, eh?"

Her smile faded, and she fiddled with the pen before putting it down. "I wish not. It hasn't been very rewarding."

"I shall steal you away from it, then." He took her hand and brought it to his lips. "Perhaps you will walk with me in the gallery instead of the outdoors."

"Anywhere," she said.

He was kissing the inside of her wrist, brushing his lips across the tender skin there. "What has distressed you?" She hesitated, and he glanced at the journal. "Something in there?"

Cressida nodded, then held out the pages she had just translated. "It's dreadful. I don't know what to do about it." Alec gave her a curious look, then released her hand and took the pages.

She knew what he would learn. Her father had somehow met a French officer, and been lured into sharing what he knew of the British army's disposition. Then, in pursuit of additional funds, he had persuaded another soldier, a man of superior rank, to do the same with his greater store of knowledge about Wellington's army.

Alec smoothed the sheets and began to read. As she watched, the thoughtful crease between his eyes vanished. Faster and faster his eyes raced, and his fingers grew clumsy as he turned the page to read to the end. "Are you certain of this translation?" he demanded hoarsely. "Absolutely certain?"

"I— Y-Yes," she stammered, thrown by his demeanor. She had expected disgust, even anger, but he was as pale as snow. "Why?"

"This was in your father's journal?"

"Yes," she said in a small voice. "It is horrible. I cannot bear to think of it—"

Alec lurched to his feet and strode across the room. The door flew back and hit the wall behind it when he threw it open, making Cressida jump again. Shame suffused her. Her father was a traitor, a liar, and worse, he had enticed someone else into doing the same . . .

Her mouth fell open as the obvious conclusion came to her. Dear Lord. She had been so miserable thinking of her father's sins, she had completely forgotten about Alec. But her father was in the infantry; Alec was in the cavalry. And he had said he never knew her father at all. She shoved her hands into her hair and gripped her head, trying to physically hold back her thoughts. Alec had never told her exactly how he came to be thought a traitor, and the events Papa wrote of happened almost a decade ago, years before Waterloo. She couldn't see the connection . . . but something had sent him storming through the halls.

She jumped up and ran after him. He was striding through the corridors and calling his mother's name. "What is it?" she cried.

He shook his head, walking past her. "Mother?" He raised his voice and called again. A footman rushed up. "Where is Mrs. Hayes?" he demanded. The flustered servant stammered that he did not know. Alec motioned him away impatiently and continued down the corridor, pulling open every door he passed.

"Why are you shouting?"

Alec swung around to face Julia as she stepped out of the music room. He ignored her question. "After Waterloo, my things were sent home. You told me that." Julia frowned, but nodded. "Where are they? Did Mother dispose of them?"

"No." She glanced at Cressida, hovering anxiously behind him. "She refused to look at them, and had it all put away."

"Where, Julia?"

"In the attic," she said, her voice rising in surprise at his urgency. "Why?"

He pushed past her into the music room and came out a few moments later with a pair of lit candles. He shoved one at her. "Show me."

Julia looked at Cressida, who knew she must look as astonished as Julia did at this command. "It will be as black as Hades in there, and filthy, too. What do you need so desperately?"

He closed his eyes and took a shuddering breath.

When he opened them he looked right at Cressida. "I need to find my trunk," he said, a little more calmly. "Now."

After a moment Julia nodded. Without another word she led the way through the house, up a flight of stairs and through a series of corridors to a narrow door. Alec pulled back the bolt that held it closed, and then heaved the door open with a screech of the hinges.

The other side was indeed as black as Hades, and the air was hot and thick with dust. Cressida stepped carefully, staying close behind Alec as they followed Julia past old furniture, trunks, heaps of discarded clothing, and other detritus accumulated by the Hayes family over the decades. She stumbled into him when he stopped abruptly, and he took her hand in his for a moment and gave it a quick squeeze. Just that touch gave her heart. Whatever her father might have done to him, directly or indirectly, he wasn't blaming her.

Yet.

"It should be here somewhere," Julia said, holding her candle high and turning in a circle. "No one will have touched it since then, so we may have to—" She broke off with a gasp as Alec heaved a trunk over onto its end and bent down to examine the one beneath it. The crash shook the floorboards.

"What did they send back? My campaign trunk, the small brown one, or just the larger ones?" Alec fought down the urge to toss over everything in the attic until he found his trunks. There was a good chance what he sought wouldn't be here. Most of his baggage had been left in quarters in Brussels before the battle; only his smallest trunk had been near the battlefield, carried along with the other officers' private belongings. That trunk might have been lost, or looted, or simply forgotten in the confusion. But George Turner's words, leaping off the page in Cressida's neat writing, had finally shed light on the accusation of treason that had dogged him since Waterloo.

Turner didn't name his British officer, but he described him. With a mixture of elation and horror, Alec recognized the man in Turner's account. He didn't want to, but he did—and the sickening feeling jarred a recollection from the crevices of his memory. The night before the battle, he had seen Will Lacey. They had huddled together in the rain and shared a smoke, trying to keep warm and talking of what the morning would bring, not knowing it was the last time they would ever see each other. At the end, Will had given him a letter, a common practice among soldiers before a battle. No doubt someone had sent his mother the letter Alec had written for her in the event of his death. But Will's letter . . . With unnerving clarity, he remembered taking it and promising to see to it. Of course he hadn't been able to, but that letter . . . that letter might still be in his things. One way or another, it might answer his questions, about himself and now about Will. It also might not, but he had to *know*.

Julia, though, knew none of that, and Alec was too wild with impatience to explain. "Stop it," she exclaimed. "What are you doing?"

"Julia," he said, practically vibrating with the need for action, "I need to find that trunk. *Now*."

A cool hand touched his. "We'll look over here,"

said Cressida. She took the candle from him. "Julia, perhaps you could look over there."

Alec sucked in a deep breath to get a better grip on himself. "Yes, Julia, please."

His sister still stared at him aghast, but at Cressida's suggestion she slowly nodded. "All right." The room grew darker as she moved off with her candle.

"What does it look like?" Cressida tucked her hair behind her ears and looked around the circle of light they stood in. "Goodness, there are a lot of trunks in here."

Alec looked at her, standing in the middle of the stuffy attic with cobwebs in her hair and dust streaking her gown, not questioning his urgency or motives, but just ready to help—and he felt his chest tighten. There wasn't another woman in the world like her. He had fallen, completely and irrevocably. "It's leather," he said. "Reddish brown, about so large, with my name painted on it."

She glanced at the dimensions he sketched with his hands. "Officers take a lot of baggage," was her only reply before she turned and started poking through the piles of stuff behind her. Incredibly, Alec felt a small smile cross his face, and then he joined her, borrowing the candle from time to time to get a better look in some shadowed corner.

After half an hour, Julia's voice called out from the far eaves. "I've found it." She sneezed, the sound muffled in the cluttered room. "I think."

Alec wound his way through the attic to her, Cressida close behind him. His heart seemed to pause in his chest as he raised his candle over the small, grimy trunk, darkened now with dust but very definitely his old campaign trunk. He had carted it across Spain, Portugal, and into Belgium, learning to send most of his baggage ahead with a servant while keeping the most necessary items with him in this trunk, which was small enough to carry over one shoulder or on the back of a saddle.

He knelt down in front of it, jiggling the latch out of instinctive habit more than conscious memory. It had been dropped in a river outside Oporto, he recalled suddenly, and the latch had stuck ever since. For a moment the intervening decade fell away, and he felt again the relief at opening the trunk to see his things safe after all. Just as he hoped they would be now. Julia and Cressida huddled behind him, holding the candles up to illuminate the contents as he lifted the lid.

It had been packed in a hurry, and clearly not disturbed since; a spare waistcoat was crumpled across the top, and when he removed it, the rest of the contents were all a-jumble, as if they had been dumped inside with no thought or care. No one wanted to waste time packing up a traitor's effects, he thought, lifting out shaving items, stockings, a dented flask. He took out a small tin lantern, useful for checking on his horse in rainy weather, and lit it, leaving the shutters wide open for more light.

"What are you looking for?" Julia whispered. Cressida murmured something to her, and she didn't ask again. Alec ignored them both, too concentrated on his task.

He found his writing portfolio, the red leather cracked and dried. A small pot of ink, also dried up. He set everything aside in a growing pile on the floor.

With increasing despair, Alec dug through the trunk, past candle stubs and spare buttons and dirty linens, stiff and musty. It wasn't here. It must have been overlooked, forgotten or misplaced, even stolen—and then all would be lost—

Cressida saw his shoulders stiffen as he uncovered a small book, and unconsciously she held her breath. Was this what he sought? Slowly he reached in and took out the book, which she could see now was a journal. Her stomach twisted as she remembered the trouble her father's journal had unleashed. She groped for Julia's hand and pressed it, watching anxiously as Alec flipped open the cover.

For several minutes he paged through the book. She saw pages of writing, a few sketches, sometimes a column of numbers. Once a dried flower fell out, still vivid red. His expression somber, Alec picked it up and tucked it back into the book before turning more pages. With great difficulty Cressida resisted the urge to fidget, and bit her tongue to keep from bursting out with a dozen questions. Julia was wiggling one foot impatiently, but also was holding herself in check. As their nerves grew tighter, he only seemed to grow more deliberate. When he sat back on his heels and stopped to read a page, she almost jumped up and snatched the book away, even though she had no idea what he was looking for or where it might be.

Finally, just as she couldn't bear it anymore and opened her mouth to ask, he flipped the pages to the back of the book. There was a letter there, folded and sealed and slightly wavy, as if the paper had been wet and then dried. Carefully he slid one finger beneath the seal and unfolded it, setting down the journal without a second glance. Cressida and Julia looked at each other and hardly dared breathe, waiting as he read.

From her position opposite him, Cressida could see his face as it slowly changed from grim and tense to an expression of abject grief. Whatever was in that letter, she didn't want to know; the bottomless sorrow in Alec's eyes was wrenching to behold. When he closed his eyes and bowed his head, she felt her eyelids prickle with tears. In a burst of panic she said a quick, desperate prayer that whatever it was, her father had nothing to do with it, even though deep in her heart she was terribly sure he did.

"I put it here to keep it safe." His voice seemed to echo from the depths of a tomb. "No one knew . . ."

"What is it?" Julia whispered again, sounding as cowed as Cressida felt. Now neither was wriggling with impatience or anything else, but sitting stone-still and clutching the other's hand.

He didn't respond. Leaving the contents of the trunk strewn about the attic floor, he got to his feet and began picking his way toward the door. Cressida exchanged a nervous glance with Julia before they seized the lights and hurried after him.

Chapter 26

He was halfway down the stairs by the time they caught up to him. "What is it?" Julia asked for the third time. "Alec, you're frightening me. What did you find?"

He just shook his head. Julia stopped. "Alec!" Still he ignored her. She turned to Cressida. "What on earth?"

"I don't know," she said, watching him disappear toward his chamber. "But I don't think this is a good time to ask."

"It was a fine time to go rummaging about the attic," Julia protested. "It must be something!"

Cressida just gave her a helpless look, then followed Alec, slipping into the room as he opened the wardrobe.

"What did you find?"

He pulled out a coat and tossed it on a chair, stripping off the coat he wore. "An old letter."

Cressida chewed the inside of her cheek, then forced herself to speak. "It—It's about my father's diary, isn't it?" He didn't reply, rummaging around in a drawer. "Do—Do you know what he spoke of?

The man who . . ." Words failed her, and she stopped. If Alec were somehow the man in her father's journal, it proved his guilt. Her father's as well, but that was immaterial; he was gone, while Alec was still here to bear the shame and disgrace, and her heart was splitting in two at the thought. "I can burn it," she said a little wildly. "No one else has ever seen it—it was in code, not even Tom knew what was inside—"

"You don't have to burn it, Cressida." He took a knife from the drawer and slid it into a sheath with a strap attached. To her alarm, he swung the strap over his shoulder and buckled it, settling the knife and sheath under his arm. "Translate the rest of it. I daresay it will answer all your questions." He put on the coat he had just taken out, patted the pockets and ran his palms down the sleeves, and strode past her to the door. The dagger under his arm made the barest ridge, although to Cressida's panicked eyes it looked to be the size of a battle saber.

"Where are you going?"

"To see a dear family friend."

She wedged herself between him and the door to block his path. "Why? Tell me, damn it. It involves my father in some way—do you think I'm a complete fool? I translated that journal; I know what it said. Are you—" Her voice shook appallingly. It was impossible, but she had to ask anyway. "You *can't* be that man, the one he described."

His jaw hardened. "No."

She almost sobbed with relief. "Then what? Don't brush me aside like this. What caused you to go running off to search the attic for a trunk you could have had brought down any time in the last month?"

The dark, focused look faded a bit from his face. "Cressida, let me pass."

She set her chin. "Not until you tell me where you are going, and why you need a dagger."

Alec exhaled through his teeth. "Later. I will explain, I swear to you I will. Just . . . not at this moment." She shook her head, holding tight to the doorknob and refusing to yield. He ran one hand through his hair and swore under his breath. "I fear—I believe I know who your father describes. He . . . was a friend of mine. I thought I knew him, and yet he betrayed everything: not just his country, but his family and everyone who loved him."

"Including you?" Her question was just a breath of sound.

His shoulders tensed. "Yes."

"But this doesn't need to be done now," she cried. "Wait until tomorrow. Tell the army—write to Lord Hastings and have him send someone else to deal with it!"

"Cressida." With unbearable tenderness he touched her cheek. "For five years my life hasn't been my own. I lost everything, not just my reputation but my family, my name, my very honor."

"I know," she whispered, a tear rolling down her face. "But—"

"Do you think you could wait, and go on with your life for a day or two or ten, if you knew the answer to all your questions lay just a few miles away?"

"Let me go with you." She seized his jacket in both hands. "He's my father. I have a right to know, too."

"You do. And I will tell you the moment I return." He gathered her into his arms and kissed her, so sweetly she wanted to weep. She wound her arms around his neck and clung to him, the man she loved more than anything, and thought she might die of fear. If her father had betrayed him in some way . . . if her father had been responsible for his disgrace . . . Would Alec still want her? Could he look at her without seeing the daughter of the man who destroyed him? The premonition that she might lose the love she'd never expected to find made her hold on for dear life when Alec tried to set her away from him.

"I'm going with you," she said fiercely. "Don't you dare leave without me."

"Under no circumstances are you going with me." He raised one eyebrow at her. "I'll tie you to my bed if I must, even if I won't be here to enjoy it."

She was breathing hard, her heart galloping along. "You wouldn't dare."

"I think you know I would." He kissed her again, a hard and ruthless kiss this time that made her weaken. Her grip on his coat eased and she melted into him with a moan.

"Don't go," she begged. "Please. You frighten me. Let me finish translating the journal before you do anything. Please, Alec, if you care for me at all—"

He didn't reply, just kissed her again. With two jerks he pulled up the front of her skirt, pressing his hand between her legs. She gasped, but her body responded instantly. Love and desire, fear and desperation made her hands shake as she yanked at his trousers. By the time she shoved aside the fabric and cupped her hands around his erection, her knees were weak and she was almost on the verge of climax. He knocked her hands aside, his face drawn tight, and pushed her back against the wall as he drove up into her.

Cressida threw her arms around his shoulders and held on as he moved in sharp, hard thrusts. When he reached down to pull up her knee so he could go even deeper inside her, she came with a great shuddering sob. Her body clamped around his so hard tears sprang into her eyes. Alec thrust once more and gave a guttural exhalation as he found his release, pinning her tightly to the wall and letting his head fall to her shoulder.

One tear leaked from her eye and ran down her cheek. She stroked the back of his neck, running her fingers through the short, crisp hair. Her heart would break forever if anything happened to him. "I love you," she said in a small, lost voice.

His shoulders shuddered, and his arms slid around her, holding her tightly to him. For one euphoric moment, she thought he had relented. He lifted his head and gazed down at her with eyes as blue and boundless as the twilight sky, but filled with resolve. Without a word he eased out of her, letting her feet back to the floor and gently smoothing her skirts down. His expression was somber, and she knew he wasn't going to agree to her pleas. She closed her eyes and turned her face away when he touched her cheek, but he tipped her chin back to him.

"Cressida, my darling, stay here," he murmured against her lips. "I'll answer your every question when I return, but don't ask me not to go. If you truly care for me"—he paused, then continued more evenly—"please don't try to stop me from this."

He was telling her that she could stop him if she tried—but he asked her not to. Without opening her eyes she nodded. Gently, reverently, he kissed her once more. There was a soft rustle as he stepped away, cool air rushing into the space where he had been, and she shivered. Without another word, he opened the door and was gone.

Damn him. Damn all men who thought they could handle any problem alone. Damn him for taking her heart with him into harm's way and leaving her to suffer the agony of waiting. She opened her eyes and looked around the room. Damn her father, for whatever he had done. And damn her, too, if she stood here and did nothing to help Alec in whatever he was about to do.

She marched through the house, hoping her quarry hadn't left already. Madame Wallace, dressed in a smart blue traveling gown, opened the door at her knock. A valise sat on the floor behind her. "*Oui?*" she asked, as if it was not surprising Cressida was at her door even though they had barely been introduced.

"May I come in? I must talk to you." Cressida hesitated. "It is urgent."

"Of course, Miss Turner." Madame opened the door wider to allow her to enter. "What is the problem?" asked Madame with polite curiosity.

Cressida drew a deep breath and faced the other woman with an even gaze. "Alec has gone to confront someone who was involved in causing him to be suspected as a traitor."

"Goodness," she said mildly. "Just now?"

"He refused to let me go with him, but it may be dangerous and he would not wait."

"Men," said Madame with a sigh. "But why have you come to me about this?"

Cressida suffered a moment of doubt. Madame Wallace was so slim and elegant, with her exotic face and sensual movements. Next to her, Cressida felt like a giant, clumsy girl. Was she really here to ask this delicate woman to go help Alec? Tom was still in Portsmouth and Mr. Hayes had gone, but Mr. Wallace looked very capable . . . "I think you are more than you appear," she replied, trusting her instinct. "I think you can help him."

Something flickered in Madame's eyes. She leaned closer. "Why is that?"

Cressida opened her mouth, but realized she didn't have a good reason. "Can you not, then? Because if you can't, I shall have to go myself."

There was an odd humor in Madame's smile. "This is why I do not like to work with gentlemen," she said. "They are forever being led astray by their hearts or by their—" She stopped and pursed her lips. "Where has he gone?"

"I don't know, but I think I can figure it out."

"Go do that. I will be at your room in a few minutes." She picked up the valise and set it on a chair. "We will leave soon; hurry."

"Thank you," she said in a rush of relief. "Thank you so much—"

"You will come with us." Madame was digging through the valise and didn't look at her.

"What?" Cressida exclaimed. "Oh, no. Must I go? Alec told me to stay here . . ."

"You are bound to know more than I do, and if you stay here I will be blind. Go, and be ready to tell me where he has gone."

Cressida hoped she had done the right thing. With

a quick nod she hurried back to the conservatory to scoop up the journal and her notes. She went in search of Julia, finally locating her in her chamber, freshly washed from the attic. "I need your help," she said when Julia opened the door. "It's about Alec."

Julia waved her in without a word, her expression sharp with curiosity. Cressida handed her the pages of notes. "This is from my father's journal. He kept it while in the army. It was in a code, of sorts, and I've been translating it."

"Goodness, this is from years ago," exclaimed Julia as she glanced at the first page. "What can it have to do with Alec now?"

She laughed nervously. "I'm not entirely certain, but read it all. There is a man mentioned, an officer, I think. Alec recognized him. Something in these notes led him to the attic and his trunk, and now he's gone off to do . . . something, and I want to help but first I have to discover who this person is."

Julia stared at her. "What?"

"Just read!" Cressida pushed her lightly in the direction of a chair. Julia went, reading as she walked. Cressida pulled out the writing table chair and picked up her pen, taking up the translation where she had left off.

For several minutes they worked in silence. "Do you mean this fellow?" Julia asked, reading aloud, ' "a fair, priggish fellow from Hertfordshire?' "

"Yes, that's the one. He calls him Little Nob, or Nob. Can you guess who he means?" Julia shook her head. Cressida sighed. "He must be someone Alec knows, or did know, and it must be someone who lives within a day's ride, since he left already." Julia frowned, and they both turned back to their work.

Cressida's despair deepened as her pen marched across the page. Worse and worse, her father's behavior became. "A fine sum collected today," he noted in June 1815. "Enemy on the march again, lovely to be back in business with my old friend De Lion." De Lion was his name for the French colonel. "De Lion especially grateful today, informed him of old Blech's position," he wrote a day later. Cressida swallowed hard; old Blech was Marshal Blücher, head of the Prussian army at Waterloo. She handed the completed page to Julia and reached for another piece of paper.

And here was mention of the officer again: "Little Nob reluctant, even when de Lion offered considerable sum. Nob agreed after proof of his previous actions was displayed. Always wise to keep proof in secure location." She was skimming now, looking for the codes that represented Little Nob or De Lion. "Nob snubbed me this eve; must remind him of mutual obligations . . . De Lion pressing for more information, reward handsomer than ever . . . Saw Nob with his expensive Castilian. No wonder he's for sale . . . De Lion pays in gold now, excellent choice . . . Rebuffed by Little Nob, pompous arse; had to show him letters retrieved from De Lion to ensure cooperation . . ."

"Cressida." Julia was looking at her with fright in her eyes. "This—This is by your father?"

"Yes." The word almost lodged in her throat.

"But this—this is dreadful, what he says." Julia held up the pages, her hands stained by the ink

Cressida hadn't taken the time to blot dry. "This is—this is—"

She stretched her cramped fingers. "I know," she said quietly. "I can't believe my father—"

"No." Julia shook her head. She ran across the room and put the paper in front of Cressida, poking it with her finger. "This—*This* is what the army accused Alec of. This exactly, writing to a French officer and selling secrets. Here, it talks of letters retrieved from De Lion; letters from a Frenchman were found in Alec's things, clearly implicating him in a correspondence with the man for money. My mother begged and begged for more information when the army said he had turned traitor, because she couldn't believe it was possible, and finally some colonel spelled it out for her. I read his letter. This agrees with every particular of his account!"

"Are you saying that Alec is the officer my father dealt with?" She felt sick and disoriented. "But no—that can't be . . ."

Julia snorted. "It's not Alec. No one would ever describe him as fair or priggish, especially not then."

She pressed her hands to her temples. "Then who?"

"Let me see more." Now Julia was as fevered as Cressida. She read rapidly through the next page, then another, and her face sagged in shock. "Good heavens."

"What?"

She touched the page. "Castilian. Will Lacey married a Spanish girl while they were in Spain. It caused quite a furor in town because Priscilla Darrowby had set her cap for him before the war, and everyone knew old Mr. Lacey approved the match."

They looked at each other. "And Will might have given Alec a letter," Cressida said slowly. "Because they were such friends."

Julia nodded. "He died at Waterloo. A great hero; Mr. Lacey received a letter from Wellington himself. But this . . ." She shook the translated pages. "This is Will Lacey, I'm sure of it. He was fair and could be priggish—or rather, he could seem so, even though he was just as much a devil as Alec. But . . . What if . . . Is it possible someone mistook Alec for Will?"

"You said the papers were found in Alec's things."

She watched the realization sink in. Julia, Alec's sister, looked at her with dawning alarm. "Could— Could he have . . . ?"

Cressida knew he could have. Her father could have seen an opportunity and seized it while the battlefield was still in disarray. *Everything was chaos after a battle,* echoed Alec's words in her memory. The relief that Papa's journal exonerated Alec was eclipsed by the confirmation that Papa had been responsible for those charges being made at all. She steeled herself and picked up the journal to read some more. The code had become almost as clear as English now, and she didn't even have to write it down to know what it said. She was still turning pages when a knock sounded on the door, and Madame Wallace opened it.

"You are ready?"

"Yes," she said hollowly. She couldn't face Julia. "You are right. He writes of it here. My father put the letters in Alec's effects to cast the blame for Nob's treason onto him, and then bl-blackmailed Nob's family with the truth."

George Turner had been a blackmailer. Alec had seen that quickly enough in the journal account, and he thought Cressida did, too, even if she didn't want to say it out loud. He could understand that, and even respect it. There was little to be gained by exposing a man now, when he might well be dead but was most certainly gone, particularly when it was someone she loved so dearly and the sins had occurred so long ago.

But Turner had also been a traitor, selling information to the enemy. A common sergeant couldn't know much of interest to the French army, though. Turner had wanted more easy money, and in time he found a means to get it, in the form of a British officer in dire financial straits. Alec's heart burned with fury as he remembered Turner's account of coaxing the officer to relate intelligence, trifling items at first, then more and more important until finally the officer was writing directly to a French colonel, with Turner as the intermediary—collecting his fee along the way, of course. For money, Turner had sold out his fellow Englishmen, endangered his mates and the country they all fought to protect, and lured a decent man into dishonor and treason.

The only thing Alec didn't know was how the blame had been diverted onto him.

He knew the road to The Grange well. As a boy he had traveled this path often, and even after all these years he could still do it in the dark. Cracks of lightning split the sky with increasing frequency, but the booming rolls of thunder were far-off rumbles. The stiff breeze stung his face, and Alec welcomed it. It went some small way toward cooling his temper, reminding him that revenge, no matter how long plotted or well-earned, was rarely satisfying. It wasn't revenge he sought; nothing could bring back the years of his life or his lost reputation. It was justice, not just for himself but for everyone else mired in this tragedy.

The house was just as he remembered it. Alec's eyes went by pure habit to the third window from the left on the upper story, where he used to toss pebbles and other items to Will. What rapscallions they had been, sneaking off to swim in the river or to run through the woods at night after long days indoors at lessons. Will had been his brother in spirit if not in flesh, his thirst for adventure matching Alec's own. Will was just as adept as Alec at finding trouble, despite looking so solemn and innocent that many people thought Alec was the one responsible for leading Will astray. As soon as they were old enough, the two of them had bought commissions in the army, determined to see the world and escape stern, strict fathers at the same time. Alec's father had been relieved to see him committed to something respectable, but Will's father mightily disapproved of the whole enterprise, and let his son and heir know it. Alec could still see the somber farewell between Will and his father before they rode off to join their regiments. He had seen the tears spring into Mr. Lacey's eyes when Will turned away to mount his horse, just as he had seen the scars the old man inflicted on Will's back over the years.

He tied his horse to the paddock fence and walked up to the back door of the house, memories flooding him. How many times had he come this way, full of anticipation to see his friend? It caused a dull pain in his chest that he was here to confront a man about his son's treason.

Alec straightened his shoulders. The dagger under his coat pressed against his ribs. He thought of Cressida, clinging to him with all her strength and begging him to stay, and her last whispered declaration of love. Then he opened the door and let himself in.

Chapter 27

17 June 1815
Near the village of Waterloo, Belgium

Those who had fought with the Duke of Wellington in the Peninsula campaign claimed that great victories were often preceded by great storms crackling with thunder and lightning. In Wellington's army, drenched and chilled to the bone by the rain that had started up the previous afternoon and proceeded to turn the Belgian hills and fields into oceans of mud, some were reassuring themselves that this storm was a sign of good fortune for His Grace. That might be true, and perhaps it did foretell another great triumph on the morrow, but at the moment, Major Alec Hayes would rather have been warm and dry.

He forged through the ankle-deep mud toward the squat little house where he was billeted for the night. There was nothing he could do for his men. They were managing as best they could, huddling under blankets thrown over their saddles and clinging to the stirrup leathers to stay upright and avoid being trampled. Cavalry always bore bad weather even harder than the infantry. Alec had gone among them, doing his best to raise spirits and morale, making certain they got their rations of gin, but now he had to get some rest himself. The morning promised the exhilaration and madness of battle, when he would need a calm, collected mind more than ever.

"Hayes! Hallo there, Major!"

He stopped and turned, swiping rain from his face and grinning as he saw William Lacey slogging through the storm. He and Will had been boyhood friends, growing up near the same town in Hertfordshire and purchasing commissions at the same time. Lacey was attached to the staff of Sir William Ponsonby, the brigade commander, and Alec hadn't seen him for several days, not since the night of Lady Richmond's ball just before the French pushed across the border. "Nice night for a stroll," he called. "Care to stop in and have a drink?"

"If you've got anything, I'd drink it," Lacey replied. He looked exhausted, his face drawn and gray. "The stronger the better."

Alec pushed open the door of the farmhouse, but it was full. A group of junior officers were clustered around the fire, where a pot steamed. He grimaced; whatever was in the kettle didn't smell appetizing in the least, not even to a man who hadn't had a decent meal all day. Combined with the smell of drying wool, the air in the house was thick and sour. Instead Alec picked up an umbrella someone had left near the door and ducked back into the rain. He opened it, and Will stepped under it beside him to share the last of the brandy in his flask.

For a while they just watched the rain. When the

brandy was gone, Will rummaged in his pockets and found some tobacco. Alec went into the house and got an ember, and they settled in for a smoke to warm themselves.

"It's going to be a bloodbath," Will said at last.

Alec blew out a puff of smoke that evaporated at once in the wet air. "Worse than usual, you think?"

His friend was quiet, then plucked the cigar from his mouth to gesture at the sodden darkness. "Somewhere over that ridge are thousands of Frenchmen who want to kill us all. They must know it's old Boney's great chance. If he can wipe out this army, what would stand in his way?"

Alec grunted, conceding the point. "He shan't destroy the army, I don't think. Wellington's too cagey for that. He'll fall back on Brussels and make another stand, and God help the Prussians if they don't join him there."

"They're on the way to Wavre, if the French can't get them first."

"You're awfully grim," Alec said mildly. "I hold out hope we might crush them, instead of the other way around."

Will shook his head. "I have a terrible premonition about this fight, Alec. No—that is not what I mean." He paused, seemingly struggling for words. "I have not been as—as able an officer as I should have been."

Alec glanced at him. "Nonsense. What the devil . . . ?"

"I have felt my inadequacies weighing on me of late." He was drawing hard on his cigar. "As though

I've been blinded to them all my life and only now see what they cost me."

"The lament of all married men."

As hoped, Will smiled, but it quickly faded. "My poor wife. If I should die, who will take care of her? She shouldn't have to suffer so, and now she's with child."

Will had married a Spanish beauty during the Peninsula campaign, but his father had not been pleased. From what Alec recalled of old Mr. Lacey, he wouldn't be likely to take care of Isabella Lacey and her baby if anything happened to Will. Mrs. Lacey was in Brussels now, no doubt even more anxious about the impending battle than her husband. Alec had met her on a few occasions and thought old Lacey was a fool not to embrace her. He clapped Will on the shoulder. "I will care for her. You may depend on that, although I fully expect you to ride through this battle without a blemish, and have many children to vex you well into your old age, just as you and I have done for our fathers."

Will's shoulder twitched. "Thank you. You cannot know how that eases my mind. I have your word? Whatever may happen?"

Surprised, Alec looked away from the driving rain and into his friend's face. "Do you even need to ask? You know I would."

"Your word?" Will repeated. His eyes burned and the cigar trembled in his fingers. "Whatever happens?"

"Yes." Alec wondered at Will's feverish insistence, but then told himself not to judge too harshly; he didn't know what went through a man's mind the night before a battle when he had a wife and children to think of. He didn't particularly care to think of his own death, but if it happened, his family would go along well enough without him. No one depended on him for home and happiness, and he didn't depend on anyone for his. "I swear it."

The tension went out of Will's body and he leaned against the wall at their back. "I have a letter here . . ." He drew it from inside his coat. "To my father. Would you send it to him, after my death?"

It was customary to leave a letter for one's family, to be sent if necessary. Many officers would be up most of the night writing them. Alec stared askance at Will, though, for the certainty of his phrasing. Not "if I should fall" but "after my death." He took the letter and shoved it into his pocket. "Get some sleep, Lacey. You're not going to die, not in this fight."

Will's smile was ghastly. "Perhaps not. But it would ease my mind . . ."

"Of course," Alec muttered. Of course they both might die on the morrow, or a week hence, or in their sleep tonight. It was part of the army. "I regret I have no wife and child to leave to your tender care. Perhaps you can find someone to marry Julia, if I die and miss the chance of teasing her suitors."

Will closed his eyes, smiled, and said nothing. For a long moment the only sound was the steady patter of the rain on the umbrella over their heads and the soft rush of the small river now flowing through the ditch that used to be a road. In the distance was a constant rumble, not of thunder but of wagons carrying supplies, artillery, and wounded. A man came sloshing through the mud toward them. "Captain Lacey, sir!"

He stiffened. "Yes?"

The man's eyes were barely visible in the dark; every inch of him was spattered with mud. "You're needed, sir. General Ponsonby sent for you."

Will's face relaxed, and he nodded before sending the man on his way. "Ponsonby's concerned for his horse," he said wryly, more like the Will of old. "He's been set on purchasing another to spare his animal any injury but cannot seem to strike a bargain. Perhaps I shall sell him mine and make a tidy sum."

Alec chuckled, and raised one hand in farewell as Will flicked the end of his cigar into the darkness. The glowing tip of it was extinguished before it hit the ground. "Godspeed, Will."

His friend looked at him and touched the drooping brim of his hat in salute. "And to you, Alec."

Chapter 28

1820

But I can't help," Cressida said for the fourth time. "I could tell Mr. Wallace the direction and stay behind, out of the way."

"Nonsense." True to Cressida's suspicion, Madame Wallace was proving to be far more than she appeared. She wore a pair of loose dark trousers and a dark, close-fitting jacket. Her black hair was pulled back into a tight braid that snaked down her back. Cressida caught the gleam of a knife, strapped to her forearm, when lightning flashed. She stared at it in uneasy fascination, and wondered what she had gotten herself into. Madame had swept her into the waiting carriage, and now Mr. Wallace was driving them along at a perilous speed toward the Lacey home. "Tell me more. What did you read?"

Cressida shivered again. "My father was responsible for it all," she said in a small voice. It was horrible to think, let alone say out loud. "He helped another officer commit treason, then he put the incriminating papers in Al— in Major Hayes's belongings when it appeared the major had been killed in battle. And then he blackmailed old Mr. Lacey, taking money in exchange for keeping silent about the truth."

"Then what has happened to your father?"

"I don't know." But she suspected. Mr. Lacey did not seem the type to be cowed and afraid, and blackmailers rarely met good ends. If Mr. Lacey hadn't done Papa harm, someone else probably had.

Madame Wallace didn't appear too concerned. She kept glancing out the window. The lightning was growing more frequent and brighter, and now the distant rumble of thunder rolled across the land. From the strength of the breeze that ruffled the carriage curtains, it was quite a storm coming. "What do you know of Lacey and his home?"

"Almost nothing." She raised her hands when Madame sent her an irritated look. "I told you I couldn't help! You ought to have brought Julia instead."

"No," Madame said. "You are the steadier one. Do not say you know little; tell me what you do know. You have met Mr. Lacey?"

Cressida took a deep breath and nodded. "Once. He's an older gentleman, about my height and stooped; he walks with a cane. I don't think he has any family still living, at least not at The Grange. There is a servant, a very large man named Morris, who attends him to church. That's the only place I've ever met Mr. Lacey. He scowls at everything and everyone, and he practically gave my grandmother the cut direct. He called Alec a traitor to his face in front of all Marston at church one week."

"And the house?"

"I have never seen it except from a distance. Julia

said Alec and Will Lacey were bosom friends as lads, though, so he must know it well."

"Well, that will have to suffice." Madame lifted the curtain to peer out the window again, and again Cressida caught the gleam of the knife handle.

"May I ask . . ." she began timidly. "May I ask how you know Alec?"

Madame's smile flashed in the dark carriage. "He has not told you; perhaps I should not."

"Then what . . . who *are* you?"

Madame Wallace leaned forward. Cressida leaned forward, too. "I am not someone you should know too much about."

Somehow Cressida agreed with this statement. It didn't stop her from asking more questions, though. "Why do you have a knife strapped to your arm?"

Madame gave an elegant shrug. "I hope it might remain there all night."

Meaning that Madame hoped not to draw it? "What are you planning to do?"

"I shall have a look around," said Madame vaguely. "Alec may have no need of my help. He is quite capable, when pressed."

Cressida kept looking at the knife. Madame seemed far too dainty and delicate to hurt anyone with it, small as it was. "Do you have a pistol, too?"

She laughed in genuine surprise. "Of course not. Far too much noise. I prefer a more subtle approach." She leaned forward abruptly. "Ah, this is the house?"

The Grange, the Lacey estate, lay in the hollow below them, a rambling edifice from the days of the Tudors. Cressida nodded. Madame tapped on the side of the carriage, and they halted at once. Madame pushed open the door and leaped to the ground, moving up to talk to Mr. Wallace. Cressida leaned out the window, searching for any sign of Alec during the frequent lightning flashes. The grounds appeared to be deserted, and light glowed in only a pair of windows in the house. Thunder crackled more ominously now, and the wind was sending leaves swirling from the trees. The horses were just as spooked as she was, to judge from their stamping and snorting.

Mr. Wallace jumped down from his perch and waved Cressida forward. "You'll have to hold the horses," he said, raising his voice over a boom of thunder. "The storm's put the fear of the devil into them." He held out the reins, and she took them uncertainly. "Lead them down the road a bit, there's a stand of trees. Just don't stand too close, else the lightning might get you." He laughed as he said it, looking remarkably jolly given the situation. Cressida scowled at him and he turned away, pulling up the collar of his coat to hide his grin.

"You will be fine," Madame said to her. She patted Cressida's arm. "Just wait here. Come no closer. We shall see to Alec."

Cressida nodded, and the two of them spoke a moment before heading off toward the house. Within seconds they had melted into the shadows, and even the next flash of lightning didn't reveal a trace of them.

The wind howled, and a shower of acorns fell from a nearby oak tree, bouncing off the carriage roof with dull little pops. The horses tried to rear up in alarm, nearly pulling Cressida off her feet. If she didn't tie them up, they could take off and drag her along with them, or leave her behind entirely. She managed to urge them onward, to the bend in the road Mr. Wallace had pointed out, and tied the reins to a sturdy tree branch.

But she couldn't see the house from here. Anxiously she paced along the road, finally slipping through the trees to peer into the darkness again. The lightning, when it came, was now almost as bright as day, but she couldn't see a sign of anyone—not Madame Wallace, nor Mr. Wallace, nor Alec.

What was happening? Even though she had told Madame she ought to have stayed at Penford, she was practically shaking with the desire to see better, to know what was going on inside the house. Was Julia mistaken? Perhaps the journal hadn't referred to Will Lacey at all. If they had come to the wrong house . . . She laughed out loud in despair. Madame and Mr. Wallace would be breaking into the wrong house, Alec would be off somewhere completely on his own, and she would be standing here in a thunderstorm with two terrified horses, biting her fingernails to the quick worrying about all of them.

She hadn't even begun to comprehend her father's actions. It was there in his own hand, baldly spelling out how he had persuaded Nob into treason and profited from it, then again from another man's supposed death. She thought of all the times Papa had gone off and come home flush with cash—blood money, most likely. Perhaps that was why he had gone to see Lord Hastings; he had never given them a good explanation of how he knew a colonel. Bitterly Cressida wondered what secrets the colonel might have, and if Papa had held something over him, too. Had Papa met his end there, having gone too far, or perhaps here in the house in the hollow below her? The wind whipped through the trees where she stood, making the branches creak and moan as they swayed. It was a mourning sound, wrenching and sorrowful, and a tear leaked from her eye as she acknowledged that her beloved Papa, with his booming laugh and affectionate embraces and the way he always made them all smile, had been worse than a scoundrel; he had ruined other lives and lived on money wrung from other people's guilt and shame. She had suspected for a while that he'd met his death, but for the first time, Cressida thought it might be a blessing if they never knew, if Papa just disappeared and was never heard from again.

The wind was rising. The interminable heat hadn't abated when they left Penford, but she had snatched up a cloak out of habit. It was still in the carriage, and as the wind changed and became noticeably cooler, she shivered. No rain had fallen yet, but the air was thick with it. She rubbed her hands up and down her arms, and turned to go back to the carriage. She should check on the horses, and the cloak would feel good. There was nothing to be seen in the darkness anyway. With any luck, Madame Wallace and Mr. Wallace would return soon, with Alec in tow, and they could go home.

She only made it three steps.

Chapter 29

Alec found Angus Lacey in his study, dozing off over in the chair by the fire. For a moment he stayed in the shadows, noting how much the man had aged. The hand that lay on the book in his lap was gnarled and crooked, veins standing in blue lines across the back. His head drooped to one side as he slept, and for a moment he looked almost dead.

Alec stepped into the room. He had already made sure Morris wasn't about, and the footman and butler were securely locked in the butler's pantry. Alec didn't want to hurt anyone any more than he wanted to be interrupted.

At his footstep, Lacey started awake. "Eh? Morris, close the window," he muttered, then jerked as he saw Alec. For a moment they regarded each other in silence.

"How dare you," growled Mr. Lacey. He struggled to his feet and gripped his cane. "Get off my property at once. I have nothing to say to a traitor and a liar."

Alec stood his ground. "Understood. I, however, have something to say to you."

The old man's lips curled in a sneer. "Nothing you

say can interest me. Get out." He started to walk past Alec toward the door.

"No, this time you shall not walk out on me. I have not come for my sake."

Lacey glared at him with hatred in his eyes . . . and fear. Alec saw the apprehensive loathing and it struck not fury, but pity, in his chest. Mr. Lacey suspected what he had come about. He didn't want to hear, not because of his revulsion for Alec, but because he knew Alec had come to confront him with his own sins. "I don't care whose behalf you've come on," Lacey said. "Say your piece and remove yourself from my sight. If I were a younger man, I'd thrash you myself for coming here."

He smiled grimly. "No doubt. Allow me to explain my purpose before we come to blows. I think you'll find it an interesting tale. I was sent back to Marston to inquire into the disappearance of Sergeant George Turner." The other man's flinch was small, but Alec saw it. "Sergeant Turner was, to all appearances, a man of modest means, with a few army connections and boundless ambition. From what I can gather, he traded on every favor he'd ever done anyone and his considerable personal charm to move up in the world. He took a house near Marston and set up there with his family as a comfortable man with means and expectations. No one seemed to know much what those means and expectations were, or whence they might come, but he paid his bills and behaved with propriety."

"This is hardly interesting," Lacey said, his voice freezing with contempt. A vein pulsed at his temple. "I didn't know the man."

"And then one day he simply disappeared," Alec went on. "He went to London, met an old army superior about a post he wished to take, and then vanished. No word to his family, no letter, not even funds sent on to pay the accounts due a week after he left." Alec paused, watching Lacey feign indifference. "Eventually his family grew worried enough to inquire of the man he was to meet in London and ask for help finding the sergeant. And so I came back to Marston—rather reluctantly, might I add."

"As well you should have been, bringing your treachery back on your family! The shock of it might have killed your poor mother."

Alec bowed his head. "Yes, it might have done; my treachery, as you call it, was terribly hard on my family. But that leads me to another interesting story I would like to tell you."

"I don't want to hear it." Lacey retreated, circling around the chair. Alec moved with him, always keeping between Lacey and the door, like a hunter monitoring his prey.

"I think you do, whether you believe you do or not. It begins several years ago and far away—in Spain, to be precise. When Will fell in love with a Spanish girl."

Lacey's eye had begun twitching. "Do not speak of my son." His voice was the low growl of a cornered animal. Alec refused to relent.

"He married her, and was very happy until word of your displeasure reached him. I don't know what he wrote to you, but to me he expressed his deep regret. Not for marrying her—he loved her deeply— but for the fact that he had not planned better and couldn't keep her in the comfort she deserved."

"A hot-blooded foreigner. She did not deserve my son!"

"She was a Spanish grandee's daughter, a lady from a good family, and used to a life of ease. She left it all to go on campaign with Will, and to the best of my knowledge she never regretted it." Alec paused, but Lacey merely snorted. "Of course, we were in different divisions. I didn't see Will much after Bonaparte escaped Elba and returned to Paris. Our paths crossed once or twice in Belgium, but never for more than a few moments' conversation. I was grieved to hear of his death."

"Don't you speak of his death!" There was real agony in Lacey's cry.

"The last time I saw him was the night before the great battle at Waterloo. It was pouring rain and we had only a few moments, but he was very odd that night. He made a few requests of me; he seemed to be quite certain of his impending death. I had entirely forgotten it, in my . . . difficult situation, until today, when I read the journal of Sergeant Turner."

Lacey jerked. The agony in his expression faded away at the mention of Turner's name, replaced with a look of such loathing that Alec realized the full truth of what had happened. "Stop," said Lacey viciously. "I'll tell you. Here to seek the noble Sergeant Turner, are you? You may find him in hell. That—That *offal* betrayed my son, and held it over my head ever since. I care nothing for his family; if anything, they are better off without him. And if you think to sully my son's name, I shall pursue you to the end of my days. Who would believe a traitor, after all?"

"You will," said Alec softly. "You know I speak the truth. Will needed funds after his marriage. Turner offered him a way to make money and in desperation, Will took it." Lacey recoiled as if Alec had struck him. "And when Will died on the battlefield, Turner planted the letters from the French colonel in my belongings, then blackmailed you with a threat to expose the truth."

For a long moment, Mr. Lacey simply stood with bowed head, one hand braced on the back of a chair, his body shaking with every breath. "You were dead," he said heavily. "You were supposed to be *dead*."

Alec said nothing at this confirmation of his dark suspicion. His family had not been dead, and Lacey knew exactly what he had done to them, neighbors he had once valued as friends.

"He was the lowest of men, utterly without honor. The thought of that beast using my son . . ." Lacey's knuckles were white where he gripped the chair.

"You paid him not to speak. You allowed my family and the entire country to think me a traitor." Alec's iron control on his temper was finally slipping. "Whatever Turner's sins, what of *yours*, sir? What honor is there in supporting a lie and ruining my good name? My *father's* name?"

"You were dead," repeated Lacey. "He was my only son. I had no choice!"

"When did you kill him?" Alec meant the question to startle Lacey, even goad him into a confession. All his calm and restraint were under terrible strain.

Lacey, though, was unshaken. He raised his head in defiance. "He deserved to die. It was a boon to humanity, ridding the world of his sort. I make no apologies for it. Not only did he lure my son . . . Not only that, but he held it over my head and he *reveled* in that power." He shook a fist at Alec. "He was a snake, a poisonous viper who preyed on the sorrows of others, and wasn't killed soon enough."

"Then why pay him?"

"I was weak." He glared up from under his brows. "I suppose now you'll call down the authorities on me, for the death of that—that rapacious bastard."

Quite unexpectedly, Alec felt a moment of pity for the old man. Lacey had ruined his own life with hatred and anger and now guilt. Lacey, of all people, didn't have it in him to stand up and condemn his own son to spare another. "No," he said quietly. "Not at the moment." There was little proof of the deed. The diary would incriminate George Turner more than it would Lacey; Alec doubted Turner had even used his name outright. "But you should have this." He drew Will's letter from his pocket and held it out.

The older man glared at it, then started as he recognized the handwriting. "Where did that come from?" His voice shook as he reached out to touch the letter with his fingertip, then took it from Alec's hand.

"He asked me to deliver it, in the event of his death. It was sent home with my personal effects after Waterloo."

He waited for the meaning to sink in. After a moment Lacey paled and looked up. "Then—no one has seen—"

"I read it." But Lacey knew. Will could have been exposed as a traitor at any time, by his own hand. Perhaps that was as Will intended it. Alec felt a fierce sorrow clutch at him, that Will had chosen to make his confession and ride to his death. With this man for his father, he must have seen no other honorable choice. He had done his best to atone for his sin, by asking Alec to look after his wife and child, by laying out his confession to the one man who would never have believed it otherwise, and by sacrificing himself in a last dying moment of patriotism and honor. Only through chance had the letter gone missing. George Turner had seized that chance, casting the blame from Will onto Alec, and in doing so sealed Angus Lacey's loss in a tomb of agonizing uncertainty. If Lacey had had this letter, he might have refused Turner's demands. Alec might have proven his innocence years ago, or even not been accused at all. Cressida might have never lived in Marston at all, nor asked Hastings for his aid, and then he would have never met her.

For the first time, Alec didn't know which course he would have preferred, had he been offered the choice. Innocence, without Cressida . . . or five years of guilt, but with Cressida at the end? There was no question that he had found more peace and happiness with her than he'd ever expected in his life. Knowing what he had done, even what he had been accused of doing, she accepted him and trusted him and gave him her heart. Alec had never met another woman like her, and knew he could appreciate the depth of her faith and love as he could never have done before Waterloo.

"What happened to Turner?" he asked again. Cressida and her family deserved to know his fate, whatever the man had done in his life.

"He came here late at night," murmured Lacey.

He was still staring hollow-eyed at the letter in his hands. "Some months ago. He wanted money—always money. He set up house in Marston to torment me, to flaunt his presence in my face at every opportunity. There were papers, he said, in William's hand. As this letter . . ." He turned it over, handling it as gingerly as if it were spun of glass. "Just as this letter. Papers he would sell me, one page at a time, and I paid him to conceal my son's weakness." His voice broke on the last word. "I sent Morris to try to find them, but he never could."

Alec remembered the man sneaking around Cressida's stable on that long-ago day when he had first gone to see the Turners, and another small puzzle piece fell into place. Of course; it had been Morris.

"And then that villain came and said he would sell me the last of them, save one," Lacey went on, his voice heating with fury again. "He said he intended to move to London, and I suppose defraud other men more prosperously situated. If he had offered every page I would have paid him and been done with it, burned it all and gone to my grave with the shame. That last page, though, he meant to hold forever, no doubt to bleed me even more when he had run through the money. He was a leech, a conniving, amoral excuse for a man, and I am not sorry he's dead, no matter what it costs me."

"What did you do to him?"

"Morris took him away," Lacey muttered. "I don't know where, nor do I care." With trembling hands he unfolded the letter and began to read.

Alec watched the lines of his face grow deeper, and felt Lacey's pain almost as his own. Will's last

letter was damning, in detail and in scope: how he
had married in a reckless burst of passion and love,
how devastating his father's disapproval had been,
how his finances had grown desperate. How he had
been seduced into giving information to the French,
and how he believed he had gotten away with it when
Bonaparte was sent into exile the first time, only to
realize he had compromised himself too far when
the Emperor returned and marched on Belgium. And
most tragic of all, his belief that the only honorable
atonement for him was death on the field of battle, re-
paying the blood he had cost England with his own.
Alec felt the force of his own grief for Will, and at the
same time a great emptiness where he had expected
to feel vindication. The driving need for proof had
nursed him through many a lonely and bitter night,
when he had imagined the triumph and the release
of clearing his name. He had imagined confronting
the true traitor, the one whose sins had been laid at
his feet, and never dreamed it would be his dearest
friend in the world. He finally had answers, but there
was no joy in them for him.

"He asked me to look after his wife and child,"
Alec said as Lacey seemed to shrink before his eyes.
"Do you know where they are?"

Lacey bowed his head and closed his eyes. He gave
a tiny shake of his head.

Alec let out his breath. What ought he to do now?
His instinct was to let Stafford deal with it. Whatever punishment Lacey deserved, Stafford would be
better equipped to impose it. But it was murder. He
didn't see how he could simply walk out now and
wait to see what Stafford did, knowing that Stafford

had cards in his hand that Alec knew nothing about. For all he knew, Stafford and Hastings might be well-pleased to hear Turner was dead, and thank Lacey instead of arrest him.

A shriek outside the door interrupted his thoughts. Alec spun around, flexing his hands and automatically assuming a half crouch, ready to defend himself even as he wondered who the bloody hell would be screaming. It was a woman, and he didn't think Lacey had any maids, just a footman and butler besides the all-purpose Morris . . .

The door opened and Morris stumped in, dragging a struggling female form in his arms. Alec's heart seized even before he saw her face.

"Morris," cried Lacey in astonishment. "What the devil?"

"She was lurking by the road," the servant said. He had one arm around Cressida's chest, his hand wrapped around her throat, but his other hand held Alec's attention. The man had a pistol pressed to her side. "One of them Turners."

Chapter 30

Lacey's incredulity turned to disgust as he turned on Alec. "And what do you mean by bringing her here?"

"I didn't." Alec kept his voice low and even, his eyes never leaving Cressida. She had agreed to stay behind. He couldn't believe she would follow him, yet here she was, apparently unarmed and alone. Bloody hell.

"I don't approve of shooting women, Morris," Lacey snapped. "Not even that one." The sight of Cressida—a Turner—had revived the old man's bilious spirit.

"Let her go," said Alec softly. "She had no part in any of this, and knew nothing of it." Cressida was watching him with wide, frightened eyes, but no panic. He felt an absurd spark of admiration, that she could be dragged about by her neck with a gun to her ribs, and yet not dissolve into panic. Of course, it would have been even better had she kept her promise and stayed safely at Penford. Bloody, *bloody* hell.

"It appears she's a lying, sneaking thief like her father," snapped Lacey.

"Let her go," Alec repeated, ignoring Lacey. "For your own sake, Morris."

Morris grunted. He shifted Cressida's weight more to the side, as if tucking her under his arm. Her feet swung helplessly, like a doll's, as she struggled. Morris moved the pistol muzzle to her back, right at the curve of her spine. A shot there would leave her paralyzed if it didn't kill her instantly. "You want to take her place?"

"Lacey," said Alec in warning.

The old man glowered. "Get her out of here, Morris. I never want to see another Turner on my property."

The servant grinned. "I'll put her with the other one."

"Where is that?" Cressida squeaked. She had begun struggling again at Lacey's words, twisting against Morris's thick arm.

Morris's grin grew wider. "Buried behind the privy, miss, right where he belonged." He jerked his chin at Alec. "You come along, too. It's not nice to call on a man and make threats."

"Lacey," said Alec again, more loudly. A faint buzzing filled his ears. Not even in the heat of battle had he ever been more focused on killing another person.

"Morris!"

"It's my duty to Master William, sir," replied his servant, ducking his head. "I owes him this, too. Never you mind, sir."

"Let her go, and I'll come with you instead," Alec said. Morris was a thug, big and brutal, but Alec had learned more than a few tricks as a spy. The first lesson was to abandon honor at the door, and never mind a fair fight. Morris's pistol was a single shot. All Alec had to do was make sure that shot didn't go into Cressida or himself.

Morris laughed. "Eh, no. Got you both, don't we? Led the young master into trouble for many years, you did; got him killed, too, most like. No friends of the family here tonight."

"She had nothing to do with Will," Alec said again. He was slowly moving to the side, to where he could see Cressida's face. Two spots of red burned in her cheeks, and her eyes were glittering. She was furious, he realized, so furious she wasn't even frightened anymore. "She never met him or heard of him."

"But she lived well off his death, and that's enough." Morris gave her another shake. "Let's go, miss. Time to join your papa."

With a strangled shriek, Cressida threw her head back, cracking into Morris's chin. She kicked at his knees and scratched at his restraining arm. He cursed, turning his head away from her as she twisted, and almost dropped the pistol. Alec lunged forward to grab it, but Morris, still cursing, raised the gun and tried to aim at him. Alec dodged to the side to avoid presenting a good target, reaching for Cressida at the same moment. But suddenly she crashed to the floor along with the pistol; Morris had released both to grab the rope that had appeared around his throat.

It was the moment of hesitation Alec needed. With one flick of his wrist, he pulled the stiletto from his sleeve and flung it. Morris jerked upright, his face going slack with surprise. With an awful, reedy gasp he choked and coughed, and blood spurted from the mortal wound.

Alec had thrown the knife hard and true. The weighted hilt quivered right below Morris's meaty chin, the blade piercing his throat. Morris's eyes glazed over and went blank. Angelique, clinging to his back, gave a sharp tug on her garrote, and his head went up without resistance.

"Angelique," he said. "You can let him go."

Morris thudded heavily to his knees as she relaxed her grip. She peered over his shoulder, not appearing very surprised by the knife hilt sticking out of his throat. "I was not in need of help." She whisked the black rope from around his neck and gave Morris a small push. Freed of support, his body slowly toppled to the floor. The blood gushed forth as he collapsed, staining the carpet dark red in a wide arc around him. Angelique stepped away, wrinkling her nose. "Such a mess the knife makes," she said on a sigh.

Alec turned to Cressida, who had scrambled away from Morris and now sat braced on her arms, skirts twisted around her legs, breathing hard and staring at the dead man. "Are you hurt?"

She raised dazed eyes to him. Mutely she shook her head. Alec exhaled, his hands starting to shake from the delayed fear and fury at the sight of her caught in Morris's grasp. He simply nodded, unable to speak.

"My God," cried Lacey in shock. "You've killed my man!"

Alec gave him a black look as he bent to retrieve his knife. He cleaned the blade with a sharp swipe across Morris's sleeve.

Angelique raised her eyebrows at Lacey as she

coiled her deadly garrote around her hand. "Perhaps you are next."

The old man jerked, staring at her as if she had sprouted another head. In her dark clothing, with all her hair pulled back and making no attempt to gentle her expression, Angelique might have been the angel of death, coldly merciless. When Ian appeared in the doorway behind her, looking for all the world like his fierce Highland forebears must have looked to the invading English, Lacey gave an audible whimper.

"Get him out of the way," Alec muttered to Ian. The big Scot glanced at Angelique and nodded. He shoved his pistol into his pocket and bent to heave Morris's bulk over one shoulder. Angelique stepped out of his way as he carried the dead man to the sofa. Lacey watched in horrified silence, cowering in the corner.

Alec put out his hand and pulled Cressida to her feet. She came into his arms and held him as if she would never let go. He pressed his lips to her hair. She was shaking, and he held her even tighter, to keep her still, to comfort her, to reassure himself that she was whole and well. He hadn't planned to kill Morris, but the sight of him strangling Cressida had fueled a black rage that overrode every instinct except the fierce drive to protect what was vital to him. The knife had left his hand before he'd even thought of drawing it.

"Why did you not wait in the carriage?" Angelique asked gently, touching Cressida's arm. "I did not wish you to be involved."

"I did wait with the carriage." Cressida's voice was muffled against Alec's chest. "He found me and dragged me to the house."

Alec glared at Angelique. She pursed her lips. "I am sorry, Alec."

"It doesn't matter." It did matter. Angelique should have known better than to bring her anywhere near The Grange. Based on the way she was dressed and armed, Angelique had known exactly what she was walking into, and there was no excuse for bringing an innocent, untrained woman with her. In other situations Alec would have argued the point, but this time it didn't matter. Perhaps that, more than anything, drove home to him how final his choice was. He couldn't go back to being a spy—not because he had found the proof of innocence he sought, not because he had returned home and taken up his real name and position, but because of Cressida. If something had happened to her, there would have been little at Penford to keep him from the nomadic, lonely existence of Stafford's agents. But with her . . . With her he saw not the salvation of his reputation, but the salvation of his heart and soul. With her in his arms, nothing else mattered.

"You'll take care of this?" he asked Angelique.

She nodded. "Ian will go to Stafford tonight. He will want to know."

At the moment Alec didn't give a bloody damn what Stafford wanted. He nodded once and walked out of the room, leaving it all behind—Lacey's concealment of the truth, Morris's murderous loyalty, George Turner's venal sins, and most of all Will's fatal, tragic flaw. He had Cressida in his arms, and that was all he cared about.

Chapter 31

⌒⌒

They rode home slowly, she before him on the horse. For the first time in five years, Alec realized he was free. The weight of his suspected treason that had borne down on him for so long was gone. The thirst of vengeance that had driven him was no more, washed away by the sorrow of his friend's tragic secret. The prickly solitude that had been his life for five years was over, stripped from him by the woman in his arms. He was free, to live and to love. He tilted his face up to the sky and breathed deeply.

Neither spoke during the ride. A few fat drops of rain spattered against them, but the storm was still holding off. At the Penford stables Alec dismounted and handed the reins to the stable boy. He held out his arms to Cressida, wanting nothing more than to hide away from the world with her.

She let him help her down. Through the long ride home, she hadn't been able to stop thinking about one fact: her father had directly caused Alec's disgrace and estrangement. He hadn't hesitated to destroy an innocent man's name, all in the interest of blackmailing the family of the man he helped ruin. As she huddled in Alec's arms, her life with Papa had played across her memory's eye, his cheery winks and booming laughter, his quick temper and generous nature. The time he had brought home a baby bunny for her and Callie to see. The way his face would darken when she argued with him, and the cold way he had maneuvered Callie into marriage with Mr. Phillips. She thought of him making sport of Tom, and of how he carried her grandmother tenderly up the stairs when Granny had broken her ankle. It was a bittersweet jumble of happiness and horror, that he could support them with money gained so shamefully. And now Papa was lying in the ground behind Mr. Lacey's privy, if Morris could be believed, and she was sad and angry and relieved all at once.

She looked up into Alec's face. He had borne the disgrace, sacrificing five years—and almost his very life—trying to disprove what Papa had so carelessly cast on him. It was a cruel irony that he had been sent to find Papa when all along Papa had been the one responsible for Alec's condemnation. Cressida couldn't help thinking that her father had brought his fate upon himself; he had played with fire and it had consumed him in the end. And not only had it cost her her father and her affection for him, it might cost her a lifetime of happiness with the man she loved.

"What you must think of me," she began brokenly. "Of him, and everyone connected with him."

Alec's jaw tightened, then eased. "I am sorry you were there. Angelique should never have brought you with her."

"Oh!" She waved one hand impatiently. "At least now I know the truth, not some fairy tale of 'expectations' and other rubbish Papa used to tell us. He was a liar and a thief who lived on other people's sins."

"He was your father."

"And I loved him!" she said hysterically. "I did, and he was so—so—so *unworthy*."

"I loved Will," he reminded her. "He was my brother in spirit, closer than Frederick."

"I know. And Papa ruined his life, too," she said sadly.

He shook his head. "Will was not weak-willed. What he did was unpardonable, and I don't for one moment hold your father blameless. But Will could have refused. I don't know why he didn't, but he was not likely to be swayed by a lowly sergeant to do something so heinous if his inclination had been fixed against it. French gold, I expect, won him over more than anything else.

"What your father did to me . . ." He paused. A gentle rain had begun, wetting the shoulders of his coat. "It was the coward's way," he said quietly. "Did he know me and despise me for some reason, or was I just a conveniently dead officer? He might not have even known whose belongings he hid those letters in, and it was mischance he found a man not truly dead."

"But Mr. Lacey—"

"I doubt he had any thought of Mr. Lacey when he undertook the plan, except perhaps contempt. If he'd had any respect at all for Mr. Lacey, he never would have tried to extort money from him."

Yes, she could believe that. But what contempt must *Alec* have, then, for her father—or for her?

"You told me once you cared only for the truth,"

she said. Rain ran down her cheeks and dripped from her nose.

"The truth," Alec repeated. "Yes. I do." Cressida wrapped her arms around herself, bracing for the coming blow. Her heart would never recover from this one. "The truth is that I love you. The truth is that nothing your father did, or said, or thought or felt or wrote, could change that."

"The truth is my father cast blame for another man's crime on you!"

"He did."

She laughed a little wildly in despair. "How horrified you must have been when you realized the man you had been sent to help was the very man who betrayed you."

"It was odd," he agreed.

"And—"

"And the truth is that my own actions contributed to my situation," he said over her protest. "I was rash and quick-tempered. I was well-known in the army for being as bold as brass and daring to a fault. Had I been more restrained, people might not have believed the charges so quickly. Had I been more logical and dispassionate, I might have chosen a different course of action. Disappearing for five years doesn't have the same effect as standing up and shouting my innocence for all to hear, even if in a criminal dock."

"You should not have needed to!" she cried. "Papa—"

He put his fingertip on her lips. "It is not the adversity you suffer, it is how you react to it that determines one's worth. What your father did does not reflect on you any more than Will's actions reflect on me. And in the end, it does not change where we have ended up."

The rain pattered harder around them, refreshingly cool after the suffocating heat. He touched her cheek, and she leaned into it. "How can you bear to look at me," she whispered, "and not think of him? Of all he cost you?"

"When I look at you," he murmured against her temple, "it's not your father I think of."

"I am so sorry," she said, her voice cracking.

He rested his forehead against hers. "I'm not."

Cressida pulled back to look at him in astonishment. He was dripping wet, as was she, but he was grinning at her with that endearing dimple just visible in his cheek. "If you wish to make reparation, though," he added, "I could be persuaded to accept."

Her mouth fell open. There was a wicked gleam in his eyes. A brilliant bolt of lightning lit the sky for a moment, with thunder like a cannon shot. They really ought to go inside. "Why are you not sorry?"

"I had time to think while I rode to The Grange. I read Will's letter; I knew what it said, and I was fairly certain what it meant for my circumstances." He had to raise his voice as the rain increased, drumming loudly on the stable roof and the paving stones beneath their feet. "I had time to consider if I would rather have never been accused of treason, and come home to go on my way without ever crossing your path, or if this were the happier ending for me. And I knew I would rather have you, whatever else life might bring."

She blinked, and sniffled. Raindrops clung to her eyelashes. "You're mad."

He grinned. "Barking, howling mad," he said. "For you."

"Even though—?"

"Even though." He kissed her until she forgot her question, then tipped back his head and squinted into the downpour. "I don't think we shall have a walk today after all."

She smiled through her tears. "Not without getting very wet."

Alec laughed. "It feels rather good, to tell the truth. But perhaps it's holding you that feels good, and not even the rain could quench my delight." He cupped her cheek and made her look up at him. "You said something earlier, about loving me." Cressida froze, her eyes wide with apprehension. "I was wondering . . . or really, hoping," he went on, "that you might love me as much as I love you. Or at least enough to marry me, because I really don't think I can ever let you go."

For a moment she was too stunned to reply. Then wordlessly, she began nodding, and didn't stop even when he held her close and swung her off her feet.

Chapter 32

To Alec's great surprise, John Stafford himself arrived the next day. He had never learned what Stafford's real interest was in George Turner's disappearance, and could only guess that it was even greater than suspected for him to come all the way to Marston for a report.

"Welcome to Penford," he said.

"Thank you. It is a lovely estate."

Alec smiled. It was like a boxing match, the two of them circling each other warily. He was not sorry to be leaving Stafford's employ. "You'll have heard the story from Ian, of course."

The other man's eyes gleamed. "I expect there is more to the story than Mr. Wallace could tell me."

"No doubt." Alec paused, then changed course. He had no patience to repeat what Ian had already said. "Why did you send me on this job?"

Stafford smiled his thin, dry smile. "A favor for Lord Hastings." Alec waited, just watching him. "And I suspected it might be to your benefit as well."

"Why?"

His former employer's mouth quirked. He clasped his hands behind his back and turned to walk over to the window overlooking Penford's sweeping lawns. "I realize everyone does not always recognize my methods or means, but I am not as haphazard as one might suspect. This is not a game we play. A wrong guess often leads to disaster. When I send my agents out, I do so after solemn consideration of their skills and talents and what will be needed in the circumstance at hand." He flashed a sly glance at Alec. "And, of course, I never forget why my agents have chosen to serve His Majesty."

"Did you know what Turner—?"

"Of course not," Stafford interrupted. "Certainly not with regard to *you*." His voice fell back into calm, bland tones. "Hastings alerted me that the man had gone missing; he wanted him found, although he did not particularly care if it were dead or alive. It didn't take much to persuade Hastings to reveal the true nature of his concern. I daresay Turner thought he was quite clever, but he spread his net too wide."

Alec had suspected as much. Turner had been blackmailing Hastings, or trying to. He wondered what Hastings's secret was, and then he realized he didn't care. "Cressida has her father's effects," he said. "Should you wish to examine them for anyone else's private papers. There may be more hidden at Brighampton as well, according to his journal. Turner, I gather, managed to retain both sides of the correspondence by showing the letters from one to the other, but then keeping them. Whatever he hadn't sold to Lacey might still be there. Lacey sent his servant to steal them back, but the man never found the papers."

"I should very much like to look into that," Stafford

agreed at once. And that, Alec realized, was what had brought him to Marston: the prospect of Turner's hoard of secrets being exposed. No doubt people like Hastings only trusted Stafford himself to return their shameful secrets discreetly—and freely. Or perhaps not. Perhaps Stafford would expose them in his own way. Hastings might well regret setting him on the case.

"But why did you send *me*?" he asked again, returning to his main concern.

"Your brother's death was not insignificant." A rare note of compassion entered Stafford's voice. "I recruited men like you because I wished to create a more honorable class of agent, men who had honor and could be depended upon to serve the Crown and not just themselves. Men who could testify in court and not be dismissed by the judges as tools of the government; a discreet security service of sorts for His Majesty, if you will. But when your brother died, Lord Sidmouth directed me to send you home. Your family's need was greater. As to this last assignment . . ." He shrugged. "I have seen the French colonel's letters. After working with you for four years, it seemed incomprehensible that you could have been his correspondent, but there was no proof."

It was an odd comfort to know that Stafford had kept his promise to see what he could do, even if he hadn't bothered to inform Alec about it until now. Alec bowed his head. "Thank you, sir."

"I could do nothing except vouch for your conduct these last few years. Lord Sidmouth persuaded the Duke of Wellington to suspend judgment, based on that conduct. You will be permitted to call on His Grace and explain the truth of the matter. I believe Wellington will be inclined to listen." He paused. "Lord Doncaster may have also said a word on your behalf, at his son-in-law's urging."

Alec grinned in surprise. Harry Sinclair had been his fellow spy until falling in love with the Earl of Doncaster's daughter on their last assignment together. Harry must have forgiven him for the thrashing Alec administered over that love affair, which Alec had feared would ruin everything they worked for. He'd have to send the man a note of thanks, now that they were both respectable citizens again.

"It seemed too convenient that Turner, whose regiment was also at Waterloo, who had schemed to blackmail other officers, had gone missing from your own home village," Stafford went on in the same idly musing tone. "May I simply say, it was a striking coincidence, and I hoped you might somehow find enlightenment in the course of the job." He put out his hand. "I am glad you did."

Alec shook his hand. "As am I." He knew what Stafford was doing. As a landed gentleman, Alec would be in a position to support Stafford's initiatives, to influence his friends and peers on the necessity of this security service. Harry Sinclair would as well, since Alec had heard he intended to stand for Parliament. Perhaps Stafford had been wilier than they all thought in selecting them.

"I regret losing you," Stafford said then. "Very thorough, but not prone to rash heroics. I admire that in a man."

"Thank you, sir," he replied again. Stafford had

taken him on when no one else would have considered it, trusted him and vouched for him. Becoming a spy had been a tremendous gamble, and Alec knew he was exceedingly fortunate that it had worked out this well for him. "What is to be done with Mr. Lacey?"

For a moment Stafford said nothing. "That is not my decision," he said at last, somewhat vaguely. "I suppose the magistrate hereabouts will have to decide what to do when a body is unearthed from behind Lacey's privy. The dead man's family might demand restitution, but I doubt they will require a prosecution, since the murderer is dead. A gentleman of Lacey's age might find the shock of the whole affair taxing, and choose to retire to the seacoast."

Perhaps. Alec said nothing. He didn't want to see old Lacey ever again, and yet he didn't feel the same burning need for revenge. Lacey had already lost what he cared for most, and George Turner had rubbed salt into the open wound with his blackmail. But while Lacey had smiled at Turner's death, he hadn't killed him; there was no way to know for certain if he had even told Morris to do it, or if Morris—a fanatically loyal servant for as long as Alec could remember—had simply taken it on himself. Perhaps there was no more justice to be sought, or at least none that would help anyone.

"A terrible pity, it is, that the man who administered the killing blow has already met with an unfortunate accident." Stafford's words echoed his thoughts. "How dreadful that he should trip and fall on his knife."

"Yes," Alec agreed dryly. "Terrible." Stafford had

a way with "terrible pities." A great many of them happened in connection with his assignments, yet none were held against his agents. Alec had to hand it to the old fox: Stafford demanded a great deal, but he also overlooked a great deal and he stood solidly behind his people. After an hour with Stafford, Lacey himself would swear Morris had stabbed his own throat.

The spymaster's mouth twitched. He bowed his head in farewell and walked out of the room. Alec touched Will's carved wooden horse on the mantelpiece once more, then followed at a slower pace.

Stafford had already gone out to his carriage by the time Alec reached the hall. Cressida was waiting there, pacing and wringing her hands. Her face cleared when she saw him, and she rushed forward.

"What happened? Julia said there was an odd man from London come to see you, and that Madame Wallace was leaving with him. Was that . . . ?"

He took her hand in his and raised it to his lips. "It was. All is explained."

"Then he can clear your name?" she asked anxiously.

Alec smiled. "No. He has provided me the chance to do it myself."

"Oh!" She seemed to shine with relief. "You must tell your mother at once, and Julia—"

"Hmm." He slid his arm around her waist and led her out onto the terrace overlooking the garden. Every path was a quagmire of mud from the rain yesterday, but every leaf was bright and fresh in the sun. "I wasn't thinking of them."

"No?"

"No." They stopped, in very near the same place they had stood the evening of his mother's party, when they talked in the dark and made their wary bargain to trust each other. "I was thinking that I should clear my name before I share it with you." She glanced quickly at him. "It will require a trip to London, of course, to see Wellington. I was thinking we might all go. I'm sure my mother and Julia would like to see town, and I hear they have dressmakers there who could fit a bride's trousseau in no time."

She laughed. "Don't be silly."

"You won't go?" he said in surprise. "Cressida—"

"I thought I had been quite clear, but perhaps it bears repeating, since you persist in asking questions like that." She twined her fingers through his and squeezed, smiling up into his beloved face. "I would go with you anywhere."

Epilogue

May 1821
Yorkshire

It was a tidy lane, dotted with a few small but neat houses, surrounded by carefully tended patches of garden. They had left the carriage at an inn in town and walked the rest of the way, not knowing the exact house they were seeking, but Alec's eyes immediately snagged on one dwelling. It wasn't surrounded by the usual English primroses, but by crimson blooms on tall stems. He hadn't seen carnations that bright since the Spanish campaign.

"This is her last known residence," said James Peterbury.

"It is," said Alec quietly. "Right there, I'd wager." He indicated the bright red flowers. "Carnations are everywhere in Spain," he told Cressida.

"They're beautiful," she said.

Alec smiled. "I always thought so. My mother would like them."

A few children ran by them, herding a handful of geese along with the help of a barking dog. One of the boys stumbled over a rock and dropped his biscuit almost on Alec's boots. "Beg pardon, sir," he said breathlessly, snatching up his snack and brushing the dirt off it.

Behind him, James inhaled sharply. Alec felt the same shock. It was Will's face peering up from under the mop of dark hair, darker and smaller but unmistakable. The boy had inherited his mother's Castilian coloring, but every feature was his father's. Cressida pressed his arm in worry, but he put his hand over hers in reassurance. "Are you Master Lacey?" he asked, recovering his voice.

The boy's dark eyes shone up at him, innocent and unsuspecting. "Yes, sir. Who be you?"

Alec went down on one knee to face him. "I'm an old friend of your father's."

A surprised smile burst over the boy's face. "Truly?"

"Yes. My name is Alec Hayes, and this lady is my wife." He gestured at James. "And this is Sir James Peterbury. Sir James and I grew up with your father in Hertfordshire. We're very pleased to meet you."

The lad looked between them, then turned and ran down the street. "Mama, Mama!" he shouted. "There's some men here—friends of my papa! Mama, come!"

A slender woman with olive skin emerged from the house with the carnations, shading her eyes as her son raced toward her. For all that she was older and had obviously suffered some hardship, Isabella Lacey was still lovely. Alec recognized her at once. He had last seen her at the Duchess of Richmond's ball, the night before they marched out to meet the French. That night she had been a young bride, deeply in love with a man who adored her. It must have been their last night together.

"At last," breathed James. He and Alec exchanged a glance; at last, indeed. It had taken them months to find her. Isabella had moved about frequently after Waterloo, and even the two private agents they hired to trace her had struggled at times.

She watched them approach, her aristocratic heritage evident in her proud posture if not in her appearance. Her son started to run back to them, but she admonished him with a word and he returned to her side, only dragging his feet a little.

"Mrs. Lacey?" Alec removed his hat and bowed.

"Yes." Her wary eyes darted between the two of them. She put one hand on her son's shoulder, drawing him even closer to her. Beyond her Alec could see the interior of the house, neat and clean but tiny. Her hands bore the calluses of hard work, and her clothing was faded and much mended. He felt again the sharp guilt that he hadn't been able to keep his promise to Will to take care of them, tempered only by the knowledge that the Laceys would never want for anything again.

"I am Alexander Hayes. May I present my wife, Mrs. Hayes, and Sir James Peterbury." James also doffed his hat and bowed. Cressida curtsied, murmuring a polite greeting. Mrs. Lacey returned it, but most of her attention remained on the men. "Peterbury and I were friends of your husband, Will," Alec said. "The three of us grew up together in Hertfordshire and served in the army together."

Something sparkled in her gaze, the memory of old joys and the remembrance of enduring sorrow.

"He has been dead several years now," she said softly. "Since Waterloo."

"We know, and are very sorry for it," said James. "But we have brought you some news. Your son has inherited a legacy from his grandfather."

Her lips parted in shock. Her son crept closer to her side. "What's a legacy, sir?" he asked.

Alec smiled at him. "It can mean many things, young man, but in this case it means money." He looked at Isabella, still standing in mute amazement. "Ten thousand pounds."

"Blimey," exclaimed the boy. "Mama, we shall be rich!"

Alec grinned; the boy was just like Will. "Yes, indeed."

Later, after Isabella had recovered from her shock enough to invite them in, they talked about Will. Her son, named for his father, asked dozens of questions, and as James and Alec shared their memories, silent tears began to flow down Isabella's cheeks.

Cressida made tea, keeping out of the way. As they reminisced and laughed, she sensed a subtle easing of the last tension in her husband's shoulders. He needed this—he *deserved* this, she thought fiercely. After he had discovered the truth about Will Lacey and her father last summer, Alec had been fully exonerated; the Duke of Wellington acknowledged the error and publicly denounced the rumors of treason. Suddenly it was as if no one had ever believed Alec guilty, or so it seemed from the number of people who came to call. Alec bore it all with a wry twist to his smile, and told her he almost preferred being a pariah.

But not a word of Will Lacey's true actions was ever uttered. Will had been buried a hero, and Alec had loved him too well to reveal the truth. He told only his family and James Peterbury, a confession that had sent Julia into a flood of tears before she flung herself into her brother's arms and begged his forgiveness for not believing in him all along.

For her part, Cressida had told Callie part of the truth about their father. She revealed that he had blackmailed people, including old Mr. Lacey, but she never mentioned what he had done to Alec. Callie would have been too horrified and guilt-stricken by that knowledge, and it was over in any event. Papa was dead. Cressida was content to bury his sins with him, and let her family embrace their lives to come, instead of regret the life Papa had lived.

And now, today, they had solved the last part of the puzzle. Cressida knew Alec and James had engaged investigators to find Isabella Lacey months ago. He and James had intended to provide a comfortable annuity for her and her son, until old Mr. Lacey sent them a terse note indicating his desire to settle five thousand pounds on his grandson. Perhaps it was the closest the old man could come to any apology for his actions. He had left Marston soon after that dreadful day at his house, when all the festering secrets had been spilled, and no one had been sorry to see him go. Alec and James had carried on with their plan to find Mrs. Lacey, and agreed they would contribute another five thousand pounds.

Cressida smiled as she watched Alec laugh at something James was relating, some prank the three of them had played as lads. William listened raptly, exclaiming in delight, and Alec tousled the boy's hair when he grew too excited. This was the last ghost to exorcise, the fulfillment of his long-ago promise to a friend. And to see him do it with such compassion and decency made her heart almost burst with love for the man she had married.

Finally it was time to say their farewells. Young William hooted with delight when James Peterbury promised to call on them again soon, but fell silent as Alec motioned him over.

"This is for you," he told the boy. "Your father made it many years ago, and I have been keeping it for you."

William's eyes were as round as saucers as he took the carved wooden horse. "Did my papa really make it?"

"He did," Alec assured him. "Right before he met your mother."

Solemnly the child carried it to his mother. "It is an Andalusian horse," she told him with a smile. "They live near my home in Spain." She turned to Alec, her eyes glistening. "Thank you, sir—he never knew his father, but he will never forget this day."

As they all walked out into the late afternoon sunshine, a closed carriage started down the lane. Glossy and expensive, it rolled slowly past. The driver made no sign of stopping, but as it passed Mrs. Lacey's small cottage, the curtain fluttered open. A pale face appeared at the glass for just a moment, and then the carriage was gone, continuing down the road out of town.

Cressida watched the carriage rumble away. It looked small and lonely against the wide, barren heath in front of it, as if it were driving into oblivion. "That was old Mr. Lacey, wasn't it?"

Alec nodded. "It was."

She looked up at her husband. "You let him see the boy."

"Just once. He deserves to see what he lost."

"Yes." She sighed.

He took her hand between his. "I am sorry you noticed him," he began.

Cressida shook her head. "No. Don't be sorry. I could never face him again, but you were right to let him see his only grandson."

"He gave his word not to come near them again. As far as they know, he is dead. If he chooses to leave William any more funds at his death, the solicitors will deal with it, and neither William nor his mother will ever know."

Cressida looked over at young William Lacey, pretending to gallop his carved horse over the front step. "I'm glad he relented," she said softly.

Alec took one look at the carriage, now tiny in the distance, and turned back to her. "I'm glad he's gone," he said bluntly. "I've more important people to deal with."

"Mrs. Lacey—"

"Not Mrs. Lacey," he interrupted her. "Did I not tell you? Peterbury offered to provide any assistance she needs." He glanced at his friend, still deep in conversation with Mrs. Lacey. "He's taken up the duty with commendable enthusiasm, it seems."

Cressida recognized the wicked gleam in his eye. "Then who?"

He tilted his head. "A woman without equal. Intelligent, sensible, daring, kindhearted . . . and of course beautiful beyond my dreams." Cressida blushed. "And the most seductive mouth I've ever seen," he murmured. "When she blushes and smiles at me, my heart all but bursts."

"What a woman," she said with a laugh. "You must tell me if you ever find her."

Alec leaned closer, until she could see every spark of love and happiness in the depths of his eyes. "I already have. And I'm never letting you go."

Some loves are worth waiting for . . .

Callandra Phillips locked her heart away after her
disastrous marriage. But Tom Webb has been in
love with her for ages. And love denied can burn
hot enough to melt the most cautious heart . . .

An exclusive short story extra,
available December 2009
at *carolinelinden.com* and *harpercollins.com*